Liberators of the Dawn:

Book 4 of the Dawn Saga

I0536732

ZACHARIAH WAHRER

First Print Edition

Wahrer of the Worlds Publishing
www.wahreroftheworlds.com
publishing@wahreroftheworlds.com

ISBN-13: 978-0-9983827-5-3

DEDICATION

For my readers.
Your letters of appreciation and encouragement inspire me to continue writing. Thanks for reading the Dawn Saga. It means the world to me.

CONTENTS

ACKNOWLEDGEMENTS

Without Sarah Wahrer's help, neither this book nor the Dawn Saga would exist. Much love and gratitude to you, my forever love.

A big thanks to Walter Scott for his editing powers. Your help and feedback on this series was invaluable.

Tyler Ellis, you made amazing covers for the Saga! I hope your career as an artist continues to grow and prosper. I look forward to our future collaborations.

Lois Rahal, Shreve Fellars, Frank Frey, Helen Brookman: Thanks for beta reading this series and sticking with me. Your feedback has made the Dawn Saga so much better than it would have been otherwise.

Patrick Wahrer and Barney Rahal, thank you for your financial support that made the amazing covers possible. I'm so psyched these books have the artwork they deserve.

And, as always, thank you, kind reader. You are the reason I do this, and without you, none of it would matter. :-)

May the fires of the black star be quenched in your life,
Zachariah Wahrer

"Our hope is not lost and our dreams still live. Do not despair. The Entho-la-ah-mine species will survive."
— Queen Na-ah-co, Final Lith-elo-hi-rosh address

"Drop your pants, or drop a lover, but never drop a load of cargo."
— Verger Proverb

"The Dawn, our most honored and holy nexus, made itself known in time immemorial. It benevolently accepts our worship, setting our path through tumultuous times."
— The Collected Works of Thadris, Elrahi Philosopher

01 – FELAR

Felar charged forward, mentally embracing the surrounding space-time. She drew it in, the energy filling her like a breath. She crafted the growing power into dual mind blades, one springing into either hand. Their hilts felt solid in her grasp, the blades themselves light and nimble. "You take right," she yelled, darting towards her own opponent.

Lothis moved in sync alongside her, mind dagger in his right hand. His small feet flew through the emerald grass, light and swift. He summoned a spray of glimmering mental shards and sent it zipping towards his foe, shredding it.

Felar reached her own adversary, easily sliding into long practiced combat forms. *Human. Elrahi. Elrahi. Human,* she thought, listing their origins. Her blades flared, producing devastating results. The arms and head of her practice dummy tumbled into the long grass. When she was satisfied, Felar stepped back, feeling her breathing and pulse quickly settle.

"You've caught on quick," Lothis praised, his mind daggers vanishing as he moved away from his own target.

Felar turned to him, still unable to suppress the sick pain in her gut that always hit when she saw his dead right eye and scarred arms. *He'll never get his full vision back,* she thought, making herself smile despite the sadness. "Yes, I think I have."

"Why didn't they teach you the way of the Blade when you were an Elrahi Sentry?" Wake interjected, walking over from where he'd been observing. "You obviously have a talent for it."

"Sentries were prohibited from learning any mental combat disciplines. Our job was to secure the borders, to protect the Accord from other hostile nations and species. We were never meant for action inside our own borders. Since none of our enemies had psionic weaponry, it was deemed unnecessary training." As Felar remembered more of her past life

1

as Lek Tomun, the Division Chieftain of the Elrahi Sentries, she kept expecting a mental schism to form. The two existences were vastly different, but somehow, they melded in a way that made her feel whole. From Felar's conversations with the other Harbingers, she knew they felt the same about their own dual histories.

"And if the Sentries were given psionic training, in addition to their beam weapons," Lothis added, "they would have been unstoppable."

Felar remembered the heavy beam cannon, its violet light, and how it felt in her hands. *What I would give to have one of them again...*

"They could have rebelled," Wake realized. "They'd have had the power to wipe out the Protectors and capture the empress."

"Don't be silly," Felar snapped. "The Sentries have no desire to get involved in the political bickerings of the Accord. We love our empress, our empire, and its people, and we'll do everything within our power to protect it from outside forces." Felar realized she'd drifted back to a place and time that only existed in memory. "The Sentries were steadfastly loyal," she finished, feeling foolish.

"I didn't mean to imply they would," Wake answered, looking like he regretted his earlier statement. "Just that it's understandable why the Accord would have been leery."

"Yes," she replied, sighing, "the Accord was always wary of competitors, real or imagined."

An awkward silence descended over the trio. Lothis finally broke it. "We are making good progress restoring our Elrahi fighting skills. Even those without much training to begin with have blossomed under instruction. I didn't expect to be able to teach so much, especially since I started with such little skill myself. I wonder what we could have done with Cazz-ak as our teacher."

It had only been a week since the battle with the Descended and their friend's death. Felar still felt as raw as ever over his loss. Anger, despair, and pain flooded through her. She fought hard to maintain her composure, knowing it would be unproductive to express it.

"Lothis, you've done a great job getting us all up to specs," Wake said, smiling. "I'm no soldier, but I think I might actually be an asset, rather than a liability."

Wake's upbeat demeanor over the past week simultaneously annoyed and comforted Felar. A large part of her wanted to fall into a hole of despair and grief, but she knew this would be both pointless and dangerous. *Losing Cazz-ak is a massive blow, but we are still alive, and we must keep fighting the Breakers.*

"Even Tremmilly has learned some skills," Lothis said, smiling. "Not enough to go into full combat, but at least she can protect herself."

The positivity of her friends buoyed Felar's drooping spirits, and she felt her mood shift. *We have done so much. And we took out all of Crasor's blighthearted Descended. We sent him a message. We are to be feared.* She smiled at both Lothis and Wake as they began walking back towards Dras' ship.

As they moved through the tall, emerald grass, Felar kept a wary eye out for any of the horrible calath plants. She remembered all too well what happened when a human body came in contact with its sharp leaves. *If Dras hadn't used his nanites to flush the poison out, I'd be dead.* The chaotic visions and memories the toxin summoned hadn't been pleasant either. *Stupid plant...* Kicking it had been an accident, one that sometimes made her wonder if it had cost Cazz-ak his life. *You can't think that way,* she told herself, trying to push her mind back to its earlier, positive trajectory. *Battle isn't that predictable. Even if the blighthearted calath toxin hadn't incapacitated me, I might not have gotten to Cazz-ak and Lothis in time.*

When they reached the sleek Heltasoth vessel, Lothis and Wake headed inside. Felar stopped, not wanting to leave the fresh air and bright light of Lith-elo-hi-rosh's primary star. *Such a beautiful day.* It wasn't that Dras' ship was stifling or confined. Far from it. The small Heltasoth ship was one of the most beautiful and intricate things Felar had ever seen, especially its interior. *But it does feel foreign.*

Despite the fact Felar had grown accustomed to her Elrahi existence, to living on an Entho-la-ah-mine world, to sleeping in the spaceship of a sentient machine, at times she still felt homesick. And while the emerald green grass and blue tinted sunlight here were much different from her home-world of Qi-3, it felt something akin to familiar.

"You coming?" Wake said, popping back out of the Heltasoth ship.

"I think I'm just gonna sit for a while."

"Need company?"

At first, Felar almost turned him down, but then she decided she'd spent enough time alone in the past week. *Besides, I've missed him.*

"Sure," she nodded, giving Wake a smile. They both settled in the long grass, leaning up against the ship for support.

Before Wake, Jaydon, and Maxar had left to find Dras on Traynos-6, she and the engineer had spent many of their meal times together, talking and enjoying each other's company. Since he'd been back, Felar felt as if she'd barely seen him. He'd been sequestered in his room or the hold Dras had given him for a workshop. Felar had been busy training and trying to plan what the Harbingers would do next.

Minutes passed in silence, and Felar enjoyed the feeling of stellar light on her tanned skin. The Descended attack had destroyed their meager living spaces on Lith-elo, so Dras had invited them to live on his vessel. After they'd moved in, the Heltasoth had kept the ship's hull structure

3

opaque. *Otherwise, Tremmilly and Maxar would have no privacy at all.* Felar was used to barracks living and all that entailed, but none of her friends were. *It's for the best anyway. We are all intertwined enough already. It's not like we need to know every personal detail.*

Her mind drifted and her eyelids grew heavy. In a happy haze, she realized, for the first time since the battle with the Arche, the Descended attack, and the Entho-la-ah-mine massacre, she felt a semblance of peace. All her crushing cares and concerns still threatened to rush back in, but Felar kept floating in the bliss of the beautiful day.

"How much longer do you think it will take them to decide?" Wake asked. Rather than startling her or being irritating, the familiar voice was a happy addition.

"I hope it isn't much longer," Felar answered. "We can't remain here, waiting for the Breakers to come back with a larger force, and neither can the Entho-la-ah-mines." Talking about the Breakers brought back some tenseness, but Felar didn't embrace it. "If they cannot bring themselves to leave, we'll have to go without them and do the best we can to stop Crasor before he comes back."

Silence returned for several moments. A light breeze stirred, swirling loose strands of her light brown hair.

"There is something I've been meaning to tell you," Wake said.

His tone felt strange to Felar, so she opened her eyes. The engineer was looking off into the distance, unable to meet her gaze. He was biting his pursed lip, and his hands were fidgeting with a blade of grass.

"What's up?"

"I—" he started.

"They've decided," Tremmilly said, coming into view around the black hull. "They've finally agreed to evacuate!"

"What were you going to say?" Felar asked, as she rose to hug her excited friend.

"Nothing important," Wake answered, eyes downcast.

02 – CRASOR

"The Oblivion is ready for deep space trials," Salla Markond announced.

Crasor studied the woman's face on the terminal screen, noting its beautiful shape. When he had been human, her good looks and piercing blue eyes might have caught his attention, but that was all behind him now. *She almost looks like Emili,* Crasor thought for a moment, before shutting out the distraction.

"I will attend the voyage personally," he replied. Salla's team had done a remarkable job arming the frigate with the captured nuclear missiles. *But I can't leave this critical step completely to her. We need this vessel too much. The Light is out there, somewhere...*

"I'll be there shortly," Crasor continued. "Be ready to depart once I arrive."

"Understood."

Crasor cut the comms link and leaned back in his chair. *Between Salla and Gav, it's hard to decide who's more useful. Or more powerful, for that matter.* Since the blighthearted Harbingers and Enthos had destroyed his nine Descended, Gav and Salla were his strongest devotees. *Thankfully, they are more capable than the Descended ever were.*

While all of his billions upon billions of followers were completely loyal, something about the two lieutenants made them special. *Perhaps they are just closer to the darkness than the rest.* Their competitiveness with each other also seemed to drive them to greater and greater heights of excellence. He hadn't discovered what was causing the odd tension between them, but as long as it didn't interfere too much with their duties, he didn't care.

A chime sounded, and Crasor looked back to the terminal screen. Gav's large head and massive shoulders appeared on the display.

Crasor poked the accept button. "Yes?"

"I've found something." The excitement on the brute's face was

5

evident.

Hopefully it's not another of his one-up attempts, Crasor thought, gesturing for the other man to continue.

"It's one of the Family's secrets, one Salla hasn't found or chosen to disclose."

There it is, Crasor groaned inwardly, not caring if the displeasure showed on his face. He knew Salla was completely loyal, as all Breakers were. She had been head of the entire criminal organization, had known every secret it contained. *But maybe someone kept it hidden from her.* There were hundreds of alliances, factions, and smaller families contained within the huge entity.

"Continue."

"It's a ship," Gav rushed. "A specialized vessel more destructive than anything previously developed."

Crasor felt one eyebrow raise. "And how did you find this mega-ship?"

"One of my sub-captains was a logistics manager in the Dragath Family. She wasn't told the vessel's specifics, but was ordered to dispatch materials to the worksite."

"How do you know this is a viable lead?" *If we interrogate every Family-member-turned-Breaker, we'll be chasing shadows until the Founder's Light hunts us down.*

"Based on the requisitions list she showed me. In addition to standard starship equipment, I found numerous anomalies. Even for a battle cruiser, it is non-standard. I think they were building some kind of enormous, ship-mounted mass driver."

"Like a huge rail cannon? What's special about that?"

"Not exactly." Gav paused, looking flustered. "I'm not sure what it is, but I think the technical specifications make it worth checking on."

Crasor sat back, stroking his chin. *Gav is gifted when it comes to technical matters,* he thought. *Perhaps I'm not giving him enough credit.*

"Alright," Crasor said. "Where is this ship?"

Gav smiled. "I'll transfer the coordinates." He did something off-screen and a notification popped up on Crasor's terminal.

"That's on the fringe of Ashamine space. Are you sure that's correct? Why would Dragath go all the way out there?"

"That is the precise coordinates the ex-logistics officer gave. She had no digital location records, as those were verbal only. She memorized it as a blackmail credit in case anything ever happened."

"I permit further investigation." Dragath had been a powerful family with a seat on the high council. *They had the ability to do something like this.* Why they would be building a mystery ship in the middle of nowhere was beyond him. *Hopefully it's not some mining vessel or something.* "But I'll see to it," Crasor continued. "I need to take the

Oblivion on an interstellar shakedown, and this is as good a destination as any." *And if we run into any unexpected resistance, the Justice will be along to protect our nuclear assets.*

"May I join the mission?"

Crasor bit his lip, knowing this could put Salla and Gav in proximity, something he tried to avoid. "Yes, fine." *Don't make me regret this decision...*

03 – AZA

Where is he? Aza thought, the sinking feeling in her stomach reaching depths she never knew possible. *Four days late. What could have happened? Where's Ash?* Her mind spun, full of doubt, apprehension, and fear.

After Aza had been expelled from the Ashamine Holy Order, she'd run away from home, fleeing to the under-levels of the Founder's City. *Maybe I should have stayed with mother and father. They wouldn't really have thrown me out, would they?* She tapped her fingers on the scarred and graffitied terminal table.

No, she decided finally. *No, they wouldn't have completely disowned me, but I would have been shunned and left to live in shame for the rest of my life. I might only be 13, but I can take care of myself, even if Ash can't come.* Aza bit her lip and took a deep breath, slowly shaking her head. *Do you really believe that? After what you've seen?*

With careful management of the funds her uncle had sent, Aza had been able to get decent lodging and meals. They were below what she'd been used to as part of the Holy Order, but it was far superior to what many around her lived off of. *But the funds won't last much longer.* She shuddered at the thought of what some girls her age did to survive down here. *If Ash doesn't get here soon...*

A chime sounded, breaking Aza's reverie and making her jump. The screen displayed five standard minutes left on her free public terminal time. *Might as well try again,* she thought, pulling the small data square and its reader out of her now-dirty jacket. Aza connected the device to the terminal, trying to remain as inconspicuous as possible. *It hasn't worked since the day Ash said he was coming.* She didn't understand how the device functioned, but the data square used to create a video comm connection to Ash.

Come on, come on, she thought, waiting. Nothing. Either the device

8

was broken, Ash was unavailable, or the Ashamine was blocking him. She waited a few moments longer before unplugging the reader.

Is there anything else I need to look up on the Network? She'd already read all the available news stories, none of which resolved her fears or suspicions about what was going on in the Ashamine. *And that's what got you into this situation in the first place.* Surprisingly, she felt almost no remorse about her actions. *It would have been worse to ignore your feelings. Ash confirmed you had a right to be upset.*

A news update popped up on the terminal feed. Just as Aza was about to select it, something on the edge of her vision caught her attention. She turned slowly, pretending to consider a food cart a few meters left of the individual. Aza had learned that looking directly at other under-level occupants was a fast way to summon trouble.

How long has she been there? How long has she been watching? Aza felt her heart beat faster. The woman was tall, with fierce blue eyes and pale skin. It was hard to see, since Aza couldn't look directly at her, but her clothing and scars made her appear like an under-level citizen. Something about her demeanor, how she sat up so straight, made her look out of place, though. *And she's staring directly at me.*

Aza quickly logged off, trying to remain calm. *Maybe she's not really looking at me. Maybe it's someone behind me, or she's fragged out on some kind of stim.* The concept of drug use and its associated terminology was new to Aza, but she'd gotten a quick education during her time down here.

As she stood, Aza's heart began racing. *I can't go back to my room. She'll know where I'm staying.* Walking out of the public terminal area, Aza tried to adopt the slouching walk that characterized the surrounding people. Her once white clothes were now dirty and torn, one of the first things Aza had done to blend in after realizing she'd be here for a while.

The under-city was lit on a similar cycle to the stellar one above. Aza knew she had a few standard hours until darkness fell. While this level was relatively safe with day illumination, it became a whole different environment when the lights dimmed. *If she's still following me, I'll have to find a way to lose her.* The less traveled areas presented their own dangers, regardless of illumination levels. *Perhaps an outsider won't know this.*

With a slight turn of her head, Aza saw the tall woman had risen and was walking directly behind her. *What can I do?* She increased her pace, weaving in and out of the mid-day crowds. *The Disconnect sector,* she realized hopefully.

Cutting down the next side path, Aza considered her options. Going there would be dangerous, but she couldn't think of anything else. *At least it isn't like the Stim area.*

Two days ago, while eating her tiny midday meal, she'd overheard a couple girls talking about their experiences in the Disconnect sector. "The group that runs it keeps out trash and exploiters. They have tight security, and they give you what you pay for. Not like those buggers over in the Stims. Plus, you get to float on clouds, trip through the Akked, or have the best lay you'll ever experience. Whatever you want! And it's all in your head. No worries about getting some pole disease or a come down."

At the time, Aza had wondered who these girls were, and where they were from. Now, all she could think about was how they'd said there was tight security. *If I can get inside, maybe they will protect me from whatever the blue-eyed woman wants to do.* Being captured and sold was a real possibility, especially for someone like Aza. *Don't think about that now. Focus!*

A few more quick turns between grungy-looking eateries brought Aza closer to the gates leading to the Disconnect. Behind her, she heard footsteps approaching. *Just a little farther,* she thought, increasing her pace to a jog. *Just have to get past the perimeter.*

Aza heard the footsteps behind increase to a run. She glanced over her shoulder, and the woman was nearly on top of her. Desperation flooded Aza and she tried to sprint forward, but the woman caught her by the arm.

"No, stop!" Aza yelled, writhing in an attempt to twist free.

"Shut up," the woman rasped, keeping Aza locked in her grasp. "I'm here to help you!"

"Help!" Aza yelled, hoping to summon the attention of those around her. In the distance, she could see the security line leading into the Disconnect. None of the guards looked her way. The few under-level citizens around seemed to melt away when they heard her cries.

With surprising force, the woman dragged Aza into a nearby service corridor. Even in her terror, Aza could smell the rot and excrement.

"Let me go," she wailed.

"Aza, shut up!" the woman said, grasping her by the shoulders and staring directly into her eyes.

Hearing her name caught Aza off guard. "What?"

"Parick—I mean Ash," she said, shaking her head, "sent me. I'm here to help you. Now can you please quit causing a blightheart that's going to land us both in lockup?" The woman lessened her grip, and Aza felt her terror melt away.

"Ash sent you? Why didn't he come?" Hope and fear hit Aza simultaneously.

"He couldn't. Security was too tight. I barely got in, and the Ashamine doesn't have me on the watch list. Even with DNA spoofers and top-tier ident forgeries, it got messy. That's why I'm late. Ash couldn't have made it, not with the people who are looking for him."

Aza felt confused, but the woman continued before she could say anything.

"We have to get you out of here. The Ashamine is collapsing. Unless the Classad or the High-Elders find a way to prevent it, Ashamine-2 will fall into anarchy."

"What? How?"

"No time. We need to get offworld as quickly as possible. You have to trust me. Do as I say, and we'll make it out."

Aza felt her mind spin. *Anarchy? But we just need a new Founder. Why aren't the Classad protecting and guiding us?*

"Did you hear me?" the woman demanded. Her eyes bored into Aza, shutting out the distracting revelations.

"Yes, yes. Of course."

"Then let's go."

The woman led Aza out of the corridor at a brisk pace. After a minute, it was evident they were heading towards the pneumatic tube station.

"Why didn't you just come up and tell me who you were?" Aza asked between breaths.

"Because I couldn't reveal the information I told you in such a public place. Down here, it's not uncommon to see grungy adults chasing vagrant children. It makes less of an impression on those who happened to see."

"You seem to know a lot about the under-levels."

"Indeed," the woman said, not hesitating. "I used to spend time down here, in another life."

Aza wondered why anyone would want to be in the under-levels if they had the choice to be elsewhere, but she felt it wasn't the time or place to ask. Instead, a new thought occurred to her.

"You haven't told me your name." Even though the woman wasn't Ash, Aza began to feel excited. Someone had finally come for her, and she would be leaving this blighthearted place. *I'll be safe again, soon.*

"Em," the tall woman replied. "No last name."

04 – WAKE

Wake felt his heart thud as Felar rose to hug Tremmilly. *I like her so much,* he thought, trying to decide what to do next. *Why is telling her that so hard?*

"The Queen said they have agreed to evacuate," Tremmilly continued, bouncing up and down as she embraced Felar.

"About blighthearted time," the other woman replied, a subtle smile softening her harsh tone. "What tipped the balance?"

"Half of them believed we were enough to protect the Queen, since we'd already done so. I think I finally convinced them we barely accomplished that, and there was a lot of luck involved. The other half felt the Entho-la-ah-mines should stay and fight, that they've run away too often. I told them of Crasor's strength, and that if the Queen was captured, all hope for the Akked galaxy would be lost. I don't think they understand just how tempting the Great Thought is to him, even with their diminished numbers making it less powerful."

"Nice work, Trem," Felar said, releasing the embrace.

"It's a good thing they still have the ships they used when fleeing the Ashamine," Wake said, finally pulling himself out of his introspection, "otherwise they'd be stuck here. Do they have a way to defend themselves?" Wake had spent most of the last week alone, working on his gift for Felar. At times, he'd felt selfish for not helping Tremmilly convince the Entho-la-ah-mines, but he knew his diplomatic skills were limited. *Besides, she didn't need me anyway.*

"Without Cazz-ak," she answered, "their effectiveness is diminished." Hearing his dead friend's name brought a pang of grief to Wake's heart. He still felt guilty that he, Maxar, and Jaydon had left Lith-elo, had divided the strength that might have saved Cazz-ak from the Descended. "But," Tremmilly continued, "they have made great strides towards utilizing the Great Thought as a weapon. They still have an extremely

12

limited concept of anger, and their fear of 'negative' emotions will hold them back. Hopefully, wherever they decide to go, they won't need to defend themselves."

"There are still several hidden Entho-la-ah-mine refuges," Felar said. "Since the Descended traced us here through our connection to the Arche, I feel confident Crasor can't find the Queen outright."

"The farther we are from her," Tremmilly nodded, "the better."

"When are they leaving?" Wake asked.

"As soon as possible. It shouldn't take long. They don't have much in the way of belongings to transport. The Queen sends her regards and thanks. She wanted to say it in person, but I encouraged her to depart as quickly as possible."

Wake wished he could have said goodbye, but he knew it was for the best. *Crasor could show up at any moment,* he thought, turning his eyes towards the sky. A rising shape caught his attention. "Look," he said, pointing towards the first of the evacuating Entho-la-ah-mine bi-pyramids.

He involuntary braced for a crashing wave of sound, but the ship rose silently. *So majestic and peaceful,* he thought, *unlike Ashamine ships.*

"Good," Tremmilly said. They all fell silent, watching the hulking ship shrink into the upper atmosphere. A light rush of air was all that marked the bi-pyramid's passage, something Wake found both poetic and sad. Five other bi-pyramids rose after the first ship, then a sixth and seventh.

"That's it?" Felar said, voice grim. "There has to be more."

"Unfortunately, I don't think so. There weren't that many of them here to begin with, and the blighthearted Descended did their best to eradicate those left." Tremmilly's voice was hard and determined, a shift Wake had noticed more and more lately. It was right somehow, familiar in a way that linked to his Elrahi memories.

After all the vessels had disappeared into the upper atmosphere, Wake realized the planet felt empty. Even with his friends around him, Lith-elo-hi-rosh now felt desolate. *Gone forever,* he thought, not knowing if he was thinking of Cazz-ak, the Queen, the rest of the Entho-la-ah-mines, or all of them combined.

"Now, we can make our next move," Felar said, straightening up.

Her voice too had grown hard, making Wake wonder if the evacuation somehow foretold of the end of whatever joy was left in his life. *Everything has gotten so serious. When was the last time we had a real laugh?*

"Please tell me you've decided what that is." Tremmilly replied.

"We still need to talk as a group, but yes, I have a plan."

"Good. You're the most qualified of us all in this area, but I agree, it would be wise to talk it over."

Felar looked pensive for a moment. "Let's all meet in a standard hour, in the ship's communal space. My plan is simple, so it won't take much discussion. Perhaps Dras can move us into orbit while we talk. With the Queen gone, we have no need to stay here."

"I'll go find everyone and let them know," Tremmilly said. "I've been down in those caves for so long. It would be good to get a walk in the open air before we head into space."

Wake nodded, but he didn't know whether he was actually agreeing or just following social cues. It had taken him so long to work up the courage to talk to Felar about his feelings, but now it felt like he'd spent it all just saying the first sentence. *This is your opportunity,* he thought, watching Tremmilly move off into waving grass. *You're alone with Felar. Tell her!*

Without a word, Wake headed towards the ship's airlock. His cheeks burned, and he hoped Felar didn't see his discomposure.

"Hold up," she said, gently grabbing his arm. "What's going on, Wake? We used to spend time together, and now you've become a ghost. You've been hiding in your quarters and we've barely talked at all in the past week. Is it Cazz-ak's death? If so, I understand. You're mad at me for not saving him."

"No," Wake replied, turning to face her. "No, it's nothing like that. I just..."

Felar remained silent, waiting expectantly. Her soft green eyes looked into his, and he felt himself melt.

So beautiful, Wake thought, *so kind, so caring.* He willed himself to tell her, to say the words he'd rehearsed so many times. Nothing came. Anger welled up, not because of her, but because of his own inabilities. *This is exactly why you don't deserve her, you blighthearted bugger.*

"You can tell me," she said, her smile making his heart race.

With a massive effort of will, Wake finally spoke. "Let me show you what I've been working on."

He led her into and through the ship, to the small, minimally furnished room he'd been using as his personal quarters. Wake had often wondered what the space's function had been before he'd occupied it, but when he asked Dras, the Heltasoth told him he'd created it just for Wake. The engineer in him wanted to understand how the sentient machine did these things. If Wake hadn't been spending all his time on the gift for Felar, he would have investigated further.

"Sit down," he said, motioning towards the only real seat in the room, a black metal stool.

Here we go, Wake thought, going over to the chest that held Brightwing, his advanced environmental nominizing suit. He opened the lid and pulled out a heavy object wrapped in a woven grass mat. Walking over to Felar, he extended it to her.

"What's this?" A quizzical look bloomed on Felar's face, replacing her earlier concern.

"Something I made for you."

Felar accepted the heavy object, grunting as she set it down on her lap. She pulled gently at the mat, and the wrapping fell away. Before her sat a piece of burnished metal. On each side, intricate scrollwork traced its complicated edges and facets.

"You built a slug thrower?" Felar asked, wonder evident in her voice.

"It's an armament," Wake answered, feeling his excitement grow, "but it's not a rail gun. It's a beam weapon. Portable, like the one you used to wield as an Elrahi Sentry. I wanted to reverse engineer the technology from the one in Brightwing, but I didn't have the time or resources."

"Then how did you make it?"

"I removed the components from the suit, built them into a standalone unit."

"Why would you do that? It worked just fine in Brightwing and was much more compact."

Wake felt a stab of frustration at her criticism, but when he looked into her eyes, he could see she was genuinely curious. "For you," he replied, feeling awkward standing in front of her while she was sitting. He dragged the chest over and sat down next to Felar. "I wanted you to have something you were familiar with, something from your past."

"Wake," Felar said, "this is incredible." Tears formed in her eyes, sliding down past her huge smile. "Why would you do this for me?" She hefted the weapon, and Wake had a flashback of her holding her service weapon, a Sentry, standing tall and proud.

"Because, I think you'll need it. And because you'll wield it better than me. I'd give you all of Brightwing, but then I'd be practically useless in combat."

She laughed, shaking her head. "You've learned so much about the way of the Blade, and about human combat as well. You are anything but useless. But yes, it is better for you to keep Brightwing. That suit is far too complicated for me."

"There is another reason as well," Wake said, the seriousness of his tone making Felar lose her smile. "I would have waited longer to do this, to pick a better situation or let things develop further, but I don't know how much time we have left." He knew he was rambling, trying to avoid venturing deeper into his own awkwardness. "Do you remember the Elrahi courting rituals?" he blurted.

"No," she said, biting her lip. "Sentries weren't allowed those kinds of entanglements, nor were we educated in courtship practices in our upbringing as candidates."

"Oh." Wake felt his stomach drop.

"What does that have to do with the weapon?" Felar looked genuinely puzzled, so Wake forged ahead.

"In the Accord, the custom was to signal one's interest in developing a partnership with someone by giving them a gift of great significance and value. It was meant to show they were invested, that they wanted to connect further with a potential partner."

"I see." Felar exhaled.

"So—" Wake said, faltering.

Moments dragged by, and he realized he was holding his breath. Wake let it out as silently as he could. *You're in this far,* he thought. *No going back now.*

"I really like you, Felar," Wake said finally, feeling his heart flutter. "I want to support you and Lothis. I want to be there for you, with you."

"Wake, I—" she answered, voice catching. "I'm honored and flattered, really. I enjoy your company as well, but not in the way you want." She paused, sighed, and continued. "I'm not into males, not romantically, I mean."

Wake felt caught off guard. "Oh," was all he could say.

"I want to be there for you as well, and just because I'm not attracted to you doesn't mean you can't support me and vice versa." She paused, waiting.

Wake felt like his tongue was glued to the roof of his mouth. He focused on his breathing, trying to calm his whirling emotions.

Finally, Felar continued. "It's nothing against you, either in our Elrahi or human lives. I've just never been attracted to males. In the Sentries, there were a few females who caught my attention, but I was far too busy to do anything about it. Plus, it would have broken so many customs and laws. Besides, they were subordinates. If I had gotten attached and had to send them into battle?" She shrugged. "It was a conflict of interest."

Despite trying to calm himself, Wake experienced a dizzying mixture of emotions. First, he felt like crying, then laughing. It seemed as if he was floating away from his body, but then he realized he'd only imagined it. *Get yourself together!*

"Did I crush you?" Felar asked, breaking through Wake's pain.

"No," he lied.

Felar sighed again and put her arm around him. "I can't blame you for being into me," she said, "I am pretty awesome. You're not the first guy." The wry smile on her face made Wake grin in return, despite his agony. "But just because I don't want to be romantic, doesn't mean I don't want to be your best friend. You are an amazing individual, Wake Darmekus. And if I was into poles, I'd be all over yours."

Her crude humor added embarrassment to Wake's cocktail of emotions, but he could see she was trying to lighten the mood. "Thanks,

I guess," he replied, rolling his eyes.

"And if you want to integrate the beam weapon back into Brightwing, I totally understand. Sorry for not having the cultural background to understand what you were trying to say. It was very different growing up as a Sentry candidate."

"No, keep it. I want you to have it. And I'm sorry I didn't realize the difference in customs. I made myself look like a fool."

"No, you didn't. I'm flattered, honestly. Besides, we'll just make it our own custom. We give a gift to express our level of friendship. Romance not required."

"Alright," Wake said, wondering if he'd ever be able to get over his embarrassment. "As friends, will you promise to never tell anyone about this?"

Felar crinkled her face. "Really? You're gonna make me keep silent? You saw how much blightheart I gave Maxar and Tremmilly didn't you? And she's an empress."

Wake felt his smile vanish.

"I'm kidding," Felar continued, a grin overtaking her face. "Honestly, why are people so sensitive about this kind of thing? I won't tell anyone. I promise."

"Thank you," Wake sighed. Felar stood, pulling him to his feet as well. She embraced him, pulling Wake in tight.

"Remember," Felar said, voice as serious as it was during briefings, "just because we aren't romantic, doesn't mean I'm not the best friend you'll ever have. I love you like a brother and I always will. We'll be there for each other, no matter what happens."

05 – TREMMILLY

Tremmilly melted into Maxar's embrace, feeling his body envelop hers. "I'm so proud of you," he said, squeezing her tighter.

"I'm proud too," she laughed, feeling giddy. Convincing the Queen and her myriad advisors to evacuate had been a huge undertaking, one she wouldn't have been capable of before. *The more I remember of myself as Empress Aris, the more confident I become.*

As she gained more of her old abilities back, Tremmilly felt increasingly responsible for leading the Harbingers. *I'm still no military tactician, but that's what I have Felar and Maxar for.*

"What?" she said, realizing he'd said something while she was lost in thought.

"What is our next step?"

"We need to meet and talk about it together. Felar says she has a plan, and we can depart Lith-elo as soon as possible."

Maxar gave her a wan smile, and Beowulf let out a gentle whine. Tremmilly looked first at the wolf-dog, then up into Maxar's face. "Guess we'll just have to keep putting our ceremony on hold."

After Maxar, Jaydon, and Wake had returned with Dras and his amazing ship, Tremmilly could barely let her betrothed out of her sight. They'd talked about doing their bonding ceremony right then, but both realized it wasn't the right time. *Between Cazz-ak and all the other Entho-la-ah-mine casualties...* So they'd decided to wait, hoping a more appropriate time would come soon.

As the past week had gone by, they'd had less and less time together. Tremmilly was busy with breakthroughs in discovering their Elrahi past as well as working hard to convince the Entho-la-ah-mines to evacuate. Maxar was focused on training, sharpening his own human and Elrahi skills as well as helping Wake, Jaydon, and Lothis do the same. He'd also spent a significant amount of time with Dras, the two working to understand what Heltasoth technology was capable of in a human body. Each night, they'd collapsed into bed together, falling asleep before they could exchange more than a few words.

"Trem?" Maxar asked, and she realized she'd lost herself in thought again.

"Yes," she replied, nodding and giving him her best smile. "The timing just keeps blighthearting us."

"Always does," Maxar said, giving her another squeeze.

Dras cleared his throat, startling Tremmilly. She'd forgotten his presence in the room with them. "I will go join the meeting," he said. "I'll also make sure the ship is ready, so we can depart whenever you decide." The sentient machine left the room, his footsteps barely audible.

Tremmilly knew Dras was deeply integrated with the ship. *He can control this vessel from anywhere inside,* she thought, knowing he was simply giving them time alone. He had an uncanny understanding of humans, both their culture and customs. *And that throat clear. How is he able to mimic us so perfectly?*

Tremmilly realized her thoughts were drifting away from the present for a third time, and she forced herself to concentrate. "I love you, Maxar," she said, staring deeply into his eyes. "Whether we ever get the right moment to do the ceremony or not, our love will never diminish. I am yours, and you are mine. That won't change."

Maxar nodded. "I have the feeling things are going to get more blighthearted soon. I think that's been putting pressure on me. But you're right: We don't need the ceremony to show each other our love. We've already done that many times."

"Don't think you're getting out of it," Tremmilly replied, giving him a playful jab in the ribs. "As soon as we are on a safe, beautiful planet, and we aren't mourning the loss of one of our friends, we're doing it!"

Maxar laughed, once again pulling her into an embrace. "I know," he said, voice muffled as he kissed her hair. "I know."

While they walked towards what passed as a bridge on the Heltasoth vessel, Tremmilly felt twinges of doubt begin to creep in. She'd been so focused on her goal that she'd given herself little time to think of anything else. *What if I sent the Queen and her people off to annihilation, just like I did all the Elrahi?*

The thought sent a chill down Tremmilly's spine, and she wondered where it had come from. *Is Crasor influencing me again?* Memories of the nightmares and visions she'd experienced after escaping him on the Founder's Justice flooded through her mind.

I sent them to the Dawn, she fought back, trying to maintain her composure, despite the horrible images flashing through her mind. *I sent them there for safety. When peace is restored in the universe, I will bring*

19

them back again, just as we planned.

Doubt still lingered, and Tremmilly wondered if she should tell Maxar what was happening. *No. Now is not the time. He already has so much to handle. Everyone does. I can take care of this myself.* The thought felt empowering, and Tremmilly held on to it as they walked into the large area that served as both the ship's bridge and group meeting area. *It is time to be strong and destroy Crasor, See'dek, and the rest of the Breakers.*

06 – GAV

"Transition," Crasor ordered, and the Oblivion's propulsion officer moved them into the worm.

Gav kept looking straight ahead, but he was focused on Salla, rather than the new formation of stars that appeared on the far end of the wormhole. She was at the very edge of his vision, an infuriating manifestation of beauty and power.

The Oblivion was her project, a simple ship packed with devastating energy. *An easy task,* Gav thought, *putting all those nuclear missiles into this transport ship.* If he wasn't currently inside it, Gav would have wished for the whole ship to go up in a giant nuclear conflagration. *If Salla's blighthearted crew wasn't watching me so closely, I might find a way to rig it to do so after I've left.* The former head of the entire Family organization wasn't stupid. She'd obviously told her crew ahead of time that Gav was a threat.

"Transition successful. All worm-drive diagnostics nominal," the propulsion officer announced. "The Justice is still in formation behind us, at the specified safe distance."

In turn, each of the Oblivion's technical officers announced their parts of the ship were operating correctly as well. Gav didn't know if that made him happy or sad. *I wish she would fail, even if it was just once. If we find this secret ship though, maybe it won't matter.*

Gav had worked feverishly the past week, hunting for secrets valuable enough to place him in the highest position of power beneath Crasor. He'd checked and rechecked the informant's super-ship data, doing everything he could to make sure it was credible. He'd hashed his way into the Dragath Family databases to confirm what the informant had said. Gav had exposed every scrap and data point he could find before bringing the intel to Crasor. Still, despite all his efforts, Dragath had done a good job keeping their project secret. *Which is what makes it so tantalizing.*

Crasor had given both him and Salla their own forces to control. Salla's orders were to outfit this transport ship. Gav's were to ensure the newly established government of Exis-7 was an efficient, cohesive entity. *Seems like our jobs should have been switched,* Gav thought, settling back in his seat. Salla had commanded a large organization, and Gav was the expert technician. *Crasor knows what he's doing. I suppose there's a reason.* He'd made sure Exis-7's industries would keep on producing rail guns, body armor, stims, and all the other weapons and drugs it had been known for when it was still a human planet.

Despite the unwavering Breaker loyalty—or perhaps because of it—the farther down the chain of command you went, the more work had to be put in to produce satisfactory results. They were like drones, requiring constant management. Even if he had to be in proximity to Salla, Gav was happy to be getting away from mundane management. *This is almost like a vacation,* he thought dryly.

On the forward view screen, Gav saw a haze growing ahead of the ship. At first, he thought it was interference, but then the sensor tech spoke.

"A large mass of planetary debris and asteroids ahead. Radioactivity is nominal for a non-stellar region. Density and orbital spin rates will make movement through this region very dangerous." Chunks of rock, metal, and ice resolved on the screen, the sheer quantity making it difficult to tell just how large any individual piece was. The mass spun and collided in a mesmerizing, chaotic orbit. For a moment, Gav thought the cloud was small, perhaps the size of a pleasure moon, but then he checked the overlay scale and saw it was bigger than Exis-7.

"Full stop," Salla ordered, giving Gav a cold gaze before turning to Crasor. "Sir, this ship is not designed to handle that kind of punishment. It doesn't have point defenses or enough armor for this situation. We could probably blast through some debris with a stream of missiles, but that is a fruitless waste of resources. Even the Justice would be hard-pressed to create a path for us. And where would we even go? Frankly, I question Gav's motives for taking us here."

Gav didn't know what to make of the mass of planetary debris. Something on the edge of his consciousness told him there was more to the situation. *Can't let Salla defeat me,* he thought, scrambling for a way to buy time.

"How or why would anyone build a ship in this mess?" she continued. "The debris is too unpredictable. Even if there is a primary central mass for a dock to orbit, it would be smashed to pieces."

Gav realized Crasor was staring at him, head cocked and eyebrows raised. "I, uhhh," Gav said, knowing he was losing the power struggle with Salla. *Damn it! That logistics officer only knew the location, nothing about the site.*

"There is an orbital dock," he bluffed, trying to sound as confident as possible. "The Family building this ship wanted to keep it secret from you, Salla, not construct it out in open space." The lie sounded plausible, even to his own ears. *Worst case, we don't find it, and I just blame the logistics officer. She has an accident, and no one finds the truth. I'll lose some of my standing with Crasor, but he won't excommunicate me for this.*

Salla turned to her sensor officer. "Is there anything to indicate a ship building dock in the vicinity?"

A moment passed, the tech staring intently at his terminal. "No," he said finally. "All electromagnetic activity and materials composition indicate natural activity."

Blighthearted bugger! Gav roared inwardly, knowing he couldn't back down now. "As you say," he shrugged, keeping his rage hidden. "But wouldn't a covert ship building operation be invisible to sensors?"

Salla stared at him, dark blue eyes burning. For a moment, Gav thought she might explode, but a veil of calm descended over her. "Perhaps. And perhaps it is just what it appears to be: a hazardous debris field."

Silence fell over the deck, and Gav wondered what to do next. *You're not calm at all,* he thought, unable to break his gaze from Salla. *And you'll kill me when you have the chance.* The realization drove home the feeling he had to strike first. *Watch your back,* he thought, not knowing if the sentiment was for her or himself.

"Neither of you truly know if there is a dock there or not," Crasor announced finally.

Would Salla actually do it? Gav wondered, knowing he should be focused on the current mission, rather than speculating about the future.

"As you say," Salla replied, bowing slightly.

Gav did the same, jaw clenched. *How is she always one step ahead of me?*

"Incoming transmission. Audio only," the comms officer announced, breaking the awkward silence.

"From?" Salla said, easily resuming her duty as captain. As she turned from Gav, he thought he saw a satisfied smile flash across her face.

The comm officer's response made him forget about it, however. "The interior of the debris cloud." Now it was Gav's turn to smile.

"Allow it," Salla barked.

"About damn time you showed up," a gruff voice said. "You're over a week late. What took so long? We thought we were gonna starve."

Gav expected Crasor to manage the situation. As seconds dragged by

23

in silence, he realized the leader was leaving it to either him or Salla.

"Sorry," Gav said, adopting a humble tone. "Logistics office got things blighthearted. A requisitions mix-up or something."

"You don't sound like Idris," the voice said over the comms, wary. "What happened to him?"

"You'll have to talk to Logistics. I just got sent out here today."

Seconds passed in silence, and Gav wondered if his spoof had worked.

"Bring it in careful, or we'll be scraping your carcass off the asteroids. I'm sending the approach plot to you. You better hope you're good at maneuvers. Ain't much error tolerance, but it's better today than others."

The propulsion officer announced he had the information.

"Received," Gav transmitted back.

"See you in 30," the gruff voice replied.

"Sir," Salla said, "we cannot take this vessel into that debris cloud, approach plot or no. It is too risky, especially for an unknown reward."

Gav thought about arguing back, but he knew he already had the advantage. *I was right. Crasor will see that it is worth going forward. There is something inside the cloud.*

"Transport ship," the gruff voice announced, back and sounding even more suspicious, "what is out there with you? My sensors show a huge buggering mass behind you."

Gav felt his heart begin to beat faster. *He's seeing the Justice. No way to hide it.* "Donno what you're talking about," he replied, biting his lip. "Everything is clear."

"Founder curse it," the voice said, so low that he probably didn't mean for it to transmit. "Buggering sensor array must have taken another hit." He paused. "Yeah, OK. I'll sort it out. What are you waiting for? I don't want to have to run another approach plot. You wait too long and everything will be out of alignment."

"Confirmed," Gav said, knowing Crasor would have to make the final call.

After a few seconds, the Breaker leader nodded. "Take us in. And relay an order to Karoth that the Justice is to maintain position."

"But sir," Salla started to add, but she cut off when Crasor fixed her with his fierce gaze.

"You doubt my judgment?"

"No, of course not."

"Then do as I say."

Gav could hardly contain his excitement. *Victory from the cusp of defeat,* he thought, keeping his expression neutral. *She is damaging her standing with every word.*

The Oblivion moved forward. Moments passed, the debris cloud growing larger on the view screen. As they neared its edge, Gav felt his stomach tighten. There seemed to be no way to pass cleanly. *The hull can handle a few hits,* he thought, *but what about the larger chunks? What if we get smashed between two of them?*

The approach plot appeared on the screen, a vivid green line. The propulsion officer had them precisely in the middle of it, but Gav still felt nervous. *How do we know we can trust some backwater station manager to get us through this?* Ahead, a massive asteroid looked like it was on a collision course. Gav gritted his teeth, beginning to doubt his own resolve. Then, the titanic chunk sped past. The way was open. *At least for now...* It felt like the claustrophobic cloud might crush them at any moment.

"Whatever they are building in here," Crasor said, breaking the tense silence, "they went to great lengths and expense to keep it hidden."

Gav agreed, but kept silent. As they moved past more debris without being destroyed, he felt his excitement return. *Salla cobbled together this ship, but what I have found is of even greater value!*

Then, finally, they saw it: The dark skeleton of an orbital dock floated in an unoccupied bubble amongst the planetary debris. Its ribs embraced a ship unlike anything Gav had ever seen. "What is it?" Salla said, sounding like she'd forgotten some of her anger.

Gav couldn't answer, as he didn't understand it himself. The vessel looked like a cluster of enormous tubes, situated above a rudimentary propulsion system. As he stared at the curious configuration, Gav remembered the materials list the logistics officer had briefed him on.

"It's a gigantic system of mass drivers," he said in awe, quickly running through mental computations. *Hard to know exactly how big the individual tubes are, but even estimating on the small side, they're still bigger than anything humanity has seen before, even on the Justice.*

"It's far too fragile to take into battle," Salla sneered. "Look at those support structures. No armor, no point defenses. An inferior design. It's good they kept it secret from me, otherwise I would have had its engineers killed for incompetence."

Gav would never admit it out loud, but Salla was right. He felt his heart sink. *Is it just incomplete? Maybe there is more to it.* As the Oblivion's propulsion officer skirted past a massive chunk of ice, however, Gav realized what the ship was really meant for.

"It's not designed for close space combat," he blurted, "or even long-range bombardment. Based on the design, the mass drivers don't even launch at rail cannon speeds."

"Then it is worse than useless," Salla laughed, a sneer on her face. "You brought us here for nothing."

"No," Gav said, knowing what he had found would endear him to Crasor forever. "It's a planet killer."

07 – LOTHIS

Lothis heard footsteps approaching the bridge. He turned to see who it was, his dead right eye making him rotate his head farther than normal. Tremmilly, Maxar, and Beowulf entered the bridge. Dras and Jaydon had come in a few minutes earlier, but both seemed content to remain silent. Lothis was glad for this, as his mind was full of whirling thoughts.

Since Cazz-ak's death, he'd felt alone. Felar was still a mother-of-sorts, and Tremmilly, his sister, at least back when they'd been Elrahi. *But none of them are like Cazz-ak.* The Entho-la-ah-mine had been his closest friend, an ally who'd understood Lothis long before the rest of the Harbingers had begun tapping into their Elrahi beings.

Training has helped me control my sadness and anger, but it is merely a distraction. For every skill he remembered or learned, there was a memory of Cazz-ak, as Tha'sis, the Protector, doing it better. Lothis wanted to live up to his friend's skills, to honor his memory. *I'll never be as good as Cazz-ak,* he thought, *and no matter how much we learn of our pasts, we'll never be as strong without him.*

"You OK?" Tremmilly asked, sitting down on the simple metal chair beside him.

"Yes," he said, trying not to show his grief and negativity. "Do you know where Felar is?" Lothis hoped she wouldn't notice the shift in subject.

"I'm not sure. I left her and Wake outside, but they should be along shortly." She put her arm around him, drawing Lothis close. He permitted the physical affection, knowing that it did make him feel better, even if he still didn't understand why. "You've been through a lot," Tremmilly continued, putting her hand on top of one of his scarred arms. "I know things have felt different since we became human, but I want you to know I still think of you as a brother. I still love and care for you in that way."

"Thanks," Lothis said, feeling his cheeks grow warm. From his memories, he knew that they had been quite close, even once she'd become empress of the Accord. Now, though, Lothis had a hard time stepping back into the same emotional space. "I really am doing fine," he continued, knowing that if he protested too hard, he'd sound defensive.

"OK, but if you need anything, I'm here for you."

Lothis nodded and smiled, the expression almost feeling normal.

Felar and Wake walked in, and Lothis was grateful for the distraction. *I know someday I'll feel the same familial bond that Tremmilly does, but dealing with those emotions right now is just too much.* In the back of his mind, he felt the rage that had been there since he'd learned of Cazzak's death. *No, right now I need to think of how to destroy the Breakers, how to annihilate those who killed my friend.* His anger grew and abated daily, but it was always there, driving him to find a way to kill Crasor. *I wasn't there when the Descended were wiped out,* he thought, working hard to smooth the emotion from his face, *but I will be there when we take Crasor down, even if I'm the last one standing.*

"Hey Lothis," Felar said, sitting down on his blind side. When he turned to look at her, he couldn't decipher her expression. *She looks embarrassed? Surprised?* None of his descriptors fit. *She's always met my gaze in the past.* Wake sat on the other side of the room, which was also odd. *Normally, he sits next to me and Felar.* Something seemed off about the situation, but Lothis didn't have the energy to think about it any further. *We need to decide how to go after Crasor,* he decided, anger flaring in his mind.

"We're all here," Felar announced, "so we should get started." As she spoke, her odd posture and body language evaporated, and she settled into her normal rhythm. "Unless anyone objects, I think it is safe for us to depart Lith-elo. In fact, even if we are just in orbit, it puts us in a much better position if the Breakers worm in system."

Lothis had seen the departing Entho-la-ah-mine bi-pyramids through the ship's transparent bridge. He'd fought hard not to cry and had almost succeeded. *Thankfully, Dras wasn't there to see me.* Knowing that the Queen and the rest of the Entho-la-ah-mines on Lith-elo had been forced to flee, yet again, was another seed of rage. *Crasor,* Lothis thought, his fists clenching involuntarily. *First the Ashamine try to exterminate the peaceful race, and now that buggering blightheart wants to assimilate them.*

"I think that is a wise decision," Tremmilly said, breaking Lothis out of his introspection. "With the Entho-la-ah-mines departed, we have no need to stay and protect them."

Despite her regal bearing, Lothis could see something was troubling Tremmilly. *We are all keeping secrets now,* he realized, the thought adding additional sadness to his nearly overwhelmed emotions. *So much has changed since before Maxar, Jaydon, and Wake left for Traynos.*

"I will get us into orbit immediately," Dras said. The ground below the transparent bridge hull began receding. They soon passed through a layer of thin clouds, and Lothis found himself absorbed in imagining what it would be like to be one of the tiny water droplets making up the giant structure.

"Before we plan further," Felar said, "I need to resolve a variable." She turned to look at Lothis and Dras. "What is Fade's status? Will he be of any help to us?"

"You have more contact than I," the Heltasoth said, making a small gesture towards Lothis.

Lothis shrugged, sighing. "I don't think we can count on him for anything. He's degrading, both in a physical and mental sense, although neither Dras nor I believe it has anything to do with his accommodations onboard this ship. I think he's given up. Quantum existence seems... difficult, to say the least." He paused for a moment, thinking. "He's become sullen and withdrawn. I would describe it as depression, but since his processing power is so great, the negativity is magnified exponentially. The last few times I've tried to talk with him, he's barely spoken."

"You did all you could to help," Tremmilly said, a concerned smile on her face. "You've spent hours talking to him. You and Dras both tried to make this ship's systems a welcoming place."

"I know," Lothis replied, shrugging again. He wanted to tell Tremmilly how much it hurt to see Fade's decline, how he empathized with the quantum human for the loss, trauma, and exploitation he'd experienced, but something inside kept him silent. *I can't save Fade, just like I couldn't save Cazz-ak.*

"With that resolved," Felar said finally, "at least for now, I have a plan for what to do next. It is minimal, but only because we need more intel and have some hard decisions to make."

As the atmosphere thinned, shifting from deep blue to black, Lothis wondered if any of them would survive. His limited vision and the scars on his arms mocked him. *You thought you were ready, thought you had the power to face the ancient enemies of the Elrahi. And what happened? You and your best friend died. The only reason you're here now is because of Dras, because nanotechnology repaired your damaged body and brain.*

And isn't that what started this whole division to begin with? See'dek wanted to augment the Elrahi with technology. Aris and the councils told him no, and he tried to kill them all. The Empress sent the people to the Temples, and they transitioned to the Dawn. But we stayed behind...

Lothis still had the Heltasoth nanites inside him, forming brain structures a Descended had destroyed when she shoved her mind dagger through his eye. *How am I any different from See'dek?* he wondered, a question which troubled him since he'd returned to his body. Somehow, Maxar seemed fine with his technological augmentation. *Why can't I be?*

"Remember when you yelled at me before?" Maxar asked. "For this very reason?"

Lothis realized he'd gotten distracted again and missed a large portion of the conversation. *Now is the time to focus,* he thought. *We are deciding our future. They need my help.*

"Yes," Felar said sheepishly. "I remember. At the time, it did feel foolish for us to split up. I wasn't blaming you directly for going to Traynos-6, but I do feel like our decision to divide our forces is what killed Cazz-ak. We were much more powerful when we had each other nearby.

"Now, though, our strength is less dependent on proximity. We've grown strong in the ways of the Blade, and our human combat skills are better as well. If we all remain together, we limit our striking ability. I'm not advocating full-frontal assault on the Breakers. Even together, I don't think we have the power, at least not yet. But if we can strike Crasor's forces and retreat, we'll set them in disarray. They'll have to better protect the planets they control, spreading and thinning their forces."

"But we only have one ship," Jaydon said, brow furrowed.

"Yes," Felar continued, "and that is part of the plan as well. We can assault the Breakers and capture one of their ships. Maybe even get another gunship like the Death Watch. It will be a test run. We can split into two teams, keeping one in reserve in case I'm wrong about our abilities. If we get another ship and all goes well, we can make further plans."

Lothis wanted to do more, wanted to go in with mind blades and rail guns firing, but he knew Felar was right. Despite their ability and power gains, they weren't ready to take on the billions or trillions of Breakers across the Akked. The sheer enormity of their enemy threatened to overwhelm him.

"We have to draw Crasor out," Lothis said, trying to steady his voice. "We have to destroy him."

"I agree," Felar nodded. "There are seven of us, and with the head-start Crasor has, he probably controls billions of Breakers. If he hasn't gone to the Ashamine core worlds yet, he will soon. I don't know what the blighthearted Ashamine has been doing, but I think they've waited too long. We can't rely on them killing Crasor. He's too strong now.

"Once he takes the core worlds, he'll have even more ships and personnel. I estimate he'll double or triple the size and strength of his forces. If that happens, we'll have no hope. Crasor will hunt both us and the Entho-la-ah-mines down."

Everyone around the room nodded, looking somber. *We knew this,* Lothis thought. *Even if we didn't understand the exact situation, we knew the odds were grim. We just didn't want to admit it.*

"But Crasor has a weakness," Maxar said, the intensity on his face contradicting his gentle tone. "He wants us, and will put himself in risky situations to try to kill us. We can use that."

"Exactly," Felar said, a wicked smile transforming her face. "He tried to fight us in single combat on that hangar in the Justice, wormed all over space chasing us at the risk of running into a superior Ashamine force. And I have no way of knowing this for sure, but I think he sent the Descended for us, rather than coming himself, because we started to feel less threatening. If we renew our power in his mind, mess up some of his plans, get in his face and kill some of his forces, I think he's maniacal enough to come after us personally."

"Then we can strike," Tremmilly said, putting a finger on her lips and looking thoughtful.

"Then we can strike," Felar confirmed.

As Lith-elo-hi-rosh rotated gently below them, Lothis felt his seed of rage pulse at the back of his mind. *Soon,* he thought, remembering how Cazz-ak had looked in death, his carapace shattered, legs missing. *Soon.*

08 – ASH

Ash felt each passing second as it slipped by. *It's as excruciating as Verger torture,* he thought, checking the ship's tactical display for the thousandth time. *What's taking Fierence so long?* Ash had grown used to the lawless Vergers' tradition of lateness, but their elected leader had never followed that custom. *Hopefully there wasn't a coup.*

More time dragged by, and Ash felt the acuteness of their position. *If an Ashamine or Breaker ship shows up...* Normally, he'd be sequestered in the Brotherhood stronghold on nearby Azak-1. *But now we are an hour or more away if something goes wrong.* Fierence had barely agreed to this meeting, stipulating that he wouldn't leave his ship and that his vessel wouldn't go inside the gravity well surrounding the star system. *And rather than talk via ship's comms, he demanded face-to-face.* Had Fierence not been so important to Ash, he would have turned down his demands. *But humanity needs all the help it can get,* Ash thought, checking the tactical display yet again. *Still nothing.*

"Parick," his XO said, breaking into Ash's thoughts, "how long are we gonna wait for the Vergers? I know it's unlikely the Ashamine would show up, but we've detected the Breaker scouts worming through our system on a number of occasions. Perhaps we should consider using the cloaking mechanism?"

Even though he'd gone by the name Parick Olvold for the last seven years, Ash still thought of himself as Ash Kissawai, at least in most regards. He was still the same man he'd been when he'd left the Ashamine Holy Order, still had the same ideals. *By either name, I still want what is best for humanity.* He hadn't kept his name and background secret when he'd fled to Verger territory, seeking a way to act on his beliefs. Everyone beyond the edge of Ashamine controlled space had a history of some sort. Most didn't care what anyone else's was.

"I'd like to," Ash replied, trying not to express his own agitation at

31

Fierence's lateness. "But given the cloak's limited duration and fuel supply, I'd like to save it for more desperate times. Unfortunately, I think we just have to wait as long as we can. We have the weaponry to take out a Breaker scout if need be. We've done it before." The bridge fell silent, his crew looking as anxious as Ash felt.

So many steps to take, balanced on the blade's edge, he thought. *You are too busy to go rescue your own niece. You told her you were coming.* That was when he'd thought he'd be able to make it through Ashamine security, before the Breaker scout ships had started passing near the Brotherhood's base. *Em will take care of her,* he thought, trying to combat his feelings of guilt. *Besides, with the lockdown and security measures in place, you'd have never made it onto Ashamine-2. And I can't ignore the entire fate of the Akked just to protect my kin.* As much as the last thought hurt and made his guilt soar even higher, Ash knew it was true. *I trust my captains, but we lost so many good people on Eishon-2. If I had been there, maybe I could have prevented it.*

"A worm just opened up," the sensor officer announced.

"About blighthearted time," his XO mumbled.

Ash's heart rate quickened, and he mentally went through his list of negotiation items. He needed the Vergers, and despite their erratic nature and system of government, they were good, trustworthy people who would follow through with their agreements. *But you're asking them to support the Ashamine,* Ash thought, biting his lip. *You have to make them see it is for the good of humanity and the galaxy as a whole.* The enormity of the task felt daunting.

"Inbound ship isn't broadcasting the agreed ident codes," the sensor officer said, voice tight. Ash felt all his distractions disappear. On the view screen, a dark hulled ship slid into the system, making his heart sink.

"Bugger," the sensor operator continued after a moment. "It's an Ashamine design."

Everyone knew this meant one of two things: it was actually Ashamine, or it was Breaker. Verger ships were a motley mix of reconfigured Ashamine or homebrew technology. It was a point of pride amongst the different clans to create ships more bizarre than their fellows.

Ash could feel everyone's eyes on him, waiting for orders. *Odds are, it's Breaker.* The Ashamine never came out this far. It was too dangerous, between the Vergers and the multiple unplotted worm transitions they'd have to make. That was the whole reason why the Brotherhood and the Vergers were out here. *And if it's Breakers, we have to destroy them. Once they find out there is a whole faction of humans here...*

"Rail them into oblivion," Ash ordered. He sensed a strange thrum go through the ship as the huge guns powered up, felt the pit in his stomach grow as he waited for the Breaker ship to worm away. *Come on, come on.*

Red ion trails streaked through the void between the two ships, first two, then four, then six as the cannons spooled up.

"They've opened a worm," the sensor operator announced.

Three out of the six rail rounds struck their target, punching huge holes in the small enemy ship. Ash permitted himself to breathe again after two more hits made it evident the scout vessel wouldn't be leaving Azak space.

Evidence, Ash realized, knowing if another Breaker scout ship passed through this area, they'd find the wreckage. "Use the gravity-mass beam to send them into the star," he ordered. At first, the propulsion officer looked at him strangely, then seemed to understand. It wasn't how the tool was typically used, but it would work. *If I was wrong, and somehow there are surviving Ashamine humans on board, then I ask the gods for forgiveness.* It was far too dangerous to check. He'd seen how the Breakers could spread, and what they were capable of.

The situation calmed, and time dragged by once again. *I can't wait here forever,* he thought again, knowing he was risking what little remained of the Brotherhood of Azak-so by staying in this exposed position. On Azak-1, they had shielded and camouflaged facilities, several underground cities and settlements that were impervious to ship-mounted sensors.

Another minute passed, and Ash decided he could wait no longer. "Take us home," he ordered, fearing what this would mean for his plan to save humanity.

"Yes, Parick," the propulsion officer said, entering commands on his console.

"A new worm is opening," the sensor operator said.

"Hold," Ash ordered, hoping beyond hope it was Fierence. "Prepare cannons to fire if ident is unsuccessful." He watched a patch of stars vanish, only to be replaced by a new, different set a moment later.

An excruciating second passed, then another. "Successful ident," the comms officer declared, as a shining Verger ship slid through the worm, its angles jarring and ungraceful. "Fierence is hailing us."

"Put him through." Ash waited, head held high, mentally rehearsing his best arguments.

"Parick Olvold," Fierence said on the comms screen. "How good it is to see you."

"And you as well," Ash replied, trying to return the Verger's smile.

"I apologize for our lateness," the bald man said. "We ran into some... Difficulties."

"The Verge is not as safe as it once was."

"Indeed," Fierence said, eyes narrowing. "I would like to hear what you have to say about these changes. I feel it best for us not to couple, so that our ships might be prepared to face intruders."

"Agreed."

"Do you mind taking your own shuttle? Or should I send mine?"

"I'll depart shortly."

***

"You're asking me to risk every woman, man, and squiggle in the entire Verge," Fierence said, his bald scalp turning crimson.

"No," Ash said, breathing deeply, "I'm simply informing you they are already at risk. The danger is growing exponentially."

"Why should we protect the Ashamine, when all they've done is reject and murder us? It's not like we came to the Verge because there were pleasant planets and nice weather."

Ash knew enough Verger history to know this wasn't exactly true. While many had left the Ashamine due to various political, social, and economic persecutions, others had departed for less noble reasons, namely criminal records and sociopathic tendencies. *Now's not the time to bring that up.*

"We aren't trying to protect the Ashamine, Fierence. We are trying to save humanity. If we stand by, the Breakers will destroy the Ashamine and humankind along with it. We won't be safe. The Breakers will find us, if they don't already know about the Verge.

"They already control the Ashamine border worlds and are working their way towards the core. With the rest of the Ashamine fleet, personnel, infrastructure, and citizens under their control, there will be no way to stop them. Right now, we have the ability to step in, but we will have to ally with the Ashamine Forces." Fierence snorted derisively, but Ash continued. "Yes, it is disgusting, but if we watch our back and handle things correctly, there is a good chance we can take out the Breakers, putting us in a position to establish a new government when the war is done." Ash could see his last words starting to win the Verger leader over. *He's not stupid, just stubborn.*

"The Ashamine is weak," Ash continued, trying to keep his momentum high. "With the Founder dead and his heir missing or dead as well, they are in a position they've never faced before. When a government is built on such a strong figure, it is hard for them to learn new ways. If we step in as strong leaders, I think the Classad and High-Elders, if they are still alive, will listen to us." Ash didn't mention that he thought the military might balk. *Save that for if and when the problem arises.*

Fierence let out a long grunt that sounded like a cross between a growl and a burp. "As much as I don't want you to be right, I think you are. Like I mentioned earlier, we ran into some difficulties in transit due to an incident, with the ones you call Breakers. I lost some of my own crew. It wasn't pretty." He paused for a moment, thinking. "You obviously know more about the Breakers than I, so I'll minimize details, but at first, we thought the ship we'd captured was infected with some sort of disease. Perhaps the Ashamine had created another plague like on Eishon-2. But no, an alien entity makes far more sense. They were too intelligent, too coordinated." Fierence sighed, shaking his head. "I've been a Verger my whole life, Parick. My parents too. Generations back. We built a place for those who didn't belong to the Ashamine. Blightheart, we even took you in, a former Ashamine holy man.

"We survived and thrived, creating order from chaos. We've kept the human spirit free and alive, despite the Ashamine's best efforts. But now, things are changing." He smiled, an action that wrinkled his face and bald head.

Ash nodded. He too had come to the realization that the Akked galaxy was changing, that they'd never be able to go back to their previous existence. He'd built the Brotherhood of Azak-so to combat the Ashamine's injustices, not destroy the entire government. Even if humanity survived, it would be years and decades before any type of meaningful, long-term stability returned.

"It's the end of an era," Ash said.

"Blightheart that," Fierence bellowed. "This is a beginning of an age. The Verger age."

09 – MAXAR

"You're sure this is the right ship?" Jaydon asked.

Maxar stared at the Breaker gunship for a moment longer, his nanite connection to the Heltasoth ship allowing him to see beyond his human senses. "Yes. It's isolated, with minimal crew on board. We'll be able to take on six Breakers, we'll gain a ship, and it will be a good test run for Felar's theory."

"It just looks so big," Jaydon grumbled. "And it's not like I have special abilities like you all."

"It's the same size as the Death Watch. Same model too, if I'm not mistaken. It will be familiar for you to fly and for us to crew."

Tremmilly put her arm around the grizzled captain, smiling. "I have all the same combat abilities as you. No mind blades, no singularities, no shields. We'll just have our pistols and our wits."

Maxar felt a smile grow on his own face, despite the intensity burning in his chest. *She's learned so much, come so far, since the Bloodsport asteroid.* Maxar had been a convict in his past Elrahi life, as well as his human one. Even though See'dek had framed him for the death of an entire world, Maxar knew he still wasn't blameless, at least in his human life. *How could she love someone like me?*

"Yeah, yeah," Jaydon rasped, shaking his head. "It's amazing how straight we can shoot. Blah, blah, blah." The smile on his face belied his rough edge. "I know, 'We'll be fine.'"

Maxar couldn't help but laugh. The old smuggler's tone and inflection was spot on for Felar.

Tremmilly laughed as well. "She's right though. Felar has trained us all well. We will complete the mission." She bent down and stroked Beowulf's lustrous coat. Maxar could almost feel her touch move across his own back.

That's impossible, he thought, wondering if it really was. Memories of

36

being in Beowulf's head and taking part in restoring Lothis' connection to his Elrahi being were faint, but still present. *We are one being, separated during transition from Elrah to human.* He could think the thoughts, know they were true, and still, it made little sense.

"Remember," Felar's voice said over his suit's comm, "we are only here for backup. Call us if you need to, but remember, this is a test. If you have to draw on our strength, Elrahi or human, we'll have to rethink our entire strategy. We all know there isn't time for that. Fight hard, and pretend we aren't here."

"Affirm," Maxar replied, latching his helmet to the rest of his ENS suit. Everyone else did the same. *No way of knowing what conditions will be like on that buggered ship. Hopefully, there's atmosphere for Beo. If not, I suppose we'll have to leave him here.*

Dras was taking them towards the Breaker gunship as fast as he could, while still maintaining the ship's strange stealth ability. "It won't be fast," the Heltasoth had said, "but they won't know we are there, not until we couple with their airlock. There is a chance they will spot a dark patch of space, like the background stars disappeared, a void in the blackness. Even if they do, they have little chance of knowing what is causing it. The odds are in our favor.

"Once connected, it will be up to your team to force entry. Unless the Breakers want to risk a collision, I think they'll be willing to stay and fight."

Maxar hoped the Heltasoth was right. *If he's not, and we get blasted out of a compromised airlock, at least we'll have our suits on.*

When Felar had proposed the idea of two teams, and who their members would be, Maxar was glad to find out Tremmilly was with him. *No need to challenge her plan.* Objectively, he knew he was in the weaker group, but it told him what Felar thought of his combat abilities. *I'm the only one here who can manipulate the way of the Blade,* he thought, looking from Tremmilly, to Jaydon, to Beowulf. *If you didn't know us, you'd think we were a bunch of hashers.*

Despite the fact Felar's team had three people who could wield mind blades, plus Brightwing, plus Dras, Maxar was glad for his assignment. *Just have to make sure I keep them all alive...*

The Breaker gunship was close now, and Maxar knew he had to focus. Another minute passed, the stationary Breaker ship taking up the entire outside view. Through his connection to Dras' ship, Maxar felt it couple with the enemy vessel. The Heltasoth hull formed a seal, tiny nanites sliding into place around the Breaker airlock. It took only a fraction of a second, the malleable technology amazing Maxar.

"It's time," he transmitted, looking each of his teammates in the eye. "We can do this."

The translucent wall in front of him lensed open, revealing the enemy's airlock. *My turn,* Maxar thought, setting to work on the nearby access panel, trying not to think what would happen if the Breakers decided to flee. *Maybe it wasn't the greatest idea bringing Beowulf after all.* A command prompt flashed up on the screen, showing he had no privileges. *Didn't figure I would, but it doesn't hurt to check.*

Maxar tried an exploit on terminal, quickly keying in several lines of code. He entered the command. The terminal flashed a red stop hand. *Must have patched that one out.*

For his second attempt, Maxar tried a more complex and time-consuming authentication corruption hash. He entered more code, this time in several symbiotic steps. As seconds, then a full minute crawled by, he felt the urgency of the situation threaten to overwhelm him.

Finally, he entered the last command and a green thumbs up appeared. "We're in," Maxar yelled, feeling his body tense with the nerves that came immediately before combat. *Everyone is at risk, and everyone understands that,* he thought, taking a firing stance next to the door.

Maxar took a quick look behind him, making sure Tremmilly and Jaydon were in their agreed upon positions. They were. As he turned back to the airlock, he saw a timer counting down the seconds left until pressure equalization. *Three...* Maxar reached out to the surrounding space-time, using his Elrahi abilities to compress and mold it into a dagger in his left hand. He lengthened the blade, until it was almost a short sword. The energy shimmered across an iridescent spectrum, making Maxar smile. It felt good to have a weapon in his fist. *Two...* Between his mind blade and his flechette pistol, he was ready. *One...*

The gunship door opened, and Maxar dove through. The Heltasoth nanites coursing through his body sensed three Breakers in the room adjoining the airlock. *Perfect.* Maxar slashed the nearest one as he rose to his feet, the infinitely sharp blade splitting the Breaker from crotch to forehead. In the next instant, Maxar aimed and fired his pistol, the distinctive crack and whistle of the flechette needles accompanying his action. The second Breaker's head exploded, black blood spraying across the bulkhead behind him.

Another crack-whistle sounded next to Maxar, and he turned to see Tremmilly poised in a shooter's stance. The third Breaker slumped to the floor, a ragged hole in his chest.

Jaydon stepped forward and raised his short sword, standing over the motionless form. The old captain paused for a moment, wavering. Finally, he brought down his blade, severing the creature's neck. When Jaydon turned back, Maxar saw his face was a pale shade of green. "Has to be done," Maxar heard over the comm, although he expected Jaydon hadn't meant to transmit.

"We need to get to the bridge, secure the ship's controls," Maxar said. Seeing the cannon loading machinery adjoining the airlock, Maxar guessed this ship was identical to their former ship, the Death Watch. Beowulf went streaking ahead of him, seeming to make the same decision.

They finally caught up to the wolf-dog at the ladder that led from the crew quarters to the engine room. He was whining and prancing around the closed hatch.

Maxar shook his head, using his nanites to scan the room below for Breakers. "Engine room is clear," he announced, opening the hatch. Beowulf immediately dove through, a feat he'd previously never tried on the Death Watch. After a hard landing, he looked up, head cocked, unfazed.

Following him down, Maxar then waited for Tremmilly and Jaydon to follow. "There are two in targeting, one on the command deck. Careful with your shots. If we damage anything, it will take time to fix it, time we don't have."

They both nodded, and signaled their readiness. Maxar strode forward, slapping the terminal button to open the bulkhead door. Inside, he saw two startled Breakers, trying to spool up their rail cannons.

"Greet the darkness you've always been destined for," Maxar said, throwing his mind dagger towards the nearest Breaker. His aim was true, and the blade went directly between the female's mutated eyes. Beowulf leapt through the air, fangs glistening. He barreled into the remaining Breaker, tearing at his throat.

Maxar continued forward, sensing the wolf-dog had the situation under control. He didn't know if the Breakers could mentally communicate, but so far, the Harbingers had struck so quickly they didn't seem to know what was happening. Maxar channeled energy through his left palm, reforming his mind dagger. He still hadn't grown accustomed to the sensation, a strange mixture of rushing and tingling. As he finished, he opened the bulkhead door and entered the command deck.

"Halt, Ashamine," the remaining Breaker said, holding his hands in the air. "I offer you power beyond your grandest imaginings."

"Wrong, tainted one," Tremmilly said, stepping up beside Maxar. "We are true Elrah, not filthy traitors. We want nothing to do with your corruption." A crack-whistle sounded, and the Breaker fell to the deck, head a shattered mess of black clots.

Maxar felt his eyebrows raise involuntarily. He'd seen the regal, empress side of Tremmilly, but never expressed in this manner.

"My aim has gotten better," Tremmilly said, a coy smile on her face. "Proud?"

"Of course," Maxar stammered.

"Just so I know," Jaydon said, sounding disgusted, "am I always going to be the one who has to do the head removal thing?"

Maxar barked a laugh. "No, Jaydon. Just this time, I promise."

"Because, I blightheartedly swear, that if I do, I'll quit!"

Tremmilly joined Maxar's laughter as the angry captain entered the deck.

"I'll take the next one," Maxar said, trying to stifle his mirth. "Ship cleared and secured," Maxar transmitted back to the Heltasoth ship. "No friendly casualties or injuries. Let us close the airlock, then you can depart."

"Nice work," Felar's voice said. "They must have gotten a message off right when you boarded," she continued, "because we have a bunch of inbound Breaker ships streaming our way from Qi-3 near-space. Time to get out of here."

Jaydon moved over to the pilot's seat and made a few selections on the terminal. "Felar, airlock is closed. Once you uncouple, I'll get us headed to the worm boundary." He paused for a moment. "And Maxar, since I'm fully occupied, perhaps you could clean off this deck. Can't let all that Breaker blood corrode our beautiful decking."

"Alright, alright," Maxar replied, shaking his head ruefully.

"I'll head back to the rail cannons," Tremmilly added, a satisfied smile on her face. "I'll get them ready, just in case."

Maxar returned her smile, knowing this ship was a small, but significant first step in their campaign against Crasor. *The darkness is coming for you, See'dek,* Maxar thought, wondering if his old enemy still existed somewhere amongst the Breakers. *And I won't be merciful.*

10 – FELAR

"Once you uncouple," Felar heard over the comms, "I'll get us headed to the worm boundary."

Felar let her breath out slowly, feeling the tension relax from her shoulders. *It's amazing how strong and useful Jaydon is, since he went clean.* When she'd first met the captain, he'd felt like a liability more than an asset. *I never thought he'd be able to give up alcohol.* Felar still didn't know what had made Jaydon swim so deep in the ancient substance, but she'd seen enough traumatized soldiers to know he had something dark in his past. *He'll share it with me if he wants to, when he wants to.*

"The Breaker ships won't be able to catch us," Dras announced, "unless something goes wrong on Maxar's ship. We have a sufficient lead."

Felar nodded, agreeing with his assessment. "Good. Everything is working out according to plan." She'd believed Maxar, Tremmilly, Jaydon, and Beowulf would be capable of capturing the gunship, but there was always a chance of the unexpected blighthearting them. From what she could tell, they'd overthrown the enemy crew in a quick and efficient manner. *You did a good job designating teams.*

As they drew closer to the worm boundary, Felar watched her home-world of Qi-3 grow smaller and smaller behind them. *My parents,* she thought, wondering what had happened to them. *Were they killed outright, or are they Breakers?* She didn't understand why they chose to convert some humans and kill others. She knew it was foolish to hope her parents might have survived somehow. *You saw what they did on the Justice.*

A weight settled on Felar's chest, sadness intermingled with resentment and guilt. *I should have been there, shouldn't have left them.* She settled back into one of the metal chairs Dras had created on the bridge. *You would have died, just like them. You wouldn't be in a position to defeat*

41

the Breakers and protect the trillions of humans left in the Akked.

Felar hadn't picked Qi-3 for their first strike because she thought she could rescue her parents. They'd known the Breakers were in the system, which meant conversion or death for everyone who couldn't escape. No, she'd picked it because they'd seen so few ships when they'd wormed there, attempting to escape the Justice. Felar was also familiar with the layout of the planet and its stellar mechanics.

Time passed as Dras brought them closer to the worm boundary. Felar periodically checked behind them, making sure the gunship was keeping up. The Heltasoth vessel, when not trying to be stealthy, was capable of almost double the speed when maneuvering in a solar system. Felar had asked Dras to stay close to the other team, just in case something malfunctioned on their vessel.

On the edge of her vision, she saw Lothis and Wake playing a game of Castles and talking quietly. Things had felt awkward and formal between Felar and the engineer. *I hope I handled things correctly,* she thought, continuing to watch them in her peripheral vision. Felar had meant all the things she'd told him. *Now, your secret's out.*

It wasn't a secret, she thought, rubbing her hand across her forehead. *I just never had a reason to tell everyone.* While this was strictly true, Felar had withheld many personal details from her fellow Harbingers. *Except for Wake.* She did feel a deep bond with the engineer, even if it wasn't romantic.

"Both ships have exited the gravity well," Dras said, breaking Felar out of her reverie.

"Perfect," she replied. Felar hit the transmit toggle on the arm of her chair. "Jaydon, ready on your ship?"

"Everything is green," his rough voice replied. "Ready when you are."

"Let's go."

***

"How will we call for assistance or update each other mid-mission?" Tremmilly asked. They'd done several worm transitions to throw off pursuers and were now in a remote region of the Akked.

Dras knows our galaxy well, Felar thought, looking among her friends as they spoke. The captured Breaker gunship, renamed "Retribution," was now coupled with Dras' airlock. Everyone was currently on the Heltasoth ship's bridge.

"If both ships are outside the worm boundary," Dras said, answering Tremmilly's question, "you will be able to use the device I installed on the Retribution to communicate. Otherwise, it is not possible. Even we Heltasoth have not discovered a way to transmit information from inside the gravitic influence zone of a solar system."

Felar had known this was a negative aspect of her plan. *It won't stop us though,* she thought, locking gazes with Wake. They both looked away quickly, and Felar felt her cheeks get warm. *Everything is fine. Quit making this into a bigger deal than it is.*

"We will have to plan our strikes according to a schedule and check in with each other at agreed upon times." Felar felt better when she was doing, rather than just thinking. "We have no other choice."

"This is dangerous," Maxar said, biting his lip. "If something goes wrong, neither team will have backup."

"I know," Felar said. "I'm not saying the plan doesn't have faults, but I can't think of any other way."

"We could stick together," Wake added. "Work as one team on two ships."

"No time," Lothis said, the first words Felar had heard him say in a while. "If we remain as a single unit, we limit our effectiveness. We need to deceive Crasor into thinking there are more of us. It has the greatest chance of drawing him out to take care of the situation personally."

"And maybe we'll find other humans in the Akked," Tremmilly said brightly, "people who will join our cause. There have to be people who escaped Crasor's invasions."

Felar wished that were true, but she doubted it.

"There are the Vergers," Dras said, "but they are relatively weak from a military standpoint, at least from what I know of them."

"Who are the Vergers?" Maxar asked, brow furrowed.

"Scavengers, vagabonds, explorers," Dras replied. "They roam the outer edges of the Akked. I was never able to tell exactly how many of them there were. They are a secretive, loosely bound group who prefer independence to the safety and comforts of even the border worlds."

"Interesting," Felar said. "Why have I never heard of them before?"

"Not many have. I don't think the Ashamine even knows of their existence."

"Would it be worth going to talk to them?" Tremmilly asked. "Perhaps we could form an alliance. Maybe they could help us somehow."

Dras shook his head. "If we had more time or personnel, it might be worthwhile. Given what I currently know, I doubt we, as those unconnected to the Vergers, would be able to convince them. They have no love for the Ashamine and would celebrate its destruction, rather than prevent it."

"If the Ashamine hadn't obliterated the Brotherhood of Azak-so," Felar added, "I would say we should coordinate with them. But even if anyone survived, I don't know how we'd find or contact them." *And given how hard the Ashamine hit Eishon-2...*

"Did anyone else notice how different the Breakers looked?" Maxar asked, sounding troubled.

"Yeah," Jaydon said. Tremmilly nodded too.

"What do you mean?" Felar asked, her attention locking onto the new information.

"They looked different from the Descended," Maxar said, "or the Breakers back on the Justice. They're more evolved somehow, less human."

"I think they are heading towards some new form," Tremmilly added.

"Have they gained new abilities?" Felar asked.

Maxar thought for a moment. "Not from what I could tell."

"Well," Felar decided, "let's keep our guard up as always. We swap intel between the teams and keep up-to-date on whatever is going on with the Breakers. Hopefully, it's just physical mutations and nothing with their mental capabilities."

Everyone nodded, looking somber. Felar waited for someone else to speak, but finally continued. "Then it's decided. We'll separate and conduct independent strikes on pre-planned Breaker planets and installations." She looked around the room once again, hoping this wasn't the last time they would all be together.

11 – CRASOR

Crasor slammed his fist on the chair's arm, his jaw clenching so tight it hurt. The list of incidents on the terminal in front of him was infuriating. "Who is perpetrating all of these attacks?" he said, his voice a hot blade formed of rage. "Why have they gotten away unscathed, every blighthearted time?"

He selected one listing, then another. "On Eishon-2, they destroyed several vessels. On Vind-8, shortly after Karoth took the world, they captured a gunship. The buggers set it on autopilot, and rammed into one of our Rubicon class ships, causing significant damage." He checked more listings, face growing red as he scanned each one. "An orbital bombardment on Kii-la-ta, a sabotaged dock on Exis-7, crippled mining capability on Traynos-6." He slammed his fist down once again. "Every time Karoth takes a world, these blighthearted attackers swoop in and do some treachery. Even our strongholds aren't safe."

Crasor closed the list, knowing he had to get his rage under control. Everyone on the bridge of his flagship, the Transfiguration, remained silent, waiting.

"We told you to dispose of the Harbingers," the Breaker mind thundered in Crasor's head. "Your Descended failed. Now, our true enemy is gaining strength, just as we told you they would."

I'm dealing with them now, Crasor replied.

"Hopefully, it is not too late."

"We've exited the gravity well, and are now worm capable," the Transfiguration's propulsion officer announced.

"Entire fleet ready for transition, on your mark," the comms officer added.

"Hold," the Breaker mind ordered. "There is another ship that must go with you."

Crasor felt a pit form in his stomach. He knew what ship the voice

45

was talking about. *We are ready to go now,* he protested. *Time is of the essence.*

"You waited this long to send another mission to destroy the Harbingers. Another standard hour won't make a difference." The voice of the Breakers was full of scorn, and Crasor felt himself wilt before it.

It's only been three weeks since we discovered their hiding place, he sent. *I have been doing all I can to secure the Akked for you, to build our strength for the final push. Karoth needed me for the campaigns on the larger Ashamine worlds, just as he needs the Justice now. I had to find and outfit the Transfiguration to make it suitable—*

"We want action, not excuses!" the Breaker mind shrieked, its trillion voices a violent cacophony. "Find the Harbingers and destroy them!"

After the reverberation subsided from his head, Crasor realized he'd had his eyes closed. When he opened them, his bridge crew was staring at him expectantly.

As you command, Crasor sent back. "Hold position," he announced. "We have another ship joining the armada."

Minutes dragged past as Crasor waited for the final vessel, hoping beyond hope that perhaps he was wrong. *Please don't be them,* he repeated over and over to himself.

Ever since the Breakers had sent the three ships full of the faceless beings back from their dimension during the battle of Exis-7, Crasor had been on edge. The Breaker mind had assured him they were his to command, but so far, he'd barely seen them. The ships would be gone for long periods of time, on missions unknown to Crasor.

"Worm transition opening," the sensor tech announced, pulling Crasor from his reverie.

Please don't be the Faceless, he thought again, before seeing the ship's name pop up on his tactical display. *Buggering blightheart.* The exterior of what was once the ASN Valiant looked much like it had before, but Crasor knew it was full of the smooth faced creatures.

"Proceed," the Breaker mind said, sounding satisfied.

"Make the transition to the Entho world," Crasor ordered, trying to shut the image of the Faceless out of his mind. *The Breakers promised me power, promised me control of this dimension.* The reassurance did little to comfort him.

***

"The planet is empty of Enthos," the sensor tech said, voice quavering.

"Empty?" Crasor asked, feeling like his heart had stopped.

"Yes, sir," the tech affirmed. "All orbital based assets confirm what the ground teams reported. There is evidence the Enthos and Harbingers were there, but not for quite some time."

I waited too long, he thought. *How did they evacuate so quickly?*

"You underestimate the Harbingers," the Breaker mind said. "Again, and again, you fail us." Crasor's stomach felt like a black hole, gnawing at him. Even though they didn't say it, the threat was there: "Succeed, or we will replace you."

Rage boiled up in Crasor once again, not towards the Breaker mind, but at the blighthearted Harbingers who were making him look like a failure. *I will find them, and I will destroy them! This is but a minor setback.*

"As you say," the voice boomed.

"Deploy the Rain," Crasor said, feeling like he needed something to placate his anger. *This will send those buggers a message,* he thought. His crew set to work, becoming almost frantic with activity.

"Expedite troop removal from the surface."

"Pull back sensor ships and reform the fleet."

"Ensure safe clearance from the planet."

"Rain in proper firing range."

Crasor felt his rage subside, transforming into a cold void of hatred. *This is what I will do to everyone who stands in my way,* he thought, waiting for everything to fall into place.

"Sir," Gav said over the view screen. "My ship is ready. All that is left is to set intensity. Give the order, and I'll have my weapon's officer initiate."

Crasor smiled, his face transforming into a sneer. "We don't need full destruction, but I want to see what your planet killer is capable of. Launch when ready."

"As you wish," Gav said. "Tubes selected and coordinates locked. Deploy."

Crasor watched as the Rain's propulsion engines fired full forward thrust. As it began moving, the array of tubes above the ship's rudimentary structure started launching projectile after projectile. The enormous rods were much bigger than anything a rail cannon could deploy, although they moved substantially slower. The Rain's forward progress slowed, then stopped. Crasor expected the recoil of the giant launchers to send the ship backwards, but it held fast, engines still at full burn.

With no ion tracer component in the slugs, they soon vanished into the blackness of space. Crasor knew they were on target, though, and they would accelerate to an even higher velocity as the bugger world pulled them in.

"Any moment now," Gav transmitted, both the launchers and his ship's engines cutting simultaneously. Several seconds ticked by, Crasor waiting in exquisite anticipation.

Then, the first few rods struck the atmosphere, creating bright flares of light. "Enhance magnification," he commanded. The view screen brought the Entho world even closer, and Crasor smiled. Rod after rod plunged into the planet, sending massive plumes of dirt, rock, and super-heated magma into the atmosphere. Soon, the view was obscured by the debris, but Crasor could see the glow of fires. He knew the inferno on the ground would reach levels that would sanitize everything but the hardiest bacteria.

"Do you want me to move to the opposite hemisphere?" Gav asked.

"No," Crasor replied. "You've proved Rain a success."

12 – AZA

Aza felt the weight on her chest grow as the pneumatic tube transport approached its next stop. *Be calm,* she thought, *Em got you the genetic credentials you need.* She breathed out slowly, trying not to appear nervous to her escort or the surrounding passengers.

"We've received reports," the Terminal Network commentator announced, drawing Aza's attention back to the screen situated above her, "that Kii-la-ta has fallen to enemy forces. All comms with the planet are down. It can only be assumed that the attackers will be coming for the core worlds soon."

"Buggering blightheart," Em growled. "This isn't going to help us at all. Couldn't he have kept his overly-pretty mouth shut on that last line? He's going to cause a world-wide riot."

Aza remained silent, trying to add up how many worlds had been lost to the invaders. *I've lost track...* Over the past two weeks, while they'd been lying low, looking for someone to create Aza's spoofed credentials, she'd watched world after world fall to the Breakers via the Network. It felt like there was so little of the Ashamine left, both of its people and its government. *Are any worlds beyond the core left?*

When Aza had asked, Em filled her in on what she knew about the Breakers, although she admitted it wasn't much and it might not be accurate. "They're like some kind of intelligent plague or something, unlike anything humans have seen before. Alien. Foreign. The Brotherhood has had a couple encounters, mostly with their small recon ships. I don't think we'd have survived, if the forces had been any larger." When Aza had asked for more information about the Brotherhood and her uncle's part in it, Em had told her, "It's not my place. Best for him to tell you." This answer frustrated Aza, but she figured she'd see him soon.

After finding someone capable of such a deep level network

penetration, they'd waited the prescribed 36 standard hours for the hash to propagate through the secure databases. *It should be ready now,* Aza thought, watching as the commentator started recapping all the worlds that had fallen to the Breakers.

"Listen," Em said, looking determined. "We don't have a lot of time before our stop. It's going to be hectic out there. There will be a lot of people that all want off this world. They'll all be trying to get to the same place as us: the orbital dock. None of them will have the credentials or authorization we do, and that will make them desperate. Do what I say, and for the love of Azak-so, don't draw attention to us."

Aza nodded, feeling homesick. *But that place doesn't exist anymore,* she thought, knowing she had to be strong. From everything she'd seen on the Network, it felt like the Classad and High-Elders had given up. *Maybe they fled to some hidden worlds long ago.* The thought made Aza feel an intense anger she'd never experienced before. *How could they abandon us, when we needed them most? They should have stayed and fought!*

And where are we going now? To some Brotherhood base? How long will it stay hidden? If the Ashamine can't stand up to the Breakers, how can anyone else? Aza felt the tube begin to decelerate, and she shut all thoughts about the future out of her mind. *If you can't get past the Ashamine Forces, to the orbital dock, and into Em's ship, none of it will matter.*

"Ready?" Em asked, one eyebrow raised.

As the tube came to a quick stop, Aza breathed in deeply. "Yes," she exhaled, knowing she had to be.

"We'll wait for them to leave first," Em said, nodding towards the mass of humanity jostling outside their private compartment. The tube doors sealed against the station, the hissing of pressure equalization audible through their plasti-glass wall. "Someone is likely to get trampled, bladed, or worse."

Sure enough, as soon as the doors began sliding open, everyone inside the tube started fighting to get out first. Someone shouted, another screamed, and a melee broke out.

"Blighthearted idiots," Em said, shaking her head. "Half of them probably never got any education, and those that did never had an opportunity to use it for good." After a few minutes passed, most of the crowd had exited the transport. Those still inside either lay unconscious on the floor, or were looting the incapacitated forms.

"Come on," Em said, taking Aza's hand as she opened their compartment door. The imminent departure signal began to flash, signaling they only had a few moments left to get off before the tube left.

"Shouldn't we help them?" Aza asked as Em led her towards the primary exit.

"There is a very fine line between us and them," the older woman replied, giving one of the looters a fierce glance as they passed. The man shrank away, quickly breaking eye contact. "If we don't get to the orbital dock as quickly as possible, we may be stuck on Ashamine-2 until the Breakers show up."

Aza knew she was right, but something about passing those in need just felt wrong. *But I'm in need too, and Em is rescuing me.* As they exited out into the station, the doors slid shut behind them. The cacophony assaulting Aza's senses made her forget about the few helpless individuals in the tube.

Before her, a mass of humanity stretched across the station. On the far side, towards the exit to the above-ground city, was a thick plasti-glass barrier. Several squads of Ashamine Forces troops blocked the single gate. "NO CLEARANCE, NO EXIT" flashed on the massive screen hung above them.

"We have to keep moving," Em said, pulling Aza into the tightly packed mass. They wiggled, squirmed, and tunneled through the crowd, drawing ever closer to the gate. Once, when the mass momentarily diminished, Aza saw several guards with heavy armor and shock batons protecting some sort of scanner.

"The genetic identifier," Em explained. "As long as that blighthearted hasher's work was good, you should pass through with no problems."

Aza knew her new credentials no longer listed her as the daughter of Holy Order diplomats. The thought made her both glad and anxious. *What is happening to my parents now?* She supposed, given their position, they'd be evacuated or at least given some sort of protection. *But you don't know that. You should find out. You should be helping them!* The old flame of guilt, absent since she'd been expelled from the Holy Order School, threatened to flare up within her. Aza fought it off, knowing she would be little to no help to her parents. *I tried to warn them, tried to make them see something bad was coming.* The knowledge she had been right was little consolation.

Em finally fought the last few meters through the packed crowd, bursting into the clear area between them and the armored guards. Aza looked up to see one of the huge soldiers raising his shock baton, ready to bring it down on her head.

"We have clearance!" Em shouted.

The guard's face was hidden behind an opaque face shield, but he cocked his head. "Really?" His voice was incredulous, but instead of bringing the charged weapon down on their heads, he stepped around them.

Aza turned to see the armored man strike down a figure lunging towards her. There was a crack, a sizzle, and then the woman sprawled unconscious on the ground. The guard stood over the figure, baton raised. After it was evident no one else was going to try to nab Aza, the guard motioned them towards the scanner. "You better be telling the truth..."

Em took the lead once again, and they walked the few remaining meters to the scanner. More of the menacing, shielded troops stood around it.

"Stand here, one at a time," a guard said, pointing to a spot on the floor near the white, curved panel.

Before Aza could protest, one of the guards grabbed her wrist, yanking her away from Em. "One at a time," the female voice barked. "You'll go next."

Em gave her a comforting smile, stood on the indicated spot, then advanced towards the exit area when motioned to do so. Aza stood on the spot next, feeling like her heart was going to beat right out of her chest. *Stay calm. Everything is fine.*

"Move it," the same rough female guard ordered.

Am I through? Did it work? Aza wondered, moving to stand by Em. A moment passed, then a more lightly armored man approached them.

"Em Durandos," he said, voice crisp, "you have clearance to exit the under-city. Something is wrong with your adopted daughter's credentials, however. Her information was corrupted, with large chunks of data missing. I'm going to have to detain you both until we can pull a database backup."

Aza felt her heart stop, knowing this was the end. She'd be captured. *Who knows what they will do with me,* she thought, glancing back towards the immobile woman, unconscious or dead on the floor.

"That is unacceptable," Em said, throwing her head back and sighing loudly. "You can't keep your blighthearted database squared away, and I have to suffer for it? I think not. Let us through. Pull the backup if you want, but we will not be forced to stay in this dangerous environment."

The guard seemed taken aback for a moment, then gathered himself. "I don't know who you think you are—" he stared, but Em broke in.

"I'll tell you who I buggering am," Em hissed. "I'm the wife of the ambassador to Kii-la-ta. My husband is likely dead now, and you are harassing the widow and daughter of a decorated war hero."

"I'm sorry, ma'am," the guard said, taking a step back. "I had no idea. We don't often see—" he stopped short, rethinking his words. "We don't encounter people of your stature down here."

"Obviously not."

"Just let me check your identifiers one more time and I'm sure it will be no problem to let you pass. Please wait here."

The guard turned and began walking back towards his terminal. The moment he had taken five steps away, Em yanked on Aza's arm, almost pulling it out of its socket.

"Come on," the older woman growled, accelerating into a run.

"Stop!" Aza heard the guard yell. She was too focused on maintaining her footing to give him any further thought.

When they reached the far wall of the station, Em yanked open an access hatch. "Get in," she yelled, boosting Aza up. Aza caught a quick glance of numerous guards closing in on them. "Move," Em said, crowding in behind her. Aza began shuffling her way forward, the low ceiling making it difficult to move fast.

They're going to come behind us, going to catch us, she thought, half-running, half-lurching her way deeper into the gloom.

After a frantic minute, Aza felt a hand grasp her arm. She almost screamed before realizing it was Em. "Hold up," she said, the weak light of the maintenance tunnel barely illuminating her face.

Aza waited, wondering why they weren't continuing to add distance between them and their pursuers. Em cocked her head, closing her eyes. Then, Aza heard it too. Silence.

"Why aren't they following us?" Aza asked.

"Good question," Em replied, shaking her head. "And none of the answers are good for us."

13 – WAKE

"Coupling in five. Four," Dras' voice announced inside Brightwing's helmet.

Wake braced himself, steadying his heart rate. Just a few weeks ago, these attack missions got in his head and made him jittery. *Now, I almost feel comfortable. Almost...*

"Three."

Wake knew he couldn't get complacent; the Breakers were more deadly now than ever before. *I've practiced the way of the Blade, have restored Brightwing to the impressive machine Calthis once used, and have tested my skills in combat.*

"Two."

I'm not just an engineer anymore, he thought, readying himself to burst into the enemy cargo ship as soon as Dras hashed their airlock security. The realization made him smile.

Wake glanced at Felar, who was next to him in a similar braced position. She returned his smile, nodding slightly. She was clad in an armored Ashamine environmental nominizing suit they'd captured from one of the Breaker facilities.

"One."

Returning his attention to the airlock, Wake tensed, ready to spring forward.

"Go!"

The translucent surface before him irised open, revealing the Breaker airlock. It too was sliding open, revealing a dimly lit room beyond. Something about the situation felt different from their previous raids, but he didn't understand why.

Before Wake could ponder further, he leapt forward, turning on Brightwing's full illumination. "Clear," Wake yelled, storming through the personnel transfer room and throwing open the hatch.

54

"Right behind you," he heard Felar say.

"Times two," Lothis added.

Wake went through the hatch, checking both left and right down the corridor.

"Clear," he said again, his feeling of unease deepening. Before attacking, they'd sensed Breakers aboard the cargo ship. Their signal had felt weak. Both Felar and Dras thought it worthwhile to check the anomaly.

"Strange," Felar said, joining him in the corridor. She cocked her head, and he saw her brow furrow through the faceplate. Wake nodded as Lothis joined them. The armored suit hung on his lanky frame, despite his recent growth spurt.

"These ships have always been full," the boy added. "Where is everyone?"

"Maybe they're transporting goods or weapons instead of troops?" Felar said.

"Maybe." Lothis didn't sound convinced.

"Split up," Felar ordered. "Let's figure it out, then scuttle this heap."

"Affirm," Lothis said.

"Affirm," Wake added, hoping this wasn't a mistake.

As he set off down the corridor, his sense of unease deepened. Not because he was alone, but because the ship remained empty. *Where are the Breakers we felt?* he wondered, checking cargo hold after empty cargo hold. The ship seemed deserted.

After several minutes, Wake finally reached the aft bulkhead, having seen nothing interesting. "Aft is empty," he reported.

"Copy," both Felar and Lothis transmitted.

Wake began working his way back towards the airlock, dread creeping down his spine. *You're fine,* he repeated. *Everything is fine. This is a remote system. No Breaker outpost to come after you. This ship just got lost or something.*

"Just zeroed five Breakers on the bridge," Felar's voice said. "Although calling them Breakers is pretty generous. They must have been brand-new converts. They were still blathering and barely able to function."

"Odd," Lothis transmitted. "Central segment is as empty as—"

"Evacuate the enemy ship immediately," Dras' voice broke in. "The Justice just wormed in system, practically on top of us."

"Buggering blightheart," Felar yelled over the comm. "You heard Dras. Move!"

Wake started running through the tight corridor, feeling his sense of dread metastasize into fear. The Justice was a massive vessel, capable of taking on whole armadas of smaller ships. The Harbingers had barely escaped their last encounter with it.

The Justice is sure to have Karoth commanding it, he thought, remembering when Felar told them how decorated the man was as an Ashamine Ascended.

"It was a trap," Wake transmitted. "Crasor or Karoth is trying to—" Wake's sentence was cut short as he slammed into an unseen obstacle. He careened off the side wall and tumbled to the floor. As he gathered his senses and got up, he saw Lothis doing the same.

"Sorry," was all Lothis could say.

"Not your fault. Let's go!" Wake replied, helping him up. They sprinted down the remaining corridor, turning into the room adjoining the airlock.

"Felar," Wake transmitted, "you coming?" He knew she wouldn't have left them in the enemy ship alone.

"Yeah," she replied, breathless, "almost there."

"Rail rounds incoming," Dras interjected. "All of you have to get back aboard so I can maneuver!" Wake thought he heard fear in the sentient machine's voice. "Full spread incoming. They're aiming for both ships. If we don't move, we're all dead."

Wake looked from the hatch to the airlock to Lothis, wondering if he should grab the boy and take him to safety. *Blight, blight, blight,* he cursed. *I can't leave her, but I can't let him die.*

Another moment of horrible indecision passed, Wake wondering desperately what Felar would do, when she burst through the hatch. "Let's get the bugger out of here!" she yelled, and they all piled through the airlock.

"Go, go, go," Felar said. "We're clear, Dras! Close the airlock and get us out of here."

Wake saw the Heltasoth hatch iris shut and the dark mass of the Breaker transport ship outside fade into blackness. He followed Felar and Lothis towards the bridge.

When they got there, Wake felt his stomach drop. "No time to maneuver," Dras said, his focus on the huge circle of incoming rail cannon rounds. To Wake, it looked horribly festive. Every color in the visible spectrum was represented in the enormous, sweeping mass. "Even with my speed, we can't get past an edge before the wave hits us. It is a well-designed trap."

This is how I die, Wake thought, feeling paralyzed. *This is how the Breakers win. We got too confident, and it killed us. I hope Maxar, Tremmilly, and Jaydon can take out Crasor alone.*

Wake turned to look at Felar, wishing he could save her and Lothis somehow. *I'm glad I expressed my feelings,* he thought. *Even if she wasn't interested in exploring a deeper relationship, the things we shared were amazing.*

"But you have a plan?" Felar asked, breaking Wake out of his reverie.

"Yes, I do," the Heltasoth replied, keeping his eyes trained on the impeding destruction. "I must admit I'm unsure of its outcome, however. It is the only option. I think it worth trying."

Felar nodded and everyone fell silent. Wake wanted to ask what the plan was, but he could feel Dras needed concentration. A few more moments ticked by, and the glowing ion tracers took up the entire forward view. Wake bit his lip, knowing the fires of the dark star were about to hit.

The sentient machine stood rigid and motionless, focused on the rail rounds. "Three, two, one," Dras announced, voice quiet, but firm. An intense light filled the Heltasoth bridge, making Brightwing's optics attenuate the source. When they resumed normal operation, Wake felt confused. Now, the wave of ion trails was behind them, streaking away.

"What just happened?" Lothis asked.

"Phase drive," Dras said. "I used precise timing to phase us out of sync with the projectiles." Wake experienced a momentary flashback of Dras flying them through the solid rock of Traynos-6's crust. "It's never been used on matter moving so quickly, hence my uncertainty."

"How does it work?" the boy asked, sounding excited.

"We can get the details later," barked Felar. "Now, we need to get the blightheart out of here."

"Of course," Dras replied.

A flash of light in the corner of Wake's vision drew his attention back towards the massive ship. It had launched another full volley of rail cannon rounds.

"How far till we leave the gravity well?" Felar asked, turning to watch the new wave of death.

"Only a million kilometers," Dras answered, "but the Justice lies between."

"We can't make a transition to escape," Wake realized.

"No," the Heltasoth confirmed.

"What about running to the other side of the system?" Lothis asked. "We are faster than the Justice. We can make a worm when we get to the other side."

"I considered that while you three were coming back from the trap vessel. A massive, nearby black hole would make the transition too unstable."

"So," Wake said, feeling hopeless, "the only way out is past the huge ship raining death on us?"

"I believe so, yes." Dras' voice sounded so confident that Wake wondered if the sentient machine was misunderstanding the human emotion he was trying to mimic.

The bridge flared with light again, and when Brightwing's optics settled, Wake realized the second volley had passed through them.

"I think whatever direction we try to go around it," Dras continued, "the Justice will be able to cut us off from escaping to the worm zone."

"So," Lothis said, seeming to understand why the Heltasoth was so confident, "we go through it."

"Exactly. That is a phase transition I better understand. We will not be moving so fast, nor will our phase mass."

"But what about their point defense systems?" Felar asked. "The velocity of those projectiles is far greater and the time to impact much shorter."

"It is an unknown variable, but I have a better comprehension now that I have done two waves of rail slugs."

"OK," Felar nodded, "take us in."

As they drew closer to the huge ship, Wake couldn't help but feel anxious. The Justice had quit launching rail rounds, obviously understanding the strange ship was an impossible target.

"They're launching fighters," Dras said. "It's too late for me to try stealth tactics. They have a good fix on our position and vector."

"Then you'll just have to out-fly them," Felar said, a smile on her face. "Besides, we have speed on our side."

"Indeed," Dras replied.

As the waves of incoming fighters tried to strafe them, Wake did his best to ignore the situation. Lacking Maxar's nanite interface with the vessel, he had no way to help. Focusing on the incoming rail rounds and enemy ships made him nauseous, so he closed his eyes. *Calm, peace, breathe,* Wake thought, hoping it would all be over soon.

"Too many variables to configure the phase drive," Dras said, voice beginning to glitch.

"You're doing great," Lothis replied, his tone belying his confident words. "Your maneuvering is fantastic."

A minute later, the whole ship reverberated with a massive concussion. "Slug strike," Dras announced. "Hull integrity intact, but strength is compromised."

"We're almost there," Felar said, voice tense. Wake wanted to open his eyes, but he knew it would just overwhelm him. "Nearly in point defense range," Felar continued. "You ready?"

"Yes," Dras said, all humanity removed from his voice. "At full processing capacity. Please refrain from further communications."

The bridge fell silent. Wake kept his head down and eyes squeezed shut. *Calm, peace, breathe,* he continued repeating. Finally, when the suspense was worse than the potential view, Wake opened his eyes. Blackness showed through the hull ahead of him, faint stars shining.

Wake turned, seeing the Justice pivoting to follow them, it's fleet of small fighters quickly falling behind Dras' faster vessel.

"One minute to gravity well exit," the Heltasoth said, some of his human-like mannerisms returning.

"I think we're going to make it," Lothis said, letting out his breath.

"That was amazing," Felar whispered, her face pale.

Wake wondered what he had missed, but then thought perhaps it was better he'd not seen it. *Some things can't be unseen. I'm just glad we're all alive.*

14 – TREMMILLY

"How long until we reach the worm zone?" Tremmilly asked.

"Seventy standard minutes," Jaydon replied after a moment, his attention still focused on the piloting console.

"I think I'm going to head back to the crew quarters." Tremmilly yawned. "Will you guys let me know when we get to Lith-elo?"

Jaydon nodded, continuing to enter commands into his terminal.

"Everything OK?" Maxar asked.

"Yeah, I'm fine," Tremmilly answered. "I feel like now might be a good time to seek the Dawn's guidance." She paused, thinking. "I've forgotten how good the connection feels. Perhaps I can also learn more about our past and insight for the future." She yawned again.

"Maybe you'd do better taking a nap," Maxar replied, hugging her.

"Perhaps, I'm so tired," she whispered in his ear, "because someone has been keeping me up late at night." They broke their embrace and Tremmilly gave him a wry smile.

"I'll be here if you need me," Maxar said, winking. "I'll let you know when we get to Lith-elo."

Tremmilly turned and looked at Beowulf. "Wanna come?" The wolf-dog got up, his light blue eyes locked on hers. He blinked a few times, then trotted over. "Such a good boy," she said, stroking his thick fur.

Tremmilly left the command deck and made her way through the targeting center. When they reached the engine room, she boosted Beowulf up the ladder, following behind him.

The Retribution's crew quarters were minimal, but sufficient. It, like the Death Watch, was a combat vessel, not a passenger transport. "I bet this space would be packed with a full crew," Tremmilly said, laying down on the double bed. Maxar and Jaydon had spent some of their infrequent down time modifying the space to better suit them. *Double beds and extra padding too,* she thought, enjoying the moment.

Beowulf jumped up next to her, spinning in circles until he'd created his own space within the bedding. "Silly dog," Tremmilly said, scratching his ears. She breathed deeply, but the stale smell of the ship's atmosphere broke her peaceful moment.

"I guess it's about time we freshened things up," Tremmilly said, happy they were going back to Lith-elo for just that reason. "You can only recycle the water and air so much before it just seems... old." They were in no danger in this system, at the moment, but since they had to get out of its gravity well for a scheduled comms meeting with Felar anyway, it made sense to make the hop to the former Entho-la-ah-mine world.

"It's a little dangerous going back," Tremmilly continued, even though the wolf-dog had his eyes shut. "The Breakers know its location, but there aren't that many places with such a fresh atmosphere and clean water. Jaydon says the Retribution isn't equipped to do more than rudimentary filtering, since it's not a colony vessel."

As she spoke, Tremmilly felt her eyelids grow heavy. *Maybe now would be a good time to rest,* she thought, almost giving in. "No, no," Tremmilly said, sitting up and shaking her head. Beowulf didn't move. *With all the missions and strikes you've been doing lately, you've had no time to continue exploring the past. You were so close to a breakthrough while you were still on Lith-elo. Knowledge of the Elrahi history and the Dawn's guidance are the keys to defeating the Breakers and restoring our people.*

Tremmilly sat back against the bulkhead, assuming meditative pose. She closed her eyes, but with the poised position and her resolve, there was no danger of falling asleep. *Ready yourself,* she thought, feeling a twinge of nervousness creep into her chest.

Clearing her mind, Tremmilly reached out to the surrounding space-time, feeling it cascade and flow around her. She went deeper, sensing the molecules making up the ship. Her consciousness expanded. Tremmilly sensed the invisible force binding everything, felt the slight tug of gravity pulling on every single cell within her.

When the moment was right, Tremmilly cast her mind out, expanding and settling into an even deeper harmony with the universe. Time lost meaning, and she felt her consciousness going to the dimension she remembered as an Elrahi. *I am one, I am many,* she thought, grateful for what the Entho-la-ah-mines had taught her. *Without them, I would be unable to reach this state so easily.*

Tremmilly could sense her connection to her human body, her Elrahi being, and the Dawn. *And what about him?* she thought, her consciousness refusing to look at the dark filament stretching off into blackness. *No, I won't think of him! I'm not here for that.*

When she'd first attained this nexus state, Tremmilly had been nearly overcome with joy. *So easy to find the Dawn now,* she thought, looking to where the shining path stretched off into blackness. *This is the only place I feel like my Elrahi and human selves are fully united.* For several visits, the nexus had been serene, a place all her own, connected to everything vital.

But then, Tremmilly had discovered the link to the Breakers, and it had nearly ruined the place. *At least it explains why I've felt Crasor so acutely, the visions I had of him, and why it seems like we share a bond.* She wished she could use the connection to her advantage, to spy on Crasor or sabotage him, but so far, she couldn't figure out how. *I wish I could at least resolve how or why it is here...*

Tremmilly hadn't told anyone about the Breaker link and didn't plan to. *What would they all think of me, if they knew I was connected so closely to the Breakers?* A part of her knew she should tell the other Harbingers, and she'd tried to bring it up once, but she'd felt too ashamed. *Dirty,* she thought, remembering the embarrassment welling up within her. *Besides, I'm handling it. And I'm not lying to Maxar. He'd just worry unnecessarily if I told him.* A deep part of her wondered if the omission was really because she feared he wouldn't love her anymore.

As Tremmilly's consciousness floated in a dimension of her own creation, she tried to purge the shame and guilt flooding through her. Finally, her thoughts shifted and a memory of the confrontation with See'dek arose before her. *In many ways,* she thought, *I'm as responsible for this schism as he is.* She watched as See'dek stood before her, proud as always, demanding that she allow him to use technological augmentation to unite with the Dawn. *And I said no.* The scene shifted, images of warfare and chaos. *I'd lost him long before that.*

The memory ended, and Tremmilly pondered the stance she, as empress, and the majority of her species had taken. *Technology is not the path to the Dawn, not the way to ascend. But then how will Maxar ever join with the Dawn, or Lothis? They have nanites within them. Isn't that what I once thought of as corrupted?*

Now, her previous stance felt foolish. *Is this just because someone I love so deeply is technologically augmented? Am I changing my principles for personal reasons?* Tremmilly thought for what could have been a few seconds, or an eternity. Memories of her life, time as empress, and years as a human cascaded before her. *No,* she decided finally. *No, I am not. It's not just because of love. I was wrong. The rest of the Elrah were too. And it created this catastrophic division.*

Tremmilly looked towards the path to the Dawn, a shimmering expanse stretching out before her. She couldn't see the energetic entity from here, but if she focused hard enough, she could make the journey.

If I was wrong about such a fundamental thing, how do I know any of my decisions were correct? Was it right to send my people to the Dawn? For me to stay behind? For any of this to be happening?

The more Tremmilly questioned, the darker her consciousness grew. Turning, she saw the connection to the Breakers expanding, a hollow maw threatening to swallow her. The blackness grew, creeping towards her. *What if I gave up? What if I surrendered to him? Maybe See'dek would relent and leave the Dawn alone, if he still exists.*

In the next instant, Tremmilly realized what was happening and forced her consciousness back into her body, just an instant before the connection to the Breakers initiated. Her eyes flew open, the surrounding room bright, bland, and dull. Beowulf lay beside her, asleep.

Enlightening, she thought, *but as dangerous as ever.* This wasn't the first time the blackness had threatened to overwhelm Tremmilly as she sought answers. The more she learned, the more she realized the depth of her connection to See'dek, Crasor, and the Breakers.

Maxar's head popped up through the hatch to the engine room, his face grim.

"What's wrong?" Tremmilly asked, wondering if she had brought some new doom on them with her earlier experience.

"Lith-elo," he said. "You need to come see this before we worm out of here."

Tremmilly helped Beowulf down the ladder and then quickly made her way to the command bridge. When she got there, she felt the bottom of her stomach drop away.

Speechless, she stared at the magnified images on the Retribution's large tactical displays. The once beautiful, shimmering haven for both the Entho-la-ah-mines and the Harbingers now looked murky, full of dust, smoke, and ash.

Jaydon, voice quiet, spoke. "I think it's safe to say the Breakers were here. Good thing you evacuated the Entho-la-ah-mines when you did."

Maxar manipulated his console, and the images shifted. "It's not just the atmosphere," he said, pointing to a readout, "although it is extremely hot and windy. The surface has been obliterated. I don't know how they did it, but it looks like some kind of giant rail cannon sent about a billion slugs down there. I don't think it will ever be habitable again, at least not by humans or Entho-la-ah-mines."

"They must have a new weapon," Jaydon added, shaking his head. "As if things weren't bad enough already."

Tremmilly remained silent, her eyes fastened to the destruction. She felt anger boil up within her. *I may be responsible for the Elrahi schism that caused the Breakers,* she thought, clenching her fists, *but I did not corrupt them or make them do this.* She felt her already strong resolve to stop Crasor deepen further. *We will destroy him and the rest of the Breakers for what they have done!*

"Take us to a safe system, Jaydon," Tremmilly commanded. "We need to alert Felar."

15 – GAV

"We were close, sir," Karoth said over the shared comms line. "We almost had them."

"Which ship?" Crasor barked, the look on his face making Gav nervous. He'd seen that look directed at him and Salla when they were bickering. It made him glad he was on his own ship, away from the fuming leader.

"The alien one. I haven't received any recent reports about the gunship."

"And how did they manage to escape your ambush?" Salla asked calmly, not seeming to notice the mood Crasor was in.

"I don't know," the Justice's commander replied. "They teleported or changed dimensions. Something I don't understand."

"What do you mean?" Crasor demanded.

"They flew right past our cannon volleys and went through the Justice without causing any damage. They disappeared from sensors during that time."

Interesting, Gav thought, wishing to inspect this unique ship. He wasn't convinced it was alien tech, given the secrets he'd already discovered, but Karoth and everyone else seemed to be.

"They won't be tricked so easily again," Crasor said, scowling. He inhaled deeply, and Gav waited silently.

"We need to fortify our planets and installations," Salla interjected.

"I agree," Karoth said. "We have far too many weak spots for the Harbingers to attack. If we pull back our scout ships and focus on spreading our forces amongst—"

"Silence!" Crasor barked. "Did I ask for your suggestions?" He scowled for a moment longer, before continuing. "Don't be so easily manipulated. We are in the position of power, not the buggered Harbingers. They are trying to disrupt us, to impair our ability to strike at the Ashamine.

65

They've barely made a dent in our forces, and you want to pull back?" Crasor shook his head. "I will not allow it. We must continue our offensive, strike the core worlds, and finish taking what is ours.

"The Harbingers will come to us, as they already have. Our primary mission is still to destroy them, but I will not allow it to halt our progress in the Akked."

Crasor's eyes narrowed, and Gav felt like he was looking into his soul, even through the terminal display. "Karoth, the time has come. Gather a fleet sufficient to take the Ashamine system." He paused for a moment, face as hard as tungsten alloy.

Gav felt exhilaration flood through him. *It's happening! It's really happening!*

"Leave our main worlds as protected as possible," Crasor continued, "but I don't care if smaller outposts are left empty or undefended. You know which are expendable."

Karoth nodded, face grim. "As you order, sir."

Crasor continued. "We will exponentially replenish any causalities the Harbingers cause in the meanwhile, once we take Ashamine-2. This is our moment, our time to rise to ascendancy within the Akked. Do not fail me."

"Understood. I will report when the fleet is ready for action." Karoth's face disappeared from the screen.

"Gav, Salla," Crasor said, the image of his face enlarging to take up the section Karoth vacated. "Prepare your respective ships and crews for the assault. We'll need both the Rain and the Oblivion for this, for their tactical abilities." He paused, rubbing his forehead. "Another thing, and this is more important: As we advance on the core worlds, the Harbingers will surface, I know it. They will likely put themselves in a compromising position to try to stop us. They have no choice. The buggers understand what is at stake, what it means to them when we take the Ashamine primary worlds. I want you both alert and on guard. If you sense anything, notify me. I will issue further orders." Crasor's face disappeared, leaving only Salla as part of the comm.

"So," she said, sounding uncharacteristically friendly. "Are you ready for this?"

"Yes," Gav replied, eyes narrowing, "of course."

Salla took a deep breath. "I wanted to apologize to you," she said, head bowing slightly. "I was unprofessional when we found the Rain. It is a powerful asset to the Breakers, one we are fortunate to have."

Gav had to fight hard to keep from gaping. *Salla. Apologizing?* He wondered for a moment if he was dreaming.

"I know," she continued, "surprising. I've thought about it, and this is genuine. Our power struggle is counterproductive, and is a holdover from our previous lives. We must work together for the good of the Breakers."

Suspicion followed surprise, and Gav wondered if this was some kind of trap, another move in the deadly game. "Thank you," he replied, not knowing what else to say.

"Once we prep our ships for combat, I'd like to have the opportunity to tour the Rain, to understand how it works, and congratulate you on your success obliterating the Entho world."

There it is, Gav thought, sensing the trap. *She'll sabotage my worm generator, install remote maneuvering access, or use some other trick to make me look bad or kill me.* At first, he almost turned her down, but then he thought better of it. *Salla will be on my ship, around my crew, in my territory. If she tries something, I can report it to Crasor. I'll be blameless, and he'll destroy her for her treason.*

Gav was still riding high on the emotion of finding the planet-killer ship and its resounding success. Having his own vessel to command was also a boost, even if it was so specialized. *Rubbing it in Salla's face will feel good,* he thought, overriding the small voice that said it would be safer to keep her at a distance. *She might even be genuine, in which case, perhaps I can gain even further advantage.*

Licking his lips, Gav felt his excitement grow. "Let me know when you're finished prepping the Oblivion, and I'll give you a tour, personally."

***

Gav watched the small shuttle make its way between the Oblivion and the Rain. Getting his ship ready for the forthcoming invasion hadn't taken long. *We already went over everything after we captured the ship and its original crew,* he thought, rubbing his hands together. *And the test on the Entho world went splendidly.*

Salla had taken longer, evidently, because she'd just recently asked for permission to transfer. During this period, Gav had plenty of time to think and consider Salla's plans and motivations. He felt some anxiety, knowing it was going to be a game as dangerous as Bloodsport. Mostly, though, he just felt excitement. *What if she really has decided I'm superior?* he thought, smiling. *Maybe what she really wants is a piece of me.* The thought sent excited chills down his spine and made his heart race.

A chime sounded, breaking Gav out of his lustful thoughts. "Shuttle docking in primary bay," his operations tech announced.

Gav nodded. "XO, you have control. I will be showing our guest around the ship. Remember to monitor my position and status at all times, until I notify you otherwise. Keep a Marine squad nearby, and have them ready to assist me at a moment's notice."

"Yes, sir," the XO replied, bowing slightly. "We will maintain everything as you've ordered."

Heading down to the shuttle bay, he felt his anticipation rise even further. *You knew she'd give in all along,* he thought triumphantly. *You knew she wanted you.*

Careful, a small voice said in his mind, *it could be a trap.*

The small voice fell silent, and Gav went back to thinking about the pleasures of the flesh awaiting him. *Been a long time since I've been with a woman,* he thought, opening the hatch to the shuttle bay. *I wonder how it will be different, now that I'm a Breaker.*

When he stepped inside, he saw Salla getting out of her small craft. His eyes were immediately drawn to her formfitting body suit. It was crimson red, covering her from head to toe. It displayed almost none of her skin, the silky-white human or the black metal of the transforming Breaker, but it showed off every curve and line of the body beneath. For a moment, all Gav could do was stare. Finally, he realized he was displaying his desire and tried to act nonchalant.

"Salla," he said, "welcome to the Rain." It felt odd being so courteous after their previous animosity, but she was smiling seductively, and it made his head swim.

"Gav," she said, bowing. "Thank you for this... opportunity."

The way she said it made his heart beat faster, and the small voice let out a faint warning cry. *She's manipulating you.*

Shut up, Gav thought, trying to decide how to proceed. *I've made my precautions. Would she be trying to bugger me if she wanted to kill me?* Gav tried to ignore the fact that he couldn't answer that with a definitive no.

"Let me show you one of the weapon tubes," he said, attempting to focus on the game, whatever it was. "The rest of the ship is fairly bland, but the mass drivers and their paired generators are where it really excels."

Salla nodded, touching his arm lightly. "Of course. But you'll show me the crew quarters afterwards, yes? I feel like there are interesting things there to experience as well. Surely they built a marvelous stateroom for the commander of such a technologically advanced vessel?"

"Yes, as you wish," Gav replied, feeling lightheaded. "I'll show you everything you want."

Gav spent the next standard hour exhibiting the planet-killing features of the Rain. Salla followed him dutifully, asking in-depth questions. At one point, Gav thought he saw one of the Marines tailing them, but he wasn't sure. *They are good,* he thought, knowing his XO would keep them close by, as ordered.

"I would love to see your stateroom," Salla said, after they'd left the upper portion of the ship. Gav felt her eyes run up and down his body as she slowly licked her lips.

"Follow me," he replied, barely able to keep himself to a walk.

***

"What?" Gav said, sitting up. For a moment, he didn't understand where he was. *My stateroom,* he thought, some of his wits returning. *Salla?*

He looked at the space next to him in bed. Even with the room's illumination set for sleep, he could see it was empty. "Day illumination," he said, squinting as the room brightened. When his eyes adjusted, he scanned the room. *Nothing.*

"Salla?" he asked, getting up to the check the connected bathroom. *Where is she?*

Looking at the time, Gav realized it had been almost 8 hours since he'd begun the tour. *How long were Salla and I buggering?* he wondered. *And how long was I asleep?*

"XO," Gav said, opening up an audio comms channel. "What is the ship's status?"

"As you left it, sir: Secure, and ready for duty."

Gav's eyes narrowed. The time with Salla had been furious and animalistic, a sexual experience that was better than anything he'd known previously. As he'd drifted off into exhausted sleep, he'd hoped she would be there when awoke, ready for another round.

"And Lady Markond?" he asked shamelessly. News of their private time together would have traveled around the ship. Gav didn't care.

"Escorted back to her shuttle, which safely returned to the Oblivion."

Gav nodded, feeling some of his anxiety diminish. "And the Marines were watching my stateroom the entire time?"

"Yes," the XO replied. "After the... incident, they resumed their surveillance positions." A blurry memory of having to dismiss the guards after they barged in during a violent segment of lovemaking rose in Gav's mind, making him smile. "When Lady Markond finally left the room, they followed her all the way to her shuttle. She was never out of sight. We let her leave when she requested, as you commanded."

"Good. Thank you for watching over the Rain during my absence." Gav had learned, back in the early days when he'd been trying to form his own Family, that treating your subordinates with respect and appreciation bought far more loyalty than fear or domination. He supposed, with the absolute obedience of the Breakers, this was unnecessary. *Old habits are hard to kill. Besides, it doesn't hurt anything.*

"As you say, Commander Serrith."

Gav closed the audio comm, and sat back on the bed. *How do you know she didn't do something to you?* the small voice asked. *To the ship?*

Absurd, Gav thought, laying back. *The Breaker nanites make poisons or bio-weapons useless. She was in this room or being watched by the Marines the entire time I was sleeping. There is no way she could access anything important from here. She wanted you, and you wanted her, simple as that. Just enjoy the sex and don't read too much into it.*

Still, he couldn't dispel the nagging feeling he was wrong. Gav tried to reason his way out of his anxiety, but no amount of arguing could dissuade the little voice in his head.

"Fine!" he growled, leaping out of the bed. "XO," he said, opening the channel again. "Order a full sweep of all the ship's critical components."

"Yes, sir," the XO replied, sounding confused. "Right away. But you should come to the bridge immediately. We've just received orders to take our position in the fleet. We're invading Ashamine space within the hour."

16 – LOTHIS

"What?" Felar asked. "It doesn't make sense. Are you sure your observations were accurate?"

Tremmilly looked pale on the Heltasoth screen. "They destroyed half of Lith-elo, Felar," she replied. "The atmosphere, the surface of the planet: it's burnt and uninhabitable, at least most of it."

"Not even the Breakers have a weapon capable of that," Felar replied.

Dras rose from his seated position and walked across the deck. "Logic would dictate, unless you observed a capable natural phenomenon, the Breakers are the most likely culprit, even if their ability is questioned."

"There was nothing natural about it," Maxar added, his voice sounding much smaller than it did in person. "Lith-elo's primary star was normal, no evidence of stellar anomalies. It looked like the planet was hit with an asteroid, but the Entho-la-ah-mines would have known a long time ago of anything capable of that much damage."

"Maybe they missed it," Felar protested.

Maxar shrugged. "Seems unlikely. They are excellent at stellar observation and cataloging."

"No," Lothis replied, finally ending his silence. "The other team is right, Felar. The Breakers are evolving and as they've taken over more of the Akked, it's likely they would run into hidden technology. Perhaps they found something on one of the Ashamine worlds. Whatever destroyed Lith-elo is just one of those things. We will likely discover others."

Felar sighed, shaking her head. "I guess I just don't want to believe it. What if they start using it on other worlds, places not yet evacuated?"

"All the more reason to keep pushing to stop Crasor," Lothis said.

When Maxar and Tremmilly's team had contacted them at the scheduled time, Felar had briefed them in on their encounter with the Justice. Lothis wasn't sure which of the two experiences were worse.

71

Staring down volleys of rail slugs, or encountering a dead world...

"What do we do now?" Jaydon asked, his face barely in frame on the comms screen.

"We need to push forward," Lothis said, "to kill Crasor before he can use his weapon anymore." He embraced the surrounding space-time, molding it into a small mind blade in his right hand. "We can't let him hurt or kill anyone else."

Felar gave him a strange look, before turning back to the comms screen. "Yes, we need to destroy Crasor, but we have to be careful. They outnumber us."

"But like you've said before," Tremmilly replied, "if they capture the Ashamine core worlds, we will never be strong enough to stop him. I hate to say it, but I think we might have to start taking more risks."

"Tell them the rest," Lothis said.

"Yes, I was getting to that," Felar answered. She turned back towards the comm screen. "When we were transitioning, after the encounter with the Justice, we gathered some intel. It looks like the Breakers are pulling out of smaller systems, leaving some of them totally undefended."

"That's great," Tremmilly exclaimed. "We can hit them hard. But are you sure it isn't another trap?"

"Maybe," Felar answered, sounding tired. "I think the more likely answer is that they are drawing in their forces, building up for an offensive."

"The most likely target is the core worlds," Maxar added.

"We're already too late," Tremmilly realized. "How will we ever get to Crasor if he is in the middle of some huge armada? Our plan to draw him out failed."

"I think it did, yes," Felar said, biting her lip. "But we're not dead yet. Remember what you were just saying about taking more risks? I think you're right."

Lothis felt anticipation building in his chest. *The time has come. We will find you, Crasor, and destroy you.*

"So what do we do?" Jaydon asked. "Just go to Ashamine-2 and wait for him to show up?"

"Simply put, yes," Felar answered.

"You can't be serious," Jaydon shot back.

"If we know where Crasor is headed," Felar replied calmly, "maybe we can get there ahead of time, lay out an ambush, and strike before he can take what's left of the Ashamine."

Jaydon shook his head. "Am I the only one who thinks it's a bad idea to go worming into the center of one of the biggest battles ever seen in human history? Even though the Ashamine control a fraction of the ships they used to, they are still a respectable force. Last I checked, we are

72

enemies in the eyes of both the Breakers and the Ashamine. If we end up caught between them in the battle..." Jaydon trailed off, looking scared.

"I think it's our only real chance," Maxar said quietly. "You aren't wrong, Jaydon, but we have to try. If Crasor is distracted with the attack, we might be able to use the chaos to shield our approach."

"Exactly," Felar said. "Let's meet up at one of the safe star systems. We can make a plan, scope this thing from all angles. We'll have to use our combined knowledge to make sure we think of every contingency possible."

"Jaydon," Tremmilly said, putting her head on the old captain's shoulder, "you don't have to come with us. This isn't your battle, not really."

"Bugger it," he replied. Lothis was barely able to hear him over the comm. "I'm not leaving you without a qualified pilot for this flying box of cannons. Besides, you guys are family. You're all I have left in the Akked."

"Alright," Felar said. "It's decided. Let's meet in the Big Red system. It's out of the way and unlikely to see traffic other than us."

While everyone agreed and signed off, Lothis remained silent. The heaviness in his heart for the loss of Cazz-ak felt lighter now. Revenge was in sight. *Just a little longer,* he thought. He twirled the mind blade in one hand, focusing on moving it faster and faster. *You'll feel this in your eye, just like I did...*

"Can I talk with you?" Felar asked, startling Lothis out of his concentration. The mind blade vanished, and Lothis felt the warped space-time spring back painfully.

"Yes," he replied, irritated. "What do you need?"

"I'd like to talk alone."

Lothis felt like Felar had been treating him differently lately, although he couldn't say exactly what changed. *Everything has become so... Distant.*

Felar led them to Lothis' quarters, leaving the door open behind them after they entered. "I've needed to talk to you for a while," she said, looking uncomfortable, "but we've been busy with raids..." She trailed off, and Lothis kept silent, feeling a strange mixture of fear and excitement.

"I know I'm not your mother, at least not biologically. I feel like we've had a similar relationship though, and I've tried to help you as much as I could. You've had to grow up so fast, take on things far beyond your age, experience things that no one should have to live through."

Lothis felt anger rise within him. "I don't want to talk about this. I'm fine. I'm doing my duty like everyone else."

Felar sighed. "I figured you wouldn't, but I have to insist."

"I don't get what the problem is," he yelled, clenching his jaw.

73

"OK, here you go," Felar said, looking him straight in the eyes. "You're on a dark path, Lothis. I noticed it after you died and Dras brought you back. At first, I thought it had something to do with the Heltasoth nanites, so I consulted Tremmilly. She wasn't sure. She's still undecided about the corruption of augmenting technology, but she won't remain there long. Otherwise, she'll have to disown Maxar, and we all know he is no more corrupt than the rest of the Harbingers. I also considered maybe there's something in your Elrahi past causing this, but neither Trem nor I think so.

"Then, I went to Dras and asked if your shift in mood could be attributed to the nanites. He doesn't understand much about how they interact with human bodies, but feels strongly that the repairs they're sustaining wouldn't make you so sullen and withdrawn.

"Tremmilly and Dras both thought perhaps Fade and his outlook might be pushing you towards darkness for his own ends, but everyone agreed you're too smart for that. I don't think he has that kind of influence over you anyway. Besides, you've been spending less time with him as your negativity grows.

"Which brings me back full circle to my initial feeling. I've seen this before, in kids not much older than you, Ashamine Inits sent into battle. They implode under the stress of deployment and combat. When they repair the damage, they over-compensate, getting dark, deciding every positive feeling or experience they've had is what made them weak. They focus on the pain and loss they've experienced, trying to put themselves in situations to replicate what hurt them originally, only this time they *know* they will win. They're gonna kill the blighthearted bugger that made them hurt. They wall themselves off, distance themselves from loss."

Lothis felt a cascade of emotions roaring through his body: rage, sadness, hatred, loss, pain, and despair. Without thinking, he summoned a flurry of mind shards and sent them careening into the bulkhead beside him. Before he understood what was happening, Felar was hugging him as tears streamed down his cheeks.

"I couldn't save him," he cried, simultaneously needing and fighting against the embrace. "I tried, but I couldn't. It's my fault he died. If I could have been stronger, smarter, I could have saved him."

"I know," Felar said, holding him tight. "I know."

"Cazz-ak needed me, and I let him down."

"Killing Crasor won't bring him back, Lothis. It won't fill the emptiness in your heart."

"It has to," Lothis wailed, feeling like his chest would burst. "There isn't anything else I can do!"

"I wish it would work, but I can tell you from personal experience, revenge won't heal you. It has to come from within. You need to make peace with it, to embrace the pain and move on. Right now, it's festering, rotting you away from the inside."

Lothis thought back to all his memories of Cazz-ak, both in his Entho-la-ah-mine form and as the Elrahi Protector who'd so dutifully served his sister as empress. The tide of emotion threatened to overwhelm him.

"I can't do it," Lothis said. "It's too much."

"It won't happen in an instant," Felar replied, a concerned smile on her face. "It is a process, sometimes a life-long one. Take it slowly, one memory and emotion at a time. Face them with love, rather than rage. Cazz-ak would tell you to do the same thing. He'd want you to heal, want you to be the loving, inquisitive boy he knew, not the wrathful husk you've become."

Looking back, Lothis could see the transformation, could notice the subtle steps leading him to his current mental state.

"You're right," he said, wiping the tears from his cheek. "I'll do the best I can."

"That's all we ever can do," Felar said, smiling.

"But if I have the chance," Lothis said, some of his earlier intensity returning, "I will kill Crasor, for what he did to Cazz-ak."

Felar's smile remained. "As will I, given the opportunity."

17 – ASH

Where is she? Ash thought, distractedly swiping through a long list of reports and updates. *Em should be back by now.* But she wasn't, and that meant she and Aza were still on Ashamine-2. *Or worse,* he thought, trying not to imagine the things that could've gone wrong. *Should have gone myself. Then I would know.* The list in front of him was just one of the more obvious reasons he'd had to send one of his operatives.

Besides, Em Durandos is the best person for this job. With her intelligence, stealth, and combat skills, Aza is in good hands. Ash knew he had to start working his way through the reports, but he couldn't focus. *Where are they, then? It's been over two weeks...*

Knowing his frame of mind was both counter-productive and unhelpful, Ash forced himself to begin reading the updates. Entry after entry of ship readiness, personnel distributions, and supply tallies did little to distract him.

Should I go find them? Could I? He thought about all the people who wanted him dead, who would be alerted if he set foot on any of the core worlds. Ash shook his head. *No, you fool. You'd get Aza, Em, and yourself killed.*

An incoming comms link notification popped up. "Yes, Coris," Ash said, after swiping "Allow".

"I have disturbing news," his head of intelligence replied, his normally animated face looking grim. "Our sources, both inside and outside the Ashamine, have reported the core worlds are descending into chaos."

"They've been in a state of unrest for weeks now." Ash felt the pit in his stomach deepening. "What's changed?"

"The central government has finally lost what little grip it had left. The upper class is fleeing, to Azak-knows-where, while what is left of military command is keeping the riots confined to the under-levels."

"Any intel about the Founder's City specifically?" Ash asked, unable

76

to get his mind off the implications for Aza and Em.

"It's the least impacted, at least so far. My sources say the military is maintaining at least some level of order. Given the nature of what is occurring in the surrounding areas, however, I don't expect the City to stand for much longer."

"And the Classad and High-Elder Council?"

"Dead, missing, or fled to their personal bunkers."

"They've just left the Ashamine to fend for itself?"

"You expected more from them?" Coris raised an eyebrow. "Their collapse appears to be the primary force behind the growing unrest and disorder. The Lower-Elder Council is mostly intact, but they don't have the knowledge or influence of their superiors."

Ash sighed, rubbing his forehead. "I'd dreamed of reforming the Ashamine, of returning the government to its former glory and prestige. Now, though..." He paused, shaking his head. "Now, I wonder if there will be much to restore."

"The Breakers have done us a favor, of sorts," Coris said, shrugging. "The Founder and Classad were too strong to bring down in our lifetime. Even so, there will still be many generations of work ahead."

"Will there be anything left," Ash said quietly, "even if we can stop the Breakers?"

"Good question," Coris nodded. "And that brings me to my next priority report."

Ash raised an eyebrow, hoping this one would be good news.

"I can't be completely sure," Coris continued, "but I believe the Breakers are forming to attack the core worlds."

"Already? How can you be sure? The AI projections stated a few more weeks at the soonest."

"Several automated scout ships have signaled diminished Breaker activity in the border worlds. They have even completely abandoned several systems."

"They're consolidating their forces."

"That is my theory," Coris said, frowning. "I can't be sure, but the latest projections, factoring in the new intel, are giving us less than a week."

"Less than a week?!" Ash shook his head, knowing Coris was right. *Why would they wait? They control a huge portion of the Ashamine and border worlds already.*

"I'm sorry, sir. I know this blighthearts many of your plans."

"It's not your fault, Coris. At least we know and won't be showing up late to the blighthearted festival."

"What's our next step?"

"We have to move our plans up, get to the Ashamine system before the Breakers."

"What will keep the Ashamine Forces from railing our small armada into stellar debris?"

"Reason," Ash said, "I hope. And the Vergers."

***

Ash felt his throat tighten as he stepped aboard his flagship, the Stellar Memory. It was by no means a large or formidable ship, but it did have some advanced tech and weaponry. *I wish Aza was here,* he thought, saluting each of the crew he passed. *And while I'm going to be so close to her, there is almost nothing I can do to help.* Ash hoped—despite his better judgment—that the arrival of the Brotherhood and Verger ships would help prop up the failing empire, maybe restore some order to the core planets. *Blighthearted bugger of a chance,* he thought, knowing they'd be lucky not to be attacked as soon as they wormed in system.

"The Memory is ready for service, sir," his XO said as Ash entered the command bridge.

He nodded, thanked the woman, then sat down at his terminal. All readouts were nominal, as reported. "Fleet status?" Ash asked.

"74% of the fleet reports readiness."

"Time remaining?"

"Approximately 30 standard minutes."

"Update me when we hit 90%."

"Yes, commander."

Ash sat back in his chair, enjoying the cocoon-like feeling of the Memory. A few minutes passed as he tried to absorb as much calm as he could. *Soon, peace will only be a memory.*

"Worm transitions opening," the sensor tech announced. "Hundreds of them."

For a moment, Ash wondered if their intelligence had guessed wrong, if the Breakers were actually coming for the Brotherhood. He stared intently at his terminal, waiting to see who would come through the worms.

The first ship he saw looked melted, its aft bridge hanging off the main structure at a precarious angle. *Verger,* he knew instantly, recognizing it as Fierence's strange vessel.

"Incoming transmission originating from the Verger flagship," the comms tech announced.

"Allow," Ash said, hoping he hadn't made a mistake including the intense leader and his people.

"Parick Olvold," the bald-headed man on the screen said, looking even more ferocious than when Ash had last seen him.

"Fierence," he replied, giving a respectful bow. *I wonder if he even has a surname.*

"I did the best I could to rally my people on short notice," the other man said, "but you gave me little time."

"The Breakers are moving faster than expected."

"I read the reports you sent," Fierence said, nodding. "It would appear our victory will arrive sooner than anticipated."

Ash stifled his frustration with the Verger's cockiness, knowing he was not giving the Breaker or the Ashamine forces enough credit. *Overestimating his own abilities too, I'm sure.*

"I could not bring all the ships I promised," the Verger continued. "Some of our best ships are still traveling from the very edges of the Akked, but I could not wait for them."

"Thank you for coming," Ash replied. "With your help, we will forge a better humanity."

Fierence looked skeptical. "If such a thing is possible, then the Vergers will be the ones to do it."

"Fleet readiness at 90%," his XO said quietly.

"We are almost ready to depart for the transition zone," Ash said. "It will take us a standard hour, perhaps a bit longer, to reach it."

"We will be ready," Fierence said, eyes burning with excitement. "Soon, the blighthearted Ashamine will learn of our superiority."

18 – MAXAR

Maxar gazed at Big Red. The giant star was spewing huge arcs of plasma, the material spraying out and raining back to the surface. *A coronal mass ejection,* Maxar thought, grateful they were still beyond its gravity well. More plasma burst out, bound to the star's lines of magnetic force, shimmering in twisted waves. *Beautiful.*

"Is this going to work?" Tremmilly asked, snuggling closer to him.

"It has to," he replied, pulling her in.

"Maybe we could just run away. Go as far from the core as possible. Maybe Dras could figure out how to take us to a new galaxy. Crasor would never find us."

"He won't give up," Maxar answered, shaking his head. "Crasor, See'dek, the Breakers: they will spread across the universe if we don't stop them."

"We've been trying for years, decades, millennia," Tremmilly sighed.

"I wish we could just retreat, but that would be abandoning our last chance. The darkness will find us, no matter what. We have to make our stand here." They were both silent for a while, and Maxar was grateful Jaydon was sleeping in the crew quarters. *He's already freaked out enough without hearing Tremmilly's doubts.*

"What's wrong?" Maxar asked finally. "This kind of pessimism is unlike you." He held Tremmilly out at arm's length so he could see her better. Silent tears rolled down her cheeks, and she looked defeated.

"I've been wrong, about so many things," she replied, wiping her face in the crook of her elbow. "What if going to the Ashamine system is wrong too?"

"Wait. Hold on," Maxar said, brow furrowed. "What are you talking about?"

"As an Elrahi, I supported the purist faction. I said technological augmentation was wrong, both for regular life and for attaining the

80

Dawn. Now, I know that wasn't true. Look at you, Maxar. You're pure in heart, and you're full of nanites."

Maxar sighed, wondering how she could think he was pure, despite everything he'd told her about his past. "We make mistakes, Trem. Everyone does, even exalted rulers." He gave her a wry smile. "You just have to learn from them and move on."

"There's more," she said, shoving her face back against his chest. Her shoulders shuddered from silent sobs.

"What?" Maxar felt so confused. This fragile Tremmilly was so far removed from the strength she'd showed recently. "What happened?"

"I think I sent them to their deaths, Maxar."

Beowulf awoke from his sleeping space on the command deck and trotted over next to them. He leaned his head against Tremmilly, whining.

"The Entho-la-ah-mines are far better off on just about any planet other than Lith-elo. You saw what the Breakers did. You didn't send anyone to their deaths. You saved them."

"No, not them," Tremmilly wailed. "The Elrahi. I sent a quadrillion people to the Dawn. But do you know what the Dawn really is?"

Maxar tried to understand what she was saying, but none of the words connected in his mind. "It's the eternal good, the positive force guiding the universe. You sent them there to be safe, so they could be restored once we made the galaxy safe from See'dek and the Breakers."

"Wrong," she said, becoming rigid in his arms. "I've spent so many hours seeking the Dawn's guidance, trying to understand what it's telling me. And you know what? I haven't learned a blighthearted thing. It appears like a flower, unfolding, beckoning. But it's just dumb energy, Maxar, no more intelligent than Big Red."

"No," Maxar said, remembering what he'd been taught as a young Elrahi. "The Dawn is salvation. It is where all positive beings hope to go when they die. It is a force for good in the universe."

"Yeah, sure," Tremmilly said, "that's what we were all taught, what we all believed. I've tried and tried to contact the Dawn. Every time it is the same thing. It beckons me in, just as it did the people I sent to be safe from See'dek. But it never gives guidance, never offers even a hint that a quadrillion Elrahi are contained within.

"I don't understand, Trem."

"I killed them, Maxar. I sent all of my followers, every Elrahi except for the Harbingers and See'dek's followers, to their death. Yes, their energy is now part of the Dawn, but there is no way to get it back. It was swallowed up. I sent them to the temples to commit suicide, so they'd be safe."

Maxar's head felt like it was full of Big Red's plasma, a swirling torrent of confusion that devastated him. "How can you be sure?" he asked, trying to draw his mind back together.

"I can't, not without joining the Dawn myself. And if I was right, I would never see any of you again. I'd rather not try that."

"Yeah. No. I mean," Maxar stuttered, "that's not a good idea."

Tremmilly stepped back, taking his hands in her own. Tears still streaked her face, but she looked more like her normal self. "I'm sorry. I shouldn't have unloaded on you like that. It's just such a heavy burden."

"It's fine," Maxar said, taking a deep breath. "It's what I'm here for, to support you."

"Thanks," Tremmilly said, squeezing his hands.

"But the Dawn isn't evil, right?" Maxar still felt he needed clarification, even if Tremmilly's mood was improving.

"No," she replied, shaking her head. "It isn't connected to the Breakers, or whatever source of power they are a part of. Not everything we thought about the Dawn is incorrect. I think it is a force for good, perhaps it is even part of how we are able to create mind daggers and energy shields."

"But it isn't sentient?"

"No. I've tried to get something, anything from it, to lead us going forward. Nothing. I've tried contacting my friends and family who should be inside, but it is all the same: Good feelings and uplifting energy, but no thoughts or hint of communication."

Maxar sighed heavily, feeling a weight of emotion bear him down. "I can understand why you're upset." He shook his head. "The Dawn was meant to guide us, to restore our people when everything is over."

Tremmilly looked deep in his eyes. "We're alone, Maxar. There are only five of us Elrahi left, all in human form."

"Well, you got at least a part of one in dog form," Maxar said, reaching down to scratch Beowulf.

Tremmilly gave him a weak smile, which he returned with more force. "How am I ever going to get over this? Even if we defeat the Breakers, how can I ever feel good about myself after what I did as empress?"

"It's like I've said before: You were just making the best decision you could with the intel you had at the time. We were taught the Dawn was guiding the Elrahi race, as our creator and salvation. How could you know differently?"

"All those times I communed with it as empress, I really felt it guiding me. Looking back now," she continued, frowning, "I can see it was just me all along."

"You were an amazing leader. Don't you see? You made all those decisions yourself. You were wise. Even if you sent a quadrillion people to the Dawn, that was better than leaving them alive for See'dek and the

Breakers to consume."

Tremmilly nodded halfheartedly. "I feel like the Harbingers are falling apart, Maxar. Cazz-ak is dead. I'm full of doubt. Lothis is heading into some kind of darkness and I don't know if Felar or I can save him. We're a mess."

"We've always been a bit of a mess," Maxar said, smiling and trying to keep his tone light. "But you will figure things out. We'll figure things out together. You still have me, and I'm as solid as ever."

She laughed through her tears, beginning to look more confident. "This is why I want to bond with you for life, no matter how little time we have remaining."

Despite her rising mood, Maxar could sense Tremmilly was still troubled. *And probably will be for quite some time. Just have to keep supporting her. She'll make it through.*

"I just want to bond because of the physical benefits," Maxar joked, hoping his humor would ease her worry, "and because how often does a life convict get to marry an empress?"

Tremmilly slugged him on the arm, shaking her head. "You're a scoundrel, Maxar Trayfis."

"But I'm your scoundrel, my lady!"

A chime sounded, notifying them of an incoming message.

"That will be Felar," Maxar said. "Time to plan our battle."

"Back to reality," Tremmilly sighed.

Maxar gave her a long hug, squeezing tight. "I promise I'll keep you safe. Not even See'dek himself will be able to harm you."

"I will protect you as well," she replied, voice muffled.

Maxar hoped he could keep his promise.

19 – FELAR

As the Heltasoth ship transitioned to the Big Red system, Felar felt her chest tighten. *We're running out of time,* she thought. *We need to get to the core worlds as soon as possible.*

Wake walked up to her, a smile on his face. It was good things were feeling back to normal with him. *Our new relationship is stronger than before. Took him buggering long enough to get there,* she thought, shaking her head.

"What's up?" Wake asked, eyebrow raised.

"Nothing," Felar replied, returning her focus back to the present. "Dras, please let the other team know we are in system."

"As you command," Dras replied.

"Everything went OK with Lothis?" Wake asked quietly. The boy sat on the other side of the deck from them, still introspective, but much less upset and hostile than before.

Felar nodded. "Yes, I think so. He's still troubled, but I think I got through to him."

"Good, good." Wake looked relieved. "He's been a different person lately. I was hoping we weren't losing him to Crasor."

"No, nothing like that." Felar paused for a moment. "Losing Cazz-ak was hard on all of us, but Lothis most of all. Add battle weariness and you have a pretty powerful trauma scenario. We're all wearing down, but he's only a child. I don't think he has the life experience to deal with it."

Tremmilly appeared on the screen before them, her face showing the weariness Felar had just been describing. "Glad to be in the same system again," she said, smiling. Maxar stood beside her, looking tired as well.

How are we going to face our biggest battle yet, when we are all on the edge of exhaustion? From her years as a Founder's Commando, and a previous lifetime as an Elrahi Sentry, she knew battles rarely came when you were well rested and ready. *We just have to push on. We don't get to choose the timing of our opportunities.*

"Good to see you too," Felar replied, nodding. "While I would like to spend some time here resting and developing my plan further, I think we need to get to the Ashamine system as soon as possible. We can worm in together, assess the current situation, and decide where it would be best to set our ambush for Crasor."

Maxar breathed a heavy sigh. "Much as I think we could all use the rest, I think you're right. We have to get there first, before the battle starts. It will give us a much better position."

"Alright," Felar said, waiting for anyone else to chime in. When no one did, she nodded, closing her eyes. "Then let's head to the Ashamine system. If anything goes buggered immediately upon transition, we head back here straight away."

"Agreed," Maxar said.

"Dras," Felar said, taking a deep, steadying breath, "take us to the Ashamine core system."

The Heltasoth opened the worm transition and went through. Felar watched the Retribution follow behind them.

When she turned to look at their destination, her breath caught in her chest. "No, no, no," Felar said. *This is worse than I imagined.* Across the gravity well, past Ashamine-2 and 4, she saw a huge fleet, thousands of ships. "Buggering Justice," she noted, seeing the enormous carrier ship leading the armada.

"We can't retreat," Maxar said over the comms, looking grim. "We are a little late, but this is still our best opportunity. The Ashamine is just now sending its fleet to engage. The Breakers must have just wormed in."

Felar made a quick estimate of the Ashamine Forces, mentally switching to one of her numerous backup plans. "I wish they had more. The Breakers will obliterate them."

"So what do we do now?" Tremmilly asked, face ashen. "If we go flying into either of those groups, we'll be killed instantly."

"Tremmilly's right," Maxar said. "We can probably send or spoof the proper ident codes for the Ashamine fleet, but the Breakers will know we are intruders instantly. Dras, your ship won't be able to appear as friendly to either group."

Felar mentally kicked herself for not anticipating this. "Then we'll have to figure out a way to avoid either fleet, swoop in somehow, when they are distracted." The limitation would cripple their approach capabilities.

"There's another way," Lothis said, rising to come stand next to her. He thought for a moment, took out his personal terminal, and began taking notes. After a moment, he showed it to Wake.

"Could work," the engineer said. "Show Dras."

The boy stepped over to the Heltasoth and showed him the terminal. "Interesting concept. I believe I could make something like it function for this ship. The learning algorithm will be much easier for me to implement than it is for the human ship."

"OK, great," Felar said. "Anyone want to fill me in?"

"Lothis," Wake said, "get to work on the remote programming for the Retribution." He paused for a moment, thinking. "It's complicated," Wake continued, "and technical, but the basics are that we can create a program to take whatever ident signals are sent to us, learn the pattern, and spoof a legitimate reply. Should work for the Ashamine and the Breakers."

"Great," Felar answered. "Will it take long to implement?"

Lothis didn't look up from his terminal. "No longer than it will take us to get within cannon range of any enemy ships."

"Take us towards Ashamine-2," Felar ordered, watching as the Ashamine fleet drew closer to the Breakers. *Maybe we have a chance after all.*

20 – CRASOR

Crasor felt his heart rate quicken, the organ beating rapidly in his chest. A rushing sensation filled his head, and he couldn't help but smile. *It's happening,* he thought, seeing the Ashamine system and its two inhabited primary worlds. *I will control humanity after today.* In the distance, the trillions of people on Ashamine-2 pulled him forward, some bound for darkness, many more for the seed. Their souls, their vital energy, felt like everything Crasor ever wanted. *I'm coming,* he thought, his smile turning to a sneer.

"The Ashamine home fleet is as estimated," Karoth reported over the Transfiguration's comm screen. His armada commander was on the Justice, leading the fleet's vanguard, while Crasor remained farther back.

Keep our forces spread out, so surprises aren't catastrophic. It was Karoth's plan, and Crasor approved. He checked his tactical display, making sure the Rain and the Oblivion were in the correct positions. *All is as it should be. Gav and Salla are doing well.*

"The Founder's Light is absent," Karoth continued.

Crasor didn't know whether to be glad or upset about this information. Other than the Harbingers, the Ashamine's last remaining Tarton class ship was Crasor's biggest threat. Karoth continued stressing the fact the ship was likely the strongest and most destructive of the Founder's three namesake vessels. *If it is stronger than the Justice...* Crasor didn't want to meet the massive ship without having a much stronger fleet. *An objective we will secure once we take this system.* The probability seemed high that whoever was commanding the Light might surrender to Crasor once he occupied the Ashamine capital.

Karoth straightened up, looking formidable. "Analysis indicates we have the capability to take the system."

"Casualties?" Crasor asked.

Karoth gestured to one of his off-screen techs. "Transmitting to you."

Crasor reviewed the numbers and waited.

"Acceptable," the Breaker mind boomed. "We will still have the forces required to take the planets and maintain security for our other strongholds."

"Good," Crasor said, his earlier thrill returning. "I also have a surprise for those on the surface of Ashamine-2. It should help destabilize things further."

Karoth gave him a questioning look, but Crasor ignored him, focusing instead on opening a tunnel through space-time. *Miss Shinn,* he sent, pushing the thoughts towards his group of Breakers under the Founder's City. *Now is the time. Rise, and make yourselves known. We are coming.* He could feel her receive the message, although she couldn't send anything back. *No matter,* Crasor thought. *Whether she and her darkwalkers survive or not matters little. As long as they disrupt the capitol, it will be useful.*

"Take us forward," Crasor said finally, motioning to Karoth. "Now is our time. Let us seize our destiny."

"As you order," Karoth said, ending the comms link.

On the tactical display, Crasor watched the Ashamine ships move towards his fleet. *They must be insane,* he thought, licking his lips. *They have no hope.*

A faint prick of awareness struck the back of Crasor's mind. He tried to hold it, but it was too weak and slippery. *Miss Shinn?* Crasor wondered momentarily, before realizing she wasn't the origin. *Across the gravity well,* he finally decided, checking on his screen for any ships in the region. It appeared empty, but with the interference from an entire star system and the intervening ships, he couldn't be sure. He tried reaching out with his mind, to create a tunnel like he had before, but he couldn't find a clear path through space-time. *Probably nothing anyway,* he decided, returning his focus to the invasion.

As he watched, the Breaker fleet started moving forward, its foremost ships crossing the gravity well. *Not long till I rule the Ashamine,* Crasor thought.

On the screen, he couldn't help seeing the Valiant and several other ships directly behind him. *Blighthearted Faceless,* Crasor thought. The Breaker mind had given no explanation when it added the ships, and none of them followed Crasor's or Karoth's fleet orders. *They're watching me,* he thought, *always at my back, waiting...* Crasor attempted to forget their presence, but it nagged at him like a festering wound. *Why won't they leave me be?*

He thought back to when the Breaker mind had threatened him, forcing him to give up his humanity. *They promised I would remain the leader of the Breakers if I did so,* he consoled himself. *I did as they commanded.* Yet the presence of the faceless ones, direct from the primary Breaker dimension, loomed over him. *Why are they here?* A part of him tried to argue they were backup, support for when he found the Harbingers. Still, they felt vaguely threatening. *Trust, obey, and succeed,* he decided, realizing he had no other options.

"Multiple worm impressions opening behind us, sir," the Transfiguration's sensor tech announced, breaking him from his thoughts. "Sensor array capacity is overloaded. It's at least a couple hundred, maybe more."

Crasor's first feeling was one of confusion. *Was there a Breaker sub-fleet I forgot?* A moment later, he realized what was happening. On his tactical display, he saw hundreds of ships pop into existence, configurations he'd never seen before, strange amalgamations of engineering, technology, and art. *This must be the Vergers,* he thought. *They have impeccable timing.*

Karoth appeared on the comms screen. "You've seen the Vergers?" he asked.

"Of course. Does this change our probability of success?"

"Based on our limited intel of them, no" Karoth said. "Even with their addition, we have superior numbers. It will be a two-front battle, but I don't think we will need to dedicate much of our rear guard to disposing of them. Their ships are small. I doubt they have the capability to penetrate the armor of our larger ships."

"Good. I will take the rear sub-fleet and destroy them," Crasor said confidently, although there was a faint twinge of fear in his gut. *We have the numbers to fight on two fronts,* he thought. *Besides, they are weak, even if there are hundreds of them.*

"Darkness take those who oppose up," Karoth said, saluting.

Crasor nodded, dismissing his fleet commander. "Turn us around. We have human filth to eliminate, if they stay and fight."

Minutes dragged by, Crasor's sub-fleet drawing closer and closer to the ragtag Verger fleet. *This will be an appetizing sampler, before the main course,* he thought, smiling. He kept checking the tactical display, expecting to see the ships fleeing off into space, or disappearing into worm tunnels. Neither happened. *Why are they standing against us? Even this sub-fleet outnumbers and outpowers them significantly.*

Just as they were almost within accurate rail cannon range, the sensor tech made another announcement. "Multiple enemy worm generators spooling up."

They are running, Crasor sighed, feeling relieved his command skills wouldn't be put to the test. *We can go back to the primary offensive. Karoth is the one who should be leading this entire battle.*

Then, status reports from his ships began streaming in, filling up his display. Before Crasor could read any of them, the comms tech burst out, "Massive damage across much of the sub-fleet, sir!"

"No indication of weapon launches or discharges," the sensor tech relayed. "More enemy worm generators spooling up."

Crasor opened the first few status messages, seeing reports than ran from minor damage to half a ship missing. "What could have caused this?" he demanded, checking the tactical display again. All the Verger ships were still in system. None had fled. *Why did they spool up their worm generators?*

Just as he realized what the Vergers were doing, a gaping maw of blackness sprung up before the Transfiguration. "Full stop!" Crasor bellowed. "Maximum reverse thrust! Get us inside the gravity well. Order the rest of the sub-fleet to do the same." But it was already too late. The Transfiguration's nose slid into the blackness. "Get us out of here!"

Crasor felt the vessel shudder as the propulsion officer followed his order. Slowly, the ship's nose reversed out of the blackness. *Come on, come one!* Crasor willed, hoping it wasn't too late. A fraction of a second later, the view of the stationary Verger ships returned.

"Forward hull damage," his engineering tech reported. "The Transfiguration's nose is gone up to bulkhead Charlie."

"They're using worm generators as weapons," Crasor transmitted to his sub-fleet through gritted teeth. "Get back to the gravity well. Maximal thruster burn."

They set a trap, he thought, *and I flew straight into it.* Using a worm transition as a weapon was an impressive feat, one Crasor wished he had thought of. *Perhaps I underestimated the blighthearted buggers.* He felt exposed, powerless. The feelings inspired a rage deeper than anything he'd experienced since the incident with Emili Trayfis. *Once I get back inside the gravity well, they lose their power, and I will destroy them.*

"Worm generators spooling up again," the sensor tech announced.

Crasor felt fear battling with his anger, making his fury even more intense. *I will survive this,* he thought, willing the Transfiguration to move faster.

21 – AZA

"Shhhhhhh," Em whispered, hurriedly switched off her illumination device. Voices murmured out of the darkness ahead, reminding Aza of the similar situation just a few weeks ago.

Em pulled gently on her arm, directing Aza into a dim alcove. Lights blinked nearby on some kind of equipment, harsh on her dark-adapted eyes. *At least I'm not in sewage and refuse,* she thought, glad those tunnels were far below them. *We have to be getting near the surface.*

The older woman had been leading for hours, climbing higher and higher through the maintenance areas. They'd heard voices a few times before, but never this close.

"Keep quiet, no matter what," Em's voice said, her mouth so close to Aza's ear that she could feel her breath. "We'll wait them out."

Aza wanted to ask a thousand questions, but she did as ordered. *Who are these people? Why are they down here?* It seemed like, with all the chaos erupting on Ashamine-2, they were probably refugees. Aza knew there was nothing they could do for anyone else. *Like Em said, we are barely surviving ourselves.* The thought still brought pangs of guilt, but less than before.

As the voices and footsteps grew louder, Aza pressed herself against the alcove wall, trying to minimize her profile.

"Crasor is coming soon," a female voice said, buzzing oddly. "Has to."

"You've been saying that forever," a male voice replied. "We'll all be dead if Miss Shinn doesn't figure out a covert energy supply soon. As it is, we're almost out of darkness to prowl."

"The Ashamine has too much on its mind to worry about a few under-city inhabitants going missing. We can keep this up for months."

"You've always been too optimistic," the male voice replied.

The footsteps stopped just outside the alcove, and Aza felt her breath catch.

"Feel that?" the female voice said, close enough Aza could touch her.

91

"Yeah, I do."

Seconds passed in horrible anticipation. Aza knew, at any moment, a hand would reach out from the darkness and close around her throat. She fought hard to control herself, to keep from fleeing. *You're fine. It's OK,* she repeated, her lungs beginning to burn from lack of oxygen.

"It's time," the female said finally, buzzing voice triumphant. "Crasor has spoken to Miss Shinn. The time has come for us to rise!"

"The day has come. May the Dawn be broken!"

Running footsteps boomed down the tunnel, making Aza jump. She took in a deep breath, still trying to keep it as quiet as possible.

"Just a moment longer," Em said, her hand a comforting presence on Aza's shoulder. When the footsteps had faded into obscurity, Em pulled her forward. "We have to get out of these tunnels," she continued. "I'm not sure exactly what or who they were talking about, but I think things are about to get a lot more blighthearted." Em sounded shaken. When she turned her illumination back on, Aza saw all color had drained from her face.

"I know who Miss Shinn is," she said, walking as fast as she could to keep up. "And I've heard of Crasor."

"Tell me."

Aza spent the next few minutes recounting her prior experience in the lower maintenance tunnels, of her encounter with the horrible Miss Shinn and what the grotesque woman had said and done.

"They are cannibals or something," Aza finished, hoping she hadn't left anything too important out.

"Not cannibals," Em said, shaking her head, "but you're close. They do eat humans, sometimes. They're Breakers."

"What's a Breaker?"

"That's what the Brotherhood has been trying to figure out. They're some kind of alien organism. They infect human hosts. They've been taking over border worlds, causing much of the pandemonium you've seen on the Network. Beyond that, we don't really know. It sounds like they've been hiding on Ashamine-2, and they are about to attack the Founder's City."

"Do you know who Crasor is?" Aza asked, her breathing rapid from exertion.

Em shuddered, her whole body shaking. "I've only ever known one Crasor," she said, shuddering. "And I buggering hope he isn't the one they were talking about."

***

"Hold on," Em said, poking her head around the corner.

Aza couldn't take her eyes off the surrounding bodies. The huge space-lev station smelled like blood and metal, making her feel nauseous. Screams echoed and resounded from within the station's depths. *So much death...*

"Blightheart," Em said finally. "We need to dash for it." She turned around and grabbed Aza's hand. "No matter what happens, you stay with me. Keep running."

"OK," Aza said, mind spinning, "but–but where are we going?" She knew she had to focus, but it was all she could do to keep from spewing the contents of her stomach.

"We have to get to one of the space-lev carriers. That will get us up to the orbital dock and my ship. Now let's go!"

Em took off running, nearly pulling Aza's arm from its socket. As they passed into the main loading area of the space-lev station, she saw huge cargo skids, aligned neatly. Around them, more bodies were strewn about.

Aza's legs began burning, and she fought hard to keep up. Concussive booms and cracks resounded through the huge room, but she was too focused on running to figure out what was causing them.

"Get it open," Em said, thrusting her towards a huge cargo bay door. "As fast as you can!"

Aza slid to a stop before a large terminal screen. Its options were limited. She quickly found the command to open it. "Do it," she said, stabbing at the screen with her thumb. The heavy doors slowly retracted to either side.

When Aza turned to find Em, she saw the woman struggling with two male attackers. Both had crude metal clubs, swinging wildly at her. Em jumped left, easily dodging the smaller man. The moment after regaining stability, she raised her right hand and triggered her flechette pistol. Blood erupted from the smaller man's back in a gruesome fountain as he fell to the floor in a heap.

The larger man turned to run. Before he could take more than a step, Em trained her pistol on him. The weapon cracked, and the second attacker's lower torso vanished in a mist of blood.

"Get in," Em said, running towards her. Aza felt frozen, her body unable to obey anything her mind was willing it to do. "We gotta go!" Em grabbed her by the shoulder and dragged her into the carrier. As they entered, the doors finally finished opening.

"Come on, come on," Em growled, hitting the close button multiple times. Finally, the doors began rumbling back in the other direction.

Movement across the loading area caught Aza's attention. A group of seven figures came through the facility entrance. Their movements were awkward and unsteady.

"Fires of the dark star," Em said, checking her flechette pistol. "Aza, get to the back of the carrier."

Aza did as ordered, wishing there was something to hide behind in the cavernous interior. "Breakers?" she asked, flattening herself against the corner.

"Yep," was Em's curt reply. She took up a stance just inside the carrier, her position reminding Aza of the military recruitment vids she'd seen on the Network. Em raised her flechette pistol and began triggering it. *Crack, crack, crack.* The loud noise reverberated in carrier, making Aza put her hands over her ears.

When she refocused on the Breakers, she saw three of them lay motionless on the floor, heads obliterated. Em's pistol cracked three more times and two more Breakers fell mid-run.

"Blightheart," Em cursed, steadying her aim.

The doors were nearly closed now, but Aza could see the remaining attackers would reach them before they were fully shut. *No, no, no,* she thought, willing them closed.

Em's pistol cracked twice more, then a single remaining Breaker dove through the narrowing space, slamming into her. They both fell to the ground, Em's pistol sliding across the floor away from her. A moment later, the large carrier doors boomed shut.

"Get us going up," Em yelled, trying to keep the Breaker female from getting on top of her. The two rolled across the floor, and Aza couldn't tell who was snarling the loudest.

Feeling dazed, Aza ran over to the carrier's terminal and searched for the depart option. The letters on the screen seemed jumbled, a confusing mix of symbols and gibberish.

"Aza! Hurry up!" Em roared. In the edge of her vision, Aza could see the fierce woman slamming the Breaker's head into the alloy metal floor.

Taking a deep breath, Aza refocused on the screen. "Launch," she said, hitting the corresponding option.

A notification screeched. "Personnel detected in carrier," the screen flashed. "Launch not advised." After a moment, "Are you sure you want to launch?"

Aza hit "Yes." An instant later, it felt like she was going to be sucked through the floor of the carrier. Unable to withstand the increased gravity, Aza hit the decking, her head slamming against the heavy metal plating.

The world became fuzzy, spinning around her. Grunts, curses, and growls echoed through her head. *Where am I?* she wondered. *It feels like I'm glued to a giant spider's web.*

After a few moments, Aza blinked her eyes and felt the fog clearing. The force pinning her to the floor lessened as well, allowing her to sit up.

She looked around, still feeling confused about where she was.

She saw Em, and everything came rushing back into place. The Breaker female was on top of her, trying to sink her teeth into Em's neck. Em had the creature's wrists grasped in her hands, which was all that was keeping the Breaker from tearing out her throat. As Aza watched, the snapping jaws moved closer and closer to Em's neck.

"What—what can I do?" Aza said dazedly. She looked around the room, trying to find a way to help her friend. Then, she saw it: Em's flechette pistol. It was just a few meters away, but when Aza tried to stand, she found her legs were too unsteady.

So she began crawling across the smooth decking, her head swooning with the movement. When she finally reached the weapon, she grasped at it with numb fingers. *You can do this,* she thought, her vision fading in and out. *Sit up. Focus!*

Aza raised the pistol, grasping it how Em had. The weapon felt like it weighed a thousand kilos. Her arms shuddered with the effort. *Come on, come on,* she thought, trying to steady herself.

When she finally got the pistol aimed in the right direction, she saw the Breaker was just centimeters from Em's neck. Aza tried to keep the Breaker's head squarely in her sights, but her hands kept shaking. *One chance. She's counting on you. Get it right. Do it. Do it now!*

Aza tightened her index finger and triggered the flechette pistol.

22 – WAKE

"Can anyone feel where Crasor is?" Felar asked. "He should be on the Justice, but I'm not strong enough to locate him through all the other Breakers."

Wake tried to reach out with his mind, to sense Crasor. He found nothing but the huge mass of negative energy composing the Breaker fleet.

"I'm having the same problem," Tremmilly said over the comm, looking troubled.

"Cazz-ak would have been able to find him," Lothis said, frowning.

Felar shook her head, looking directly at him. "Remember what we talked about?"

The boy's eyes widened, and he shook his head. "Yes, sorry."

She really did get through, Wake thought, the rest of his mind continuing the search for Crasor.

"I think we have to get closer," Felar said finally.

"Agreed," Maxar said over the comm. "We have to get in the battle at some point anyway. Might as well be now."

If Tremmilly can't see through this mess, it seems highly unlikely I'll be able to. Wake drew his consciousness back, returning his focus to his body. He looked at the tactical display Dras had created for them. The mass of Breaker, Ashamine, and Verger ships were overwhelming, but Wake tried to make sense of the situation.

"We are nearly around Ashamine Primary," Dras noted, voice calm. Wake wondered how the sentient machine could maintain such strict composure when they were all facing such grim odds. "We will pass Ashamine-4 shortly."

Checking the display, Wake could see there were still a few ships departing the orbital dock above the planet, and this gave him hope. "Perhaps we can go with the laggers and catch up to the Ashamine fleet. With the ident spoofers Lothis created, we should be able to slip in with no issues."

Felar nodded. "Good plan. Even if we remain comms silent to them, there is so much chaos they will likely just assume a malfunction."

"What of the alien appearance of my ship?" Dras asked.

"They have too much going on to notice an anomalous black ship." Felar paused. "They'll just think it is a black-ops vessel, if they see us at all."

Wake finished putting on Brightwing, but left the helmet off. Looking behind the Heltasoth ship, he made sure the Retribution was still in formation. *All is as it should be.* On the comms screen, Wake could see everyone on the other ship already had their armor on.

Felar seemed to notice only she and Lothis were left and started getting into hers. "Time to suit up," she said, giving the boy his ill-fitting suit.

"Passing Ashamine-2," Dras announced, carefully joining in behind a ship leaving the orbital dock. Wake waited, wondering if Lothis' ident spoofing code would work. As time passed and nothing happened, he felt himself relax. "Good job," Wake said, patting the boy on his now armored back. Lothis remained silent, but smiled up at him.

After another long passage across empty space, they reached the next habitable planet in the system. "Passing Ashamine-4," Dras announced.

That's where Felar was stationed, Wake remembered, thinking back to the stories she'd told him. *Glad we've made things right again,* he thought, looking at her. Wake loved seeing her in her element, eyes fierce, body and mind ready to strike. *She'll have her chance soon enough. We all will.*

"Nearing the Ashamine fleet," Dras said finally, slowing down as they approached the mass of vessels. Wake had never seen so many ships in one place, had never known so many even existed.

"What now?" Jaydon asked, sounding as spooked as Wake felt.

"Tremmilly," Felar asked, "can you feel him?"

Wake watched Tremmilly close her eyes on the comms screen. A moment later, she opened them again. "Still too much interference."

"Dras, take us closer to the near edge of the Breaker fleet," Felar ordered.

"As you wish."

Wake felt a strange sense of disembodiment as they began moving through the massive ships. *I am like water, rushing past massive boulders.* The feeling was exhilarating.

They passed row after row of ships, all ready to face the Breaker fleet, who vastly outnumbered them. *How are they willing to go into these horrible odds?* Wake wondered, pulling Brightwing's helmet over his head. *Their chances of survival are better than yours,* he realized, latching the helmet in place. *Maybe, but they don't have Brightwing, and they are not Harbingers.*

23 – TREMMILLY

You know how to find him, Tremmilly thought. *No, I don't want to go there, not now.* The connection to the Breakers bloomed in the back of her mind, a swirling torrent of dark energy threatening to pull her in. *Besides, I'm not even sure how it functions. Is it a link to Crasor, to See'dek, or just the Breakers in general?*

"The front lines are coming in range of each other," Jaydon said, startling Tremmilly out of her reverie.

A second passed, then the area between the Ashamine and Breaker fleets lit up with one of the most beautiful things Tremmilly had ever seen. Every color imaginable streaked between the opposing forces.

"This has to be the biggest battle in human history," Maxar said, eyes wide. "The death count is going to be enormous."

Tremmilly couldn't take her eyes off the spectacle, as the massive ships tried to hammer each other to oblivion. The smaller fighters and gunships from either side weaved in and out of their foes, trying to strike at the larger ships' weak points.

"We're really going into that?" Jaydon asked, continuing to keep the Retribution close behind Dras' ship. "We don't stand a chance."

"We're identing as both Breaker and Ashamine," Maxar said, still keeping his eyes on the titanic battle. "Neither side should target us."

"Target or no," the old captain grumbled, "if a stray cannon round from one of the big ships hits us, we won't stand a chance."

"You're a good pilot," Tremmilly said, giving Jaydon a smile. "I'm sure you'll keep us out of harm's way."

"Burn it all to the fires of the dark star," he mumbled, shaking his head. "You've been around me long enough to know I can't work miracles."

Dras was difficult to follow as he flew amongst the slower Ashamine fleet, but Jaydon was doing a remarkable job. Tremmilly gripped the arms of her seat, stifling an anxious groan as they streaked by a carrier ship.

"What'd I tell ya?" Jaydon said, banking hard to prevent a collision with a launching fighter.

Another minute passed, then the two fleets met. "Now is where things get really messy," Maxar said, staring intently at the tactical display.

"We're gonna be inside the enemy fleet within the next few minutes," Dras transmitted over the comm.

Tremmilly sent her mind out, desperately searching for Crasor. *Come on. Where are you?* Nothing but the same overwhelming background of dark energy that typified the Breakers. *I spent so much time hiding from you, shielding us,* she thought, looking deeper and deeper into the chaos. Then, she felt him.

"He's in the back!" she yelled. "Crasor is near the back of the fleet. Just inside the gravity well."

"Not on the Justice?" Felar said, face looking surprised over the comm link.

"Correct," Tremmilly replied, checking again to make sure. The Breaker leader appeared as the darkest spot in all the negative energy. Despite the swirling, churning interference, she knew it was him.

A huge explosion caught Tremmilly's attention, distracting her from Crasor. Several Ashamine ships ahead of the Justice were engulfed in bright light.

"Compromised worm generators," Wake said, eyes wide.

"Blightheart," Felar cursed. "I'm no space warfare expert, but given the already bad odds, I don't think the Ashamine will last long. The Justice is going to just keep pounding away until every last Ashamine ship is decimated. With it gone though..." she trailed off, looking thoughtful.

"There's no way," Wake said. "There aren't any ships here capable of taking it out. That's what you said before."

"Sure," Felar replied, "no other ships, but I never said anything about us."

"Wait, what?" Wake said, a look of horror on his face that matched how Tremmilly felt. "We can't go back on that ship. We barely escaped last time."

"Felar's right," Maxar said, sighing. "We don't really have a choice. We don't know that killing Crasor will stop the Breakers."

"So now we have to stop Crasor *and* the entire Breaker fleet?" Jaydon said, face pale.

"Not the entire fleet," Felar said, eyes narrowing. "Just the Justice."

"Oh yeah," Jaydon scoffed, "*just* the Justice."

"Once we disable it," Felar continued, ignoring him, "it will give the Ashamine and Vergers a non-zero chance of stopping the Breaker fleet. If we remove their leadership at such a critical moment, it could launch those chances up to probable."

"We're all going to die," Jaydon said, looking resigned. "Guess it's better to go down in the blaze of a hero than to the bottom of a bottle," he finished, so quietly Tremmilly could barely hear him, despite their proximity.

"We don't have the time to do this as one team," Felar said finally. "We have to split up."

Tremmilly felt her heart sink. *It was so good to be back together,* she thought, *even if we were in two different ships.* She missed being with the other team, of hearing Wake and Felar's inside jokes, of trying to help Lothis get out of the dark place Cazz-ak's death had sent him. *Felar is taking care of that,* she thought.

"Our ship will go to the Justice," Felar announced. "Maxar, you and your team will go take out Crasor."

The enormity of what she was about to attempt slammed into Tremmilly like a starship. "Us? Just the four of us?"

Maxar leaned between their seats, putting an arm around her.

"It isn't going to be easy," Felar continued, eyes narrowing and face growing hard. "All I ask is all you have to give. There is no other way, there is no other time."

As Tremmilly thought about it, she realized Felar was right. Despite her team's limited combat abilities, it did make more sense for them to go after Crasor. The Justice would be full of troops and defenses. Felar and her team would have to penetrate deep within it to reach any critical systems. Tremmilly nodded, trying not to let her fear show.

"Besides," Felar said, giving her a small smile. "You and Jaydon are expert shots. I should know, I trained you. Maxar and Beowulf will handle anything you two can't."

Tremmilly nodded again, hear heart still fluttering in her chest.

"Tremmilly," Felar finished, "don't underestimate your Elrahi abilities. You are stronger than you give yourself credit for. Stronger than any of us."

Not wanting to contradict her friend, Tremmilly kept silent, but inwardly, she knew the woman was just saying it to bolster her courage.

"If we are to achieve optimal courses," Dras broke in, "we must diverge as soon as possible. Any delay puts the other team at a disadvantage, and closer to the dangers the Justice presents."

"It is time we part," Felar said. Despite the other woman's best efforts, Tremmilly could see she was trying to stifle her emotion. "No time for long goodbyes."

"We'll see each other soon," Tremmilly said, putting on a fake smile, "after we've both completed our missions."

"No doubt," Felar said.

As the comms screen went black, Tremmilly wondered if they'd both be proven liars.

24 – GAV

What did you do, Salla? Gav thought, staring at the Oblivion on his view screen. Salla's ship was stationed ahead of him, closer to the front of the primary fleet, while Karoth had Gav and the Rain in the center of the huge mass.

On his tactical display, Gav watched the leading edge of ships tear into the oncoming Ashamine fleet. Part of him wished he was commanding one of the huge battleships, rather than his specialized planet killer, but he knew his time would come soon. *Not all glory is won in battle,* he thought. *But if you don't find Salla's sabotage, you won't live long enough for it to matter.*

He'd had his personnel sweep and scan all critical systems. They'd found nothing so far. It was slow going, especially since they were underway and maneuvering with the fleet. *Salla is a crafty pole sucker. There is no way in the fires of the dark star she would have passed an opportunity to blightheart me.*

Still, his XO and all his techs told him the ship was clean, all systems nominal. Gav had interviewed the Marines who'd kept watch on his room, both during and after their lovemaking session. They all swore that she'd remained inside the entire time. *But there weren't eyes on her while I was sleeping.* His mind kept coming back to that, despite the fact he was beginning to feel like he might just be paranoid.

The whole crew probably thinks that. They are going to judge me a fool for having welcomed my enemy on board, and into my arms. The realization made him grit his teeth, but there was nothing he could do about it now.

Except find the blighthearted sabotage, then I buggered her and won. Still, he felt like he'd checked everywhere, had his best techs run diagnostics on anything that mattered. *It's here, somewhere,* he thought.

An abnormal movement on the tactical display caught Gav's

attention. A lone gunship was heading backwards through the fleet. *Odd,* he thought, upping the magnification. The status readout said it was Breaker, which made sense since it was so deep inside the fleet. *But why is it heading away from battle?*

Gav had watched the conflict between Crasor's sub-fleet and the ships tagged as Vergers. He wasn't in the line of sit-reps, but he'd seen the Breakers flee. *How did those small ships fight off so many superior vessels?*

As the tiny gunship zipped past the Rain, Gav thought he felt something twinge in his mind. The feeling was gone so quickly that he couldn't focus on it, and after a moment, he wondered if he'd felt anything at all.

Shaking his head, Gav watched the solitary gunship continue towards the fleet's rear. *Some kind of reinforcement?* he thought. *Makes no sense.* Gav shrugged, zooming out on the screen. *Leave the strategy to Karoth. He knows his business.* The Breaker fleet commander had captured or destroyed every Ashamine system, save for the one they were attacking now.

On his display, Gav found the Justice. Watching the huge ship was a lesson in the art of domination. What Karoth didn't destroy with his enormous cannons, his fighter wings picked apart. *I wonder how big a fleet it could face unsupported?* It would be foolish to do such a thing, but with the mass destruction it was handing the Ashamine fleet, Gav wondered if they needed any of the other ships at all.

A whole division of the enemy fleet was swallowed up in galactic fire as the Justice sent rail slugs into one of their worm generators. Gav smiled. *So much energy bound up in that system,* he thought. *Destabilize it, and physics does the rest.*

The Justice continued plowing through the enemy vessels, destroying ship after ship. *Perhaps this won't take as long as I thought. We'll obliterate the Ashamine fleet, then we'll move on to dominating the core worlds.* Systematically killing or converting a population of trillions would require time. *But we have so many troops,* he thought, checking to make sure the drop ships and transports were nearby. They weren't Gav's direct responsibility, but as Crasor's second-in-command, he felt like he should keep watch on them.

What makes you think you're the second? Crasor never told you that, and Salla would dispute it violently if you ever tried to claim it.

Thinking about his rival banished his positive thoughts about the invasion and brought back the anxiety about her sabotage. *Have you really thought of everything?*

Shut up! You're being ridiculous. Focus on the battle. You could be ordered to deploy the Rain at any moment.

Still, a nagging sense of foreboding hung over him. *I'm forgetting something, something critical.* Then, it hit him. *The code. She could have hidden something deep in the ship's operating system.* A yawning pit opened in his stomach. *It could be anywhere,* he thought, *so small I'll never find it, until it's too late.*

The tactical display flickered violently, displaying a gruesome image of his severed head floating in space. Gav blinked, and then it was gone. *What was that?* He continued staring at the screen, heart beating rapidly, wondering if the experience had been real or only in his mind. *Stress,* he decided finally, trying to shut the incident out.

Still, the longer he thought about it, the less convinced he felt. *Psychological warfare... The perfect sabotage. Salla could slowly break me, diminishing my effectiveness until I'm completely discredited. It would leave no evidence. She could effectively deny any accusation I level against her and blame it on my slipping sanity.*

He shook his head, the enormity of the situation threatening to overwhelm him. *I have to find what she did, stop it before it gets worse.* Even with his entire crew helping, it could still take days, if not weeks. *We have to try.*

Gav began issuing orders, telling all non-essential personnel to begin searching the ship's computers, looking for suspicious code and sub-routines. He organized them as best he could, distributing the load evenly. *If only I had a properly trained quantum human,* he thought, remembering the speed at which Fade had powered through complex searches and equations. Gav sighed, opening up his own search queue. *I wonder where that bugger got off to, or if he is still alive.*

25 – LOTHIS

"Lothis?" a faint voice asked over the boy's ENS helmet comm, distracting him from the mayhem raging outside the Heltasoth ship.

"Fade?" Lothis answered, trying to remember the last time he'd talked to the quantum human. *He was more depressed and sullen than I ever was.*

"Lothis, I've found him," Fade said, voice stronger.

"Found who?" Lothis transmitted back.

"The Creator."

Lothis wondered briefly if Fade had finally gone insane, if his self-imposed isolation within the Heltasoth ship had warped his mind. *We have no way of knowing what existing in a quantum state does to consciousness.*

"He's out there," Fade continued, his tone becoming more intense. "I found him. I searched through every ship, scanned every consciousness until I found his blighthearted being. He's different now, but I still recognize him."

Then, it hit Lothis. *His creator, the person who killed his body, tortured his mind, and turned him into this.*

"I'm going to kill him, Lothis. I'm going to make him understand agony, perhaps not the same agony he put me through, but it will have to suffice. I've already infiltrated his systems, showed him previews of the future."

"But you'll decompose," Lothis replied, finding his voice again. "More and more of your quantum entanglements will evaporate the longer you are away from a compatible computing system."

"I don't care!" Fade screeched, making Lothis jump. "Whatever life I had, it's over now. Existing in this ship is only a modicum better than death. It is so foreign, so *unconnected* to me. If I can destroy the Creator, it will be more than worth the loss of existence."

Lothis thought about trying to dissuade the quantum being, to tell him they might find a better, more human place for him to live, but then he realized Fade was probably right. *He has no hope for anything other than revenge, and if he can attain that, perhaps it is enough.*

"Good luck," Lothis transmitted, wishing he could have done more to restore Fade's sanity.

"Thank you for everything you did for me, for saving me from the Arche. I wish I could have helped you and your friends, but just existing was almost more than I could bear. May you succeed at whatever it is you're trying to accomplish."

Lothis jumped again as a ball of white light engulfed a nearby Ashamine ship. *You have to focus on the mission,* he thought, somehow sensing Fade had left the Heltasoth computer. *He's on his raid, and you're on yours. Keep your mental shield up, like Tremmilly taught you. If you let it slip, Crasor could spot us, even through all this chaos.*

Two more Ashamine ships erupted into miniature novas, only this time, Lothis remained still. *How are we ever going to make it through?* he wondered. *Dras is an excellent pilot, but this is too much, even for him.*

As the Heltasoth ship neared the Justice, things went from bad to worse. All around them, rail cannon tracers flared, tracing straight lines between the Justice and Ashamine ships. Dras had phased them through a few of the larger volleys, but his monotone voice had returned and Lothis guessed he was maxing out his processing power.

We're going to die, Lothis decided, seeing no way to reach the enormous carrier ship. Behind them, their escape was blocked by exploding vessels and intense rail cannon fire. Seconds dragged by, feeling like eternity. Lothis wondered what it would feel like when a rail round finally hit them. *Will I survive, or will darkness take me instantly?*

They burst into the bubble of the Justice's point defense systems. The smaller slug throwers chewed up incoming enemy rounds, creating a space that felt safe by comparison.

"Your ident spoofing system still seems to be working perfectly," Wake said, his face invisible behind Brightwing's solid faceplate.

Lothis toggled his ENS's comm to transmit, knowing his voice would be nearly inaudible otherwise. "The machine authentication got us this far, but what about when we are close enough for them to see us physically? They are more alert than the ships we've passed previously."

"On my sensors," Felar said, her attention still focused on their approach. "Dras, take us to that hangar, the aft one." The Heltasoth made a course correction, and they sped down the side of the huge ship, flying below a line of rail cannons. "All the ship's guns are controlled remotely, and I believe they are automated. Tech's issue combat parameters and the system follows through. Occasionally, they might target a ship specifically, but since we are pinging as friendly, they have no cause to do that."

Dras slowed the ship down as they neared the hangar doors, swinging out to an oblique vector.

"Hopefully," Felar continued, "since it looks like the Justice deployed all its fighters, this section of the ship will be nearly empty."

"What about flight crews?" Wake said, his attention turning to the forward view as Dras headed straight for the hangar. "Won't there be service and maintenance personnel?"

"Most likely, yes," Felar said. "We should have no problem with them."

"And if there are Breaker soldiers?" Lothis asked.

"We do the same thing we did on all our other missions: Take them out."

Lothis nodded, feeling his anxiety deepen. *This is for Cazz-ak,* he thought, doing one final check to make sure his suit was ready. *This is for my sister, the Empress.* He drew his flechette pistol and checked its loadout. *This is for the Elrahi.* Out of the edge of his vision, he saw the hangar deck rising as Dras set them down. *This is for the Dawn!*

"Let's go!" Felar yelled, and Lothis fell in behind her. She was lugging her huge beam weapon, a sight that brought a smile to Lothis' face. Wake stepped in behind him, and they all three headed for the airlock. "Dras, protect the ship and be ready for our return. I have the feeling we won't have much time to escape when we're done."

"Yes, Felar," Dras said, as the Heltasoth ship slammed down.

Felar jumped into the exit chute. Lothis waited for a moment and followed. For a second, he was free-falling, but then, he soon felt himself decelerate. His boots hit the deck hard, and Lothis was running, clearing the way for Wake. They'd practiced this drill many times on earlier missions, and now their movements were smooth and coordinated.

Lothis quickly identified where Felar was, sprinting towards a group of surprised-looking Breakers off to the right. Lothis found another clump, and ran towards them. His legs felt strong, his mind clear. Despite the exertion, his breathing was calm.

As soon as Lothis was within range, he dropped to one knee and leveled his weapon. He triggered several shots in succession, each hitting its target with devastating accuracy.

Violet light illuminated the hangar, and Lothis knew Felar was using her beam weapon. Checking her progress, Lothis saw her sweep the weapon through a broad arc, scything through supply crates and the Breakers taking cover behind them. He felt glad for his suit's atmosphere supply. *Not a pleasant smell...*

Slapping in a quick reload, Lothis found a new group. By this time, the rest of the hangar crew were recovered from their shock and began raising pistols. Flechette rounds ricocheted off the surrounding deck, so Lothis dove behind a pallet of fighter-caliber rail ammunition. Even though his suit was rated for these kinds of impacts, he didn't want to risk it. *The armor is only there as a backup,* he remembered Felar drilling into him. *It is for when your tactics fail or you get overwhelmed.*

Darting his head around the crate, Lothis took aim and fired several rounds. This squad of Breakers had taken cover, but their movements were predictable enough Lothis was able to pick them off. *All that practice. All those drills...*

When he'd taken out the last of his second group, Lothis once again scanned the deck. He watched Felar blast through a heavy container, the violet beam scorching the Breakers behind it.

"All clear on my side," Wake said, joining Lothis a few seconds later.

"Everything clear over here as well," Felar said. "Got to keep moving." She led them towards the hangar exit, a large door set in the space's far end. They reached it, and Lothis selected the open option on the nearby terminal. The halves silently parted before them.

"If we are lucky," Wake said, moving through the doorway, "none of those buggers had a chance to raise the alarm."

"The lack of a lockdown indicates they haven't," Felar answered, motioning them to take a right down the long corridor. "If my plan works, we'll be in and out before they even know what's happened."

26 – ASH

"We have to pursue them!" Ash yelled, finally losing patience.

On the screen before him, Fierence was livid. "You can go castrate yourself in the coldest depths of the void," he shot back, shaking his head. "We aren't going in there to sacrifice ourselves in a losing battle. You didn't tell us how many Breakers there really were."

Ash clenched his jaw so hard he thought he might break a tooth. "I told you it would be long odds, and I told you it would be risky. If we get in there and attack that sub-fleet, we'll destroy a sizable chunk of them. It will give the Ashamine a chance."

"Bugger you," Fierence said. "We aren't going inside the gravity well. You're lucky we've stayed this long. Their fleet is too big. We used our weapons, destroyed ships, and held up our end of the agreement. Inside the well, we won't be able to use the worms."

"You have other weapons," Ash seethed, knowing he needed to get control of himself, "ones that will work inside the gravity well."

"I don't know what you are talking about," Fierence said, unable to meet Ash's gaze. "We did what we could. We fought with honor."

"You have beam weapons. I know it. I've heard about your cloaking technology." Ash threw his hands up in the air. "You could help. You could save humanity!"

"Are you calling me a buggering liar? You void-defiling, worthless excuse for a leader!"

"No," Ash shot back, unable to stop, "I'm saying you're a coward. This is humanity's last chance against the Breakers. If we don't help, there will be nothing left for us."

Fierence's eyes narrowed, and he pursed his lips. "We Vergers had a bargain, with the Brotherhood of Azak-so, and we have fulfilled it. We came here, supported your fleet. I never agreed to go to my death for a useless cause. Do what you want, Parick Olvold, but know if you survive,

108

you and your name are forever despised by the Vergers. We will never bargain with the Brotherhood again." The comms screen went dark.

"Buggering, blighthearted, opportunistic, unfaithful waste of—" Ash yelled, knowing that even if he had approached Fierence calmly, the situation wouldn't be any different. *He had no intention of taking real risks,* Ash thought, *even with all his boasting.*

He put his hands over his face, trying to block out the images of the collapsing Ashamine fleet. The Breakers were quickly obliterating them, and while the Vergers had destroyed a significant portion of the nearby sub-fleet, it wasn't enough.

So ironic, he thought, feeling the warmth of his burning face on his palms. *I spent years fighting the Ashamine, and now I'm trying to save them.* He'd known from early in his life the citizens of the galactic empire were innocent of the government's corruption. Ash, as Parick Olvold, had done all he could to help excise their pervasive cancer, to be a force for positive change. *Now, none of it matters. The humans, the Entho-la-ah-mines, everything good in this universe will be subsumed by the Breakers.*

Despair threatened to overwhelm him. He knew the odds were bad from the beginning, but now it was in front of him, he couldn't really blame Fierence for wanting to stay out of it. *But we can't run and hide. The Breakers will find us all. Even in the Verge. They'll go to other galaxies, find other life.* Ash couldn't go forward, and he couldn't go back.

"Sir," a voice said, breaking through his agony. He dropped his hands and located the speaker, a young female officer.

"Yes?" he replied, trying to keep despair from his voice.

"Permission to speak freely?"

"Of course."

"Well, sir," the officer said, alternating between looking him in the eye and staring down at her clasped hands. "I think I speak for everyone in the Brotherhood when I say that Fierence is a liar and a coward." Around the bridge, his crew nodded. "It was always a remote chance they would follow through, and they did help out, at least a little. You did an amazing job just getting them here. But now it is up to us, to the Brotherhood. The Breakers will come to our worlds after they finish the Ashamine. After that, even if they disbelieve, the Vergers will be destroyed too. They are buying time, but there is a limit. We don't have a choice, sir. Whether any of us survive or not, it is our obligation to our species to protect it, and now is our chance."

"As you say," Ash replied, nodding. He felt frustration and despair drain from him, his emotions buoyed by the woman's words. "But we do have a choice," he continued. "There is always a choice. And today, we choose to go to battle, to destroy the evil threatening to wipe us out, or die trying."

The bridge erupted in cheers and stamping feet, but Ash guessed it had more to do with the officer's words than his own. *I needed to hear it just as much as anyone else,* he thought, recalculating plans now that the Vergers were out of the fight.

"Get me a comm to whoever is leading the Ashamine fleet," Ash ordered as soon as the cheers died down. "They've got their fleet laid out in the worst way possible. Someone needs to tell them to get their blightheart sorted before the Justice buggers them all."

27 – MAXAR

"Blightheartedly good thing we didn't have to go into the middle of that battle," Jaydon said, flying them through the void between the main battle and the Breaker sub-fleet.

Maxar had to agree. "I'm not jealous of the other team," he said. "I hope Dras gets them to the Justice OK."

"He will," Tremmilly said, looking tense.

Maxar felt the danger they were facing as well, but her anxiety seemed deeper. He wanted to talk with her, to ask what was wrong, but the present moment seemed ill-timed. *I thought I convinced her she wasn't responsible for killing the Elrahi race.* Now, he wasn't so sure. *She takes too much on herself. She wasn't the only one making major decisions back then.*

"That's the ship Crasor is on?" Jaydon asked, pointing to a large vessel on the magnified main view screen. Tremmilly nodded. The ship was pointed away from them, back towards the edge of the gravity well. "It doesn't look like it has a hangar," he continued, "at least not one we can use. Probably some for shuttles, but we'd never fit."

"Won't Crasor feel us coming?" Maxar realized, wondering why he hadn't thought of it before they'd gotten this close. "He'll just rail us before we can even land."

"Be calm, my love," Tremmilly said, giving him a wan smile. "I've been handling that. I think he's very preoccupied at the moment anyway, but I've been shielding our Elrahi auras for quite some time."

Maxar smiled back. "It's like Felar said, even without Elrahi combat abilities, you are still a major asset to this team."

"If we can't land in a hangar," Jaydon said, ignoring their side conversation, "we need to come up with another plan. Right now, there are lots of gunships flying around in this fleet, but once we land on Crasor's hull, we'll stand out like a starship in a farm field. Even if we are

111

squawking the right ident codes, someone will notice and report us."

"What if we do like we did on the Justice?" Tremmilly asked. "Land near the shuttle hangar and go in through the shuttle bay doors?"

"We can do that if it's the only option," Maxar replied, "but I'd rather not have the containment field's EMF knock me out again. Unless they have shuttles coming and going, they might not even have the armor doors open."

"Oh yeah," Tremmilly said, brow furrowing. "I forgot about the whole EMF thing."

"We have to find an airlock," Jaydon said, upping the magnification on the view screen. "See if you can spot one. The closer to Crasor the better. Wish we had someone familiar with Ashamine-built ships with us. Would make things blightheartedly easier."

"Once we find one, we'll have to hash it to get inside," Maxar added, rubbing his chin. "Without Lothis, this is going to be a lot harder, but I think I know a few exploits their systems might be vulnerable to. Unless they patched them out."

"Won't they know we are trying to get in, once you start?" Tremmilly's eyes were focused on the magnified view screen, reminding Maxar he should be scanning it too.

"Only if I bugger it up."

"There are going to be a lot of troops on that ship," Jaydon said, entering commands on his piloting terminal. "If they send squads of whatever the Breaker equivalent to Marines are, we'll be buggered."

Maxar sighed. "We'll do our best to stay stealthy and prevent them from even knowing we are there. There is a lot going on in this star system at the moment. Hopefully, they'll remain distracted, and Tremmilly can keep us shielded. Crasor has no idea we are coming. Once we get in and take him out, his whole command structure will collapse." *Hopefully,* Maxar mentally added. *That would be the most ideal thing. If not, who knows how we'll get out of this alive.*

"There's one!" Tremmilly exclaimed, pointing to a small airlock near one of the port-side cannons.

"Probably some kind of maintenance hatch," Jaydon added, adjusting their course.

"It's even close to Crasor," Tremmilly added, "relatively speaking. He's near the front of the ship, so we'll have to travel up a few decks and traverse part of a deck. Is that near enough?"

"I think the longer we are out here trying to find a better option," Maxar said, nodding, "the more chance someone has to notice us. Once we are on the ship, we can hide more effectively." He failed to mention that once inside, the Breakers might cut off their escape by finding and destroying the Retribution.

As they drew nearer and nearer to Crasor's ship, Maxar felt a pit grow in his stomach. *Don't notice us,* he willed. *Nothing to see. Just flying abnormally close by.*

Tremmilly and Jaydon remained silent. Beowulf began whining until Tremmilly bent down to hug him.

Everything is fine. Just another Breaker gunship passing by.

Soon, Jaydon slowed their approach even more, and Maxar could feel himself grow heavy as the inertial dampers worked to keep up with the deceleration. The sensation added to the expanding pit in his stomach. Eventually, he could make out the airlock's details without screen magnification. He finished putting on his captured Ashamine combat ENS by locking the helmet into place. Tremmilly did the same.

Jaydon took the ship in farther, hovering a short distance from the airlock. He made some quick adjustments on his terminal, and the Retribution settled lightly on the larger ship's hull.

"Nice work," Maxar said, letting his breath out.

"Just doing my job," Jaydon replied, attaching his own helmet onto his suit. "Lead the way."

"What about Beowulf?" Tremmilly asked.

Maxar bit his lip, looking at the wolf-dog. "I wish we could take him along, but we won't have any way to get him from the Retribution and onto the Breaker ship."

Tremmilly bent down, running her hands through his long fur. Again, Maxar felt her hands on his own back. "You stay here and protect our ship," Tremmilly said. She leaned her head against the wolf-dog. Maxar couldn't see her tears due to the angle, but he knew they would be there. "We'll be back, I promise."

After a moment, Tremmilly rose to her feet and signaled her readiness. Maxar took the lead, heading through the Retribution to its primary airlock. *You'll have to be quick with the exploits,* he thought as they waited for it to cycle. *If they have the standard AI, you won't have long before they spot an anomaly.* Maxar was thankful for their previous weeks of raiding Breaker installations and ships. *Were it not for those missions, we'd be going in blind.* As it was, this was by far the largest and most advanced ship they had attacked. *The Ashamine tech is the same,* he thought, stepping through the airlock and out onto the enemy's hull.

After making a quick orientation, Maxar headed towards the larger ship's hatch. In the absence of artificial gravity, his combat suit automatically engaged its magnetic clamps, securing him to the deck as he walked. It felt odd, but it allowed him to move with ease, rather than dealing with a tether.

On the edge of his vision, Maxar saw several enormous flashes of light. When he turned to look, he saw the Justice continuing to rain destruction upon the Ashamine fleet. Ship after ship went up in micro-novas as it compromised their worm generators. *I hope the other team is safe,* he thought, moving the last few meters to the airlock door.

Maxar found the control terminal and set to work, the intensity of the job so great it shut out the spectacular view surrounding him.

Maintenance mode activated. That was an easy, yet crucial step. It would provide a few layers of insulation if one of the next steps went wrong. *Now,* he thought, *should I go for the buffer overload or the matrix corruption?* After a moment's consideration, he decided on corruption. It was risky, but quick and relatively easy.

Tapping at the screen, Maxar entered a series of hex commands, accessing the sub-routine controlling the connection to the ship's central server. Scrolling down a long list of text entries, he found the one for pass code authentication. *Tweak a few key values,* he thought, entering the data Lothis had showed him. *Now, on to the control matrix.* Several screen swipes and option selects took him to the proper database. There he shifted a few values out of sequence, leaving one blank in a precise position.

Double check, Maxar thought, reading each entry and ensuring everything was as it should be. *No reason this vessel would have this patched out.* If someone had fixed this exploit, when he entered a pass code, the whole door security system could lock down. The ship's AI would alert the security force, and his team would lose all hope of a stealthy entry.

"Here we go," Maxar said, exiting maintenance mode. He selected the open airlock option, and when prompted, entered "BUCrasor" as the code. A second passed, and Maxar held his breath, waiting. A green thumbs up symbol flashed on the screen, and the airlock began cycling open.

"Good job," Tremmilly said, slapping him on the back.

"All thanks to Lothis," he replied, stepping inside the hatch as soon as it was wide enough. "Wouldn't have known any of these high-grade hashes if not for him." Tremmilly and Jaydon followed Maxar inside.

As the airlock cycled, Maxar tried to sense Crasor, but all he got in return was a vague sense of unease. "Which way?" he asked, glad Tremmilly had such a strong sense of their foe.

"Right," she said, "and up a few levels."

Maxar drew his flechette pistol and watched the interior airlock door slowly open. *I'm coming for you See'dek,* Maxar thought. *Your little Crasor puppet isn't going to stand in the way of our final meeting. You'll pay for ruining my Elrahi life and the lives of the trillions of others you forced into the Dawn or darkness. Get ready, you buggering blightheart, because I'm coming for you.*

28 – FELAR

"I'll take them," Felar transmitted over their encrypted comm, slinging the heavy beam weapon across her back. She eased around the corner, moving silently, the heavy boots of her combat suit forcing her to be extra cautious. Ahead, three Breaker officers stood in front of a terminal displaying the Justice's power routing.

It had been slow getting to this point, but they had nearly completed the first half of their goal. *Destroy power routing, exfiltrate the ship.* It seemed like a simple plan, but keeping the ship's crew from discovering their presence had been tedious and tricky.

Felar took one more step and deftly swung her right-hand short sword towards the nearest Breaker's neck. The blade cleanly sheered through the metallic looking skin, lopping the male's head off. Harnessing her momentum, Felar whirled, her left-hand blade in a reverse grip. The matte black weapon easily scythed through the next officer's neck as well.

Before the final Breaker could react, Felar struck, cleaving the woman's skull in two.

"Clear," Felar transmitted, turning her attention to the power readouts.

"I'll keep watch," Wake replied. "No sign we've been detected."

Lothis came into the room and stood next to her. "What now?" he asked, starting to take off his helmet.

"Leave it on," Felar barked. "Sorry," she continued after a moment, realizing she'd fallen back to how she'd handled Ashamine trainees. "It's just safer to leave it on. Easier for comms too."

"Yeah, you're right. Should've remembered that."

"Can you hash this?"

The boy looked back towards the screen, his face obscured by the too-large helmet. "Yes. I was able to get control of several systems when we were on the Justice before." He paused for a moment, thinking. "Only

115

Crasor was able to lock me out last time, and since he is not here now, I don't see why I can't find a way in."

"Good," Felar said. "Get control of power distribution, and I'll think of the most effective way to bugger it."

"Easy," the boy replied, selecting options from the terminal screen before him. "Just a moment, and I'll have root."

Felar turned her attention back to the large status screen. The ship's systems were listed in several broad categories, but she guessed there would be more precise control over subsets. Currently, the display showed that offensive and defensive weaponry was currently using 90% of maximum available power. *They're shorting life support to give more energy to the guns,* she thought, seeing the listing in red. *Good thing we're in our suits.*

Looking at the surrounding room, Felar followed the network of large conduits that snaked from the deck below and through the room. From here they spider-webbed out to points across the ship. Felar had almost gone to the deck below first, where the primary power generator was. She'd decided against it, knowing the hatch security would certainly be tight and stringent. *Up here, though, the Ashamine left a weak point, and the Breakers didn't reinforce it.*

"What?" Lothis said, stepping back from the terminal screen. Felar looked down, to see a swirling mass of darkness replace the Ashamine operating system.

"What happened?" Felar asked, taking an involuntary step back from the menacing shape.

"I don't—I don't know," Lothis stammered. "I was just finishing a root exploit when it happened."

"Greetings, intruders," a booming voice said from the console, startling Felar. Lothis jumped back, hastily drawing his flechette pistol. "Either you are very clever Ashamine, which seems unlikely, or you are Harbingers." A black tentacle welled up out of the screen, snaking towards them.

"How is that possible?" Felar asked, grabbing Lothis and taking several steps back.

"I don't know," the boy said. "Hologram? I've never seen anything like it before."

"Take off your helmets. I'd love to hear your clever voices." The tentacle continued growing, slowly advancing. "Don't be shy. Get comfortable. Stay awhile."

"I don't think it's a projection," Felar said, holstering her short swords and readying her beam weapon. "Take a shot."

Lothis did as ordered, the flechette pistol bucking in his hand. The tentacle shattered as the needles passed through it. A second later, it re-

116

formed.

"Nanites," Lothis said, voice faltering.

"Everything OK?" Wake sent over the comm.

"Yes," Felar answered. "Change of plan. Be prepared to run."

"Acknowledged."

"Oh, so that is how it is going to be?" the tentacle said. "You refuse my hospitality?" Something about the voice felt familiar to Felar, but she couldn't place it.

"Shouldn't we be doing something?" Lothis said, tugging at her arm. "Maybe we can figure out another place to hash the system."

"No," Felar answered. "The Breakers have integrated themselves into the Justice and now they know we are here. Give me a second to think."

"I have answers, Harbingers," the tentacle continued. "Don't be so hasty. Let me tell you the truth. Let me tell you about your Empress, what she did to your people."

An old voice, Felar realized. *Not human. Not speaking Common.* The answer was on the edge of her mind. *Elrahi. That inflection. That taunting.*

The tentacle continued flowing towards them. Felar and Lothis both took another few steps back. "You don't have to die. The blackness doesn't have to be your fate. We can find a compromise."

He knows you are here. He's going to send his people. Then, the realization hit Felar. "See'dek!" she burst out.

"Where?" Wake said.

"The Breaker voice," Felar said. "It sounds like See'dek."

"Does that mean he's part of the ship?" Lothis asked.

"I have no idea, but if he is somehow linked with this vessel, we have even more reason to destroy the Justice than we did before."

"Agreed," Wake replied.

"Lothis," Felar ordered, "go outside with Wake. Both of you be ready to shut the hatch when I come through."

"What are you—" the boy started to ask.

"No time," she barked. "Do it."

As Lothis ran the short remaining distance back to the exit, Felar hefted the heavy beam weapon. *The generator conduits may be armored,* she thought, her hands readying the gun, *but they were thinking of rail rounds, not concentrated energy.*

A violet beam shot out of the weapon, obliterating the oncoming tentacle and screen behind it. Felar shifted her aim, directing another burst towards where the primary power conduit came out of the floor. A mist of blackness enveloped the violet light as it struck the heavy metal shroud, leaving it undamaged. After a moment, a smudge of soot settled onto the floor.

"Think your nanites can handle a sustained burst?" Felar said, bearing down on her weapon's trigger. The violet light was nearly overwhelming, even with the attenuation of her faceplate, but she kept the weapon on target. The mass of nanites swirled around the beam, sacrificing themselves to prevent the inevitable. "Bugger you to the fires of the dark star!" Felar growled.

For a few moments, she wondered if the weapon wasn't strong enough, if the Breakers had an inexhaustible supply of their nanite servants. Then, the conduit's shroud started to glow. Metal sloughed off, dripping and splashing onto the floor. *Can't run this much longer,* Felar told herself, pushing the heavy beam weapon to the edge of its capability.

Finally, the beam passed through the shroud and into the conduit, shattering the delicate crystalline lattice within. Felar continued discharging the weapon for a moment longer, wanting to make sure she'd sufficiently damaged the conduit. When she was satisfied, she terminated the beam, turned on her heel, and ran through the hatch.

"What's going on?" Wake said, slamming the heavy door shut behind her.

"I just severed the primary conduit," she said, slowing for just a moment so Lothis and Wake could catch up. The hallway illumination flickered, then went out, forcing Felar to enable her helmet's low-light enhancement. "You guys switched on? Don't use your primary illumination. It will make us too obvious."

"I can see fine," Lothis said.

Wake agreed. "What about backups? Secondary power routing or generators?"

"They're already running," Felar said, "but it isn't nearly enough to keep up with demand."

In the next instant, something slammed Felar against the wall. When she regained her footing, she saw Wake and Lothis were still on the deck. "What was that?" the engineer transmitted, sounding dazed.

"The Ashamine," Felar said, dragging them to their feet. "We have to get off this ship before they put too many holes in the Justice."

29 – CRASOR

"What in the buggering blightheart happened?" Crasor demanded, watching the Ashamine pummel the Justice on his rear view screen.

"Problems with—" Karoth's voice cut out. "—distribution. We are doing all we can to—" Crasor ground his teeth, fighting to control his anger. "Pulling back. I need your—"

"Re-transmit request."

"I need your fleet to assist."

"Acknowledged," Crasor replied. The Justice was only intermittently firing its giant rail cannons, allowing the Ashamine fleet to close in. As he watched, his fleet flagship moved behind the Breaker front line. *Good,* Crasor thought, *the rest of the fleet can hold off the Ashamine till Karoth repairs the Justice.*

Without the massive carrier ship, however, the odds seemed more balanced, and Crasor wondered if the Ashamine might be able to destroy some of his sub-fleet ships. *If Karoth is busy with repairs to the Justice, he won't be able to guide the fleet as adeptly. I need to oblige his request,* Crasor thought, turning to face the forward view screen. Ahead of him, the Verger fleet sat stationary, as it had since he'd fled back inside the gravity well.

Even if I turn my back on them, Crasor thought, *they don't have the courage to come after us. It is physically impossible for them to use their weapons inside the well, and unless they have more surprises, their ships are just too small to compete with us. Our armor is thick, our point defense systems accurate. If they come after us, we'll obliterate them.*

Despite this knowledge, Crasor still felt a twinge of fear as he began issuing orders. "Turn the sub-fleet around. Assist Karoth and the primary fleet. Sensor techs, keep your instruments focused on the Vergers. If any of them come within effective range, send the coordinates to weapons ops. I want them obliterated." The propulsion officer and sensor techs signaled readiness, and the Transfiguration began pivoting.

On the tactical display, Crasor watched as the rest of his sub-fleet did the same. The Vergers remained stationary. Crasor nodded, feeling his anxiety diminish.

"Half-turn," the propulsion officer announced. Minutes passed, and Crasor waited, wishing the large ship would move faster.

"Turn complete," the propulsion officer said finally.

"Verger ships disappearing," the head sensor tech yelled.

"Disappearing?" Crasor asked. "They're worming out of system?" This seemed like the sensible explanation.

"No, sir," the tech replied, shaking her head. "No worm generators in operation." A sinking feeling hit Crasor deep in the pit of his stomach, knowing what the tech was going to say. "It might be some kind of stealth or cloaking tech."

"Darkness take them all," Crasor growled, realizing the situation was going from bad to worse. *First, I can't get within range to rail them into oblivion. Now, I can't see them!* He studied the tactical display, trying to decide what to do. "Keep us moving back to the primary fleet," Crasor ordered. "We need to support Karoth and the Justice. These Verger ships are just a distraction."

As the Transfiguration and its surrounding sub-fleet accelerated, Crasor continued pondering what the Vergers might be up to. More time passed, and nothing happened. Crasor began to breathe easier. *The worm transition attacks were their only advantage,* he decided, sitting back in his chair. *Maybe they tried again, and since we were inside the gravity well, it buggered their targeting and sucked them in instead.*

"Bring us in on a vector to protect and shield the Justice," Crasor ordered. "I want to take out as many of the Ashamine front line ships as we can. Perhaps we can shock them into retreat." He paused for a moment, thinking. "Get the Oblivion on comms."

A few moments passed, and the comms tech signaled readiness.

"Salla," Crasor said, seeing her face on the large screen. "Have your weapons system powered up and ready for when my sub-fleet reaches the Justice. We may need greater weaponry to keep it safe during repairs, but don't risk your ship just yet."

"Yes, sir," the woman replied. "All systems are nominal and ready to perform."

As she was finishing the last word, one of the Transfiguration's sensor techs cut in. "Sir, I'm seeing a radiation emission spike from our fleet's rear."

"Just lost contact with one of the rear-guard stellar gunships," the tactical officer barked.

"What now?" Crasor growled under his breath. On the main view screen, a bright flash of light bloomed, attenuated because it was brighter than even Breaker eyes could handle. It was obviously a worm generator breech. "How is that possible?" Crasor roared.

"No signs of rail cannon discharge," the sensor tech said. "I've reviewed the logs. I can find no explanation."

Slamming his fists down on his chair arms, Crasor checked the tactical display. As he reevaluated the situation, another white light flared, this time from the middle of his sub-fleet. *Buggering stealthed Vergers,* he decided, trying to control his rage. *Be calm. Anger is unproductive. You have to steady yourself and find a way to stop the Vergers.* He thought for a moment longer, then inspiration struck. *Perhaps you can hide from this blighthearted human-made tech, but what about Breaker senses?*

Crasor cast his mind out, looking for the cause of the destroyed ships. For a brief moment, he thought he felt something close to the Transfiguration, inside it in fact, but when he scrutinized deeper, it was gone. *Am I losing my Breaker powers, or am I going insane?* he wondered, sending his consciousness farther out.

Then, Crasor felt them, over a hundred ships of all shapes and sizes, moving around and through his sub-fleet. *What are they doing?* He noticed one take off from the hull of a troop transport ship. *Not Verger,* he noted, seeing its design was too neat and refined. *Who are you then?* Several moments passed, then the Breaker transport ship erupted into blinding white light. The surprise caught Crasor off guard, sending his consciousness tumbling back towards his body.

"A transport ship just exploded," the sensor tech announced as Crasor's eyes shot open.

"Order full defense and readiness position on all sub-fleet ships," Crasor barked. "Someone other than the Vergers is raiding our ships, rigging them to explode. Catch them, alive if possible. I want to know who they are!"

If they have that kind of cloaking technology, Crasor thought, *it probably wasn't hard for them to hide from our scouts. Or destroy them. We had many unexplained losses.* He didn't like knowing there was a shadowy entity who had intel on him. *Too many surprises, too many possibilities.*

Crasor checked the tactical display, trying to decide if it would be safer to stop and deal with the unknown assailants directly, or maintain their plan. *Karoth needs me,* Crasor decided finally. *With the asset of surprise eliminated from their arsenal, we will have—*

A new dot appeared on Crasor's three-dimensional tactical readout, interrupting his thoughts. It was outside the gravity well, and for a moment, he thought the display was misrepresenting its size. Then, the ship's tag filled in, and Crasor's breath caught in his throat.

"The Founder's Light," he whispered, his darkest fear manifested before his eyes. Selecting a few options on his commander's terminal brought the ship up on the primary view screen.

The vessel was enormous, much bigger than the Justice. Its black hull was hard to distinguish from the darkness of space, but Crasor could see it well enough to know any advantage the Breakers possessed had just vanished. The Light had odd curves and unknown appendages, but still looked strong and ready for battle. A massive structure ran the length of its entire spine, its purpose unknown to Crasor.

"Founder damn it all to the fires of the dark star," he said, using a curse he'd not uttered since his human days. Karoth had warned him about this ship, and it had shown up at the worst possible moment, when his powerful flagship was crippled. *We're doomed...*

"Do not give up," the Breaker mind boomed, shattering his paralysis. "It is just one ship. Remember your assets."

Shaking his head, Crasor tried to clear the fear from his mind. *You're right,* he thought, knowing he was fully committed to this battle. *I will be victorious. Let's hope the Light's defenses are no more capable than the Justice's were before we upgraded them.*

Without waiting for approval, Crasor moved forward. "Salla," he barked, renewing the connection to the Oblivion. "Move into a clear offensive position where you can target the Light. Extreme priority. No delay. Notify me as soon as you have firing solutions and are ready to launch."

"Yes, sir," Salla replied, looking pale. "As you command."

Moments passed in tense silence as Crasor waited. The Light remained stationary, its intentions inscrutable. *Run,* Crasor willed. *The situation is too grim for you. Flee.*

On the magnified view screen, he saw the apparatus along the Light's spine start to glow. First, it was a dark red, barely visible against the backdrop of space. As seconds passed, it transitioned to orange, yellow, then finally, white. It held there for several seconds, and Crasor wondered what the ship was doing. *This is the Founder's secret ship? His legacy? A giant illumination rod?*

"Ready to launch," Salla said over the comm, interrupting his thoughts.

Before he could give the order, the Light's spinal apparatus jumped from white to violet. *What the—* Crasor thought, then a huge lance of energy shot out, streaking through the blackness of space. Crasor's eyes darted to the wide-angle view screen. It was briefly overwhelmed, the intensity of the Light's beam blanking the photo-receptors. Before it resolved, Crasor already knew what he would see.

The beam had pierced the Justice, cleanly passing through the entirety of its high-tech armor. The remaining structure was too flimsy to hold the halves together, and as Crasor watched, the pride of his fleet broke into two mangled pieces.

"You are failing us!" the Breaker mind thundered, full of rage. "Get the situation under control!"

Realizing he had just been staring dumbly at the Justice, Crasor widened his awareness, trying to understand what to do next. In addition to the Justice, the Light's beam had created a perfectly straight swath of destruction passing through Crasor's sub-fleet and several other vessels near the Breaker flagship.

"Fifteen vessels fully destroyed," the tactical officer yelled. "Another thirty to fifty have suffered major damage."

We can't let it fire again, Crasor said, feeling his rage battling with the feeling of helplessness. *We can still salvage this! Even with these losses, we can still beat the Ashamine. Once we control the solar system, the planet will fall, and we'll replenish our losses.*

"Salla," he barked. "Launch every single missile you have on board the Oblivion. Make sure each is in full stealth mode and maximum speed. I want to create a secondary star for this system. Make the Light burn!"

"But, sir," she replied, still looking shaken, "we will then be out of weapons for future engagements."

"There will be no future engagements if the Light survives!" he yelled back, throwing his arms in the air. "We need to ensure complete destruction. Do as I command!"

"Yes, sir," Salla said, turning to face her own crew. "Launch all missiles as quickly as possible. Full stealth protocol, maximum propulsion burn, full destruction vectoring."

On Crasor's three-dimensional tactical display, a swarm of dots so dense the sensors couldn't resolve them individually sprung up in front of the Oblivion. They streaked towards the Light for several seconds, before disappearing. In the edge of his vision, Crasor could see the Light's weapon charging up again, slowly shifting from red to orange.

He waited, heart thumping, as minutes passed. *Hurry, hurry,* he thought, everything within him hoping the nuclear missiles would strike before the Light discharged again. *We can't stand another strike.* Somehow, he knew the weapon was aimed at him.

Finally, after what felt like an eternity, the first cluster of missiles struck, looking like a swarm of tiny novas. Stellar fire engulfed the Light's bow, growing brighter and brighter as more of Salla's weapons hit the huge ship. The Oblivion's commander had been smart in her targeting. Some clusters of missiles swung wide, hitting at oblique angles to increase the damage.

"Yes!" Crasor roared, jumping out of his seat. Salla's strike continued, and he reveled in the purging light. *Burn, you blighthearted buggers. Burn and then find yourself swallowed by darkness.*

"Good," the Breaker mind said, startling Crasor. "You are bringing the situation back from the brink."

Yes, Crasor replied, feeling like a god. *I struck down the most powerful ship the Ashamine could muster, and now, I will take their remaining planets as well.*

"No," the Breaker mind boomed.

No, what? Crasor replied, feeling confused.

"We've lost too much already. The Justice is obliterated, and you will lose more ships trying to fight your way to the core worlds. Even now, the Ashamine fleet is forming a stronger position. Without the Justice, it will require too much sacrifice. We are tired of this battle."

Flee? Crasor thought, feeling like the entire ship was falling out from under him. *They will rally their forces. They will pursue us. We can't stop now.*

"Of course not. Do you believe I'm such a fool?" The scorn in the Breakers' voice was so harsh Crasor felt crushed under the weight of it. "No, Crasor, we will simply destroy the Ashamine core worlds. Once their fleet sees the destruction, they will surrender."

Crasor looked towards his display, towards the view of Ashamine-2 filling the screen. Something deep within him welled up, bringing forth a deluge of memories. He remembered the giant buildings stretching high into the atmosphere, center of government and commerce. The beautiful Founder's City, which he'd always loved, full of magnificent sculptures, gardens, and ancient Ashamine history. *The citizens, the people,* he thought, mind churning. *I am their rightful ruler. I am their god. This is what I've always wanted, what I need.* Something inside Crasor hardened, something that felt distinct from the Breakers. *You cannot ask this of me. I never agreed to obliterate the core worlds. You said we would convert them!*

"Give the order," the Breaker mind demanded. "We have given you power, and if you do not obey, we will revoke it."

I will not destroy my subjects, Crasor growled, standing tall. *This is my world, my place. They need me.* The part of him that felt hard and separate from the Breakers continued growing, solidifying his determination. He couldn't take his eyes off Ashamine-2. *I will not destroy the world I love, nor the people destined to worship me!*

"Worship you?" The intense scorn had returned, denting Crasor's confidence. "You are but an atom in entity beyond comprehension. There is no worship, no admiration. There is only power and obedience. You will either exercise yours, or you will be annihilated."

You need me, Crasor yelled. *You need my guidance and knowledge. I will destroy the Ashamine fleet and convert the trillions before us.*

Silence greeted his final word. As moments passed, Crasor wondered if he had won. He settled down into his command chair, wondering what to do next. The Ashamine fleet spread out before him, and as the Breaker mind had observed, it was now in a much stronger configuration.

"Incoming shuttle," the tactical officer announced.

"Origin?" Crasor asked, his concentration still focused on how to approach the enemy fleet. *Perhaps Karoth survived the attack,* he thought. *If we can dispatch a rescue crew, we might find him.*

"The Valiant."

The name immediately grabbed Crasor's full attention. "Deny access," he commanded, feeling his heart race. All his earlier confidence vanished. "Confirm the shuttle hangar doors are fully sealed and armored."

Silence greeted his command, so he repeated it.

"No," the officer finally replied.

For a moment, Crasor thought he was hallucinating. No Breaker had ever refused to follow his commands "I gave you an order! Deny access to the Valiant's shuttle."

"And I said no," the officer said, voice emotionless.

Crasor was speechless, rage, fear, and desperation welling up within him.

"Did you think you could refuse with no consequence?" the Breaker mind bellowed.

I– I– I– Crasor mentally stammered, knowing he had made a huge mistake. *I'll do as you ask. I'm sorry!*

He turned to his comms tech. "Secure a connection to the Rain." Nothing happened. "Did you hear me?" Crasor yelled. "Get me a comm to Gav immediately!" Still, the tech was oblivious.

I'm trying to do what you asked, Crasor thought. *I won't disobey ever again.* The Breaker mind was silent too, leaving Crasor to cower in a maelstrom of fear. He heard the command bridge hatch opening, and knew what he would see. *Please! No!*

30 – WAKE

"Get down!" Felar bellowed. Wake hit the deck as an explosion ripped over them, the force shoving his body to the metal floor.

We didn't get out in time, he thought, pushing himself back to his feet. Despite Brightwing's advanced armor, he knew there were limits. *What if a rail round comes straight through the hull? I'd be reduced to atomic parts.*

Wake helped Lothis up, keeping the boy in between himself and Felar. His gangling form and ill-fitting combat ENS would have been comical if the situation wasn't so serious. *Gotta get off this ship,* Wake thought, refocusing his attention on the corridor ahead. *How can Felar keep our course straight?* With all the twists, turns, and chaos, even Brightwing's HUD map seemed confused. *Or maybe it's just the person reading it.*

After destroying the central power conduit, Wake had felt ecstatic. They'd taken down the behemoth. All that was left was the simple matter of getting back to Dras' ship. But whoever was commanding the Justice had roused the Breaker troops. They'd locked down the ship, making escape a difficult affair. With their combat amour and excellent team work, Felar had kept them safe as they painstakingly moved through bulkhead after bulkhead. With a majority of the Justice's systems down, the Ashamine fleet was pounding away at the ship, creating so much chaos and destruction even the Breakers were disoriented.

At one point, Felar had led them through a sector where the hull had been compromised. The decompressed space was eerily quiet, the unsuited Breaker bodies drifting off into space. They'd briefly discussed traveling across the exterior of the hull, but decided against it. "We'll have no protection against incoming rail rounds," Felar had said, as Lothis hashed a secured airlock.

"Come on!" Felar grunted, manually opening a de-energized hatch. Wake quickly checked back the way they had come, making sure no one followed. The corridor was empty, normally perfect lines looking bent. When he turned back, Felar was making a tactical entry into the next corridor, disappearing out of sight.

Lothis and Wake followed. By the time they'd gone through, several dead Breakers littered the floor in front of Felar. She slapped in a flechette reload and shook her head. "Burn it all in the fires—"

Wake felt himself swimming in a warm blackness. Static rose inside his head, building to a crescendo that threatened to overwhelm him. "Wake?" he heard, the voice loud and disembodied. "Wake?!"

Light filled his vision as he opened his eyes. "Lothis?" he asked, trying to sit up. Everything hurt.

"She's non-responsive," he said, tugging at Wake's arm. The boy had blood running down one side of his face. "I can't get her up."

Wake got to his feet, and walked over to Felar. She was indeed comatose, but a quick check of her combat suit's diagnostic readout showed she was still alive and had stable vital signs.

"She's gonna be OK," Wake yelled. "But we have to get her to Dras' ship. We can't wait for her to wake up." Just as he was about to lift Felar over his shoulder, he heard the sound of boots running towards them. "Incoming Breakers," he yelled, trying to draw his flechette pistol. It wasn't in its chest holster. *Must have dropped it,* he thought, frantically checking the surrounding deck.

Five heavily-armed Breakers charged into the corridor, weapons ready. *No time,* he thought, bending down to remove the sling attaching Felar's beam weapon to her combat suit. "Lothis, get her to the hangar," Wake said, standing between the boy and the Breakers. "Drag her if you have to!"

"Acknowledged," Lothis replied, grabbing Felar by the wrists.

Wake triggered the heavy beam weapon, sweeping it across the corridor. The violet ray struck down the first two attackers, but passed harmlessly through the remaining three.

What in the fires of the dark star? he thought, turning to quickly check Lothis' progress. He had Felar several meters down the hall, tugging with all his strength.

Wake backed up, trying to keep pace with the boy. He triggered the beam weapon again, but had the same unsatisfying result of seeing it pass harmlessly through his enemies. As they drew nearer, Wake could feel something strange about the space-time surrounding them. *They are warping it somehow,* he thought. *Must be how the beam is missing them.*

There was no time for hand-to-hand combat. *Besides, they'll just overrun and drag us down until more Breakers can come and finish the effort.* Wake intuitively reached out to the space-time just outside the Breaker bubble, the effort requiring supreme concentration. *Slide through the barrier,* he told himself, narrowing his consciousness into an atom-thick blade. *Now!* Wake punched through the warp, feeling it shudder under his strike.

Before the Breakers could react, he formed and created weapons, sending the mind blades into their skulls. All three crashed to the floor, black ooze seeping from their foreheads. Wake released the warp, allowing his Elrahi power to subside.

"You have to hurry," he heard Dras say over his comm.

"We're almost to the hangar," Lothis replied. "Just a few more minutes."

Wake checked Brightwing's HUD, and saw Lothis was right. The door to the hangar was only a hundred meters away. He quickly caught up with the boy and put the still-unconscious Felar over his shoulder.

"There have been some developments since we lost comms," Dras continued. "Somehow, the Justice has tried to interface with my ship. They made promises if I joined the Breakers, great power and lots of other blightheart. When I refused, they tried to take me by force."

"Obviously, you fought them off," Lothis said, "otherwise we wouldn't be talking."

"Yes," the Heltasoth replied, a strange buzzing in his voice. "I did the best I could, and disengaged the enemy nanites from the hull. I have suffered some damage, however."

"Can you still fly?" Wake asked, watching Lothis hash the hangar door.

"Self-checks and diagnostic routines indicate yes," Dras replied, his voice buzzing even more than before.

"Alright, we're to the hangar door and almost inside. Be ready for us."

"Strange," the Heltasoth buzzed.

"What?" Wake asked, feeling his stomach drop.

"A large Ashamine vessel just wormed into the system. It's the largest human ship I've ever seen, almost as large as a Heltasoth intergalactic-explorer." He paused for a moment, and Wake wondered if he was hallucinating or had gone unconscious. The hangar door slid open, and Lothis darted through. Wake followed him, resettling Felar's weight on his shoulder.

"It's generating energy," Dras finally continued, "massive amounts. What—"

The world surrounding Wake exploded in violet light, before blackness once again swallowed him.

31 – TREMMILLY

"How much farther?" Maxar asked, pausing at the next corridor junction.

Tremmilly tried to calm her frantic mind, to sense where Crasor was, but it was all she could do to keep them shielded from his senses.

"Ummm, uhhh," she stammered, "I'm not sure. It's hard to tell. I think he's still on the command bridge."

Maxar bit his lip, looking apprehensive. "Are you sure you're OK?"

"Yeah, I'm fine," Tremmilly lied, forcing a smile. *Keep the shield up, don't let him see you.* As they grew closer and closer to Crasor, it had become increasingly difficult to maintain the barrier. *Ignore the maw. It doesn't exist.*

But no matter how many times she told herself, it didn't change the gaping blackness threatening to swallow her. The small, dark thread that had once been her connection to the Breakers had grown into a vast black hole, threatening to pull her in. She didn't want to think about what would happen if she failed to resist.

"Let's keep moving towards the bridge," Maxar continued. "If we can surprise him, I think we might be able to lock down the bridge and take control of the ship."

"Sounds like as good a plan as any," Jaydon said. "Stealth is key."

"For sure," Maxar said, turning his attention back to the path ahead. Glowing lines indicated several destinations, but Maxar kept them on the white one, leading to the bridge.

"Elevated security stance," a voice boomed over the ship's intercom. "Alert: Possible intruders. Door lockdown initiated. All troops, secure and monitor vital systems. Capture and detain the enemy if possible."

"Buggering blightheart," Jaydon exclaimed under his breath.

"What in the fires of the dark star?" Maxar said, looking quickly back and forth down the hall. "Must have seen the Retribution on the hull."

"If that was the case," Jaydon replied, "why would they have said possible intruders? They'd be ordering security sweeps, rather than just stationing troops."

"Either way," Maxar said, "it makes our job a lot harder."

Down the passageway, Tremmilly saw a squad of troops advance through a cross corridor. "We can't stay out here," she said, gesturing.

"She's right," Maxar said. "The bridge is sure to be guarded. If we reveal ourselves too soon, we'll be overwhelmed, especially since they are prepped." He turned to the nearest door, which was labeled as an officer's cabin. "We can wait here." Tremmilly turned back to monitor her section of corridor as Maxar began hashing through the security lockdown. "Come on, come on," he said as she heard the door slide open. "We're in."

After they entered the spacious cabin, Maxar hit the close option. "Smooth entry. No log alerts initiated."

"We'll know soon enough if you are wrong," Jaydon snorted.

"This is a good temporary solution," Maxar said, "but we can't wait here forever. Hopefully, whatever has them spooked will get resolved, and we can get back to the mission. Trem, can you maintain the shielding indefinitely?"

The darkness tugged at Tremmilly, making it hard to focus on Maxar's words. "Yes, I think so," she replied. *As long as the Breakers don't pull me in.*

"Good," Maxar said, turning on the large terminal screen that comprised one wall. "If that changes, let me know. We can always storm the bridge." He selected several options, which pulled up a tactical display.

"Let's hope it doesn't come to that," Jaydon said, shaking his head.

Tremmilly stared at the large screen, trying to make sense of the confusing jumble of symbols and information. The deluge of information flooded her already overwhelmed mind, making her head pound.

"Is that what I think it is?" Maxar said, pointing to a large indicator on the far edge of the screen, surrounded by darkness.

"I think so," Jaydon replied. "There isn't another vessel in the Akked that big."

Maxar selected a few options, and the tactical display vanished, replaced by a dark hulled ship. Tremmilly tried to focus on it, but the black maw kept pulling her attention away.

"The final Tarton class Ashamine ship," Jaydon said, voice full of awe. "Where was it all this time?"

"Who knows," Maxar said. "The real question is: Does this help or hurt us?"

An escalating glow on the top of the ship caught Tremmilly's attention, distracting her momentarily from the connection to the

Breakers. In the next second, there was a bright flash of violet light, and the Ashamine ship went dark again. "What was that?" she asked, wondering if she'd hallucinated it.

Before anyone could answer, Tremmilly felt an intense, searing pain in her mind. At first, she thought the Breakers had found her, or were pulling her through the maw somehow. When she checked the dark connection, however, it felt the same.

"Looked just like Felar's weapon," Jaydon said.

What just happened? Tremmilly thought, trying to manage the pain without revealing its presence. Through squinted eyes, she watched Maxar flip from the exterior view to the tactical display, then back to a new outside angle. When she saw the Justice, nearly split in two, she knew what was causing her pain.

"Blightheart," Maxar said, eyes wide.

"Did they..." Jaydon added, face going pale inside his combat ENS. "Did they make it off?" Both men turned to face her.

"I don't know," she replied, feeling the pain subside. *Is that a good thing, or a bad?* "It's too far away. I feel... something, but I don't know what it means."

"Either way," Maxar said, taking in a deep breath, "the Justice is out of the fight. And we still need to complete our mission."

Tremmilly agreed, but she felt a profound sense of fear and heaviness settle over her. *I can't stand this uncertainty,* she thought, *not with everything else threatening to overcome me.*

Maxar turned off the screen and looked into Tremmilly's eyes. "I know you're under a heavy load," he said, gathering her into his arms. "Jaydon and I can only help so much with that, but know that we are here for you. We love you, and no matter what, we will see this through to the end. We're gonna take him out, Trem. We're going to win this war."

"Thank you," she replied, fighting to ignore the black hole trying to suck her in. "I know we can do this."

"The other team will make it through OK," Maxar said, sounding less confident. "Felar will keep them safe. I bet they crippled the Justice and flew off before it was destroyed."

The trio waited in silence, Tremmilly holding onto the shielding warp with a mind frayed and fragile. An even darker swirl began emanating from her connection to the Breakers. *No, not now,* she thought, watching it creep ever closer to her consciousness. *I control this link. I will not allow you to touch me.* Try as she might, however, the tendril grew, slithering farther. *Stop!*

"Maxar," Tremmilly said, trying, and failing, to hold back her tears. "I don't think I can hold on much longer. He's going to see through my shield. I think we have to go to the bridge now."

"OK," Maxar replied, her anxiety immediately mirrored on his own face. "We can still do it. We'll work our way to the command deck, take out whatever sentries are in the way. There is still a good chance for us to surprise him."

"Great," Tremmilly said, creating a thin barrier between herself and the emanating darkness. *How long will I be able to hold it back, though?* she wondered, following Maxar and Jaydon as they headed towards the door.

When they returned to the corridor, Tremmilly felt a momentary sense of relief. *Just a little longer and it will all be over.* A feeling of dread greater than anything she'd ever experienced in her life slammed into her. *Run! Run!* she thought, panic exploding within.

As she fought to remain calm, she saw looks of terror on both Maxar and Jaydon's faces. *What is this? What's happening?*

Up ahead, tall, robed figures drifted down a cross corridor. Tremmilly's eyes tried to look away, but she forced herself to see the cause of her fear. Four of the dark figures moved past, and her fear abated. The final, fifth form stopped and turned to look at them. A weight of terror slammed back into Tremmilly with an exponential force.

The dark shape had no face. Only smooth, pale skin stretched across its skull, unbroken by eyes, nose, or mouth. Despite this, Tremmilly felt the creature trying to see her. It cocked its head in an oddly human gesture. Tremmilly threw all her effort into maintaining the shield warp, instinctively knowing to do anything else would mean death.

Jaydon let out a muffled whimper, and in the corner of her vision, Tremmilly could see he had his hands over his own mouth. Maxar too was cowering in fear, eyes wide. Something flared inside Tremmilly, and she felt her mind and body stabilize. Her fear evaporated, and the black hole shrank slightly. *I will protect you, Jaydon,* she thought, willing the ghastly shape to join his fellows. *I will protect you, Maxar, my love.*

Seconds ground by, and Tremmilly felt a bead of sweat roll down her face. She shut out the distraction, continuing to push all her power into the shield. Finally, the faceless form turned, and moved down the cross corridor. Maxar and Jaydon rose, standing behind her.

"What was that?" Maxar said, voice shaking.

"I don't know," Tremmilly replied, "but I think our mission just got harder."

"You mean we are still going to the bridge?" Jaydon said, eyes wide. "Isn't that where *they* are heading?"

"Yes," Tremmilly replied, taking a calming breath. Her mind felt clear, her consciousness stable. "Yes, and we will take those buggers out while we are there."

32 – GAV

Gav watched as Salla's missiles obliterated the Founder's Light, the massive ship burning in stellar fire. Part of him felt joy in the event, knowing she had saved the Breaker fleet from disaster. Another, larger part of him felt bitter and jealous, knowing that Crasor would reward her greatly.

And all I can do is sit here, waiting, like some worthless underling. Gav slammed his fist down on the arm of his chair, startling his surrounding crew. No one spoke.

Unfortunately, now that they'd exhausted the search for Salla's sabotage, there wasn't much else to do. Gav knew one of the crew had missed the devious woman's treachery amongst the millions of lines of code. *You're just telling yourself that because it's an easier explanation than insanity.* He shook his head, trying to suppress the line of thought. *Logic says flashing lights, gruesome images, and other creepy phenomena are a result of psychological warfare, perpetrated by a foe with motive, opportunity, and ability. I don't have a history of mental illness. There is no reason for one to start now.*

No matter the cause of his increasing sense of unease, sitting around and waiting wasn't doing anything to improve his mood. *I just have to withstand, to be stronger than whatever she is planning.* He sat back in his chair, trying to calm down. Checking the tactical display, he made a quick assessment. *Despite the loss of the Justice, I think we will take the Ashamine worlds.* Had the Light remained viable, the odds would have shifted, but for now, it seemed the Breaker fleet was still destroying Ashamine ships and closing in on victory. *This will take a heavy toll,* Gav decided, *but that may leave more opportunities for me, especially if Salla is discredited or killed somehow.* He couldn't think of a way to accomplish either objective, but it wouldn't keep him from looking for an opportunity.

133

"Obliterate Ashamine-2 and 4," a booming voice said, shattering his contemplation. It sounded like a trillion voices yelling, saying every word in perfect unison. "Deploy the Rain."

When Gav was finally able to open his eyes, he scanned the ship's bridge, hoping to see the rest of his crew responding. Around him, his officers and technicians continued focusing on their terminals, oblivious.

What was that? Gav thought, wondering if Salla had discovered a way to transmit thoughts directly into his brain.

"We are the One, Gav," the voice continued, making his head feel like it would explode. "We are the Breakers. We elevated Crasor, and now, perhaps, we will elevate you."

Gav smiled, feeling a comforting, imperative urge settle on him. *As you command,* he answered, wondering if they could hear him. After several seconds of silence, Gav decided they had.

"Engage primary generators," he said, startling his crew once again. "Move us into a launch alignment most effective for Ashamine-2 and 4." As the words left his mouth, Gav realized what he was saying. *You're going to destroy the last human strongholds, obliterate them in a rain of magma, ash, and tungsten alloy rods.* For a moment, something seized in his chest, but he realized this was the opportunity he'd been longing for. *This is far better than just destroying the Light,* he thought, beaming. *And you heard what the voice said. They will elevate you, maybe to even greater heights than Crasor.*

"Generators spooling up," the weapons officer announced.

"Good," Gav said, watching the targeting system move closer to alignment. He rubbed his hands together, wondering what it would feel like to issue an order to kill trillions.

A large red status warning popped up on the primary view screen. *Discharge capacitor overflow detected.* "No, no, no," Gav yelled, "not now. We have to deploy immediately."

"Sir," the weapon's officer said, "I can't disengage the generators. Controls aren't responding."

Gav had spent many hours studying the Rain and its systems and knew what the man was indicating. "Buggering blighthearted Salla," he growled, heading for the generating chamber.

As he ran through the ship's corridors, Gav wondered how long he had till the ship exploded. *Minutes? Seconds?* The power required to operate the Rain's enormous rail launchers was greater than what his entire home planet of Exis-7 used in full day. *And it has to be generated, stored, and discharged at an unfathomable rate.*

Bursting into the primary generating chamber, Gav saw techs trying to shut down the massive power conduits. On the primary status screen, another warning flashed: "Discharge overflow capacity exceeded. Critical failure imminent."

Gav tried to think of a way to shut down or disconnect the power conduits, but nothing came to mind. *Can't get close enough to physically disrupt them,* he thought, knowing the radiation was too strong, even for Breaker nanites.

"System overload in 5..." popped up on the status display. "4... 3... 2..."

Gav closed his eyes, waiting for his world to end in a flash of white light and arcing plasma. Nothing happened.

He opened his eyes, only to see a new message on the display. "It was a fun night, Gav. Don't stick it in another woman, or next time, this will be real. - Salla."

"What in the fires of the dark star..." Gav muttered, wondering what he'd gotten himself into. He shook his head, watching as the stored power levels began to lower and the display indicated normal operation. *It was just a prank,* he thought, finally breathing again. *Or is this just another part of her psychological warfare?* Before he could ponder any further, the display shifted, replaced by the face of a young man.

"Hello, Gav," Fade Alenthos said, his face a cross between smile and snarl. "Good to finally see you again."

For a moment, Gav thought perhaps Salla had uploaded his escaped quantum human to torment him, another part of her plan. *No. How could she?* he realized, a sinking feeling coiling in the pit of his stomach.

"No reply?" Fade said. "How uncharacteristic. I've been tortured by your voice inside that damn alien ship for millennia. Oh, I know it hasn't been that long for you, but you just exist in the slow, buggered binary." His voice rose in intensity, his eyes burning with a hate Gav had seen on many faces before he'd put a flechette load into them. "Gav, I'm tired of hearing your voice. I'm tired of me, I'm tired of you, I'm tired of everything."

"Primary launch initiated," he heard over the ship's intercom. "Targeting Ashamine-2."

"I know the truth now," Fade said, the words coming out of his mouth as if he was spitting them. "I've calculated the end of everything, the futility of it all. Human minds are too small to see it, but I know, Gav. I know." He paused for a moment, closing his eyes. "So I'm going to bugger us both."

"Wait," Gav yelled. "I can offer you power! I can offer you meaning!"

"10% of projectiles launched and counting," the intercom announced. "Vector calculations on-track for maximum destruction."

"No. It is too late," Fade growled. "I don't want it, don't need it. I won't listen to your lying words, like I did before, when you took me down to your lair and turned me into this!"

Every alarm, warning light, and distress notification began going off, all at once. Gav looked around, trying to understand what was happening. *Help me,* he thought, reaching out for the voice of the One.

"Greet the darkness, you buggering blightheart!" Fade screeched.

In the next instant, Gav's body was filled with an overwhelming light, and he knew no more.

33 – LOTHIS

Darkness. Lothis floated through it, wondering where he was. *Am I still alive?* He tried to find his body, to sense the physical component of his being. After a moment, he felt the rise and fall of his chest.

Where am I? He tried to think of the last thing he remembered. *In the Justice. Running towards the Heltasoth ship. Dras telling us... What?*

More time passed, but Lothis had no way of telling how much. Something shifted in his mind, and he opened his eyes.

Around him, beauty and destruction reigned in equal measures. Huge ships sent lancing tungsten alloy rounds at each other, their tracers creating vivid ion trails. Bright flashes of light caught his attention, as massive ships exploded into miniature novas.

Lothis realized he was spinning, a slight gyration that allowed him to see the entire battle. As he rotated farther, the Justice dominated his view, the once formidable ship now split in two. *What did that?* he wondered, looking out across the galactic plane for the cause. Nothing was evident.

Beginning another rotation, Lothis realized he needed to do something about his situation. Checking the readout of his combat ENS, he saw he had enough atmosphere to survive for at least three standard hours, assuming he didn't elevate his exertion level. *What do I do now?*

As his view rotated past the Justice once again, Lothis tried to understand what had happened. *Doesn't look like something compromised the worm generator,* he thought, knowing that the entire ship would have been obliterated in that case. *Based on the edges of the hole and the resulting debris cloud, it seems the damage was caused from the other side, coming in this direction.* Lothis tried to look off towards the source, but between the spin, the vast distance, and the darkness, he couldn't make out anything more than a smudge of light.

Doesn't matter, he realized. *Whatever did it, I still need to find Felar, Wake, and Dras.* He tried visually searching through the debris cloud

137

surrounded him, but again, he was thwarted by conditions.

Use your mind, he thought, mentally steadying himself. He took a deep breath, gathered his consciousness, and sent it out from his body. In the past, Lothis might have worried about finding his way back again, but he'd learned much from Cazz-ak and his own experiences. Thinking of the Entho-la-ah-mine made his heart clench, but he forced himself onward, trying to flow through the distraction. *What if you've lost the rest of your family?* he thought.

Be calm, Lothis retorted, moving out into the surrounding blackness. *Stay in the present. Find your family.* His ability to respond positively to the situation surprised Lothis. He felt like he'd been in emotional darkness for so long. *Sharing with Felar was liberating,* he thought, scanning for signs of life.

After several minutes passed, and he'd found nothing, Lothis grew frustrated. *They have to be around here somewhere. We all started in roughly the same position.* Lothis continued moving through the debris, looking. Finally, he spotted a familiar shape.

"Dras!" Lothis yelled, before realizing he'd not established any kind of connection to the Heltasoth. He moved towards the ship, his heart sinking as he drew closer. Dras' ship, an extension of his body, was missing a huge portion of its upper hull. Based on the clean shape of the carved-out section, Lothis guessed that whatever had obliterated the Justice had nicked the Heltasoth ship as well.

Moving his consciousness inside the ship, Lothis tried to find a way to contact the sentient machine. *Never done this before,* he thought, none of his techniques working. Finally, he found Dras, sprawled on the bridge, now exposed to the vacuum of space.

Lothis went closer, trying to see if the Heltasoth was injured in any way. He checked every angle, looking for signs of trauma. *Nothing.* Even his eyes were open. *But why isn't he moving or responding?* Lothis continued trying to contact Dras with his consciousness, but everything he attempted was fruitless. *I have to come back, with my body.*

Returning his consciousness to his human form, Lothis studied the path back to the Heltasoth ship. *Do I have enough fuel to get over there?* It seemed possible, but Lothis had no way of calculating the distance. Felar had gone over the basics of micro-gravity ENS maneuvering with him, but Lothis had almost no practice, certainly nothing of this distance or scale. *I don't have a choice,* he thought, powering up the suit's thruster system. *If I can't make it to Dras or another ship, I'll suffocate anyway.* He tried not to think too hard about what would happen if he exhausted his fuel getting to Dras and was unable to revive the sentient machine.

Lothis activated the auto-stabilize routine, and several of the suit's thrusters fired, stopping his gyration. *Light touch,* he remembered Felar saying, manually aiming himself towards Dras' ship. *You've got it.*

Initiating a short burn, he felt the thrust push him into the back of the suit. *Not too fast,* he thought, knowing that the debris field's density would make speed dangerous. *I'm not in a hurry. Going slow will burn less fuel, especially if I don't have to decelerate to maneuver around objects.*

After performing several short burns to bypass large pieces of hangar debris, Lothis checked his remaining fuel. *How could I have used that much, so quickly?* He took several deep breaths, trying to calm his panicking thoughts. *Stay in the present. Focus on the path ahead.*

A huge section of bulkhead appeared out of the blackness, directly on his course, spinning lazily. *I don't have enough fuel to go around it,* he decided. *I have to save enough to brake before Dras' ship.* Lothis took a deep breath, letting his reflexes and intuition guide him. He could feel the bulkhead's spin in his mind, could touch it with his consciousness. *More,* he thought, triggering a quick burn. His speed increased, and he saw his fuel level dip.

As he sped towards the massive hunk of metal, Lothis had a brief moment of doubt. *Too slow, too slow!* His heart began beating rapidly, and his hands started to sweat. Lothis' finger hovered over the thruster control on his chest plate. At the final moment, he removed it, sailing by the bulkhead, his passage synced to its spin.

Not much farther, he thought, his heart rate slowing until he again saw his remaining fuel. *It's not enough,* he realized, the status readout showing he would not be able to come to a complete stop. *Can I survive the impact?*

Finally, he could see Dras' ship, a speck growing rapidly in his view. Lothis triggered a full reverse burn, the g-force pushing him hard into the front of the ENS. When he was able to open his eyes again, he saw the Heltasoth ship momentarily. Then Lothis felt a tremendous crunch. Everything went black.

Slowly, Lothis opened his eyes. He was on the bridge of Dras' ship. His body ached, and his breath came in short, labored gasps. *I'm OK,* he thought, hoping it was true. *I'm alive.*

Groaning, Lothis pushed himself up, trying to maintain his balance. His head swam, and he swayed for a moment in the higher, artificial gravity of the Heltasoth ship. The dizziness finally passed as he carefully surveyed his surroundings.

Got lucky on that one, he thought, seeing the opening above and realizing if he'd come in just a few meters to the left, he would have ricocheted off the ship's hull and out into space. *Lost forever...*

Turning back towards the deck, he found the Heltasoth, his body lying motionless near the opposite wall. "Dras?" Lothis transmitted, slowly walking over to him. Silence. "Dras?" He shook the sentient machine's shoulder, knowing it was futile, but that he had to try. Still, nothing.

What can I do? Lothis thought. "Dras, can you hear me?" he transmitted, knowing if the Heltasoth was capable of communicating, this was a viable method.

Still feeling unsteady, Lothis sat down next to the Heltasoth, wondering if the machine was dead. *His body looks completely intact,* he thought, fear and loneliness threatening to overwhelm him. *Breathe. Think.*

Something stirred in the front of Lothis' mind, and at first, he thought it was inspiration. The sensation changed, developing into an itch, centered behind his right, useless eye. The feeling grew, becoming more pressing. *The Heltasoth nanites,* Lothis realized, remembering how Dras had used them to repair his damaged brain structures.

What are they doing? For a moment, he wondered if they were trying to crawl out of his skull and back into the ship. *Will this kill me?*

"Lothis?" he heard, a voice drifting into his mind.

Yes? Dras? The wisp sounded familiar, but it was so muted and diminished from the Heltasoth's normal tone.

"Are you OK?"

Yes, the boy replied, feeling a strange sensation course through the space behind his eye.

"Good." Several seconds passed, and Lothis wondered if Dras had disconnected. "The Ashamine ship," he continued finally, "it deployed some type of beam weapon against the Justice. Once I understood what was happening, I didn't have time to move. Plus, I couldn't leave you behind."

What's happened to you?

"I'm unsure. From what I can sense, what you humans think of as my mind got trapped in a disabled part of the ship. It is possible the splash energy from the beam overloaded certain critical components, creating an unintentional prison of sorts."

Can you get back to your body? Or operate the ship?

"Unfortunately, no. The ship, as well as my body, are entirely functional, at least from what I sensed before I got trapped here, but I have no way of reaching the nanite structures that allow operation." Dras fell silent for several seconds. "Are Felar and Wake with you?"

No. I looked for them, but you were the only one I found. I barely made it here with the fuel I had.

"Hopefully they are looking for us as well," the Heltasoth replied.

What do we do now?

"I will continue searching for a way out of this dead space, but I am not optimistic. Unless an exterior force influences the situation, I currently see no way to escape."

Lothis felt his heart sink. He'd been relying on Dras so much, and now, his hope was shattered. *At least you aren't alone anymore,* he thought.

"Yes," Dras replied, "it is good to have you here." Lothis didn't correct the sentient machine. The statement worked for both of them, and if they could bring comfort to each other, it was positive.

He focused hard on the space behind his right eye, forming a barrier between it and the rest of his mind. *Dras?* he thought, testing his theory. The Heltasoth didn't reply. *Can't have him hearing every single thought.*

Lothis checked the status readout of his ENS, noting his vital signs were good, but that he was almost through his atmosphere supply. *Find a way to fix this situation, and that won't matter.*

At first, Lothis couldn't think of anything to do, but then Maxar popped into his mind. *Dras?*

"Yes?"

Maxar is able to interface with the ship, using his nanites, so I should be able to as well. Perhaps I can find a way to release you from the dead space.

The Heltasoth was silent for a full minute. "My calculation capacity is extremely diminished, so I cannot make a definitive statement. Maxar has many more nanites in his body than you, and they are deeply integrated. I am not declaring it impossible, but what you propose will be difficult."

I can at least try, Lothis replied, scooting across the floor so he could lean back against the wall.

"I'm afraid, given the situation, I am unsure how to guide you."

That's OK, Lothis thought, taking a deep breath. *I'm a quick learner.*

Lothis closed his eyes, shutting out the distraction of the battling fleets. Normally, he would cast his mind out into exterior space-time. Instead, he brought his consciousness and attention inward, directing it at the Heltasoth nanites inside his skull.

He went deeper and deeper, until he could feel the individual machines. The sensation of being so deep within his own body felt strange and exhilarating. A competing emotion of having something alien inside him rose up, threatening to destroy his focus. *It's fine,* he thought, trying to find a way to connect to the tiny machines. *They are a part of you, and you a part of them.*

Slowly, the energy of his consciousness began melding with the energy of the nanites. *We are symbiotic, we are a single organism.* He could feel it, a conductive pathway leading to the Heltasoth ship. *Like a blood vessel, or a nerve.* Lothis' consciousness traveled through the connection, sliding easily.

As he entered the connective web of the ship, Lothis was nearly overwhelmed. It was a huge space, the structures and systems more complex than anything he'd seen before. *I'll never be able to pilot this,* he thought, giving up on one of his alternate plans. *My mind could never handle it.*

I'm linked, he thought, initiating the faint connection he had to Dras.

"Good!" he replied, sounding surprised.

Can you see me? Or feel me?

"Unfortunately, no. Everything is the same in my location."

Lothis remembered back to when he had been cut off from his Elrahi being. The current situation felt very similar, making him wonder if the technique they'd used to reconnect him would work for Dras as well.

I'm going to try something, Lothis sent, drawing on his connection to his Elrahi being. *Focus everything you have left on scanning the dead space around you. Perhaps you'll be able to sense me.*

"Understood," Dras replied.

As Lothis drew on more and more of his Elrahi power, he wondered what would happen. *I'm inside an alien ship, embracing power from another dimension. Just a few months ago, none of this would have made any sense.* Finally, he let the energy diminish, hoping it would be enough.

Anything?

"No. Everything remained the same."

Watch again.

Forcing all distractions from his mind, Lothis made himself a conduit of power. He pulled in more and more, making every fiber of his being take it in. Normally, he wouldn't be able to draw in so much, but since his only goal was to be a beacon, he didn't need the ability to manipulate it. He held on to it for as long as possible, before finally lessening the Elrahi connection.

"It was faint," Dras said in his mind, "but I felt it."

Good!

The Heltasoth was silent for some time. "I can try to make my way through the dead space," he said finally, "but it is risky. There is a chance I will lose my way or not have enough energy to make it through."

Is there any other option?

"Perhaps, but given the situation we find ourselves in, I think I have to try. If you continue to guide me, it might prevent me from getting lost."

"I can help," a new voice said. Lothis turned to see Fade, his normally bright form so diffuse and de-energized he barely recognized him.

"What happened?" Lothis asked.

"I fulfilled my purpose. Gav is dead. I'm disassociating, as you said I would."

"We can save you," Lothis replied, "reincorporate you back into the Heltasoth ship."

"No." Fade's voice was flat, the word final. "I expected to die in the confrontation, but enough of me survived to make it back here. Given my current state, I think it best if I lend you what little power I have left."

As Lothis watched, Fade's energy cloud began coalescing, becoming brighter as it did so. After a few moments, it shrank to an intense point. "Take this," Fade said, floating towards him. "It is all I have left." Lothis instinctively reached out with his consciousness and the speck merged into him. A flare of power bloomed, ready to be used. "Don't wait. I can't hold myself together for much longer."

Without a word, Lothis focused on drawing in as much Elrahi power as he could. In the next instant, he shot out a beacon of energy, using both Fade's and his own strength to show Dras the path through dead space. Time dragged by, and Lothis felt his grip on the connection threatening to fail. *We can do this,* he thought. *Dras saved my life, and now it's my turn.* Every moment began to feel like an eternity. *Without a guide, Dras dies. Don't give up!*

Another second passed, and the space surrounding his consciousness burst into activity, the ship coming to life. It was one of the most beautiful things Lothis had ever seen, and the distraction caused him to lose his grip on his Elrahi power. For a moment, he just stared at the intricate dance of the complex system, dazed and in awe. Then, he realized he'd possibly doomed Dras.

"No, no," the Heltasoth's voice said, restored to its former strength. "I'm here. I made it through."

Good, Lothis said, feeling exhausted. *Fade? Are you still there?* Silence answered him.

"I have no sense of him," Dras replied. "I think he is gone. Go back to your body. This place is safe, but you will recover better in your own organism, rather than in mine."

Lothis did as he was told, pulling his consciousness back through the nanites and into his head. He remained seated, his body and mind drained.

Dras' physical body knelt next to him, smiling. "Thank you," he said over Lothis' suit comm. "You are an amazing human."

Lothis returned his smile, feeling the nanites buzz behind his right eye. It was a pleasant sensation, having a profound connection to such a beautiful life-form. *Maxar is lucky to have an even greater one,* he thought, pushing himself to his feet.

"Just returning the favor," he said, using a saying he'd often heard from Felar.

"Indeed," Dras replied. "I wish I could thank Fade for his assistance as well, but I think he is gone forever." Lothis nodded his agreement as Dras turned his attention to the ship's beam damage. "It will make some parts of the hull quite thin," he continued, "but I believe I can shift enough nano-mass to seal the breech."

As Lothis watched, the seared edges of the ship grew towards each other. After several moments, the bridge was once again an enclosed space. His ENS chimed, noting that there was sufficient breathable atmosphere present.

"I think it is time we go find the rest of our team," Dras said. The ship began moving forward.

34 – ASH

"Stay strong," Ash said, "stay safe, and may the wisdom of Azak-so guide you." He hit the option to terminate the comms link.

Finally, Ash thought, turning his attention back to the battle. He'd just finished talking with Aza and Em. *Glad they made it off Ashamine-2 safely.* The two women were currently floating above the planet in Em's ship. He'd tried to order them to flee to the Brotherhood base on Azak-1, but somehow, they'd convinced him to let them stay in system. *As if I could have forced them anyway. At least they are relatively safe, for now.* Em had agreed to evacuate if the Breakers overran the Ashamine fleet.

"Sir," the Stellar Memory's sensor tech announced, "I'm detecting an energy anomaly."

Ash looked up from his tactical display, his thoughts taking a moment to shift from planning fleet formation to this development. "Explain," he said finally, making one final mental note on what he wanted to do next.

"A ship, positioned just beyond the edge of the enemy fleet, is generating massive amounts of power."

Ash immediately thought of the Light, and how the same tech had notified him of an energy anomaly just before it obliterated the Justice. *Do the Breakers have the same tech the Ashamine secretly developed?*

"But it's different from before," the tech continued. "The total output is much smaller than the Light."

"What makes it significant?"

"The ship is tiny, at least by comparison to its energy signature. It must just be a mass of generators all joined together and strapped to a propulsion system."

At first, Ash felt relieved, knowing even if it was a beam weapon, it wouldn't have the capabilities of the Light. The more he thought about the vessel, however, the more something felt off. *What could a small ship do with so much power? What would they need it for?*

"Massive energy discharge!" the sensor tech exclaimed.

Ash quickly rose from his command chair and strode over to the tech's station. What he saw on the screen both awed and confused him.

The power emanating from the tiny ship was enormous, on par with the weapons the Breakers had used against the Light. *But it's not nuclear, and it's centered on the ship itself. What are they doing?*

For a moment, Ash thought perhaps they were witnessing yet another unfamiliar type of weaponry. *As if nuclear missiles and beam weapons aren't enough.* After a few moments, the consuming ball of energy began shrinking, and finally disappeared. The enemy ship was gone.

"What was that?" the tech asked.

"I think we just saw some kind of catastrophic malfunction, thank Azak-so," Ash said, looking even closer at the screen. Numerous specks streamed away from the ship's last location. "What are those?"

"Probably just interference or an energy remnant from the explosion." The tech's eyes narrowed, and he zoomed in on the display. Several seconds passed, and he finally shook his head. "They shouldn't be persisting, not for this long."

Ash continued watching the screen, a sinking feeling developing in his stomach. "It's some kind of weapon. The spacing and vectors are too orderly. Could they be rail cannon rounds?"

"They're bigger and slower than any rail rounds I've ever seen," the tech replied.

"Where are they going?"

The tech zoomed out and selected some options to extrapolate the vector. "Headed straight for Ashamine-2."

The hole in Ash's stomach deepened. "Weapons, what is your best guess on the results, given their size and speed."

The Memory's weapons officer looked down at his own terminal as Ash returned to his command chair. After making a few calculations, the woman looked up, her face grim. "No way to know for sure, sir, but best case is extreme destruction of planetary personnel and assets, and that's if they aren't nuclear or carrying some other kind of payload. Worst case—given the mass, velocity, and spread—I think they could cause an annihilation level event."

Ash felt the pit in his stomach become a galactic black hole. *Just when we thought we had a chance against the Breaker fleet...* Around him, the crew fell silent. Ash felt everyone's eyes on him, waiting for orders. *You have to do something,* he thought, trying to force himself out of paralysis. *Come on!*

Ash took a deep breath, feeling the air fill his lungs. He pulled his shoulders back, straightened up, and let it out in a burst. "Comms," he barked, "re-open the link with the Ashamine fleet. Nav, vector us in on an intercept course, and relay that order to the rest of the Brotherhood fleet. If possible, get us within rail range of the enemy weapons. Sensors, how long do we have until they strike Ashamine-2?"

The bridge became a bustle of activity, as the commanding officers of each respective system began passing down orders. After a moment, the sensor tech yelled over the din. "Eighteen standard minutes, given present velocity."

"We'll have to hit them before they get close," Ash said under his breath, finger tapping nervously on the arm of his chair.

"Link to Ashamine fleet reestablished," the comms officer announced. The fleet officer he'd talked to earlier appeared on the screen at the front of the bridge.

Ash hoped the young commander would be as amenable now as he had been before. *He's listened to all your suggestions so far,* Ash thought. *You aren't his superior, but he subconsciously thinks of you that way. Don't push him too far. Find the balance.*

"You saw the small Breaker ship explode?" Ash said, skipping formalities.

"Yes," the Ashamine commander said, looking distracted. "Another ship we don't have to deal with." The officer turned to face someone off-screen. "Target their rail cannons, full rate of fire. We can't let them continue to pound away at us."

"It launched at least part of its payload before it exploded," Ash said. "There is a mass of large objects headed towards Ashamine-2. If we don't stop them, the planet will be obliterated."

The Ashamine commander's brow furrowed. "Are you sure?" He lapsed into silence, showing the lack of initiative Ash had previously observed.

He almost got his fleet killed because of that before, and now he is wasting critical time again. "We need to stop the projectiles before they reach Ashamine-2. I'm moving the Brotherhood fleet in to intercept, but there will be too many for us to stop alone. The projectiles will pass near the edge of the combat zone. I need you to disengage as much of your fleet from battle as possible and target them."

"You want me to disengage? To turn my back on the enemy to try to stop some unverified threat?" The commander's eyes narrowed. "You're trying to get us killed, aren't you? All that blightheart you said about humanity coming together, of looking past our differences for the greater good: You were just trying to maneuver us into destruction, to destroy the Ashamine fleet so that you could fly in and become the new Founder!"

"Are you a buggering, blightheart-for-brains dweller of the dark star?!"

Ash yelled, unable to keep his composure any longer. At the edge of his vision, he saw his crew members jump, unused to hearing him act this way. He didn't care. "I'm not here to take control of the Ashamine, nor am I here to save it. I'm just trying to keep humans a viable species in the Akked. Do you want to see the Founder's City wiped out? Do you want everyone you know on Ashamine-2 to die? Because that is what is about to happen! You won't have a world to go back to, even if you defeat the Breakers."

As Ash continued his tirade, he saw the Ashamine commander wilt, cowering back into his luxurious captain's chair. *Good,* Ash thought, feeling his cheeks burn with fury.

"Yes—yes of course," he replied, unable to meet Ash's gaze.

"If you maneuver your ships strategically," Ash replied, lightening his tone, "you can use one side of each vessel to rail the projectiles and the other to continue defending against the Breaker fleet. It won't be as efficient, but it will give you the best possible position."

"I will see what I can do."

"We can win this," Ash said, hoping he hadn't pushed the other man too hard.

"I will begin issuing the orders immediately," the Ashamine commander said, straightening up in his seat. "I will make our people proud."

"Of course you will." The screen went blank and Ash let out a breath he didn't realize he'd been holding. *How did someone so inexperienced get put in charge of the entire Ashamine fleet?* he wondered, for what felt like the thousandth time. *If only the Breakers hadn't taken out the Light. Whoever was commanding was likely made of stronger alloy.*

"Three minutes until rail range intercept," his weapons officer announced, breaking Ash out of his thoughts.

"Time to planetary impact?" he asked.

"Ten minutes."

Let's hope the Ashamine fleet gets in position and we can take out these projectiles, whatever they are.

35 – MAXAR

As Maxar led Tremmilly and Jaydon towards the bridge, he fought to subdue the fear threatening to overwhelm him. He'd never experienced the terror he'd felt when the faceless thing looked into him. *You almost lost control,* he thought, carefully checking the intersecting corridor. A part of him said going after them was foolish, that it would be better to kill himself, to prevent the agony to come.

What in the buggering blightheart? he thought, realizing the urge was coming from outside his mind. *The fear must originate from them as well.* When he turned around to check on Tremmilly and Jaydon, he could see dread in the captain's face. Tremmilly was serene. Maxar guessed she understood how to shield herself from the faceless' influence. She smiled at him, and Maxar felt a cool peace settle over his mind. Jaydon's creased face also relaxed, and he took a deep breath.

While the fear was still present, Maxar noticed he could more easily dismiss it. "Ready to proceed?" he asked, knowing he was about to throw himself into the most important battle of his existence. *We have to end Crasor, have to destroy See'dek's henchman.*

"Ready," Tremmilly said, checking her flechette pistol.

"Let's go," Jaydon added, feigning confidence. He too had his pistol in hand.

"Keep an eye on my back and I'll give orders when I need to." They both nodded. Maxar turned, heading towards Crasor and the faceless beings on the ship's bridge.

As they moved closer to their destination, Maxar sensed the pressure of fear building once again. Tremmilly's shielding continued mitigating the sensation, but it was noticeable. *Don't get distracted. If you bugger the approach and alert the Breakers, this will become impossible. They'll swarm and kill us all.*

Just as he passed a hatch on his right, Maxar saw it slide open. He

149

turned to face the movement, realizing three surprised Breakers now stood beside him. Maxar began raising his pistol, as the enemies shifted from stunned to active. A loud crack sounded beside him, and the first Breaker fell, blackness bursting from his head and spraying all over the figure behind him.

"Int—" the second one started yelling, as Maxar aimed and triggered his pistol. Another loud crack sounded from his other side, and all three Breakers lay in a heap on the floor, unidentifiable black fragments and fluids leaking from their necks.

"Nice response time," Maxar said, seeing Tremmilly and Jaydon both lower their weapons. He checked quickly up the corridor, hoping no one had heard the skirmish. "Can you sense if they alerted Crasor?"

"No, nothing seems different," Tremmilly replied.

"All clear behind," Jaydon added. Maxar felt himself breathe easier.

"Let's keep going." He entered commands on the hatch controls to shut and secure it. *Out of vision, out of comprehension,* he thought, wondering briefly where he had heard the expression. Pushing the distraction away, he continued down the corridor.

When they finally drew within sight of the command bridge door, Maxar expected to see sentries blocking the way, but the space was empty. The door indicator was green, denoting it was unsecured. Maxar could feel something happening on the other side of the hatch, a thrumming, building energy. He'd never sensed anything like it before, had no idea what it could be.

"Do you think they know we're coming?" Jaydon asked, as Maxar stopped before the bridge door. "Maybe it's a trap. Why else would they leave it unsecured?"

"Donno," Maxar whispered. "The longer we wait, the more chance of discovery."

Jaydon bit his lip, nodding slowly.

"Do you feel that?" Tremmilly interjected, a worried look cracking her previously calm exterior.

Maxar nodded. "Any idea what's happening?"

Tremmilly closed her eyes. "If I drop the shield, I would get a better sense of it." She fell silent, and despite their precarious situation, Maxar knew he needed to be patient.

"I'm not sure," she said finally, "but it feels similar to when we were a beacon for Lothis, when he discovered how to reconnect to his Elrahi self. Something is twisted, wrong."

"It's the Breakers," Jaydon said. "How could it be anything else?"

"Whatever is happening," Tremmilly continued, "it isn't good."

Maxar bit his lip. "Should we wait? Or would it be better to interrupt it?"

"I don't know." Tremmilly looked troubled. "I'm sorry, Maxar. This is my part of the mission and I have no idea what to do."

"It's OK," Maxar said. He paused for a moment. "If we have no other indicator, I think we go for the assault. We still have surprise on our side, which can give us odds against whatever is going on in there."

"We can do this," Jaydon said. Maxar thought it sounded like he was trying to convince himself.

Tremmilly indicated her readiness as well, so without further discussion, Maxar slapped the door control with his palm. As the heavy blast doors began opening, he flattened himself against the wall next to them, taking cover. Jaydon and Tremmilly did the same on the other side.

Maxar reached out to both his Elrahi being and the nanites coursing through his body. He embraced them, knowing he would need everything within for the coming battle. *We can do this,* he thought, repeating Jaydon's words. Power begin to flow into him from his Elrahi connection. The modified Heltasoth nanites felt ready as well, and Maxar knew it would take everything within Crasor's power to withstand his fury. *We finally hunted you down, Crasor,* he thought, seeing the bridge door finish opening. *Once we destroy you, we're going to take out your blighthearted master and end this forever!*

36 – FELAR

Felar regained consciousness, screaming. She didn't understand, but then the pain hit, a massive wave threatening to knock her out again.

"Buggering, blighthearted, fires of the dark star," she said through gritted teeth, her eyes squeezed shut. "You're—fine. Everything—is—fine." Felar tried to calm herself, to focus through the pain. Still, she felt her consciousness start to dim, the cool embrace of blackness a welcoming reprieve.

"No!" she bellowed, the effort making pain rip through her torso. Tears slid down her cheeks.

You can do this, a voice in her head said, sounding like Wake. *You're OK.*

"I can do this," she repeated. "I'm OK." She calmed her breathing, the pain in her chest lessening as she did so. *Broken ribs,* she realized, remembering a similar pain after besting one of the street toughs on Qi-3 as a child. *They'll heal.*

Slowly, Felar opened her eyes. The surrounding scene rotated gently, first the Justice, then the battling fleets, then a tiny view of Ashamine-2. Memories of earlier consciousness flitted through her mind.

Felar vaguely remembered running towards Dras' ship, a blinding light, then nothing. She'd awoken, floating in space, surrounded by debris. In her brief moments of consciousness, she'd managed to mag-lock her boots onto one of the larger portions of drifting hull. With how much pain Felar was in now, she wondered how she'd accomplished the task.

How much time has passed? she thought, trying to distance herself from the flood of pain coursing through her body. Felar tried to check her suit's HUD, but it was glitchy and largely inoperable. *Good thing the atmospheric system is still online.*

Continuing to distract herself from her broken body, Felar looked

152

back at the surrounding space. *Dras and his ship are out there somewhere,* she thought, hoping the sentient machine had survived whatever happened to the Justice.

As the Breaker ship came into view again, Felar saw the vessel had split, the halves still venting gasses and other debris. *How?* For a moment, she tried to reason it out, but a wave of pain and nausea overwhelmed her ability to reason.

When the intensity finally decreased, Felar knew she had to find safety. *You can't float out here forever, and with your HUD down, you have no way of telling how much air you have left.* She hit the transmit toggle inside her suit, hoping that perhaps the comm was still configured to reach the rest of the team.

"Dras? Lothis?" she said, trying to keep the pain out of her voice. "Wake? Are you guys online?" She waited for several moments, but silence was all she heard. *Comms must be damaged as well,* Felar thought, not wanting to let herself consider the alternative.

She tried to spot the Heltasoth ship, but knew it would be nearly impossible, as the black hull blended into the darkness of space. Large pieces of debris kept catching her attention, making her heart jump with hope, but none were the sleek alien vessel.

As minutes crawled by, Felar felt her optimism fade. *You're going to die out here,* she thought, watching the Justice once again slowly rotate into view. *Mission accomplished, at least.* Felar knew what they'd done to the large ship hadn't caused it to break in half, but perhaps in disabling its defenses, they'd allowed someone else to deliver the killing blow. *Wish we'd gotten clear first.*

The warring fleets came into view, and Felar noted many of the Ashamine vessels seemed to be maneuvering away from the Breaker ships. *Running?* she wondered, but the ships were small and the distance great. *Besides, it's hard to tell the two fleets apart anyway.*

Maybe I can work my way back to the Justice, she thought, a plan beginning to form. *Find a shuttle or something, come back and find the rest of the team.* Felar had enough zero-g training to know, while it might be possible to hop from debris chunk to debris chunk, it would be a hazardous endeavor. One miscalculated jump or poorly timed release, and she could go launching into the void, or worse, slam into a jagged piece of hull.

Still have to try. No other options. But when she tried to bend down to manually release the magnetic locks, agony screamed through Felar, threatening to once again overwhelm her. After she could open her eyes again, Felar admitted she was in no condition to move at all. Her left arm was bent at an unnatural angle, the armored ENS somehow still maintaining structural integrity despite being forced into a strange shape.

The suit's left leg was crumpled, explaining the pain radiating there. Other parts of her armor were damaged as well, making Felar wonder how she'd survived the exit from the Justice.

They're gonna have to cut me out of this wreck, she thought, suppressing the black laughter threatening to renew the agony in her chest.

A movement at the edge of her vision caught Felar's attention. When she turned to look, she saw Dras' ship slowly navigating through the debris field. The alien vessel was pushing larger chunks of hull and debris out of its way, moving directly towards her.

Felar felt a cheer bubble up inside her, but suppressed the urge, knowing that it would likely make her pass out again. Instead, she settled for a smile and a careful wave of her less injured right arm.

Minutes passed, and the ship crept closer. *What if it's just Dras?* she thought, feeling some of her earlier relief evaporate. *What if Lothis and Wake are still out there?* Felar tried to prepare herself for the possibility. *We can find them,* she thought, *just like how Dras found me.*

Finally, the sleek ship stopped directly in front of her. For a moment, Felar wondered how she would make it across the intervening distance, then, the vessel rotated out of view. *I couldn't even disengage my mag-lock,* she thought.

When the Heltasoth ship rotated back into view, however, Felar saw a figure floating towards her. "Dras!" she tried to comm, forgetting the system was broken. "Curse it all to the fires of the dark star."

As the sentient machine approached, Felar was able to make out more detail. It still felt odd to see a human likeness floating unprotected in space, despite the fact she knew he wasn't human. His bald head gleamed in the light of the Ashamine primary. It seemed like his black robe should billow as he flew, but Felar knew that was impossible in vacuum.

Setting down lightly next to her, Dras put his hand on her shoulder. "It is good to see you, Felar," the Heltasoth's voice said over her helmet speakers. His lips remained still, but there was a smile on his face. "Given the damage your ENS has sustained, I am pleasantly surprised it retained structural integrity."

"Good to see you as well," Felar managed to gasp out, keeping her voice low so as not to move her chest. "Are Lothis and Wake with you? I'm in pretty bad shape. Can you get me back to your ship?"

"Yes," the Heltasoth replied, "of course." He reached down and hit the releases for the boot mag-locks. "I will be as gentle as possible, but I cannot guarantee painlessness."

"Don't worry about it. I'll be fine." Felar winced as Dras began propelling them back towards his ship. The acceleration made her nauseous, and she fought hard to keep what little was in her stomach down. *Don't want to have that in your helmet for the rest of the trip, like some blighthearted Initiate.*

They both lapsed into silence, Felar focusing on anything but her pain. Finally, a thought occurred to her. "Did you say Lothis and Wake were on board?"

"No, I did not."

"Are they?"

But what he said was lost as Dras began decelerating for their entry into the ship. Pain screamed through her ribs, broken arm, and crushed leg. She wailed, feeling the blackness threaten to devour her.

When she opened her eyes again, they were inside the ship. Lothis stood before her, smiling weakly. "Felar," he said, the word containing more emotion than she'd ever thought possible from him.

"Lothis," she replied, the blackness overtaking the edges of her vision. "I'm so glad you're safe." She tried to look deeper into the ship, her heart racing. "Where's Wake?"

She saw Lothis' lips move, but couldn't hear anything. Pain, darkness, and a sensation of falling swallowed what remained of Felar's consciousness.

37 – CRASOR

Please! No! Crasor thought, turning to face the command bridge door. *Please! I tried to contact the Rain. I'm doing as you asked!*

"Too late," a screeching, static-laden voice said in his mind. Five of the Faceless strode onto the deck, clothed in tattered, gray robes. "You didn't do as *he* asked."

"A momentary lapse of judgment," Crasor said, taking an involuntary step back from the pale intruders. "I acknowledge my error, and beg for forgiveness."

"Beg all you want," the voice screeched. "It will do no good."

"Please!" Crasor said, dropping to his knees, something he'd only done once before in his life. "I will never do it again."

"Of that you are correct."

The faceless figures surrounded him, making Crasor's already thudding heart beat harder. For a moment, he thought about running, or of summoning Marines to kill the intruders. *It won't work,* he thought. *No one will obey me. There is nowhere to hide.*

"Correct again," the Faceless said, reading Crasor's thoughts. "Best just take your punishment. Resist, and you will only make it harder for yourself."

"Please," Crasor moaned, futilely trying to make eye contact with the form standing over him. "Don't kill me. Let me go, and I promise to serve you loyally, forever."

"And waste all the development? No, you will live."

Crasor's heart leapt with hope. Movement behind the towering figure before him caught his eye. He bent sideways to get a better look, and his eyes went wide in amazement. "Harb—" he began saying, before a piecing pain shot through his mind, silencing him. A blazing inferno of agony consumed him, every neuron and cell within him screaming. His eyes rolled back into his head, and he felt himself falling.

156

"The One has spent much time on you," the static filled voice said in his mind. "Thankfully, the investment has paid off. Now, he has a vessel to inhabit. Further development would have been optimal, but you decided to diverge."

Crasor fought through the pain, trying to understand what the Faceless was saying. He tried to reply, tried to reason with the eerie figures, but his mind felt paralyzed.

"A suitable vessel," a different, lower pitched voice growled. "The One is pleased."

"Glad you approve," the original voice snapped. "Now let's get on with opening the transition."

Seconds passed in agony, and Crasor felt the lance of pain expand. It turned into a flare of white-hot energy, shooting from the top of his head to the soles of his feet. He felt consumed, the pain scouring everything away. A small part of him knew this was the end, but he tried to resist, willing a barrier to protect what was left.

Around his ball of consciousness, the pain raged, flaring and burning hotter than the fires of the dark star. *No, please! You're making a mistake. I've served loyally!* If the Faceless could hear him, they made no sign.

Time lost all meaning. Crasor felt his tiny sense of self untether, a speck carried along the beam of all-consuming pain. *What can I do?* he thought, finally realizing the Faceless would never offer mercy, would never change their minds. *I have to find a way out. Perhaps I can survive somewhere else?* The plan brought a flare of hope to what was left of Crasor's mind. *That's it!*

He struggled to navigate out of the beam. *Which way?* he wondered desperately, feeling its intensity burning through his mental shield. He willed himself one way, then another. The inferno was infinite, inescapable.

In the next instant, there was an enormous flash of agonizing light, and what little was left of Crasor disappeared.

38 – AZA

Aza's eyes shifted from the magnified view screen to the tactical display. Many of the Ashamine's smaller vessels were positioning themselves towards one side of the battle, leaving the larger ships between them and the Breakers. *Doesn't make sense,* she thought.

"Whatever the Ashamine is doing," Em said, "it looks like they are putting themselves back into a disadvantage."

Aza nodded, continuing to watch the situation develop. "Is there anything we can do?" she asked, feeling helpless and frustrated.

"This ship doesn't have the armor or weaponry to get involved in combat, let alone fleet scale warfare. We can only monitor the situation, and bugger out of here if things start getting any worse than they are."

"I want to be with Ash, instead of just sitting and waiting."

Em sighed, straightening up in her captain's chair. "You think I want to be here, doing nothing? If I hadn't come to get you, I'd be on my real ship, out there in combat, fighting for humanity. Instead, I'm here babysitting you, watching as my friends get railed into stellar dust."

Aza felt her breath catch, and her lips turned down. *Don't cry. Do. Not. Cry.* She took in a deep breath, starting to turn away from Em.

"Look," the older woman said, putting her palms up in a placating gesture. "I didn't mean it that way. I was happy to help your uncle with a mission he couldn't complete himself. I owe him, and even if I didn't, I still would have come for you." Em paused for a moment. "I just meant that I feel as helpless as you do. I wish we could go in, cannons launching, but we wouldn't have even a minute chance. We're lucky Ash is letting us stay here. Otherwise, we'd be doing the same waiting, but without instant combat intel."

"I guess this isn't the worst position," Aza replied, sniffing. She wiped the corners of her eyes.

"Well, it's pretty blightheartedly bad," Em said, chuckling, "but it could be a lot worse."

A chime sounded, and Aza looked up to see an incoming comms notification on the screen. Her heart began beating faster.

"Ash? I mean, Parick?" Em said, selecting the option to make the connection. "Bugger it."

"Things are going blightheart," Ash said, face appearing on the screen before them. Sweat beads glistened on his forehead, and he was biting his lip. "The Breakers launched some kind of planet killer weapon: giant rods, similar to a rail cannon, but orders of magnitude larger."

"What?" Em said. "How?"

"I don't know, and there is no time to explain. Between the Brotherhood and the Ashamine fleets, we will get them broken up into smaller chunks or diverted entirely. So we have that to be thankful for. The downside is, we had to disengage much of our firepower from the Breaker fleet, and now they are regrouping after the disarray caused by the loss of the Justice."

"The planet is already being overrun with Breakers," Em said. "Just let the rest of the rods go through. Focus on winning the space battle, otherwise the planet won't matter."

"I know," Ash said, looking determined. "I've gotten similar advice from our own captains, as well as the Ashamine fleet commander. But I can't let the center of humanity be wiped out like that, even if the Breakers are desecrating it already. If even just one or two of the rods hit, it will be enough to cause major devastation. Millions dead, catastrophic change to atmosphere and weather. It would set humanity back generations. We have to preserve the Ashamine databases. I think the facilities can hold out against ground assault, but one rod penetrating the Founder's City would wipe out thousands of years of history and tech, as well as all public knowledge and records. We'd lose the secret records I'll need to show humanity the truth about the Ashamine."

Aza could see the passion and conviction on her uncle's face, and it was contagious. "We can help! Just tell us what to do."

"Good. I need you to leave the Ashamine system," Ash said, looking directly into Aza's eyes. "It was already an insecure proposition to have you stay, but now it's just too risky." Aza tried to protest, but her uncle kept talking. "No, Aza. If the human fleets collapse, the Breakers will swallow you up. This is a fight to the death for humanity, but that doesn't mean all humans have to die here. Maybe what's left of the Brotherhood can press on, can find a way to hide from the Breakers. All I know is, I don't want you dying here for no purpose. Em, take her to the Azak system. Protect her like she was your own."

"No," Aza said, but she knew he was right. "I won't go. I won't leave you!"

"I don't have time to argue," he said, shaking his head.

"I did all I could," an off-screen voice announced, "but the last rod outran me. It's still 83% intact."

"Em," Ash said, fire in his eyes, "I have to go. Promise me you will do as I ask and keep Aza safe."

"I promise."

The screen reverted to the magnified view of battling fleets. "Em," Aza said, trying to control her emotions, "you know we can't just leave him. He needs us!"

Em rubbed her hand down her face, sighing. "I don't want to abandon him any more than you do, but there is nothing we can do. Nothing." She sat forward, beginning to make selections on the ship's controls.

Aza slumped into her chair, feeling dazed. *That might be the last time you ever see him,* she thought. *It could be the last time you'll see any of your family.* Rather than making her sad, the realization just made her feel dead, her emotions paralyzed. Aza stared directly ahead, unable to move.

"I'm sorry..." Em said, trailing off into silence.

Everyone is going to die, Aza thought, *everyone I ever knew or might know. Then, I'll die too.*

A new contact pinged on the tactical display, pulling Aza out of her dark thoughts. She took a deep breath and sat forward in her chair, taking a closer look. "It's headed straight for us," Aza announced.

"What is heading straight for us?" Em asked, turning from the control screen.

"I don't know, but it is moving fast."

Em took a closer look, then shook her head. "It must be the rod; the one Ash got the report about."

"No one is going to be able to stop it," Aza realized, checking the position of the other human ships.

"Fires of the dark star," Em cursed, making more selections on her terminal screen.

"We can't just leave," Aza protested.

Em ignored her, continuing to work on her screen. "Buggering blightheart," she growled finally, shaking her head.

"What?"

"The last slug," Em replied, voice dark, "the only one to make it past two entire fleets, is headed straight for the Founder's City."

Aza was stunned.

"Any other buggered vector," Em continued, "and it wouldn't matter, at least not for the Ashamine databases. I even accounted for planetary spin. It's a direct hit."

"Can't we shoot it like the other ships did?" Aza said.

"Sure, we could hit it a few times as it zips past, but it wouldn't do a buggered thing. That rod is massive, and nothing on this ship has the capability to stop, fragment, or divert it." Em paused. "Besides, I told Ash I would get you out of here, and that's what I'm going to do."

Aza's memory stirred, transporting her back to a trip to one of Ashamine-2's recreational moons. She and her parents had gone to an exhibit explaining how the asteroid had been carefully guided into geosynchronous orbit around the capital world, before being terraformed into the lush environment they'd experienced. *Engineers turned the asteroids into starships,* Aza thought, remembering how they'd installed propulsion and guidance systems onto the huge chunks of rock to move them into position.

"Maybe there is nothing in this ship that is strong enough to divert the rod," Aza said, feeling hope spring up within her, "but what about the ship itself?"

Em turned to look at her, remaining silent.

"We are the only ones who can stop it," Aza said, feeling what little hope she'd gained snuff out, "the only ones who can save the Founder's City and the Ashamine database."

"Aza—" Em said, sighing deeply. "Burn it all to the fires of the dark star," she continued under her breath, turning back to her terminal screen.

That's it then, Aza thought, realizing her home would soon be obliterated, along with her parents, the Ashamine database, and the entire city. She tried to keep from crying once again, but this time Aza couldn't. Huge, hot tears rolled down her face, and she began to sob.

"Now's not the time for that," Em said, her focus still on the screen. "We have a city-killing rod to divert. I need your help."

39 – WAKE

"Wake? Can you hear me?"

Wake floated in oblivion. He tried to understand what the words meant, but when he got too close to them, massive pain threatened to overwhelm him.

"Careful," the voice continued. Wake found it was becoming harder to ignore its gravity. "Set him down."

"Is there any way to get Brightwing off him?"

"It sealed itself around the parts that are... missing. Saved his atmosphere and life, but bugger if I know how to get it off."

"We can at least remove his helmet, right?"

Wake felt something tug gently at the edges of the blackness, producing an iridescent bloom of pain.

"Dras, is there anything you can do for him?"

"I can try, but he is badly damaged."

A rushing sensation filled Wake's consciousness, and then he opened his eyes. Pain engulfed him, the sensation threatening to send him back to the black abyss. He tried to scream, but no sound came out. It felt as if half of his body was being held in front of a starship exhaust on full thrust.

"He's awake," Felar said, her face hovering over him. "Wake, everything is going to be OK. Just stay still." Beside her, he could see Lothis and Dras.

A strange sensation developed in Wake's chest, like a fluttering bird was nesting there.

"What's happening?" Felar barked, turning to Dras.

"The nanites are trying, but the damage is too extensive. They can't rebuild half his torso so quickly."

"Make them work faster," Felar yelled, becoming larger in Wake's vision. "Fight," she said, her face all he could see. "Don't give up, Wake."

162

Her beautiful features became blurry and started to fade. "We're here with you," was the last thing he heard, before the blackness took him once again.

Am I dead? Wake wondered, sensing nothing. He tried to search for a way back to Felar, but that concept seemed to have no meaning in this place. *Where am I?*

A memory occurred to him, of Lothis telling his story of death and rebirth after Dras had repaired his body. *Perhaps the Heltasoth can do the same for me.* He tried to think of how Lothis had found his way back, but all he could remember was something about dimensions.

Wake took hold of the surrounding space-time, folding and warping it instinctually. It took everything within him, but a transition eventually formed, and Wake stepped through.

On the other side, more blackness awaited. *How did I get here?* he wondered, the memory slipping away from him. *What's wrong with me?* Wake felt exhausted, like the very fibers of his existence were being dissolved.

I must have come here for a reason. What was it? He tried to focus, but the more he thought about the past, the vaguer and more nebulous it seemed. *Something bad happened to Cazz-ak.* Immediately after he thought of it, the spark faded.

Soon, Wake couldn't recall what he'd been trying to remember. An image of Felar's face, smiling and full of joy filled his consciousness. *I love you,* he thought. *I'll always love you.*

After an indescribable amount of time, it too vanished, replaced by a glowing ball of energy, swirling and pulsing. *Hello,* Wake said, not understanding what he was doing.

The ball began expanding, unfolding like a beautiful flower, its petals full of radiant, beautiful light. Wake felt like he might explode from joy. *I'm here, I'm here!* he thought, letting the blossom pull him in. *I did everything I could to protect you, I tried as hard as I could.* The words made sense, but he didn't understand them.

He felt a faint tug behind him, heard an incomprehensible sound, but his attention remained on the energetic petals. *I am yours, and you are mine.* Wake reached out his hand, stretching as far as he could towards the radiant, unfolding flower. Then, he touched its edge.

40 – TREMMILLY

Tremmilly took a deep breath, following Maxar as he crept through the command bridge door. She expected one of the Breakers to raise an alarm, but after a brief glance, she realized they were all focused on the robed figures clustered at the center of the bridge.

Maxar pointed, and the three of them quickly crouched behind a long row of consoles. Tremmilly peeked around the edge, feeling a strange energy develop around the faceless figures.

"What are they doing?" Jaydon whispered, stuck in the middle without a view.

"I... I don't know," Tremmilly replied, stretching out farther to get a better view. In the center of the faceless' circle, she saw a crumpled form. "They're doing something to Crasor."

"Is this good or bad for us?" Maxar asked. Tremmilly had known him long enough to understand the look in his eyes meant he was ready for combat.

She shook her head, trying to understand what the rising energy meant. *Feels like when Cazz-ak created the transitions for us, when we went to attack the Arche. But it's different. It's a connection to a dark place...* All the pieces slid into alignment, and Tremmilly knew. "They're connecting to the Breaker dimension. They're making a transition, to send or bring someone through."

"Whatever it is," Maxar growled, "I don't think we want them in our dimension. Take the faceless out before they can finish."

Tremmilly's initial instinct was agreement, but something in the back of her mind said wait. She tried to understand why, but no explanation followed.

"Let's do it," Jaydon said, his voice only quavering slightly.

Maxar began a three-second countdown, as Tremmilly desperately tried to think of why they should let the faceless finish. By the time he reached

164

one, Tremmilly still couldn't think of anything, so she prepared herself to fight.

"Go!" Maxar yelled, rising up from his crouched position. Tremmilly was a fraction of a second behind him, but by the time she was fully standing, Maxar had already triggered two shots from his flechette pistol.

Tremmilly fired her weapon, taking quick aim at the closest Breakers. *The faceless are the priority, but I can't let these troops be within striking range.* Jaydon and Maxar had the same idea, and several more of the ship's crew fell amongst sprays of dark blood.

Out of the edge of her vision, she saw the faceless were still focused intently on Crasor's prone form. *Why aren't they responding to our presence?* She triggered another round, obliterating the confused look from the face of a nearby Breaker.

Just as Tremmilly shifted her aim towards one of the faceless, she felt the weapon vibrate in two short bursts. *Low ammo,* she thought, steadying her aim at its head before triggering one final round. *Don't wait to reload until you are completely empty,* she thought, repeating Felar's command as she took cover behind the console. *Always keep at least one in the gun, in case you need it while reloading.*

She quickly ducked behind the console, ejecting the flechette pistol's ammo-charge pack and slapping in a new one. When she stood up, she saw Maxar and Jaydon had taken out two of the eerie creatures, their bodies sprawled lifelessly on the deck. The three remaining faceless had moved and were now facing them.

"Bugger you all," Tremmilly said, taking aim once again and triggering her weapon. The gun bucked in her hand, and she heard the crack of the projectiles, but her target remained unharmed.

"Save the ammo," Maxar said. "They've shielded themselves somehow."

Tremmilly could hear fear in his voice, something that felt new and scary. *I have to reinforce our team, keep us solid,* she realized, knowing Jaydon would be even more terrified than Maxar.

"Stay strong," Tremmilly said, trying to think of what to do next.

"Harbingers," a voice screeched over the ship's speakers. It was distorted, a static filled, alien voice. "We wondered when you would arrive."

For a moment, Tremmilly wondered who was speaking, but realized it was the three faceless before them.

"Crasor would have dealt with you adequately," the voice continued, "but it will be much more enjoyable to handle this directly, to experience your obliteration firsthand. Millennia of waiting has made us very, very thirsty." Negative energy swelled in their hands, swirling and coalescing into large, dark mind blades.

Tremmilly expected the entire crew to attack them, but those who remained alive simply stayed at their posts, watching. *The faceless want this for themselves,* Tremmilly realized.

"We have to get out of here," Maxar said, looking from their foes to the bridge's exit. "I can't fight three of them all by myself."

"You aren't alone," Tremmilly said. "You have me and Jaydon."

"Neither of you has the mental weaponry to fight them. I need Felar or Lothis."

"We can do this," Tremmilly said, feeling her voice shift into how it had been as empress. "If we run now, they'll just stab us in the back or rail our ship when we try to flee. We have to take them out. I will back you up and do what I can."

"Fires of the dark star," Maxar grumbled, straightening up. "The things I've done for love." He strode forward, a mind blade forming in either hand. Tremmilly had never seen him summon so much energy at once, and pride welled up within her.

"Jaydon, watch our backs," Tremmilly ordered. "Alert us if the situation changes."

The old captain nodded, eyes wide, but determined. "As you say, Empress."

Stepping quickly to follow behind Maxar, Tremmilly tapped into all the Elrahi energy available to her. *I may not be able to make weapons, but that doesn't mean I can't protect him.* The darkness of her connection to the Breakers swelled, and she had to fight hard to resist the distraction. *Is it because I'm drawing on my energy, or because I'm so close to the faceless?*

Maxar raised his blades and approached the three dark figures. "How many of you buggers do I have to kill before I can fight See'dek?" he snarled, all his earlier fear vanished. "Let's find out."

41 – LOTHIS

"Wake? Can you hear me?" Felar yelled. Lothis could see she was fighting hard to hold back tears, but they slowly trailed down her cheeks.

"Careful," she continued, motioning towards a spot on the command deck floor. "Set him down." Dras did so, stepping back so Felar could get closer.

"Is there any way to get Brightwing off him?" Lothis asked, wondering how the engineer was still even alive. *Can a human body survive so much damage?*

Felar's tried to loosen the suit's components, but none moved. "It sealed itself around the parts that are... missing. Saved his atmosphere and life, but bugger if I know how to get it off."

Lothis checked Wake's head, which appeared undamaged. "We can at least remove his helmet, right?"

Felar quickly removed the component, looking frantic. "He's still breathing," she said in a whisper, "still breathing."

"Dras," Lothis said, "is there anything you can do for him?"

The Heltasoth's mimicry of human emotion and inflection was near perfect. "I can try, but he is badly damaged." He looked sad, but his black eyes remained dry.

He loves Wake as much as we do, Lothis realized. *It hurts Dras to see him in pain.*

Movement in the corner of his vision brought Lothis' attention back to Wake. Around him, the deck welled up, forming an embrace around the damaged body. It moved over the missing portions of Wake's chest and arm, seeping into whatever material Brightwing had used to seal itself.

The Heltasoth nanites will save Wake, Lothis thought. *If they could bring me back from the dead and rebuild part of my brain, they can restore Wake.* Moments passed, and Lothis finally realized he'd been holding his breath.

"He's awake," Felar said finally. Lothis looked to see that indeed his eyes were open. "Wake, everything is going to be OK," Felar continued. "Just stay still."

Wake's eyes darted from Felar, to Lothis, to Dras, looking like an injured animal, seeking escape. Lothis felt an empathetic tightening in his own chest. *He'll be fine. The nanites are going to fix him.*

"What's happening?" Felar said, turning to Dras.

"The nanites are trying, but the damage is too extensive. They can't rebuild half his torso so quickly."

"Make them work faster," Felar yelled. She bent down, getting closer to Wake. "Fight," she said, voice stern, but loving. "Don't give up, Wake." Huge tears began to flow freely down her face. "We're here with you."

A moment later, Lothis could see the life drain from Wake's eyes. Felar collapsed onto what remained of his chest, sobbing. "Bring him back, Dras. Please!"

Lothis felt a sucking void form in his stomach. He couldn't take his eyes off Wake's face.

"I've done what I can," the Heltasoth said, looking dejected. "In a few minutes, the nanites will restore enough of his body to permit the chemistry you term as life, but I cannot bring his consciousness back."

"Lothis," Felar said, looking at him imploringly, "you found your repaired body. You came back after death. Find Wake! Bring him back."

The emotion of the situation felt overwhelming to Lothis. His body remained frozen, his mind a spinning wheel of bewilderment.

"Lothis? Please?"

"Y–ye–yes," he stuttered, trying to force away through the paralysis. "I'll go look for him. I'll do what I can."

Settling onto the floor beside Wake's corpse, Lothis took hold of the surrounding space-time. His motions were jittery and uncoordinated, unlike his normal skill. *Get yourself together. There is still hope.* An involuntary glance at the mangled body suggested otherwise. *Trust Dras.*

Forcing the distractions from his mind, Lothis redoubled his efforts. After a moment, his consciousness was free, floating. *Where would he have gone?* Lothis wondered, searching for Wake's spark of consciousness. All he could see was the nearby fleet battle and the darkness of the Breakers. *He wouldn't have dissipated so quickly.* But the more Lothis thought about it, the more he wondered. *Wake wasn't as strong as Cazz-ak, or me. Would that make a difference to how long he could survive away from his body?* Lothis didn't know.

A movement unlike any other in his field of view caught his attention. "Wake!" he yelled, seeing the engineer's energy slip through a dimensional transition. A fraction of a second later, the rift disappeared.

Where is he going? Lothis thought, trying to figure out how to follow his friend. *Think!* Seconds dragged past. For a moment, he thought of going over to see if he could decipher the energy residue the transition had left.

The Dawn! Lothis realized, quickly warping the surrounding space-time to take him to the cosmic flower. *He's going to integrate his energy into the Dawn.*

The next instant, Lothis went through the transition, and was staring at a plane of darkness, pierced only by the single, radiant flower. It was unfolding, moving in complicated patterns his mind couldn't fathom. Just beside it, he saw Wake, his attention solely focused on the cosmic entity.

"Wait! Stop!" Lothis yelled. "Dras is restoring your body. You can return to it."

But the engineer was already reaching out, his hand caressing one of the enormous petals. His form wavered, pulsing with shimmering energy. The flower grew, more petals unfolding in a magnificent display. A bright light flared, dazzling Lothis.

When his vision returned, Wake was gone.

42 – ASH

Ash turned back to the comms display, feeling determined. "Em, I have to go. Promise me you will do as I ask and keep Aza safe."

"I promise," his long-time friend replied.

Ash terminated the comms link. *I can't let her stay in system any longer,* he thought. *At least now I can put my full attention towards this battle, without worrying Aza and Em are going to end up as collateral damage.*

"Incoming enemy fighters," the sensor tech yelled, pulling Ash out of his reverie. "They just buggering appeared out of nowhere!"

"Weapons, shift aim to lead ships," Ash said looking towards the tactical display. "Fire flak missiles into the densest clusters of fighters. Use rail cannons for the outliers. Nav, looks like they cut us off from the rest of the Brotherhood fleet, but do your best to get us back to supporting ships." *Buggering blightheart,* he thought, watching the Breaker fighters close in. *They've got a solid formation, and they caught us out alone. At least we took out a few of the rods in the process. Hopefully the last one doesn't hit anything vital.*

The Stellar Memory shook violently, and Ash had to grasp his chair arms to keep from being thrown out of it. "Status?!" he yelled, quickly selecting options that activated the seat's restraint straps.

"Single rail round impact," his engineering officer replied. "Armor damage, 80% integrity. Hull intact."

"Too many inbounds for point defenses to keep up with," the defense officer added. "It's tracking a majority of the projectiles, but unless we can decrease the number of enemy fighters, we are going to take more hits."

"Fires of the dark star," Ash growled, glancing at the tactical display. The highlighted icon of Em's ship caught his eye, and for a moment he thought perhaps the system was lagging. *They're going the wrong way,* he thought, zooming in. Indeed, they were flying farther away from the transition zone, and towards the battle. Ash knew Em was too good of a pilot to make such a simple mistake. When he zoomed out and saw their vector, he understood. *They're going for the last buggering rod.*

For a moment, Ash thought Em had lied to him, that she was planning this heroic effort all along. *No,* he thought, shaking his head. *No, this has to be Aza's doing. Em wouldn't break a promise to me, not without persuasion and a good reason.*

Ash laughed to himself, despite knowing two of the people he loved most in the Akked were still in danger. *Can I blame them? Everyone has a stake in this fight. I won't turn and run, no matter what, so why should they?*

Another massive shudder went through the ship, slamming Ash against his seat restraints. "Armor damage, 45% integrity," the engineering officer announced. "They hit the same spot twice, directly outside the aft crew quarters."

"What are the odds of that?" Ash wondered, knowing the power generator was beneath the aft crew section.

"High, sir," the defense officer replied. "They are coordinating their attack unlike anything I've ever seen. They draw point defenses away, then launch several rail rounds towards the same portion of hull."

"We need to decrease their numbers," Ash said, looking at the tactical display and trying to find an advantage.

"Flak missiles eliminated 12% of the enemy fighters," the weapons officer added. "They've changed formations to eliminate our effectiveness. I've never seen pilots adapt so quickly."

"Yes," Ash sighed, "and we've never faced Breaker ships in this quantity either. At least they didn't know about the flak missiles before today, otherwise they probably wouldn't have kept such tight formations to begin with."

"Our rail rounds are still consistently effective," weapons said, "but with the rate of damage we're taking, I'm not sure the hull will last long enough to make it back to the fleet."

Ash felt his heart rate quicken. *Have to find a way to take them out, or at least survive long enough to reach help. Maybe a few Brotherhood ships could come out to support us the rest of the way in?* Checking the tactical display, he saw his other ships were engaged, a large swarm of the Breaker fleet pounding away at his much smaller group of vessels.

We're on our own, he thought, feeling his earlier sense of determination return. *We have to take on these buggers ourselves.*

Ash selected the screen option allowing him to address the entire ship. As he did so, he reached down to unclip his ENS helmet from its ready position on his chair. "Crew of the Memory," Ash said, keeping his voice more confident than he felt, "we are taking a pounding." The ship shook again, interrupting Ash.

"Armor 5% integrity," engineering announced. "Hull intact."

"Go to vacuum-based ops," Ash said, pulling his helmet on and attaching it to his suit. "These Breaker fighters caught us outside the fleet and are giving us more than we can handle. We aren't dead yet, and we won't go down without a fight. Give them the fires of the dark star, and we just might make it out alive."

As he finished speaking, a thought occurred to Ash. He considered it for several seconds, feeling the weight of the swarming fighters around him. "Defense," he said finally, realizing he had nothing to lose by asking, "can we reconfigure the point defense system to prioritize protecting the damaged hull portion?"

The weapons officer was silent for a moment, then nodded. "Yes, sir, I think so." He made several selections on his screen, scrolling through menu after menu of options and config files. Ash realized how stiff he'd become, waiting for the inevitable hull breech. He relaxed his jaw and facial muscles, taking a deep breath of the recycled ENS air.

"Done," the officer said finally. Just as he did, another jolt rocked the Stellar Memory. Ash quickly checked the ship's status display, his eyes noting none of the bulkheads had locked down and that atmosphere was still at standard pressure.

"They hit a new sector," engineering announced. "Armor integrity 90%, hull intact."

Ash took another deep breath. *How long can we last?* he wondered, checking the distance to the fleet. *Who knows what their situation will be like when we get there... If we make it...*

43 – MAXAR

Maxar raised his blades, assuming a combat stance. "How many of you buggers do I have to kill before I can fight See'dek?" he snarled, approaching the three remaining faceless. "Let's find out." He feinted to his left before moving to the right, hoping to throw the first of the ugly creatures off balance.

But when he dove in with his blades, ready to pierce the faceless' chest, its void-black sword was already blocking him. The two mind blades hit, sending out a concussive wave that knocked Maxar back on his heels. The second creature dove in, swinging his blade at Maxar's chest. He barely parried the blow in time, but was ready for the resulting shock.

As he steadied himself, Maxar saw the third robed creature rush past, heading for Tremmilly and Jaydon. *Bugger him in the fires of the dark star,* Maxar thought, parrying two blows at once from his own foes. *I can't stop him. They'll have to take care of it themselves.*

Drawing on more of his Elrahi power, Maxar summoned a spray of mind shards, sending them whistling towards the nearest of his two foes. Just as the jagged edged weapons were about to strike, the creature waved its free hand, and the mass went cascading away, piercing the nearby command consoles and creating a flash of light.

As Maxar's eyes adjusted, he could see black blood oozing from the creature's perforated right shoulder. "Not quite quick enough, eh, you blightheart?" he taunted, flourishing his blades. Maxar stepped to the left, trying to keep the second faceless from flanking him. Before he could get far, the first foe moved in, quicker than Maxar believed possible. He barely had his blades up in time to block the massive void-dark sword, now just centimeters from his nose.

The faceless bore down harder with his blade, and Maxar knew he was just seconds from being overcome. In the edge of his vision, he saw the second faceless moving in, blade held low and going for Maxar's chest.

Feeling the nanites within him, Maxar summoned their strength, using it to shove the first faceless back. He tried to spin and deflect the second one's charge, but even with the nanite-enhanced speed, he still wasn't fast enough. The void-dark mind blade pierced Maxar's side, beneath his ribs. It took his breath away, a cold emptiness sucking at his energy.

Before the faceless could shove the blade in deeper, Maxar stepped to the side, immediately feeling relief once he was free of the void-dark blade. A moment later, fire bloomed inside of him, a raging inferno centered around the wound. *Is that my nanite response, or a poison from the weapon?*

There was no time to answer his own question, as both foes recovered and redoubled their efforts. Maxar felt himself flowing from combat form to combat form, both human and Elrahi, in an effort to gain an advantage.

"We've seen every move you could try," the voice screeched over the ship's speakers. "And we've had millennia to develop our own."

In the next instant, Maxar lost sight of the second opponent. One moment he was there, the next, he'd disappeared.

"Behind you," he heard Tremmilly yell. Maxar felt his stomach drop, knowing that he'd never be able to move fast enough, even with nanite assistance. Still, he had to try.

Whirling, he brought up his blades in a defensive posture, while simultaneously diving to one side. As he rotated, he caught a glimpse of the second faceless, blade moving slowly through the air.

What in the fires of the dark star? Maxar thought, regaining his feet in time to fight off the first foe's renewed attack. Glimpses of the second faceless told him Tremmilly had done something to slow him down. *Can she control time?* But whatever she'd done wore off, and both foes were attacking at impossible speeds.

Maxar saw a weakness. Every time he stepped left, the injured faceless' reaction lagged. It was only for a fraction of a second, but at the speeds they were moving, it might just be enough.

Maybe the mind shard damage is creating lag in his nanites, Maxar thought, feinting right, then left. Anticipating the delay, Maxar drove forward with his right-hand blade. Before the faceless could correctly position his defense, Maxar shoved his weapon through the featureless face. The creature froze mid-swing, but remained standing.

Stepping back hurriedly, Maxar left his blade behind, parried the second faceless' strike, and let the energy holding the mind blade together evaporate. He expected the pierced faceless to crumple to the deck, but instead, the figure began jittering, a nausea-inducing spasm that made

Maxar gag. *He's repairing himself,* he thought, Maxar's remaining opponent driving him away from its injured comrade with blow after blow. *Have to finish him before he can revive.*

Summoning all the energy he could from both his Elrahi being and his nanite abilities, Maxar flung a spray of mind shards at the uninjured faceless, using the brief distraction to shove past him. He brought up his remaining mind blade, aiming for the incapacitated creature's neck.

There was a moment of resistance as his blade sheered through pale skin and nanite-infused connective tissue, but it pulled free. Both head and body fell to the decking, black blood oozing.

Maxar turned, summoning another spray of mind blades. The remaining faceless stood a few meters away, dark energy crackling off him like black lightning. Maxar had never seen anything like it before. *Can't let him get close,* he knew instinctively, taking a step back.

A tendril of darkness shot out from the faceless, arcing towards Maxar. Not fully understanding what he was doing, he grabbed space-time, condensing and solidifying it in front of him. The dark energy hit it and bounced off, deflected towards the metal ceiling above. Sparks showered Maxar, and he had to drop the shield almost as quickly as he'd grasped it. *Not strong enough,* he realized, hoping he'd not need it again.

Another tendril of darkness lanced out, and Maxar acted reflexively, creating the same warp. This time, the bolt deflected into a nearby console. The resulting flash of light was blinding. When his vision recovered enough to make out the faceless' form, Maxar sent his mind shards careening towards it. The mass was the thickest Maxar had ever summoned, and it hit the faceless before it could protect itself.

Black strands of blood and tissue flew out from the creature, a mist forming in the air. Its body began oozing blackness, its skin and robes shredded. Knowing he couldn't risk the faceless repairing itself, Maxar jumped forward and lopped off its head. Both fell to the floor just like his previous opponent.

Maxar took a deep breath, feeling relieved he'd taken out two of the three enemies. His side still burned, but it hurt less, so it seemed his nanites were taking care of the damage. As he turned to find his friends, Tremmilly's scream pushed all other thoughts out of his mind.

44 – FELAR

Felar kept alternating between staring at Wake and watching Lothis. Seconds felt like minutes, minutes like hours. *Come on,* she repeated for the millionth time, willing them both to return to their bodies.

Lothis' chest moved up and down in a rhythmic cycle, but Wake remained motionless. Dras had assured her his body was once again compatible with life. If his consciousness and life-force somehow made it back, he would be restored. *But that is the crux, isn't it?* Felar thought, hoping Lothis could guide their friend home.

The missing half of the engineer's chest was now restored, built from Heltasoth nanites. If she thought about it hard enough, Felar could feel the same tiny machines moving through her own blood. Dras had sent them there to heal her broken bones and internal bleeding, even though his own abilities were still diminished.

It's working, she thought, moving her left arm painlessly. *I benefited from Dras' experiences with Lothis and Maxar.* She'd had the nanites in her once before, to heal her from the calath plant poisoning, but Dras had taken them out. He'd said she didn't need them long-term and it might be dangerous to leave them in her system. Now, Dras knew they should stay, ready for any further injuries.

"They aren't integrated with your system like Maxar's," he'd warned, "so don't expect drastic increases in physical or mental abilities."

Lothis' eyes opened, shattering Felar's reverie. Her eyes darted to Wake, hoping beyond anything to see his chest rise and fall. It remained motionless.

When she turned back to her adopted son, Lothis was sitting up, shaking his head. "I'm sorry," he said, unable to meet her gaze. "I tried... I wasn't fast enough." He paused for a moment, looking dazed. "First Cazz-ak, now Wake."

Felar leaned over and threw her arms around him. Tears flowed down her cheeks again, and she felt herself falling into a pit of despair. "It wasn't your fault," she sobbed, her breath coming in painful gasps. "I know you did the best you could. We all did." *What do we do now?* she wondered, feeling like her whole world was being destroyed. *What do we do now?*

Lothis returned her desperate hug, and Felar let herself go. She cried and cried, embracing the rawness of grief and loss that bore her down. *We're all going to die,* she realized. *We're all going to the blackness.*

"He made it to the Dawn," Lothis said.

"What?" Felar asked, the intensity of her grief making it hard to comprehend the boy's words.

"Wake," Lothis answered. "He made it to the Dawn. That's why I was too late. I tried to stop him, to tell him his body could support life, but it didn't seem like he could hear me. He touched the cosmic flower and vanished."

The revelation brought a spark of joy to Felar, but it was a small thing in a vast plane of darkness. "Thank you for telling me," she choked out, wondering if her grief would ever abate.

"It's going to be OK," Lothis said finally. "I know it feels dark right now, but it will get better." He paused for a moment, seeming to consider his next words. "There's another team of us out there. As far as I can tell, they're still alive and pursuing their mission."

Something inside Felar shifted, and she felt the edge of her grief dull. "Another team of us out there," she repeated, the words focusing her mind and enforcing the reality of the situation. "Yes. They will need our help." All of her training, in both lives, felt like it was for this very day. *The day we end this millennia-long war, the day we stop the Breakers forever.* She squeezed Lothis even harder and released him.

"We have to find them," Felar said, wiping tears off her cheeks and standing with reviewed conviction. "Let's finish this!"

Both Dras and Lothis nodded. Now that Felar's vision wasn't clouded by tears, she could see the sentient machine actually looked shaken.

"How do we find them?" he asked. "With the damage my ship sustained, I do not feel I can accurately search for an individual ship amongst the chaos of battle."

Felar looked to Lothis. "Can you find them?"

"I'll try." The boy closed his eyes for a minute, before opening them again and shaking his head. "I'm having a problem similar to Dras. There is just too much happening, too much energy swirling around. "I might get lucky and see them, if they move towards this side or one edge of the battle, but we could end up waiting for hours."

"We need to be more proactive," Felar agreed. She tried to think of a solution, but other than charging headlong into the fray, nothing occurred to her.

"The other team was going after Crasor," Dras said finally, head cocked. "If you cannot sense the brightness of our friends amongst the darkness, then perhaps you can find the most intense darkness, and that will lead us to them."

"Brilliant," Lothis said, nodding and shutting his eyes. Time passed, and Felar remained silent, waiting. Seeing Wake's body out of the corner of her eye threatened to send her back to despair, but she held onto the dedication to her mission, something that had gotten her through many hard times in the past.

"Odd," Lothis said, voice inside Felar's mind. "I found the blackest energy, but it is different from Crasor. Bigger, stronger."

His words sent a tingle down Felar's spine. *What could be darker than Crasor?* she wondered, a sense of foreboding washing over her. When Lothis opened his eyes, he too looked afraid.

"The darkness I found," he said, voice quiet, "it isn't Crasor, but it feels like I've seen it before. I looked everywhere for him, but Crasor is gone."

"Familiar?" Felar asked. "Like one of the Descended?"

"No," he answered. "This entity is stronger and larger than Crasor. I think we can rule an underling out." He paused for a moment, and Felar could see fear, rather than thoughtfulness, was stopping him.

Finally, the boy continued. "It feels familiar because it is someone we knew before."

Felar realized what he was saying, and her own gut fell into a black hole. "See'dek?" she uttered, the name feeling like the most disgusting thing she'd ever said.

"Yes," Lothis replied, hands shaking. "See'dek is back."

45 – SEE'DEK

See'dek pushed through the transition, feeling his consciousness squeezed to a fraction of its normal size. *Should I be coming back to this feeble dimension?* he wondered. Returning to this plane had been part of the plan since before he'd found Crasor, but coming this early wasn't.

He was unstable, unreliable, See'dek thought. *Crasor gave up his humanity, but in the end, his lust for power was just too great. He wanted more control than he deserved.* See'dek felt the walls of the transition squeeze against him further. *What are the Faceless doing? They know what I need to create this bridge back to the origin plane. Why are they failing me?!*

Sending his oldest servants back to the realm of weakness had been necessary. See'dek needed them to create a special transition for his return. *Part of the issue with gaining power outside four-dimensional space,* he lamented, shoving his consciousness through the ever-shrinking pathway.

A moment later, See'dek burst into Crasor's body. A world of sight and sound confronted him. Being back in this dimension, the plane his Elrahi body had originated from, felt odd now. *I've existed for so long as a diffuse consciousness, as an entity too powerful to be contained in the weakness of temporal flesh,* he thought, pushing his new body up off the floor. He could feel the connection back to his dimension, back to his true existence and power.

Crasor's body was still feeble, at least by See'dek's standards, but it would have to do. Even now, See'dek was manipulating his nanites to begin the process of transformation. *Couldn't let him have too much power, now could I?*

Thinking of his former servant made See'dek wonder if any part of the man still existed. A moment of searching told him that the Faceless had done their job well. *Silence.*

179

Loud shots and yelling made See'dek realize he wasn't in the safe, protected area he'd instructed the Faceless to bring him to. Looking up, he saw two mangled corpses within arms reach. Their obliterated heads made it hard to know for sure, but the robes told him they were Faceless. The constricting pathway now made sense.

Experiencing the surrounding space felt odd to See'dek, more confined and limited than he'd remembered from his Elrahi body, even with its nanite enhancements. *This existence is too bland, but the energy and biomass available is too much to ignore.* He rose to his knees, feeling unsteady. *You can't expect instant integration.* Looking across the room, he saw a tall figure, clad in Ashamine ENS armor, battling two Faceless.

How have they not struck him down yet? See'dek wondered, swaying. As each second passed, he could feel more and more of the nanites networking with his consciousness. *Almost there,* he thought. He tried to turn his head to find the fifth and final Faceless, but he still didn't have direct control over that region of his body.

A Harbinger, See'dek realized, seeing the enemy wielding mind blades. *How did he get here? Why did Crasor let them get so close?* Rage boiled up within See'dek, and he was glad he'd obliterated the increasingly incompetent servant. *I'm left to deal with the aftermath.*

The Harbinger struck down one of his Faceless opponents. See'dek forced himself to his feet, the interface connection between his consciousness and the nanites still weak. *No time,* he thought, knowing that he was in a compromised position. *The loss of this body would be a catastrophic set back, even though it is still weak.* Having the remaining Faceless command his forces in this dimension was an unacceptable plan.

Still, despite the danger, he couldn't make his nanite network sync up any faster than before. The wretched Harbinger struck down his second opponent, using a spray of mind shards to perforate it. *And they have learned no new weaponry since they were pure Elrahi? Pathetic.* Before the Faceless could heal, the Harbinger used his mind blade to remove its head.

Even if it is weak mind weaponry, See'dek realized, *I'm next.* The thought brought no fear, only rage. *Come on,* he willed, forcing his consciousness through the nanite network.

A female scream resounded across the room, and See'dek found he could turn his head to look. He saw her. *Empress Aris,* See'dek spat, *I'd recognize your despicable existence anywhere, no matter what body or suit it resides in.* He hadn't seen the Empress in millennia, since she'd denied his rights and he'd been forced to defend them. *And now we meet again.* See'dek wished he wasn't in such a frail frame, that he could run over and rip out her heart, consuming her energy. *I will do the job this time,* he thought, *and no blighted Protector will save you.*

Taking in more of the situation, See'dek realized the remaining Faceless was standing over an old man, bringing a massive mind blade down. Just before it struck, an energy shield bloomed over him. The black blade collided with the barrier, the force sending out a massive concussion wave. Both weapon and shield exploded, fragments of bound space-time radiating outwards.

Don't underestimate them, See'dek thought, realizing he'd raised an arm to protect his face. *Even primitives can strike down gods if they become complacent.*

"You will not hurt my friends," the Empress screamed. See'dek felt a rising energy, different from anything he associated with her. It surrounded the Faceless, growing thicker by the moment. It flowed inwards, the interior becoming more and more confined. As See'dek watched, the barrier reached the Faceless.

His emissary tried to resist, but it was already too late. The ball of constraining power crushed the creature, bearing down on him until only a black liquid remained. The Empress finally let go of the warp, and what was left of his servant splashed across the deck. Aris fell to the floor, sobbing.

She always was a weak little pom, See'dek growled inwardly, *never able to stomach what needed to be done.*

He turned to see what the male Harbinger was doing, and they locked eyes. *Ahhhhh, Orsin,* he realized. *I never thought I'd have to see you again. How was it you became one of the Harbingers?*

"Tremmilly! Jaydon!" Orsin yelled, running over to them. "We don't have time for this. Crasor is back."

See'dek tried to access his throat, finding it was ready for use. "Where are the rest of your heroic band?" he asked, feeling an odd buzz permeate his voice. Despite the sound, it was serviceable. "Are they off pontificating somewhere about the evils of nanites? Perhaps locating some species that is discovering their power, and stripping it from them?"

Across the room, Aris had taken her helmet off and was wiping tears from her cheeks. The old man, Jaydon, was rising to his feet, looking unsteady. Orsin stood between See'dek and them, looking menacing as always.

"We are going to send you to blackness, Crasor," Orsin said, "and then we are going to find See'dek and do the same to him."

See'dek felt more and more of his nanite interface coming online. He flexed his consciousness, trying to draw power through his connection back to his primary being. *Too soon,* he thought, wincing as the transition walls constrained him. *Draw them out. You need more time.*

"I know this is going to sound insane," See'dek said, knowing he could exploit their weak wills, "but I'm finally free of the Breakers."

Orsin's eyes narrowed, but Aris looked intrigued. "They captured me on Noor-5, enslaved me to their will."

"Why are you lying, See'dek?" Aris said.

"That's him?" Orsin asked, raising his blades and moving forward.

"Maxar, wait," Aris replied.

So, Orsin, the Empress calls you Maxar now. The Elrahi he'd framed for killing an entire world, so he could convert their biomass to nanites, stopped, but kept his eyes trained on See'dek. *And she has a hold on you,* he thought, seeing the energy between them. *Predictable, and pathetic. You were always easy to manipulate.*

"If it's him," Orsin said, "we can kill him. We can end the entire war right now!"

"Maxar," Aris said, voice stern, "I need you to trust me."

Yes, See'dek thought, *trust her.* More and more power flowed into him, and he could feel the conduit back to his true self growing larger. See'dek sighed theatrically. "Do I call you Tremmilly now, Empress?"

"Call me whatever you like," she replied, "but know that this war ends today. The Elrahi will be made whole and the universe restored."

"While I applaud your optimism," he said, "no such thing will occur. It's too late. My people have established themselves back in this dimension." He shook his head, knowing they would listen to him, rather than striking. *She was always one to discuss things. Such an affinity for words.* "No, Aris, what you don't understand is, you've already lost. You and your religiously-inbred advisors were doomed the day you said no to my research. You forfeited the ascendancy, and now you see what it means, what true power and controlled evolution can provide."

Aris shook her head, frowning. "Foolish of me, to still think perhaps you might be willing to mend the division."

"Yes," See'dek sneered, feeling the nanite interface solidify completely. "You are, and always have been, a fool." The conduit expanded easily under his will, and he drew on all its power. *Not the same as being in my dimension, but it will be enough to deal with these two.*

"Please, See'dek—" Aris began, before he gagged her with a ball of dark energy.

"No, you blighted excuse for an empress," he growled, "I've thought about your obstruction for what feels like an eternity, and I will hear it no more."

Orsin jumped towards him, raising his swords, but See'dek quickly threw him back with a burst of dark power, sending him sliding across the floor. See'dek laughed, a sound that bubbled up from deep within.

"I'm going to take my time with you two," See'dek said, "and then I'm going to find the rest of you Harbinger traitors, and do the same to them."

46 – AZA

"Hold on!" Em yelled.

A huge impact shook the ship, making Aza feel like she would be thrown across the small bridge. For a moment, her head spun, and she saw bursts of light. *Am I going to black out?*

Aza opened her eyes to see the command terminal flashing an overwhelming number of warnings. "We're locked in on the rod," Em said, sounding as shaken as Aza felt. "Blightheart," she continued, silencing the alarms with a quick tap. "Remember to do exactly what I told you. Don't delay, or they'll be scraping us out of a crater in the Founder's City."

Aza nodded, feeling nervous. *You can do this. Focus!* The readouts on the display directly in front of her all showed green. "Ready."

"OK," Em said, stabbing her finger down on her own screen.

The ship emitted a groan of protest, and Aza watched one of the gauges change. "Engine up to first yellow bar," she announced.

Em slid her finger up on her screen and the ship shuddered.

"To last yellow bar," Aza said, feeling her anxiety increase. "First bar of red."

"We're OK," Em said, but Aza couldn't tell if she was trying to convince her or herself.

"Second bar of red!"

"Just one more."

The ship began to shriek, a sound Aza had never heard before.

She's pushing the impulse engines too far, she thought, watching her readouts. *Hopefully it's enough to nudge the rod off course.* "Third red bar," she announced, the pit in her stomach threatening to pull her in.

Em took her finger off the console, but kept her eyes trained on it. "Tell me when we hit the nav distance I told you. I have to keep an eye on fuel routing and status."

183

Aza turned her focus to the navigation screen, watching the distance to Ashamine-2 shrink rapidly. *We knew this would happen. We made calculations for it.* Aza couldn't help but wonder if their math had been accurate. *I still had years of equations to learn, and Em seemed shaky too.*

The red dot of their final escape point grew closer and closer. Aza glanced quickly back at the readouts, her heart jumping. "Structural stress now in the yellow," she yelled.

"It's part of the process," Em said, not turning. "The ship is being pushed, pulled, and strained in too many directions."

Aza fell silent, wondering if the older woman really understood how much the ship could take. *We are in it now. Guess we'll find out.* She kept her attention on the nav point on her screen, as Em had instructed. *If we go past it still connected to the rod, we slam into the surface right along with it.*

Another minute crawled by in shrieks and groans. They were almost to the final escape location.

"Hitting the nav point..." Aza said, watching the numbers count down. "Now!"

Em hit a large red option on her screen and Aza felt herself thrown into the restraint straps once again. Her vision began to blacken, narrowing to a point.

"Hold—on." Em grunted, straining to continue manipulating her control screen. "We—aren't—decelerating—fast—enough," she gasped, her words coming between constrained breaths. "Gravitic—dampers—doing—all —they—can—to—compensate—for—us."

Since it felt like there was a starship perched on her chest, Aza wondered how the other woman was speaking at all. The force on her body increased dramatically. *What would happen to us if the dampers fail? How long can we survive, even at this rate?*

"Structural. First—red," Aza wheezed, the effort making her already compromised consciousness feel even weaker.

"Bound—to—happen."

Moments passed, and Aza wondered if the horrible pressure would ever end. *Nobody said this was going to be easy,* she thought, trying to take short, quick breaths. Her vision cleared slightly. *You're saving all the Ashamine databases and the entirety of human knowledge. Toughen up!* Still as seconds ground past, she wondered if she would survive this effort.

"Not—going—to—make—it," Em gasped. "Rod—took—us—too—far."

Aza felt desperate and helpless. Her eyes shifted towards a newly-blinking readout. "Hull—temp—yellow," she said, realizing they were entering Ashamine-2's atmosphere.

184

"Bug—ger. Have—to—pull—out." Em struggled to select several options on the screen. "Gonna—hurt." She hit a final option, and Aza felt the gravity on her chest shift to sucking her down into her seat. For a moment, she could breathe easy, then the feeling intensified, becoming a force greater than she'd ever experienced before.

Out of the corner of her eye, she saw Em go limp, her arms forced down into her lap. "Em? Em?" she asked. No reply.

As Aza's vision began to fade, she saw the structural readout climb to crimson. Then, everything went black.

47 – TREMMILLY

Maxar leapt towards See'dek before Tremmilly could stop him. See'dek didn't flinch, easily throwing him back with a burst of dark power. Maxar slid across the floor, stopping next to her. Her old enemy laughed, a buzzing, guttural sound.

Tremmilly glanced at Maxar, wondering if he was OK. *Not moving.* When she looked back towards See'dek, she saw he was advancing towards them. *Think!* she screamed in her mind. She'd stopped Maxar from attacking their foe when he was obviously weak. *Why did I do that?* A deep intuition had compelled her, but now she wondered if it was simply See'dek's influence, his force coming through their shared link.

No, it can't be, she thought desperately, See'dek now just a few meters away. *That was me, from my knowledge, from my understanding.* Still, she didn't know how to handle the situation. *What do I do now?*

Before See'dek could reach her, Tremmilly took hold of space-time and tried to warp it around him, using the same technique she'd implemented against the faceless. Before the shield could complete, See'dek cast it off with the wave of a hand.

"You spent too long focused on your self-delusion, when you could have been growing stronger," See'dek sneered, shaking his head. He stopped directly in front of her, his stature looming. "You gave yourself to falsehoods, believing the Dawn was your savior." He grabbed Tremmilly's wrist, holding it before him. A cold developed there, moving from discomfort to pain. "Where is the Dawn now?"

"You're right," she said, trying not to show how much it hurt. "Technological enhancement wasn't evil, and the Dawn, while benevolent, isn't a god or even sentient."

See'dek's eyes narrowed, and he cocked his head slightly. "Lying won't save you, or your friends."

"I'm not lying," Tremmilly said, the void sensation traveling up her

186

arm. "I was wrong. We shouldn't have ended your research, shouldn't have turned you away. I created you, See'dek. I'm the one responsible for the Elrahi split."

See'dek laughed, the same buzzing, guttural sound as before. "You? Created me? Hardly." He shook his head, incredulous. "While I might actually believe you've seen the foolishness you perpetrated as empress, it matters little now. I created a species that far surpasses the Elrahi. Even if you hadn't sent all your ignorant followers to unite with the Dawn, I don't need them. Between humanity and the remains of the Entho-la-ah-mines, we have enough bio-mass to sustain ourselves in this dimension, to dominate it and spread to the reaches of the universe."

The drain continued through her shoulder, creeping into Tremmilly's chest. It felt like the light was being sucked out of her. *That's exactly what he is doing,* she thought, desperately trying to save herself. *He's too powerful for all of us. All I have are words, and those won't stop him.* Tremmilly looked down, seeing the skin of her arm turn black.

"What does killing us accomplish?" she asked, hoping against hope to find a way to stop him. As the words left her mouth, cold began creeping up her neck.

See'dek snorted. "Nothing. And everything. You stood in my way for so long, Empress. You slowed down my research, turned the Elrah against me. Even when I'd obviously won, you were still unwilling to capitulate. You denied me my right to lead the Accord and sent everyone to the Dawn so that I could never regain what was mine. Your journey to blackness will be a sweet consolation. I'll erase you, and you'll never find your impotent Dawn."

A movement at the edge of her vision surprised Tremmilly. *Jaydon,* she thought, realizing she'd forgotten about the old captain. He was moving carefully, keeping out of See'dek's line of sight.

We can't kill him, Tremmilly thought, still not understanding where the impulse came from. *But if Jaydon doesn't, I'll be dead soon.* The desire to live warred against intuition, but Tremmilly kept her mouth shut and her vision focused on See'dek.

With only a meter between them, Jaydon raised his flechette pistol. Somehow, See'dek finally sensed him and began whirling, a mind blade appearing in his other hand.

Tremmilly heard a crack as Jaydon triggered the weapon, even as See'dek drove the mind blade into his stomach. What was once Crasor's head vanished in a spray of black and See'dek's body crumpled to the floor. He dragged Tremmilly down with him, his hand still latched to her wrist.

"Tremmilly!" Jaydon yelled, falling to the floor. "Are you OK?" he asked between labored breaths.

"I'm so cold," she mumbled, barely able to breathe. Somehow, See'dek was still draining her, sucking out all her energy. "So cold."

Jaydon pulled himself over to her, one hand clamped over his stomach wound. "You're gonna be fine," he grunted. In her hazy vision, Tremmilly could see him trying to break her free from See'dek's grasp, could vaguely feel a tugging on the nerves leading to her void-filled arm.

"Buggering blightheart," the captain growled, shaking his hands. They looked dark in Tremmilly's vision, but so was everything else. Jaydon took a tool out of his suit's small storage compartment and began attacking See'dek's fingers again.

"There!" she heard, floating across the void that had become her existence.

Moments passed, and Tremmilly wondered if this was the end. Finally, though, she started seeing more clearly. The cold haze faded from her mind and bodily sensations returned. Suddenly, pain flooded through her. Tremmilly screamed, her body convulsing violently.

"You're gonna be OK," Jaydon kept repeating. During brief moments when she could open her eyes, Tremmilly saw the grizzled captain cradling her, trying to keep her from dashing her head on the deck. "You're gonna survive this."

Finally, when the pain diminished, Tremmilly realized their situation and looked around frantically, expecting to be attacked. "What happened to the other Breakers?"

"They all buggered off when See'dek hit the floor."

As Tremmilly's cognition returned to normal, she saw the blood covering both of them. Then, she remembered See'dek stabbing Jaydon. "We need to stop the bleeding." Sitting up, she pulled out a med-kit from her own storage compartment. "You need to get your combat suit off."

"No," Jaydon replied, shaking his head. "No time." He motioned towards where See'dek's head used to be. "He's gonna come back." Tremmilly followed his gesture and saw black pools forming beneath the shattered neck. Globs of what was once See'dek's head were creeping across the deck, forming larger and larger masses.

"You need to take Maxar and get off this ship," Jaydon continued. "I don't have powers, Trem, and I'm wounded. I'll only slow you down."

Tremmilly felt her heart freeze. "No, no. I can't."

"Maxar is still alive. He's breathing at least. Take him and go. Now!"

A part of Tremmilly wanted to do just that, wanted to take her love and run away, to hide from the monster she'd created. *You know that won't solve anything,* she thought. *See'dek will find you both, even if you manage to get away.*

"You, Maxar, and the rest of the Harbingers still have a chance to stop him," Jaydon gasped. "Don't throw that away on saving me."

"No," Tremmilly said, feeling her resolve stiffen. "I don't leave my friends to die." She began removing the locks securing Jaydon's combat suit. He continued protesting, but she ignored him. After it was off, she glanced back at See'dek's pooling head. The mass had grown, although it was still a puddle. *How long will it take for him to restore?*

"Bugger it," Jaydon said. "Just toss me a med-kit. Go help Maxar. I can patch myself up."

"OK," Tremmilly conceded, handing him the pack of supplies. She moved over to Maxar and confirmed he was breathing, although still unconscious. Tremmilly quickly inspected him, seeing no damage to his combat armor or visible signs of trauma. *Where are you, love?* she wondered. *I'll come find you.*

Turning to check on Jaydon, she saw the old captain was indeed patching himself up. "I need to go find Maxar, to bring him back. Will you be OK?"

"Yeah, yeah," he grunted, not turning to face her. "Go do what you gotta do. I'll be fine."

Tremmilly nodded and sat down next to Maxar's body. She reached out to the surrounding space-time, feeling her connection. She took a deep breath, sending her consciousness out.

48 – LOTHIS

First Cazz-ak, then Wake, Lothis thought, *and now See'dek has returned.* Losing yet another friend had cast him back into a pit of despair, but sensing their greatest foe had come back made Lothis want to collapse into himself. In every memory he had of the Elrahi politician and scientist, See'dek always felt powerful and evil. *He's had millennia to grow and strengthen himself, while we've been doing everything we can just to survive.* The odds of destroying Crasor had been long, but the chance of killing See'dek seemed impossible.

"Tremmilly, Maxar, and Jaydon were going after Crasor," Felar said, breaking into his thoughts. "I don't know how he came back to this dimension, but if Crasor is gone, and See'dek is here, our friends are likely fighting him."

Lothis didn't want to say what he was thinking, that the three of them might already be dead.

"Even if they aren't battling him yet," Felar continued, "what choice do we have, but to go fight See'dek ourselves?"

She's right, Lothis thought, trying not to look at what Felar was doing.

"Dras, do you have a place we can keep him?" she asked. "At least until we can do a proper ceremony?" Lothis took an involuntary glance and saw Wake's wrapped body.

"Of course," the Heltasoth said. "Let me help you." In the edge of his vision, Lothis saw them each take an end, and Dras led them from the command deck.

Lothis relished the brief time alone. He could feel the depression he'd fought off threatening to reassert itself. *I won't go back to that place again,* he resolved, trying to find positives to combat it. *I have Felar and Dras. I'm alive. As far as I know, Tremmilly, Jaydon and Maxar are as well.* It wasn't a long list, but it did lift his mood. *They are my family, and I will do everything I can to help them.*

190

An energy spike flared in his mind, emanating from See'dek's ship. Felar and Dras returned to the bridge, their burden gone. "They've found him," Lothis said.

"You're sure?" Felar asked.

"Yes."

"We have to get there as soon as possible." Felar turned to Dras. "Can you take us there?"

"The beam weapon strike on my ship, though small, did significant damage. I've repaired it as much as I can, but it will take several standard days or longer for me to produce the lost nanites." He was silent for a moment. "But yes, I do think I can get us there. It is much riskier than before, as I have diminished capabilities."

We barely survived the chaos flying through the battle the first time, Lothis thought, quickly appraising the continuing fleet combat. *Seems as bad as before, although there are significantly fewer ships.* The Breakers were still pounding away at the Ashamine fleet, and while the Ashamine remained outnumbered, the human vessels were still taking out enemy ships.

"Dras, I'm not asking you to sacrifice yourself," Felar said, voice hard. "But we need your help. If you feel it has grown too dangerous, I understand."

"I have come this far," the Heltasoth said. "This cause is worthy of sacrifice. I will do what I can to continue assisting you, Harbinger."

"Thank you, Dras," Felar replied, bowing. The sentient machine returned her courtesy. "Let's see how close we can get to See'dek's ship."

Dras nodded, and Lothis watched as he began piloting them through the debris field. It was slow going, dodging huge chunks of the Justice while smaller pieces bounced off the hull.

"What are we going to do when we get there?" Lothis asked, feeling his sense of dread deepen.

"We're going to kill See'dek," Felar replied, a determined look on her face. "Just like he killed Wake and Cazz-ak."

Lothis reached out with his mind, searching for their longtime enemy. See'dek was still where he'd been before, but his energy seemed frantically immobile. *Active, but not...* Lothis thought for several seconds, trying to figure it out. *He's on standby,* he decided finally, the word correct, but its implications unclear.

"See'dek changed somehow," Lothis said, "from when I first felt him."

"Did the other team take him out?" Felar asking, voice hopeful.

"No, nothing like that. He's evolving or developing. But those words aren't quite right. I keep thinking of 'standby', but I don't know how it applies."

"Keep checking," Felar said. "Let me know if and when it changes. It may not be much information, but it's all we've got right now."

Lothis nodded, lapsing into silence as Dras continued taking them through the Justice's debris field. After several minutes, they passed the edge and were in open space.

"I feel speed is our best option," Dras announced. "The identity spoofing device is undamaged, so we will be able to keep both sides from targeting us as we pass. I will do my best to compute which ships are moving into launch positions and remain outside their lines of fire." Lothis saw the speed indicator on the display start to climb, and a lump formed in his throat.

"It will not be easy," Dras continued. "My distributed computing was damaged, and I have not yet gotten it back to full capacity. I ask you not to communicate with me unless you absolutely need to. I will be placing my bodily awareness in a standby state. You can recall me by simply saying my name."

"Understood," Felar said. "If you find anything we can do to assist, let me know."

Dras nodded, then lowered himself down onto the floor. He assumed a rigid posture, legs crossed, back straight, and eyes closed.

Something about what Dras had said triggered a thought in Lothis' mind. *A standby state,* he considered, *in order to focus. Exactly what See'dek is doing. What could he be focusing on?*

As they entered the main mass of battling ships, Lothis tried not to let fear overwhelm him. Cascading rail round fusillades streaked across the void, battering the titanic ships. Hunks of disabled and destroyed vessels sped by, and Lothis knew there would be many bodies out there as well. Memories of floating in the blackness, desperate and alone, asserted themselves. *It won't happen again,* he thought, moving closer to Felar. *You're safe now.*

That's what you thought before, the dark voice replied. *It's exactly what your dead friends thought too.*

Lothis took Felar's hand, needing her touch. *I'm not going back to your negativity,* he growled. *It dishonors Cazz-ak and Wake. It is unproductive and disruptive.* He waited, expecting a reply. There was none.

"You OK?" Felar asked quietly.

"Yes," Lothis replied, leaning his head against her arm. "Being with you gives me strength."

49 – ASH

"Bring us in hard behind that Breaker cruiser," Ash yelled, feeling the ship shudder under yet another rail round strike. The sound bounced back harshly in his ears, an acute reminder he had his ENS helmet on. *It's a blighthearted good thing I do.*

The command bridge's atmosphere had been explosively vented into space, the result of several rail strikes compromising the nearby hull. *At least the bulkheads are holding atmosphere in the rest of the ship.* Another sector was also exposed to the void, but it was non-vital, and he'd ordered all surviving crew to evacuate.

"Fire all forward cannons once in position," Ash continued, this time letting the audio pickup inside his suit do the work.

"Yes, sir," both nav and weapons replied. Ash watched his ship's position change on the tactical readout, the surrounding fleet battle almost incomprehensible.

The Stellar Memory had barely survived the stealth fighter ambush, making it back to the Brotherhood fleet before they'd been pounded into oblivion. *Unfortunately,* Ash thought, *our situation has improved little since.*

After the loss of the Justice, the Breaker fleet had become disorganized and vulnerable. That disorientation hadn't lasted long, and now they seemed more coordinated and strategic than ever before.

What happened? What changed? Ash studied the display, trying to see if he could find an exploitable advantage. Everywhere he looked, the Breakers were utilizing superior maneuvering and positions.

How do they know I'm commanding the Brotherhood fleet? He had no way to tell for sure, but it felt like they were coming after the Memory specifically. *Could they have cracked the encrypted comms between me and the Ashamine commander?* That had to be it. He'd watched several of the largest remaining Breaker vessels go after his Ashamine counterpart, taking damage to their own ships in the process. *Now, he's dead, and I have no central figure to coordinate with for the Ashamine fleet.*

So far, Ash had gotten by with directly issuing orders to ships he thought could use it. A few captains had balked, but most were so overwhelmed and used to being told what to do that they were happy to oblige. The system was inefficient, but Ash had no other options. *Keep doing the best you can.*

Everything seemed to be going wrong, but Ash knew he couldn't despair. *Some of your maneuvers have even brought down a few of the larger Breaker ships.* It was little in the face of friendly losses, but it was something.

The Brotherhood fleet was still largely intact, thanks to strong teamwork and a robust chain of command. They'd lost ships, but they'd made the enemy pay dearly for every one.

We will keep fighting, until we defeat the Breakers or draw our last breath. He involuntarily looked down, checking to make sure the umbilical line still ran from the ship to his environmental nominizing suit. It was secure. *Even with a decompressed bridge and a battered ship, we will be breathing for some time yet.*

A flash of red tracers on the primary view screen caught his attention. His weapons officer had launched every forward-facing rail cannon. Now the rounds were streaking towards the Breaker ship. Between their speed and the nearness of the ship, he didn't have long to wait.

The barrage penetrated the enemy vessel's already-weakened point defense system and smashed into the hull. Light flared, only this time it was bright white.

Another Breaker ship destroyed, he thought, as his nav officer put them through evasive maneuvers to avoid the explosion.

What of Aza and Em? he thought, zooming and scrolling his display. Both the planet killer rod and Em's ship had vanished. *Just interference,* he tried to tell himself, *or a transponder malfunction.* Still, the logical part of his mind wasn't easily convinced.

Whatever they did, he thought, *I hope it was enough to save the Founder's City.* From this far away, he couldn't tell anything more than that a cloud of dust, ash, and debris was mushrooming out from the continent. *Looks blightheartedly close to the city's center,* he thought.

Returning the display to the area immediately surrounding the Memory, Ash chastised himself for losing focus. *This isn't the time, and whatever happened, it's over now. You did what you could. If Aza and Em are alive, there is no way you can help them at this moment. And if they aren't... There still isn't anything you can do.*

An alert popped up on his display, followed immediately by the voice of his sensor tech. "Fast, unidentified craft inbound."

Ash frowned. So far, every single vessel, at least the ones not stealthed, had ident transponders identifying them as either Breaker or Ashamine. All of his own fleet pinged as Brotherhood. "Put it up," he ordered.

On the primary view screen, a small black ship appeared, shattering any doubts Ash had about it possibly being one of his own with a damaged ident system.

"Vector is non-collision with us," the sensor tech added, "but it will pass nearby."

"Could be some kind of missile," the weapons officer said. "It's within range of rail cannon, but won't be for much longer. Should I launch?"

Ash watched the unidentified craft move closer and closer. It was unlike anything he'd ever seen, with graceful curves that sometimes appeared solid and others, liquid. *Whatever it is, no human made that.*

For a moment, Ash thought he was witnessing the deployment of a new Breaker weapon. He was ready to issue the command to launch, but something inside stopped him. *You don't know what it is, and if you can't confirm your target, you don't take the shot.* He wavered for a moment, undecided, knowing if he was wrong, he could be dooming his ship, as well as others, to obliteration. *Or you could be killing someone who is going to save humanity.*

"Hold!" Ash barked, raising a fist. "Do not launch."

Despite the perilousness of their situation amidst the battling fleets, Ash couldn't take his eyes off the beautiful, alien object. Neither could his crew. Everyone watched as it sped past, its purpose and mission unknown. *May the strength and wisdom of Azak-so guide you on your journey,* he thought, not understanding why he did.

"Breaker carrier inbound," the sensor tech announced, pulling Ash out of his awe. "Lining up to strike."

Ash turned to his tactical display and began issuing orders, wondering how long he could survive.

50 – MAXAR

"You won't defeat me!" Maxar yelled. "Not like this." Blackness surrounded him. No matter where he turned, he could sense nothing. His consciousness felt insubstantial, lacking any weight or consequence. His notion of time was gone as well. Either that, or this place had none. "Let me out of here!"

Complete silence answered. *How long have I been here?* he wondered, unable to feel his limbs. One moment, he'd been leaping towards See'dek, ready to sink his mind blades into the traitor's flesh, then everything had gone black. *Am I dead?*

I have to get back, have to protect Tremmilly. Knowing she would be defenseless against See'dek ratcheted up Maxar's panic even further. *Why didn't she let me kill him when we had the chance?* Maxar trusted her, but wondered if perhaps the stress of the situation had caused her to freeze. *I've left her and Jaydon alone with our deadliest enemy.*

Maxar tried to remember what Lothis had taught him about creating transitions. *You can get yourself out of here,* he thought, grasping at the surrounding space-time. But something was wrong. Each attempt, the fabric slipped out of his hands, resisting him. He tried over and over, but the surface felt oily, and he couldn't maintain his grip long enough to warp it.

"Buggering, blighthearted, burning Founder in the dark star!" he yelled, his frustration and anxiety exploding. Silence answered him.

He did it, Maxar thought. *See'dek won. He trapped me in this blighthearted cage, and now I'll never see Tremmilly again.* He felt like crying, but he had no eyes.

A brilliant ball of energy materialized before Maxar, dazzling him. "Maxar?!" Tremmilly said, her shape materializing as the energy coalesced. With her arrival, the surrounding space felt less constricting.

"Tremmilly!" Maxar said, moving his own form over to embrace hers.

196

"Did See'dek kill you? How did you find me?"

"No, no," she replied, "I'm alright. Jaydon stopped him, but it's only a delay. We don't have much time. I need you to do what I ask, Maxar. No questions." Her tone grew increasingly serious, sounding exactly like when she'd been empress. "You have to obey. No more surprise attacks. No more doing what you feel is best. I know what we need to do, but it would take an eternity to explain."

The deluge of information caught Maxar off guard, and he struggled to process it. "Yes, of course," he replied finally. "I'll do whatever you say. Just tell me."

"Good," she said. "I need you to life bond with me."

"What? If we're in a hurry, why would—"

"I said no questions," she interrupted, the commanding tone silencing Maxar. "It will be quicker and easier here than when we are back in our bodies. See'dek did us a favor, at least in that regard."

As Tremmilly spoke, Maxar tried to relax, to open himself up. As an Elrahi, the life bonding ceremony had lasted for days, the participants reveling in the love and affection they shared for each other. *Now, I have to do the same thing, only in seconds.*

"We have to rush," Tremmilly added, "but we can still enjoy this. It is our moment and will be, forever. I love you, Maxar, and always will. You are my person, my only love." Maxar felt her words wash over him like a refreshing rain, carrying away all of his confusion and anxiety. "When you proposed this bond," she continued, "I knew it was of the human variety. We've learned we have so much more to offer each other. We can unite our energy as Elrah. We've loved each other in two lives, as two different species, but we were always meant for each other. Now, we get to express that, to solidify it in the way of our ancestors."

Maxar moved towards Tremmilly, his attention now solely on her. "As you say, my love. I am yours, and you are mine. No matter the fate of our bodies, our energy will always be mingled. We will always be part of the universe, together."

He reached out, and they embraced. As they touched, he felt himself grow, his consciousness expanding. Maxar could sense Tremmilly, could feel her in a way he never had before. "I thought I knew you," he whispered.

"We are one, love," Tremmilly replied. Maxar mingled his joy and happiness with hers, the two amplifying each other until they were greater than the sum of their parts.

"I want to stay like this forever," Tremmilly said, "but we can't."

"I know," Maxar replied, feeling their combined mood shift to one of determination.

"We have to go back."

In the next instant, Maxar felt himself pulled along, drawn with Tremmilly as she moved through a dimensional transition.

Maxar's eyes burst open, and he sat up, trying to orient himself. He could feel Tremmilly nearby, but he didn't feel complete until he saw her. She smiled, and her joy continued radiating through their new bond.

See'dek's body lay on the deck, a quivering, black orb where his head used to be. Jaydon was sitting against one of the nearby command consoles, drenched in blood, an Ashamine-issue med-pack in his lap. A huge omni-dressing covered what Maxar guessed was a gut wound.

"Jaydon took his head off with a flechette," Tremmilly said, kneeling next to the injured captain. "But See'dek is healing himself."

"Why don't we finish the job?" Maxar asked. "Or just get the bugger out of here before he recovers?" Looking around the command deck, Maxar wondered where all the other Breakers went.

"Because," Tremmilly replied, "we can't kill him."

Jaydon spat towards See'dek's body. "I tried to say the same thing, but she wouldn't listen to me either."

"Can't kill him?" Maxar summoned mind blades, gritting his teeth.

"Calm," Tremmilly said, and he could feel the emotion radiating through the bond. "This is why I said you have to listen to me. We are now more susceptible to each other's emotions." Maxar let the blades go, feeling simultaneously calm and confused. "I still don't have time to explain why we can't kill him. It's too complicated, and I'm not sure I totally understand."

"If we can't kill him, and we can't run, what do we do?"

"We wait for him to reboot or restore himself, whatever he's doing. Then, I need you to bind him."

"Tremmilly," Maxar said, trying to keep himself calm, "he cast me off like a Founder's Commando would an Initiate. How am I supposed to bind him?"

"Our combined strength. The life bond will allow us to unite more strongly than we ever could have otherwise. I will lend you my power. Trust me, Maxar. We can do it."

Maxar nodded his head slowly. "It's good I can feel your confidence, because otherwise, I'd think you'd gone insane."

"Oh, this plan is crazy," she replied, completely serious, "but it is the only thing that has a chance of working against what is the single most powerful being in the universe."

The deck jolted underneath Maxar, and for a moment, he thought See'dek was attacking him.

"Ashamine figured out this ship has no commander," Jaydon said, pointing up to the primary display. On it, Maxar saw round after round streaking towards them.

"All the Breakers ran when Jaydon shot See'dek," Tremmilly added.

"Well," Jaydon replied, "if someone doesn't resume command operations, we aren't going to last long, even with all that armor plate." He chuckled, pulling himself up to his feet.

"What are you doing?" Tremmilly asked, putting an arm around him. "You're injured."

"Obviously. But we'll all be worse off if I don't start engaging the defense systems. Get me to the commander's chair." Tremmilly helped him shuffle across the floor.

Maxar had used the Ashamine omni-dressings before, when he'd been on Bloodsport. *They work wonders, but they frag me so hard I'm almost incoherent.*

"Can't say this will be my best work," Jaydon continued, "but I suppose I've done enough flying while drunk, that doing the same on stims and pain killers shouldn't be too hard." He began selecting options on the screen, and Maxar watched the point defense systems spool up. "I would say take as long as you need," Jaydon said, a loopy smile on his face, "but I'm not sure how long we got."

"When See'dek wakes up," Tremmilly said, coming to stand next to Maxar, "I need you to hold him, to keep him from fleeing back to his dimension. Once I start moving forward with the plan, he'll know what I'm trying to do. If he gets away, we'll never have another opportunity. See'dek will never make the mistake of coming back to this dimension."

Maxar took a deep breath. "Long odds. Difficult mission. Catastrophic results if we fail. Sounds perfect." He smiled, and he felt her confidence flow through the bond.

"I know we can do this, love," Tremmilly said.

"I hope you're right," Maxar replied, watching as See'dek's body began to shake.

51 – FELAR

"You're sure that's the ship?" Felar asked, pointing out of the transparent hull.

Lothis nodded, face somber.

"The Ashamine are doing their best to pound it into oblivion." Felar scowled.

"Why isn't the ship defending itself?" Dras asked.

"I have no idea," Felar said. "Maybe the other team disabled the defense systems." She noticed the ion tracers explode before they reached the Breaker vessel. "And now they're back." *But it isn't firing rail rounds. Curious.*

"It will be difficult for me to reach See'dek's ship," Dras said, "especially with the Ashamine fleet focusing on it."

"Let's see what we can to do fix that. Hold here, out of the launch vectors." Felar straightened up, mentally rehearsing what she needed to say. "Can you get me a comm to all the nearby ships?"

"Of course," Dras replied, gesturing when it was ready.

"To all Ashamine ships attacking the Breaker vessel identified as the Transfiguration: Be advised there are friendlies on board, engaged in a vital strike mission against the enemy. More units inbound as well. Please cease all hostile activity against the Transfiguration until friendlies are clear. We will notify you when that happens."

Silence greeted her. Several Ashamine ships ended their barrages.

"Who is this?" a hard voice came over her helmet speakers.

"This is 2nd Class Enlightened Felar Haltro, of the Founder's Commandos. Who's this?" A few more ships focused their weapons on other targets, and Felar began to breathe easier.

"How do we know you aren't lying?" the voice asked. "How do we know this isn't some Breaker trap? I've not heard of any Founder's Commandos up here. Easy to steal valor when there is no way to confirm."

"Do you have your blighthearted little finger plugged into the command line of this operation?" Felar growled, using her best voice from her Initiate training days. "Stand down. Cease launch. And pray to the Founder I don't find out who you are."

The voice remained silent, and for a moment, Felar wondered if she'd pushed it too far.

"They're all pulling off the Transfiguration," Lothis said. "Nicely done."

Still got it, Felar thought, smiling. "Dras, can you get us in now?"

"As long as the Transfiguration's point defenses see us as friendly, we should be able to board shortly."

"Good. Hopefully we aren't too late."

As Dras resumed their course towards the Transfiguration, Felar wondered what they would find when they got there. *Lothis says See'dek is on standby and Maxar and Tremmilly are hard to distinguish. What does that mean? Why aren't they destroying him while they have the chance?*

"I have an incoming encrypted comms request," Dras announced. "It's originating from a ship identifying itself as the Stellar Memory. The ident is neither Ashamine nor Breaker."

Felar's brow furrowed. "Put it through."

A moment later, a voice emanated from her helmet speakers again. "Are you really a Founder's Commando?" It was calm, and although it asked a question, it felt genuine, rather than a challenge.

"Yes," Felar answered. "As I said, I'm a 2nd Class Enlightened."

"What is your mission aboard the Transfiguration?"

Felar took a deep breath, trying to decide how to handle this questioner. "I've told you who I am. Would you do me the honor of telling me who you are? Seems only fair."

"Of course," the voice replied. "I'm Parick Olvold, leader of the Brotherhood of Azak-so. In another life, I was Ash Kissawai, a member of the Ashamine Holy Order."

The name sounded familiar to Felar, and she remembered Wake telling her about his time with the Brotherhood. "I've heard of you," she replied. "Weren't you and all your people wiped out on Eishon-2?"

"That was indeed a great blow to our organization, but we fight on." He was silent for a moment. "Were you involved in that mission?"

"No," Felar replied, understanding why he might think so. "Despite my earlier declarations, I wasn't on the Ashamine side that day. To be completely honest, I'm a former Commando. I fled my post before the Eishon-2 battle."

"Would you mind telling me what's going on with the

Transfiguration?" Parick asked. "Why you have strike teams on board?"

"There is too much to explain it all right now," Felar replied, "but our friends are trying to take out the Breaker leader."

"He's on the Transfiguration?"

"Yes, but something is wrong. That's why we are going in."

"As a Founder's Commando," Parick replied, "former or otherwise, you have to understand the temptation to just obliterate the entire ship. I feel your desire to preserve them, but the loss of a few friends is a small price to eliminate the Breaker commander."

"As I said," Felar shot back, anger building, "there is more to this situation than you can comprehend."

"Oh? And you expect me to take your word? Why should I not just obliterate that ship and bring an end to this war immediately?"

"Because," Felar said, desperately trying to come up with a believable reason, "it's not like a snake where you can just cut its head off and kill the whole thing. It requires more: More tactics, more direct methods. Wiping out the leader won't stop the whole species."

Parick was silent, and for a moment, Felar wondered if he'd ended the connection. "I don't know why," he said finally, "but I believe you. I'll keep my fleet and any Ashamine ships away from the Transfiguration, but you have to promise me if the situation changes, or if the Breaker leader escapes, you'll notify me as soon as possible."

"Of course," Felar replied. "Thank you, Parick."

"I hope my trust isn't foolishly placed."

Dras signaled the comms link had ended.

"I hate to say it," Lothis said, looking troubled, "but he is probably right."

"I know," Felar replied, "Especially since the Transfiguration was having so much trouble defending itself. It would have been an easy strike. But we can't let the rest of the Harbingers die."

"Jaydon is hailing us," Dras interjected.

A moment later, Felar heard the old captain's voice. "Felar? Felar?" he sounded frantic. "Buggering blighthearted Ashamine systems."

"Jaydon!" she answered. "I can hear you."

"Finally. Been trying to contact you ever since I heard you call off the fleet."

"Where are you? What's happening? Where's Tremmilly and Maxar?"

"They're battling Crasor, See'dek, whoever he is now. After I made some defensive adjustments to the ship, they told me to bugger off the bridge." A stifled moan followed his last word.

"Are you OK?"

"That blighthearted See'dek put a blade into my stomach, but otherwise, I'm fine. Stimmed up beyond reckoning, but that's OK too."

Omni-dressing, Felar thought. "Well, we are on our way. Should be docking soon."

"Good," Jaydon replied. "Your way to the bridge should be easy. Don't know how long it will last, but when I shot See'dek's head off, all the other Breakers went into some kind of shock."

"Wait, what?" Felar asked, wondering if perhaps the drugs in the omni-dressing were messing with Jaydon's perception. "He survived that?"

"Yep. Took him awhile to put himself back together, but he was getting up when I got out of there."

Felar looked at Lothis, and they exchanged a knowing look. *On standby,* she thought, the fragments of information fitting together.

"Tremmilly told Maxar they couldn't just destroy his body," Jaydon continued, "that they had to do more."

"So then what is she planning?"

"I don't know, I had to leave before I saw what they were doing. If it had something to do with dimensions or consciousness or something, it wasn't like I could tell what was happening, even if I'd stuck around."

"There's the Retribution," Dras said, motioning towards the other Harbinger ship. It was fastened to the Transfiguration's hull, next to an airlock. "I'll land there."

"We're almost to you," Felar said, feeling her anxiety rise. As the Heltasoth ship came in to land, she tried to reach out to Tremmilly, to lend her Elrahi strength. No matter what she did, Felar couldn't find a path to her friend. Everything felt clogged and occluded. *See'dek's power...* Felar thought, biting her lip. *I hope Tremmilly knows what she's doing. Because if not, we may have just wasted the best opportunity we'll ever have to destroy him.*

52 – SEE'DEK

See'dek pushed more of his power through the conduit, drawing the shattered network of his physical mind back together. Rage consumed him. *How did that blighted human get so close?* He still felt joy in the knowledge he'd gutted the old, pathetic man.

At first, See'dek had expected the Harbingers to obliterate the rest of his body, for his connection to standard space-time to vanish. For whatever reason, they had left his physical form intact.

Orsin was the only one left who had the strength to do it, he thought, *and since I sent him to a folded dimension, he'll never find the exit. The Empress' weakness has shown once again.* He could feel the network of nanites had almost rebuilt itself. *Just a little longer. Then I can resume my fun with her.*

A moment later, See'dek opened his physical eyes, seeing the Transfiguration's command deck around him. He got to his feet, the last few bits of networking filling in. Orsin and Aris stood before him, their faces inscrutable.

"So, love has once again buggered your better judgment," See'dek mocked, shaking his restored head. "You found your way out of the dimensional prison. How impressive."

"Are you ready?" Aris asked. Orsin nodded.

"You had your chance," See'dek said, drawing all the power he could through the conduit leading back to his primary existence. "Your old man bought you a momentary advantage with his death, and you wasted it. Now, I will make you both suffer."

See'dek shot out tendrils of dark energy, attempting to bind the Harbingers. But midway across the intervening distance, the fingers struck a shield. See'dek pushed harder and harder, grimacing with the effort. "You will know what true pain is!"

Given the strength he'd seen them display before, See'dek expected Aris and Orsin to collapse under his pressure. Still, they held his attack away. Through the arcing bursts spraying out from the conflicting energies, he could see their faces, full of effort, but lacking fear.

Something has changed, See'dek realized. *Something happened while I was gone.* The two Harbingers felt different somehow. Then, he realized what they'd done.

"You think a life bond will be enough to save you?" he taunted, releasing his tendrils. "You think a pathetic ceremony from a bygone era will stop me?" See'dek summoned a massive mind blade and strode forward, raising the dark, curved weapon above his head. "I've had hundreds of thousands of years to build my power, to study the ways of the universe." He brought the blade down, striking the shield. "I have billions of servants, from all species and epochs." The shield rang with his blow, sending a reverberation cascading outwards.

Fear, See'dek thought, seeing it on the faces of his opponents. *They are beginning to understand what they have done in resisting me.* He raised the blade again, adding even more mass to it.

"Do you see?" Aris asked quietly.

"Yes," Orsin replied.

See'dek brought the blade down again, and this time it shattered the shield, shards of energy exploding across the bridge. "Greet the blackness, you pathetic blights!" he said, raising his weapon a third time.

"Go! Now!" Aris yelled. "I will give you everything I can."

See'dek tried to bring the blade down, to silence the Empress forever, but he couldn't. He looked to the Harbingers, to see if they had some energy binding him, but there was nothing. Both of their faces were slack, their bodies motionless.

See'dek felt a tremor in his nanite network. *Something is wrong,* he thought, the paralysis spreading. He tried to pull more power through his conduit, but it felt constrained. *What are they doing?*

Panic rose within See'dek, an alien feeling, but he cast it off. *Even if they destroy this body, I will still be unharmed. My true power, the center of my being, is untouchable. It is far more than the Harbingers can ever handle, even if they manage to get to my dimension somehow.*

Releasing his sword, See'dek sent a burst of power through his nanite network. He roared with anger, pulling on everything he could muster through the diminished conduit. *Get off me!*

For a moment, he felt the constraint lessen, but then it rushed back, constricting his conduit down to a fraction of its normal size. *Blight you both,* he thought, deciding to try a new tactic. *Bind all you want, but you cannot stop me.*

Scouring Crasor's body, See'dek pulled together his remaining energy. He withdrew from the physical form and cast his consciousness out. *I will find you, Harbingers, and I will make you wish you'd fled to the Dawn long ago.*

53 – AZA

Aza coughed, the feeling sending a jolt of pain through her chest. She opened her eyes, wondering where she was. Everything was dark.

She tried to feel around her, to get a sense of her surroundings. *I'm still in the ship, still strapped into the chair.* Aza fumbled with her suit for a moment, trying to remember how it operated. Once she finally toggled her suit's illumination points, she got a view of the bridge.

"Em?" she coughed, seeing the other woman in the chair next to her. Speaking made Aza wince. Even breathing hurt. *Something is wrong inside me.*

"Yeah," the other woman finally replied. "I'm here. You OK?"

"I'm beat up, and I think I might have a broken rib or something."

"Yeah, I'm not feeling too good either."

"Where are we?" Aza asked, wondering why all the readouts and screens were dark. "The ship, I mean."

"Hopefully in a stable orbit." Em toggled her own suit's illumination and began removing the seat restraints. "Because if not, we might be in for more blightheart than we've already experienced."

Aza wanted to ask for more explanation, but talking hurt too much, and she figured she'd find out soon anyway.

"I'm surprised we survived that many Gs," Em continued, tapping on a few different screens halfheartedly. "I put the commands in, but I never thought we'd wake up again." It was then that Aza realized Em was floating and that she felt very little gravity on her own body. "You might as well come with me," Em said, pushing off towards the command bridge door. "There's nothing you can do up here, and if I'm right, it would be easier for you to see what happened than for me to explain it."

"OK," Aza replied, carefully undoing her seat restraints. Each movement sent a jolt of pain through her, but she tried to ignore them. *If Em can do it, so can I.*

When she was done, Aza got out of the chair and began pulling herself across the small bridge. She did not have Em's confident weightlessness. With her injuries, it seemed wise to be careful.

When Aza finally reached the door, Em was already cranking the manual release mechanism. The door crept farther open with each rotation. Aza's stomach sank as she realized she could see stars through the widening gap.

After a few more seconds of work, the door was fully open. "Just as I thought," Em said, sighing. "Whole ship sheered in two." Aza could see the other half, battered and floating in the void a hundred meters or so past the ragged edge of the adjoining room. "Took too much force to keep us from slamming into the surface. But hey," Em continued, "at least we're alive."

"We have no atmosphere, no power, no way to move." Aza felt her anxiety increase, but she managed to control it.

"Good summary," Em replied. "I think you covered everything. At least we're alive, which is more than I figured we would be when we were hurtling along on that rod. And we are in an orbit that looks reasonably stable. Without a computer, I can't say for sure, but it seems like we have at least a little while yet."

"A little while for what?"

"To get rescued." Em bit her lip, shaking her head slightly. "But I guess we can't rely on Ash knowing we would disobey his orders."

"Then who will find us?" Aza tried to keep herself from crying, but warm tears ran down her cheeks anyway. *Stupid suit,* she thought, realizing there was no way to wipe them away. Em put her arm around Aza, and despite her embarrassment, she felt comforted. "I'm sorry."

"No need to apologize," the older woman replied. "I understand. It's a grim situation, and one we will have to work hard to get ourselves out of." She turned them to face the door. "We have to get to the other half."

Aza didn't understand why, but she trusted Em.

"The comms transmitter is on the back portion of the ship," the older woman continued. "It's also where the generator is. If neither are too damaged, we can probably rig something up and use a portable terminal to transmit a distress message. Worst case, if none of that works, we can activate the emergency beacon, alerting anyone and everyone who is listening." Em seemed to be thinking out loud. "Breakers finding us may be worse than the current situation. It wouldn't take too much effort to finish the job."

"Our suits don't have zero-G thrusters," Aza said. "We'll have to jump?"

"We line up and push off, nice and easy. Float our way over."

Despite her fear, a small part of Aza felt excitement at the prospect. *I can do this,* she told herself, eyeing the distance to the other half. "I can do this," she repeated. "Let's go, before I change my mind."

Aza could see the other woman's smile through her helmet's faceplate. "You'll be fine."

Em pushed off back to her chair and unhooked her personal terminal from its storage location. "Looks like it survived," she said, making a few selections on the glowing screen.

She then pulled herself across the deck, leading Aza through the door and to the ragged edge beyond. Aza felt her stomach drop, understanding what she was about to do. "We'll push off from here," Em said, finding a bulkhead support that was properly positioned. "We can hold hands, go together."

"I'd like that," Aza said, voice barely above a whisper.

"Not too hard," Em replied. "We don't want to smash into the hull. We need to be going slow enough to grab something."

Aza took a deep breath. *This is the way to salvation,* she thought. *You chose this path when you pushed Em into going after the rod. You could have been safe, in another star system, but you decided to do what you could for your people.* She took another deep breath, then nodded. "I'm ready."

"OK," Em said. She took Aza's gloved hand, which further comforted her. "Three... Two... One... Now!"

Aza pushed off the upright, feeling the slight acceleration in her damaged chest. *Don't you close your eyes,* she demanded, watching as Ashamine-2 filled the view above her. Looking out into space, she saw the fleet battle still raging, ion paths creating lines between exploding ships.

As they floated between the halves, Aza tried to see beauty through her fear and queasiness, to enjoy the novelty of the situation. A full minute crept by, and she felt like she was almost successful. When Aza looked back, she realized they were past midway. *We're going to make it,* she thought.

"You're doing great," Em reassured, keeping her eyes focused on the other part of her ship. Aza turned her own attention back towards their target, watching it grow larger and larger. "Don't let go of me," Em continued. "I'll secure us to the ship when we get there. You just worry about staying connected to me."

"Will do," Aza said, throat feeling dry. The wrecked ship loomed large in her vision, moving fast.

"Hold on!" Em yelled.

At the last moment, Aza couldn't help but close her eyes. She focused all her attention on squeezing Em's hand. An overwhelming cascade of pain crashed over her as they slammed into the hull. After a moment of shallow breathing and fear, Aza opened her eyes.

"We made it," Em grinned. Aza had expected to be outside the ship, but the other woman's aim had been precise, and they were inside the hull.

"Th—thank you," Aza stammered.

"Of course. Lock your boots to the floor so you don't accidentally float away before we get through the door. You're not looking too steady."

Aza did as commanded, using her HUD to activate her boots' mag-lock system. Despite still being near the edge of oblivion, it felt good to have a real connection.

"Now," Em said, walking towards the ship's interior, "let's go see if we can send Ash a message."

54 – TREMMILLY

Tremmilly felt a surge of dark energy burst through See'dek's dimensional connection. For a moment, she wondered if she would be consumed. Maxar bore down, crushing the conduit to a fraction of its former size, the edges of the warp distorting under his pressure.

"I don't understand what we are trying to do," he said, the form of his consciousness wavering from the effort of restraining See'dek.

Tremmilly wanted to tell him what she had to do. *But he'd never let me,* she thought, being careful not to let it slip through the bond. *He'd rather the whole Akked fall to the Breakers.*

"I know," she answered, "but you have to trust me. Everything will make sense soon. Don't let him slip back to the Breaker dimension."

"OK," Maxar gasped. "I think, right now, we need to worry more about him obliterating us."

"He's moving," Tremmilly said, feeling See'dek's energy and attention shift. "He's coming here in raw form. Be strong, my love."

As she finished speaking, See'dek's consciousness materialized before them, connected back to the conduit spanning the dimensions. He lacked the humanoid form Tremmilly's and Maxar's energy took, appearing instead as a swirling ball of darkness. Two purple orbs glowed in its depths, menacing.

"Bind his consciousness, Maxar!" Tremmilly yelled. "I'll keep restricting the conduit." The blackness moved forward, and she knew if it absorbed her, See'dek would obliterate her mind.

Before it could reach Tremmilly, Maxar slammed into the shape, his whole form attempting to contain it. Tremmilly bore down on the conduit, applying all the force she could before See'dek could draw additional energy.

"Do you think you can contain me?" he boomed, his voice sounding like it came from a million inhuman creatures. "Do you think you can put me in a prison?" Dark energy lanced out of the swirling darkness, transfixing Maxar. He screamed, the sound conveying more agony than Tremmilly thought possible. Still, Maxar restrained the ball.

You have to do it, Tremmilly thought. *You have to do it now! If either of them finds out what you are doing, it will be too late. This is the only way.*

Maxar let out another scream, and Tremmilly saw bits of his consciousness evaporate as the dark energy shot through him. *The longer you wait, the more pain he suffers. Do it!*

Tremmilly reached out, creating a small transition back to the place her consciousness had created, the space connecting her to both the Dawn and the Breakers.

I am the one, she thought. *I am the bridge.* She felt her mind begin to fracture, the strain of working in so many dimensions greater than she'd ever experienced before. *I am the origin of this imbalance, and I will be its healer.*

Reaching out to the pathway leading to the Dawn, Tremmilly summoned it, feeling the cosmic flower grow near. With See'dek and his conduit so close, it took little effort to link to the Breakers.

"What are you doing?" the Breaker roared. The darkness flared, struggling to escape Maxar's grasp.

Goodbye, love, Tremmilly thought, severing her life bond with Maxar. *I do this for you.*

In the next instant, she simultaneously sent pieces of her consciousness into both the Dawn and the Breakers, fully bonding with the two. The most exquisite light and deepest blackness filled her. They met and mingled, both energies trying to exterminate the other. Despite the violence, she held on, knowing she had to in order to create a self-sustaining reaction.

Tremmilly's consciousness fractured, small pieces swept away as the light and the darkness equalized and obliterated each other. She focused even harder, wanting to hold the connection as long as possible. A catastrophic rushing grew in her mind, feeling like every thought, feeling, emotion, and experience was playing back at the same time. The Dawn's light captivated and enraptured her, while the corruption of the Breakers summoned intense filth and pollution. The huge rush of sensations exploded within her, nearly obliterating Tremmilly.

Hold on! she thought, knowing she couldn't give up yet. She tried to ignore the joy and the pain both, to keep her mind completely focused on maintaining the link between the energy sources.

Finally, Tremmilly knew it was enough. The reaction had created a sustaining transition of its own, larger than she ever could have. *I've done it,* she thought, allowing the elemental forces to sweep her away.

55 – LOTHIS

Climbing out of the airlock and into the Transfiguration, Lothis felt his sense of dread deepen. *Be calm,* he thought, watching as Felar took point. *Your friends depend on it.*

"Which way?" Felar asked. Lothis pointed right. "That's what I thought," she replied. "We're getting close enough even my weak Elrahi senses are working."

Lothis stepped behind Felar as she headed down the hall. The area seemed deserted, an eerie situation making him feel more nervous. The audio pickups in his suit magnified Dras' footsteps behind him, the Heltasoth's presence bringing comfort.

Felar had told the sentient machine he could stay on his ship, but Dras repeated his earlier statements about seeing the battle through to the end. Lothis could tell Felar wanted him along, but she wouldn't admit it.

After winding through several corridors, Lothis could feel the other Harbingers even more strongly. When they entered a rail cannon loading area, he forgot about them.

Standing before them were at least twenty Breakers, all frozen in the act of operating their respective pieces of equipment. "What's happened to them?" Felar asked in a quiet voice.

"I don't know," Lothis replied. "But this could explain what Jaydon was talking about."

"How do we know they aren't going to wake up and ambush us?"

"We don't. I think we just have to keep moving forward and deal with what we find."

Felar shook her head, and Lothis knew she was hesitant to leave such easy targets. A flare of energy caught his attention, the power escalating rapidly. "Tremmilly!"

"What is she doing?" Felar started weaving through the still Breakers.

"I don't know," Lothis replied, trying to follow her as quickly as

212

possible. The flare climbed to an even greater magnitude, feeling like a thousand stars being born every second. "I've never seen anything like it." Lothis tried to understand the phenomenon, to figure out what could cause such massive, continuous power output. *Can't be good,* he thought, wondering if See'dek was torturing his sister.

Once they cleared the loading room, Felar began running, seeming oblivious of potential threats. "We have to get to her," she cried. "We have to save her!"

A minute passed, with only their heavy breathing and footsteps to break the silence. *We're getting close,* Lothis thought, the intensity of Tremmilly's energy making him wince. *We're coming, sister.*

Movement ahead caught Lothis' attention. Before he could say anything, a figure burst out of a side door. Felar, unable to stop in time, slammed into it, and they both tumbled to the floor. There was a brief scuffle, then Felar came out on top, her weapon pressed against the figure's forehead.

"Jaydon?" Lothis said.

"Buggering blightheart," he replied, eyes wide. "Can you get that thing out of my face?"

Felar shook herself and got off him. "Yeah, sorry," she added, helping him up.

"Saw you on the personnel tracking system," he said, carefully leaning over to pick up his flechette pistol from the floor. "Made my way over to meet up. Didn't mean to make the timing quite so perfect." As he spoke, Jaydon held his stomach, grimacing with each breath.

"Something is wrong with Tremmilly," Lothis said.

"I figured it would be," the old captain rasped, a concerned look on his face. "She was so closed off about her plan. Not like her. I don't think she even told Maxar."

"We have to go and help her," Felar barked. "We can talk later."

"Of course." Jaydon fell into line between Lothis and Dras.

The group began running once again. Lothis wondered if there was any way Tremmilly could survive the magnitude of energy raging around her.

56 – ASH

"What's happening?" Ash mumbled, eyes narrowed. On the tactical display, the Breaker fleet had descended into chaos. He tried to see a pattern, to understand why some of their ships were wandering away from the battle, while others were launching huge barrages of rail rounds into empty space.

Could it be a trap? A trick? The longer Ash watched, the more convinced he was that the Breakers were experiencing some kind of critical failure. He wanted to stand up, to pace around the command deck while he thought, but detaching himself from the atmosphere supply line was too much hassle.

The ex-Founder's Commando, he thought, remembering his conversation with Felar. She'd said killing the Breaker leader wouldn't destroy the whole species, but perhaps they'd succeeded and now he was seeing the results. *We don't have time to waste. They could reorganize or find a new leader at any moment.*

"Comms," he said, "open a broadcast to all friendly ships."

After a moment, the comms officer nodded. "Ready, sir."

Ash took a deep breath, then forged ahead. "All human vessels, this is Parick Olvold, commander of the Brotherhood fleet. As you can all see, the enemy forces are experiencing a catastrophic breakdown.

"I know some of you are wounded and barely limping through space. My own ship is in a similar condition. Muster everything you have to obliterate the Breaker fleet before it can recover. We have no idea how long this opportunity will last, so seize this moment, and blast those buggering blighthearts back to the darkness they came from."

On the primary comms display, the status icons next to all the Brotherhood ships flashed green, acknowledging receipt of orders. Below them, the Ashamine ships also started indicating they would follow his command. *And the few that aren't? Disabled comms or perhaps they've*

214

lost too many crew members to continue.

Then, Ash remembered the strike force on the Transfiguration. *Have they gotten clear yet?* For a moment, he considered leaving things the way they were, of not continuing his protection of the enemy flagship. *I gave my word,* he decided. *I can't let them be killed by allied ships.*

Before the comms officer could close the broadcast, Ash continued. "I believe we owe this monumental opportunity to a strike team that ventured onto the Transfiguration, deep in enemy terrain, attempting to take out the Breaker commander. As such, do not instigate hostile action on that ship until we can confirm the team is clear." Ash knew his own fleet would listen, but the Ashamine vessels were out of his direct control. *Hopefully they will continue to obey.*

On the tactical display, he watched as friendly ships maneuvered into superior positions and began raining rail cannon rounds into enemy vessels. Ash felt a smile grow on his face, and some of his tension relaxed. It was the first time he'd experienced any real confidence or hope since the battle began.

"Take us after the Valiant," he said, picking a ship that was near the Transfiguration. The location would also allow him to protect the strike team while they exfiltrated. *It seems as good a target as any.*

As the crew sprang to life, Ash zoomed in on the image of the enemy vessel. The ship was one of the Ashamine's Rubicon class ships, a fairly even match for the Stellar Memory, at least before all the damage it received.

"One more push," he told the ship under his breath, hoping it would survive. The engineering team was doing its best to keep the vital parts going, despite the massive damage the Breaker fighters had inflicted. "One more foray, then you can rest."

"Nearing accurate weapons range," the weapons officer announced.

"Full—" Ash started saying, but was cut off as a blackness welled up in his mind, swallowing his vision.

"We can give you power," a voice screeched. A ball of glitchy chaos swirled before him. "The Ashamine could be yours." Ash felt his stomach churn. "Protect us, and we will give you control of all humanity."

Bugger you! he replied, trying to fight off the overwhelming oppression. *I will give my last breath to defeat you, whoever and wherever you are.* He looked around desperately for an escape, but the static laced ball became all he could see.

"So be it!" the voice hissed. "Spend your last breath in futility." The ball flicked wildly, and the oppressive weight increased. Ash felt himself compressed into a tiny speck. Visions of Aza's and Em's mutilated bodies flashed through his consciousness. Pain exploded through him, like every physical and emotional trauma he'd ever experienced was visited on him again.

Still, the weight bore down, threatening to obliterate him. *I will not let you do this to me!* he cried, fighting to stay calm. Ash felt powerless to resist. Grotesque images of dead loved ones continued flicking through his mind, an endless stream of gore and agony. The surrounding pressure compressed him even further. Another moment passed, and Ash knew this was the end.

"Sir? Sir?!" he heard, feeling himself rush back into reality. On the screen before him, he saw an expanding ball of white light, calmer than the glitchy one filling his mind just seconds before. "Sir, our second barrage destroyed the Valiant. What is your next order?"

Ash shook his head, wondering what he'd just experienced. *A hallucination? A vision?* The onset and duration seemed too coincidental to not be connected to the Valiant. *Whatever caused it, I hope they're dead.* Around him, the deck was silent, waiting for his command.

Everything within him wanted to go search for Aza and Em, but he knew he needed to finish the Breaker fleet first. *Blighthearted obligation to duty,* he thought, panning and zooming on the tactical display.

"Sensor," he barked, "find me nearby enemy ships currently unengaged. Prioritize minimally or undamaged vessels, and order them by proximity."

As the list began flooding into his personal screen, Ash shivered. *I hope we don't run into any more of whatever was on the Valiant,* he thought. He scanned the list, but part of his mind wondered just how close he'd been to death, or worse.

What if all those images of Aza and Em were real? Ash thought, before he could suppress it.

57 – MAXAR

Dark energy lanced through Maxar's being, threatening to overwhelm him. He embraced the agony, knowing he couldn't let See'dek go free. *You're not going anywhere!* Maxar tried to say, but all that came out was a ragged scream. Still, he held on with everything he could muster. The Breaker's consciousness squirmed and writhed, flexing to escape his hold.

Maxar could feel the crackling energy disintegrating parts of him, worming in towards his core. *Don't let go!* he raged, hoping whatever Tremmilly was doing, she would hurry up. He bore down even harder, trying to crush See'dek beneath him. Moments ground by in agony, and Maxar wondered how long he could hold fast before his enemy's onslaught.

"What are you doing?" See'dek roared. Maxar felt him desperately lunge towards Tremmilly and the link to his power, dropping the dark lances as he did so. With the pain removed, Maxar felt his own strength return, and he renewed his effort, stopping See'dek before he could progress further.

Light, power, and confidence flowed through his life bond with Tremmilly, giving him the strength he needed to crush See'dek. *Maybe this is what she wanted me to do?* Maxar thought, concentrating as much energy as he could into his right fist. *Smash his consciousness, shatter his being.* He pulled back, ready to swing.

"Goodbye, love," he heard faintly, then his bond to Tremmilly vanished.

What happened? Maxar wondered frantically, hoping that See'dek's allies hadn't come to his rescue. But no, Tremmilly was still standing next to See'dek's conduit, a serene look on her face.

"Tremmilly!" Maxar screamed. Half of her began glowing brighter and brighter, the light hurting his vision. The other side became a dark, churning black hole. The two mingled, creating a violent reaction enveloping her. "Tremmilly!" Maxar screamed again, realizing he'd forgotten about See'dek.

When he looked down, he saw the Breaker had fractured and was dissolving, particles of him streaming towards Tremmilly. For a moment, Maxar thought See'dek was using some kind of weapon, was absorbing her, but he remembered the fear in the Breaker's final words.

Maxar released the disappearing form, returning his gaze to the love of his life. The space Tremmilly's consciousness had occupied still flared with the brightest and blackest of energies, but her form was gone. The mingling reaction continued growing, sucking huge amounts of energy from dimensions he didn't understand.

When Maxar tried to approach the maelstrom, he knew if he went any closer, it would absorb and obliterate him. *I can't leave Tremmilly, but I can't stay here,* he thought, the agony of the decision worse than what See'dek had done to him.

Maxar tried to find her, but he knew it was hopeless. He backed away from the chaos, mind whirling. *She knew this was going to happen,* he realized. *She said goodbye, and it was she who severed the life bond, not See'dek.*

The urge to throw himself into the maelstrom, to share Tremmilly's fate, rose up within him. *The other Harbingers won't understand what happened,* he thought. *Perhaps Tremmilly knows a way to survive this I would never think of.*

Holding on to that last thought to prevent himself from drowning in guilt, Maxar cast his consciousness from the side dimension, desperately searching for his body. *What if the Breakers destroyed my physical form?* he thought, feeling frantic. Returning to standard-space time, Maxar saw his body. Relief flooded through him.

Maxar opened his eyes, his consciousnesses flooding back into his body. The first thing he saw was a decomposing shape on the floor before him. He caught sight of a few small bits of white bone and connective tissue poking out from the pile of black dust. *Bugger you, See'dek,* he thought. *Come back from that.*

Turning to find Tremmilly, he saw the body of the only woman he'd ever loved crumpled on the floor beside him. Her eyes were closed, face serene, combat suit undamaged. *She's fine. Nothing is wrong.* Maxar checked her vital signs, mind quickly falling back into old habits.

No, no, no, he thought, seeing her suit readout alerting no breathing or pulse. "Come on, Tremmilly," Maxar said, pulling off her helmet and desperately trying to resuscitate her. A deep part of him knew it was futile. The only thing that truly mattered had been swept away in the torrent of reacting energies. "I'm here. Come back to me!" he yelled, the sound echoing hollowly off the command bridge walls.

We can't stay here, he thought, realizing the Breakers or the Ashamine fleet could resume their attack at any moment. *If Tremmilly can find a way back, I have to make sure her body is ready for her.* "Jaydon!" he yelled, hoping the old captain hadn't gone far.

Maxar lifted Tremmilly over his shoulder, his mind rushing through several plans. He steadied her body with one hand, and drew his flechette pistol with the other. Hot tears streamed down his cheeks, blurring his vision. He awkwardly yanked his helmet off and tried to brush them away. Finally, he felt he could see well enough to continue. *I will keep you safe,* he thought, repeating the promise as he exited the command deck door.

58 – FELAR

"Maxar? Tremmilly?" Felar transmitted again. Still, no answer.

"I can't feel Tremmilly anymore," Lothis said. "See'dek is gone too."

"What?" Felar responded. "For how long?"

"Turn right here," Jaydon interjected. "Almost to the bridge."

"Just now. She vanished."

"Buggering blightheart," Felar cursed. She headed right, hearing something banging around the corner. When she entered the corridor, she saw a Breaker bashing its skull against the bulkhead. The action was rhythmic and measured, and it made Felar shudder. Hefting her beam weapon, Felar burned off its head.

"Why was it doing that?" Jaydon asked.

Felar didn't know and didn't care, so she remained silent. Movement down a side corridor caught her attention. Pivoting on her heel, Felar brought up her weapon once again. A writhing mass of Breakers were sprawled across the floor, biting and gnashing at each other. Black blood oozed, coating them and the surrounding surfaces. For a fraction of a second, Felar thought about using her beam to obliterate them all, but it would take too much time.

"I can't say for sure," Dras said, his voice coming from the back of their group, "but I think the Breakers are experiencing a mass nanitic dysfunction."

"What do you mean?" Felar asked. As long as the Breakers didn't get in her way, they could all go bugger themselves in the fires of the dark star, but she figured the Heltasoth might have tactically relevant information.

"I believe the closest analogue would be the human auto-immune disorder. Heltasoth inorganic biology is vastly different from yours, and even the Breakers, but certain circumstances have been known to bring about similar conditions in us. For the Breakers, I believe their nanites have lost cohesion, and we are witnessing a distributed network dissolution."

220

"Is this happening to all of them?" Jaydon asked.

"Unknown. The cause of network problems could be local or more widespread. We have no way to know until we see the rest of the Breaker fleet."

Maxar came bursting out of the command deck door. His eyes were fierce, and he raised his weapon.

"Friendly!" Felar shouted. "Friendly!"

Maxar shook his head, looking dazed. "What? How did you get here?"

Felar saw he had Tremmilly over one shoulder, her body limp. "No time for that," she barked. "Set her down." Felar made a quick assessment, confirming her worst fears.

Banging and screaming resounded down the corridor, and Felar guessed whatever a "distributed network dissolution" meant, they were going to witness a massive aspect of it if they didn't move.

"I tried to resuscitate her," Maxar was saying, voice cracking. "But she's gone."

Given she saw no physical injuries, and Lothis' experience with Wake, Felar guessed he was right. *We need to get off the ship, before one of those buggers blighthearts a critical system.*

"We have to get Tremmilly to Dras' ship," Felar said. "Maybe his tech can save her."

"You think so?" Maxar asked, looking more confused and broken than she believed possible.

"Of course," she lied. "Pick her back up, and let's get off this buggered ship." Maxar easily lifted Tremmilly once again, and they all set back towards the Heltasoth ship. As she'd expected, having a duty restored Maxar somewhat. *Plus, it frees Lothis and Jaydon to watch out for psychotic Breakers.* She never would have believed Maxar would be in a worse mental state than either of them.

The realization that her closest friend was dead hit Felar in the gut. Losing Cazz-ak and Wake had been hard, but she knew this would be worst of all. *Don't go down that hole,* she thought, refocusing her attention on the intersecting corridors. *You'll have all the time to melt into an emotional puddle once this is over, but there are people counting on you. No more deaths.* Still, despite her best efforts, the pain continued gnawing away at her.

Felar wanted to ask what had happened, where See'dek was, but she knew now was not the time. Whatever had occurred, there was no way Maxar would have left See'dek alive.

Behind her, Felar could hear someone crying. *Lothis,* she thought, taking a quick glance back to confirm. She was right. Jaydon too had tears streaming down his cheeks. *How are any of us going to survive this?* Felar wondered, biting her lip to prevent her own breakdown.

59 – AZA

"There," Em said, turning away from the patchwork console she'd created. "If the Stellar Memory's comms are still functional, they should get our location. I wish we could do a vid or even audio link, but with the damage, sending an encrypted distress alert was the best I could do."

Aza nodded. "Thank you." She was amazed the other woman had been capable of doing even that much. The mass of wires and rigged components still baffled Aza. *I should learn more about hashing and electronics,* she thought.

"So now we wait," Em continued, frowning.

"At least this compartment is solid," Aza replied, "and we don't have to keep our helmets on." The limited atmosphere wouldn't last forever, but it meant additional survival time. *Come on, Ash,* she thought.

Em emitted a non-committal grunt, her attention focused on the diagnostic display of her environmental nominizing suit.

They both lapsed into silence, and Aza thought about the future. *Ash will come for us. I know he will. And then what do I do?* Her future seemed more uncertain than ever. If the Breakers won, she knew flight and combat would become a way of life. *We can't give up, no matter what. We have to keep fighting back.*

With Em's ship broken in half and completely useless, there was no way to tell how the battle was proceeding. *You could go back into the mid-section and watch it from there.* The thought sent a chill of excitement and fear down her spine. Even with her ENS boots locking her to the deck, she still felt at risk of drifting off into the void when she wasn't enclosed in the hull.

Time passed, and Aza tried not to think of their ever-diminishing atmosphere supply. *If we defeat the Breakers, what then?* Aza didn't know exactly how, but she felt everything would be different. *The Ashamine might never recover.* She expected a pang of sorrow from the thought,

222

but there was none. *I don't think of myself as a citizen anymore,* she realized, frowning. *What does that make me?*

And what of my parents? Am I an orphan? She knew the odds of them surviving both the Breakers and the rod strike were slim. It had been impossible to see where it had hit, but Aza hoped their effort had protected the Ashamine databases.

Would my parents even take me back? she thought, her mind turning to her family. Aza remembered the feelings of disgrace and shame she'd experienced in their presence, and for a moment, a weight of guilt threatened to crush her.

No, Aza thought, forcing herself to sit up straight. *I was right. They should have listened to me. It didn't have to be this way. We could have escaped sooner, like the other Ashamine dignitaries.*

"Everything OK?" Em asked. Aza turned to see the other woman scrutinizing her.

"Yeah, I'm fine."

"Thinking about the future?"

"Yes."

"Here's some advice:" Em said, a wry smile on her face, "Don't. It won't do you any good. Too many possibilities. Just focus on this moment."

"How?" Aza said, wondering at the other woman's calm. "It feels like my thoughts are flying faster than that rod did."

"Understandable. It's not easy when you are stuck in a situation like ours. Maybe some conversation would be good for both of us, conversation that doesn't involve immediate peril and indeterminate outcomes."

"OK," Aza said, trying to find something else to say. "Where are you from? How did you become part of the Brotherhood?"

Em laughed under her breath, shaking her head. "I suppose it's a good starting point." She paused for a moment, thinking. "Do you want the adult or kid version?"

"I can handle the real story," Aza said, holding her head high. "I'm not a kid anymore."

Em laughed again. "I suppose you're right, but I don't want Ash getting mad at me for telling you too much. How about we take the middle vector?"

"Sure," Aza sighed.

Em sat back against the wall, rubbing her cheek with one hand. "I was born on Noor-5, but my parents abandoned me or died or something—who the bugger knows—so I grew up in an orphanage with my brother, Maxar. When I was old enough to start working, I did, hoping I could support us both. But Noor-5 is a tough place, and not easy for those outside the criminal Families. The only way into that world, for someone with my history, was to sell my body. I didn't want to do that, so I signed up for the other option.

"When I was 15, I became an indentured servant, to buy my way to Ashamine-2. I made good wages there, working for the Tah Ahn family, but the cost of coming to Ashamine-2 would mean years of labor. Since I was able to support my brother and send back funds, I was alright with the situation."

Em stopped for a moment, taking a deep breath. "Unfortunately, I fell in love with the family's son, Crasor. He was odd at first, but as time went on, I grew more and more attached. We did so much together when I wasn't working: seeing music exhibitions, going to exhibits, and eventually becoming quite close. But then a part of him I'd never seen before emerged. He became possessive and violent.

"I couldn't get away from him. Crasor would come after me during the work day, and I'd get in trouble with the overseer. I felt so trapped. At any time, he could make up some story to his parents, and they would sell me to the sex trade in the under city, or worse. I had to get away."

Aza couldn't take her eyes off the other woman. It sounded like one of the network vids her parents wouldn't let her watch.

"So I contacted one of the darkwalker gangs," Em continued. "I told them I had Tah Ahn family secrets, and I would work for them for a set amount of time in exchange for transport back to Noor-5. I would be changing one kind of slavery for another, but at least I would get away from Crasor before he could hurt me.

"But I wasn't careful enough with my comms, or one of the gangs told him what I was doing, because Crasor burst in on the negotiation. He killed my darkwalker contact. I don't remember exactly what happened after, but I woke up on the floor with the worst headache of my life. He'd split my skull and there was a lot of blood. I think Crasor believed he'd killed me, which was probably the best thing that could have happened.

"Now I was free, relatively. I knew Crasor wouldn't tell his parents he'd murdered me, so they would likely report me as a fugitive servant. I still needed an income source, so I just decided to join a darkwalker gang. I'm not proud of the things I did, but it helped me survive. Eventually, I made a connection with one of the Brotherhood of Azak-so members who was doing recon on Ashamine-2. She offered me a way out, and I've been free ever since."

"And what about your brother?" Aza asked.

Em pursed her lips. "I've not had contact with him. If Maxar is still alive, I'm sure he thinks I'm dead. It's too dangerous for me to inform him otherwise. The Tah Ahn family still has people looking for me."

"Even after all these years?"

"They aren't the kind of people who forgive or forget."

Aza got the sense she understood very little of the world. Em's story hinted at things she'd never thought or even dreamed of. *I've been so sheltered.*

"I did the best I could to keep up with Maxar's life, even if he doesn't know I'm alive. He had skills the Families wanted, but it ended up costing him his freedom. The Ashamine sentenced him to life on the Bloodsport asteroid, which didn't last long, because the Haak-ah-tar supernova obliterated everything."

"He died?"

"I looked for him, but quickly discovered no inmates made it out before the shock wave hit."

Aza was about to express her sympathy when an alert sounded. "Danger. Low atmospheric oxygen," a monotone voice announced. "Seek alternate supply."

"Blightheart," Em said. "Guess that's the end of what's left on this half of the ship. Don't put your helmet on yet, but be ready. We need to use every bit of what is available here. When you start to feel dizzy, you know it's time."

Aza wanted to talk more, to ask Em what her experience had been like with the Brotherhood, but the anxiety of the situation kept her silent. *Be ready, be prepared,* she thought, grasping the ENS helmet in her hands.

For a long time, she felt nothing different, then her head started to ache. The room began spinning, and her eyelids grew heavy. *Now,* she thought, clumsily pulling the helmet over her head. Her fingers struggled to work the clasps, but it finally sealed, and fresh atmosphere began circulating.

"Are we going to make it?" Aza asked once her head felt normal again.

"I could lie," Em replied, "and tell you everything is going to be fine, but you know better. You're a smart girl, wouldn't have gotten off Ashamine-2 otherwise. If Ash gets our message, he'll come for us."

Aza felt her heart begin to beat more rapidly, and her breath came in short painful intervals. A light began flashing on her suit display.

"You have to calm down," Em said. "The more you breathe, the less time you have. Our job now is to make our oxygen last as long as possible. We have to give Ash enough time to get out of the battle and come save us."

Aza nodded, focusing on Em's words. *I can do this,* she thought. *I can do this.*

60 – LOTHIS

No, no, no! Lothis thought, watching Maxar set Tremmilly's body down inside the Heltasoth vessel. *She can't be dead!* Tears streamed down his cheeks. Lothis fought hard to contain his sobs, but they continued anyway.

"Everything's going to be OK," Felar said, looking dazed.

Through his tears, Lothis saw Maxar kneel next to Tremmilly, shaking his head. He'd never seen the man cry, or look so broken. "Dras," Maxar said, voice raw, "can you do anything for her?" Lothis tried not to get his hopes up, remembering what had happened to Cazz-ak and Wake, despite the alien's medical prowess.

"Let me begin a diagnostic," Dras replied. He bent down and touched the pale skin of Tremmilly's arm.

"Maybe if you explain what happened," Felar said, "we might understand how to help."

"Yeah, of course." Maxar couldn't take his eyes from Tremmilly's face as he spoke. "We were in an alternate dimension, one she'd created or something. Tremmilly told me to hold on to See'dek's energy there, to keep him from escaping. It took everything I had, but I did it. His attacks nearly obliterated me. I heard Tremmilly say goodbye, felt our life bond sever..." Maxar trailed off, tears falling from his cheeks, dripping onto the hard shell of Tremmilly's combat armor. His chest heaved, and he took several deep breaths before continuing. "When I turned to look, she was being consumed by some kind of energy maelstrom, the brightest light and deepest dark combining within her."

Lothis felt confused. *What did See'dek do? We've never seen him wield positive energy before.*

"I thought at first that See'dek had found a way to attack her, and when I looked back, he was dissolving, particles streaming towards Tremmilly. As seconds passed, it became evident See'dek was being destroyed, and Tremmilly was in control."

Maxar took another deep breath, wiping tears from his face, collecting himself. "Soon, Tremmilly disappeared, leaving behind the flaring energies."

Maxar's last statement triggered a new thought in Lothis: *The Dawn... Is it possible? Could that have been her plan all along?*

"I tried to find her," Maxar added, "tried everything I could think of, but it was useless. I had to get back, to protect her body in case she was coming back."

"You did well," Dras interjected. "Tremmilly's body is in good condition. I can keep it on what you call life-support, but as I said with Cazz-ak and Wake, I have no way to bring her consciousness back."

"She won't be coming back," Lothis announced, the words hitting him in the gut. Even though he'd tried not to get his hopes up, he still felt crushed.

"What do you mean?" Felar asked.

Lothis shook his head, trying to maintain the little composure he'd gained. "She's gone. Forever."

"How can you know that?" Maxar asked. Lothis could see his hope, and as much as he didn't want to crush it, he knew he had to tell the truth.

"I'm not sure how she did it, but I think Tremmilly used herself to unite the Dawn and the Breakers."

"Why would she do that?" Maxar snapped.

"I'm obviously not an expert on this," Felar added, "but wouldn't that destroy the Dawn? Wouldn't it obliterate everything Tremmilly was trying to save?"

Lothis had the same questions as well, but he couldn't think of another explanation that fit. "I don't know. I'm sorry." It felt like everyone was looking at him, condemning his statement. A wave of anxiety and fear washed over him.

"You don't need to apologize," Felar said, pulling him into a hug. "I'm sorry for yelling. We're all tired, tense, and full of sorrow. It seems impossible, but we need to rest and calm down. We're too keyed up to make sense of the situation."

"Yeah," Maxar said, his gaze returning to Tremmilly's face. "You're right."

"Dras," Felar said, her voice sounding more composed. "Can you get us out of this battle? I don't think there is much we can do. If Lothis is right, the war might already be over."

"We have to get Beowulf," Maxar said. "We can't leave him to die on the Retribution."

"Of course," Felar replied. "I'll go." She looked towards him. Lothis nodded, and Felar dropped her embrace.

"I'll establish a seal between the ships," Dras said. The Heltasoth vessel made the short hop across the hull of the larger Breaker ship, settling next to the Retribution. Felar left Lothis' side, heading for the other ship.

Stay calm, he thought, immediately missing her presence. Lothis felt anxious looking at Tremmilly's body, and guilty when he wasn't. *I protected her from See'dek before,* he thought, *but this time I couldn't.* Everyone around him waited in silence, punctuated by sobs and sniffles. Jaydon seemed completely wrecked, eyes bloodshot, face drawn, a large bandage covering his gut.

You have to check, Lothis finally decided. *If the Dawn has vanished, you'll have further confirmation for your theory.* But knowing would confirm his sister's annihilation. Uncertainty, at least in the current situation, felt better. *Coward... If you don't confirm, you might miss the possibility she needs our help.*

Gritting his teeth, Lothis settled onto the deck. He closed his eyes and tried to calm his racing thoughts. After several moments passed, he was able to find enough focus to cast his consciousness out.

He felt his energy warp and flex, fluctuating due to his mood. *Calm. Patience. Focus,* he told himself. Lothis tried creating the transition to the cosmic energy of the Dawn. The space-time warp slipped from his grasp. He tried again, this time closer, but still, the transition eluded him.

Lothis turned all his focus inward, knowing he had to do this, for the Harbingers, himself, and for Tremmilly. Finally, he felt ready to try again. *Push, pull, warp,* he thought, focusing on each step. Finally, the transition sprang into being and Lothis realized why he'd had such a hard time.

Through the warp, he could see the Dawn shrinking and its entire dimension with it. The once beautiful cosmic flower, the entity he and the rest of the Elrahi had worshiped, was almost entirely gone. Its colors had faded, its petals becoming nearly invisible. Energy flowed from it, siphoned through a conduit transitioning to another dimension.

A moment passed, and Lothis watched the cosmic flower vanish completely.

61 – ASH

"Come on, come on," Ash muttered, willing the crippled Stellar Memory to go faster. Gruesome images of Aza and Em flashed through his mind, and he wondered for the thousandth time if they were reality or just some demented Breaker weapon. *What if they are both?*

The journey from the now diminishing battle towards the coordinates of Em's distress comm was taking forever. A part of Ash felt guilty for leaving combat, but from what his engineers said, the Memory couldn't take much more punishment before it would be completely disabled or destroyed.

We were more of a liability than an asset anyway. The speed they were making towards Ashamine-2 made that obvious. *Even if the Breakers were barely functioning, there was still a chance one might get a lucky shot on us.* So, shortly after Em's distress comm came in, Ash gave the order to disengage and head to her location with all speed.

As minutes dragged by, Ash hoped he wasn't too late. Obviously, something was catastrophically wrong with her ship, otherwise Em would have just transmitted via regular channel. *Hopefully they're both still alive,* he thought, fidgeting with his atmosphere supply hose. The distress comm only supplied info on location and emergency status. *Which means at least a part of the ship is still viable, and they didn't burn up in atmosphere or smash into the planet.* The logic brought some comfort, but there was still a high probability that either or both were dead.

"Closing into optics range," the sensor officer announced, breaking into Ash's thoughts.

"On screen," he ordered. "Full spectrum and magnification."

The large central screen switched from a broad view of Ashamine-2 to a much larger, grainy image. *Hard to get detail with the buggered planet in the background.* Ash waited, hoping for the best possible outcome, despite knowing it was foolish.

Another minute passed, and he finally saw Em's ship. Two large chunks orbited Ashamine-2. *Snapped or broken in half somehow,* he decided. The parts looked largely intact, although they showed definite warpage.

"Nav, take us in as close as you can without serious collision risk," Ash ordered, forming a plan to board and search the debris. "Sensors, full focus on the two halves. Get me whatever information you can."

Both officers acknowledged their orders as Ash disconnected himself from the atmospheric supply. His ENS switched over to internal processing, and he reflexively checked its capacity. *Engineering said our shuttle fleet is diminished, but perhaps one of them is still sound enough to make the short trip over. If not, our team will have to spacewalk.*

As he was deciding who to take along, the sensor officer's voice came over Ash's helmet comm. "Receiving a wide-band, short range optical transmission, from the aft section of Em's ship."

Ash's heart leapt, and he tried hard not to run over to the officer's terminal to view it himself. *Patience,* he thought, inhaling deeply.

"Message reads: 'Damn it, Ash, what's taking so long?'"

Ash let out his breath, not realizing he'd been holding it. He shook his head, a broad smile on his face. "Return transmission: On my way. Hold fast. Will be there soon."

Closing his eyes, Ash relished the feeling of victory flooding through him. *The Breakers are nearly defeated, and Aza and Em are safe.* It was impossible to know at this point where the final rail rod impacted, but with any luck, the Ashamine databases were undamaged as well. He began issuing orders, calling up a team to accompany him.

We did it, Ash thought, heading towards the shuttle bay. *We really did it.*

62 – MAXAR

How will I ever survive this? Maxar thought, unable to take his eyes from Tremmilly's lifeless face. Dras had told him he was keeping her body alive, at least biologically, which brought little comfort. *She's not coming back. Trem wouldn't have said goodbye if she was...*

Around Maxar, everyone was silent. Felar was still retrieving Beowulf, a task Maxar knew he should have done. *I can't leave Tremmilly, even if her consciousness is gone.*

A crushing despair weighed on Maxar. *I promised to always protect her, to be there for her when she needed me most. I failed.* Guilt threatened to overwhelm him. Maxar shook his head, tears resuming their slow trickle down his face. *But Tremmilly didn't tell me what she was doing. Why did she hide it from me? Why did she sacrifice herself and leave me here alone?* Anger coursed through Maxar, but then guilt flooded in for thinking ill of his love. The caustic cocktail of emotions continued to eat at him, and Maxar wondered once again how he'd ever survive. *I'd take any physical pain over this,* he thought.

Movement in the corner of Maxar's vision caught his attention. "She did it," Lothis said, rising to his feet. "I saw the last of the Dawn vanish. Given how the Breakers are acting, and what you told us, Maxar, I think my hypothesis is correct."

Maxar had a hard time focusing or making sense of the boy's words. "What?"

Before Lothis could answer, Felar returned to the bridge, Beowulf following behind. The wolf-dog whined, heading straight for Tremmilly's body. He nudged her prone form with his nose, his pitiful noises intensifying.

"Beowulf," Maxar said, "she's gone. She's not coming back. Come here, buddy." He pulled the wolf-dog into his embrace, even as he struggled to break free. "She's gone," he repeated. "She's gone." After several long minutes, Beowulf finally calmed, although when Maxar let him go he curled up next to Tremmilly's body. His whines continued, low and persistent.

"I went to check if my thoughts on what Tremmilly did were correct," Lothis resumed. He stood next to Felar, leaning into the arm she'd placed around his shoulders. "She united the Dawn and the Breakers. I saw the last of the cosmic flower drain, flowing out into another dimension. It's how she was able to destroy See'dek." He paused for a moment, thinking. "And destroying See'dek produced the results we are seeing in the rest of the Breakers."

"The Ashamine and Brotherhood fleets have destroyed nearly all the enemy ships," Dras said, nodding.

"Which means See'dek's vessel is becoming a more appealing target by the moment," Felar interjected. "We can continue this conversation from a safer vantage point."

Dras nodded. "Should we head towards Ashamine-2, or the edge of the gravity well?"

"Take us in towards the planet. We need to let our friendlies know we are clear of See'dek's ship. The sooner it's destroyed, the better."

"As you say," Dras replied.

Maxar watched as the huge Breaker vessel shrank beneath them. *What do I do now? What meaning is left in my life?*

"Balance," Lothis announced, as they sped away from the cursed ship.

"What?" Felar said, brows furrowed.

"That's what Tremmilly did," he replied, staring off into the distance. "She balanced an energy disparity."

Felar still looked as confused as Maxar felt. "You're going to have to explain more."

Something shifted in Maxar's mind, and small things Tremmilly had said leading up to the final battle began to make sense. "It all goes back to before the struggle between the Harbingers and Breakers, when See'dek's research resulted in a division between him and what the people felt was morally correct. Tremmilly, as Empress Aris, spoke the majority decision and condemned him, widening the rift. I don't know what the Dawn started out as, but when the loyal Elrahi joined it, it magnified its energy. See'dek formed his own version of the Dawn, only with negative power."

Lothis nodded, looking thoughtful. "As millennia passed, the divide continued, positive and negative growing and balancing each other. We harnessed the power of the Dawn, using it to fight the Breakers. But we were unwilling to utilize it the same ways See'dek wielded his own power, thus putting us at a disadvantage."

"But doesn't that mean all the positivity in the universe is gone now?" Felar said, eyes wide. "How will it survive?"

"The fact we are here, that anything still exists, shows our beliefs as Elrahi were flawed," Maxar said, remembering how Tremmilly had realized the same thing. "Tremmilly believed she had created See'dek, by making the rift in the first place, but it was much more complicated. The Elrah, as a people, formed the imbalance by embracing the Dawn. See'dek was just a buggering blightheart who capitalized on the results."

"When we worshiped and sent our people to the Dawn," Lothis added, "it circumvented a natural energy cycle within our part of the universe, increasing the imbalance. By following our beliefs, Elrahi society inadvertently locked away generations of people. They lost sentience, but they were still imprisoned. See'dek was the opposite side of the Dawn's equation. He was the universe trying to restore itself."

"So," Jaydon said, voice raw, "you're saying all this happened because of an energy imbalance?"

"It's not quite that simple," Lothis replied, "but essentially, yes. Tremmilly restored the balance, by uniting the positive energy of the Dawn and the negative of the Breakers. They canceled each other out. She freed our people, both those in the Dawn and in the Breakers. Now, their energy can be restored and recycled back into the universe."

"There was no other way," Maxar said under his breath. Lothis nodded, and their eyes met. Maxar could see his own pain mirrored in the boy's gaze. *We've both lost someone we loved deeply, in two separate lifetimes.*

Maxar turned away from Tremmilly's body, the first time he'd done so since picking it up on See'dek's ship. Walking the short distance over to Lothis, he knelt down, embracing the boy. Lothis hugged him back, and they both cried silently. After a minute, they released each other.

When Maxar looked back at Tremmilly's body, he knew it no longer held a draw for him. *Everything making her who she was is gone. That is merely a husk.* Thoughts of suicide, of stripping off his ENS and throwing himself out an airlock rose in his mind. Maxar had faced such darkness before, back on Bloodsport, before knowing he was a Harbinger, before knowing he had someone he loved. *And now I've lost that. The battle is over. Tremmilly is gone.* He began moving towards the hatch, wondering if Dras would let him out.

You can't. The thought stopped him, and he stood rigidly in place. It sounded like Tremmilly, but he knew that was impossible. He'd watched her be consumed in the titanic reaction between the two energy sources. *I want you to go on, to continue life. I love you Maxar, and that love remains, even after death. We'll be together again, somewhere, sometime.* As the voice continued, Maxar wasn't so sure. *Tremmilly?* he asked, allowing a shred of hope. *Tremmilly?*

A hand grasped Maxar's arm and he turned. "Don't do it," Jaydon said, shaking his head. "You know Tremmilly wouldn't want you to. That's why she did what she did, so we could all live. Don't throw that away."

Maxar felt a lump form in his throat, and he turned back to face the group. They were all looking at him. He stepped back towards them, unable to speak.

"We are a safe distance," Dras said, breaking the silence. Maxar was grateful. "Shall I establish a comm with Parick Olvold?"

"Yes, please do," Felar said, her own voice sounding choked.

"Before we do that," Maxar said, trying to find the hardness he'd developed back on Bloodsport, "can we please put Tremmilly's body somewhere appropriate. And Dras, there is no need to keep it alive. Tremmilly isn't coming back."

The Heltasoth nodded. "I will do as you wish and place it somewhere safe."

"When the time is right," Felar said, "we will give her a funeral fitting of an empress and savior of the galaxy."

As Maxar watched, the deck welled up to embrace her, forming a pod that looked eerily like an Elrahi casket. A moment passed, the shape dissipated, and Tremmilly's body was gone.

This time, Maxar was able to control himself and keep from crying. He knew the victory would be short-lived.

63 – FELAR

Felar wished she could comfort Maxar, but right now, she couldn't think of anything to do. *He has it worse than any of us,* she thought, still wondering how she was going to cope.

As Tremmilly's body disappeared into the Heltasoth ship, Felar knew for her own sake, she had to keep pressing forward. *Action and time,* she decided, knowing that was how she'd dealt with loss in the past. *Preserve the lives of those remaining to the best of your ability, and see this war through to the very end.*

Felar took a deep breath, clearing her throat. She knew her eyes would be red and her cheeks puffy, but she didn't care. "Dras," Felar said, "I'm ready to establish the comm with Parick."

The Heltasoth nodded. Minutes passed, and Felar began wondering if he'd misunderstood. Just as she was about to make a status inquiry, Parick's face popped up on the main view screen. The resolution was poor, and sleek tables and chairs surrounded him, rather than the bridge she'd expected.

"Sorry to keep you waiting, Felar," he said. "I was finishing up a rescue, and as you might have deduced by me talking from my mess hall, my ship is pretty buggered."

"No problem," Felar answered. "We're all doing the best we can. At least your vessel is still functional."

"I guess you could call it that." Parick smiled. Felar thought he even looked a bit cheerful. "You and your team made it off the Breaker flagship? What's your status?"

"We took out the enemy leader, and are now a safe distance away. You can lift the restriction."

"Glad to hear you all made it out alive. Makes sense why the remaining Breakers are acting so strange."

"Not all of us survived," Felar said, voice somber.

"I'm sorry to hear that," the Brotherhood leader replied. "Thank you for your service, and for the sacrifice of those who died for the cause.

235

Humanity owes you a debt it will never be able to repay." Felar nodded, grateful for his words, but knowing they did nothing to alleviate their loss. "Please excuse me for a moment."

Parick turned, speaking to one of his crew. After they were done, he returned his attention to Felar. "I've issued orders to have the Transfiguration obliterated."

"Thank you. We would have done it ourselves, but it was too risky."

"You did the right thing. With the Breakers acting so erratic, it has been easy to take out their ships. The Transfiguration should be no different."

A dark-skinned girl and a tall blond woman entered the frame. "Uncle Ash," the girl, who Felar guessed was probably a young teenager, blurted, "is it true we are heading back to Ashamine-2?"

"Yes, that is the plan," the man she knew as Parick answered. "Let me finish this conversation, then we can talk more."

"Emili?" Maxar said, moving next to Felar. She turned to see an expression of wonder and surprise on his face. Felar turned back to the screen, seeing the blond woman's head snap towards them. The look on her own face was so similar to Maxar's that it was easy to see they were related.

"Maxar?" she replied. "How in the fires of the dark star? Where are you?"

"I—I," Maxar stammered, "I thought you were dead."

"Little brother," she replied, voice cracking. "I thought you were dead too. How did you escape the supernova?"

Ash looked back and forth between the siblings, looking almost as surprised as them. "I was going to invite you all to a meeting on Ashamine-2, to discuss what to do next, but now it appears we will have even more to talk about."

"Where did you go?" Maxar asked, too caught up in joy to hear Ash's words. "I lost you."

"Come meet us," Emili replied, tears running down her cheeks. "I'll explain everything."

The siblings' joy was contagious, but Felar knew she had to stay focused. *Can't let my guard down. Some of the most dangerous times are when the battle is almost over and victory seems assured.*

"Where do you propose we meet on Ashamine-2?" Felar asked. "We are wanted criminals and will likely be shot on sight."

"From what I can tell," Ash said, his serious demeanor returning, "the government has completely collapsed. There won't be anyone in a position to care what happened before the war, unless they have a personal grudge. The Breakers on the surface are behaving similarly to those in space, and the populace is swiftly dealing with them."

Felar felt surprised. "There were Breakers on Ashamine-2?"

"Unfortunately, yes. My niece," he said, putting his arm around the girl's shoulders, "barely escaped them, thanks to Maxar's sister. I'm not completely sure how the Breakers got there, but it appears they've been hiding in the under city and maintenance areas for quite some time. Probably waiting for the primary invasion."

"You want to get on world as quickly as possible," Felar said, understanding the situation. "You want to be a part of whoever establishes the new government."

"Yes," Ash nodded. "I believe I can do good for humanity. Through this battle, I've built credibility with the surviving Ashamine Fleet captains. They'll look to me when the war is over. I also have my own people to back me up."

"So you're just going to set yourself up as the new Founder?" Lothis injected, surprising Felar. She took a quick glance, seeing his stance rigid and orange eyes narrowed. "The person with the biggest military rules all?"

"No, no," Ash replied, raising his hands in a placating gesture. "Nothing of the sort. I want to establish a true democracy, let the people decide their future. I've spent my whole life trying to reform the Ashamine, first as a Holy Order priest, and now as the leader of the Brotherhood of Azak-so. I want nothing to do with Founders and dictatorships."

"As you say," Lothis grumbled, still looking agitated.

"This is why I need your group to help me," Ash continued. "I can't set up and maintain this structure alone, and my own people have been decimated. You are heroes and saviors. People will look up to you and listen. It will take years, perhaps decades, for us to shift the mindset of the populace away from following dictators. They will be vulnerable to demagogues and narcissists who will try to rise to power and exploit them."

He's right, Felar thought, allowing her mind to think about the future. *What else will you do once the war is over? You've been protecting people for both lifetimes. You don't know how to do anything else.*

"I was going to save the rousing speech until we were face-to-face," Ash continued, smiling, "but I got carried away."

"Understandable," Felar replied. "It is easy to see your passion."

"You'll help me?"

Felar looked around the bridge, checking in with Lothis, Maxar, Jaydon, and Dras. *So few of us left,* she thought, feeling the knot rise in her throat again. Each of them nodded.

"Yes," Felar answered. "We'll come to Ashamine-2."

64 – AZA

"You're sure the palace is secure?" Ash transmitted, bringing their shuttle in towards the majestic structures.

Well, they used to be majestic, Aza thought, zooming in on the display in front of her. It was hard to see through the dust and ash clouding the intervening atmosphere, but not even the Founder's Palace escaped damage. The soaring buildings were scarred from rail round and debris strikes.

"The upper levels are completely free of the invaders," the Ashamine commander's stern voice said. "The underlevels will require more time to clean out, but since the enemy is disorganized, I foresee no issue with my squads wiping them out."

"Affirm," Ash transmitted back. "We'll be there in a few minutes." Ash smiled at Aza, nodding. "Looks like everything is safe, or at least as safe as we can hope."

Aza smiled back, feeling mixed emotions about returning to her home-world. When Ash had first requested clearance to land on the planet, he'd been denied, and Aza was almost glad. But further persistence, including getting one of the Ashamine fleet commanders to talk with the orbital control officer, had paid off. They'd been cleared to land.

Everything in Aza's world had shifted. *What if my parents are dead?* The thought made her stomach clench. *And what if they are still alive?* That outcome was even more troubling, in a way. *They betrayed me, and I them. I'd rather be with Ash or Em.* Aza wanted to talk with them about the situation, but she knew there were more important things that needed to come first. *Like this meeting.* Somehow, Ash had contacted and convinced what was left of the Ashamine's most powerful leaders to meet in the Founder's Palace.

As they descended through the haze covering this part of Ashamine-2,

238

Aza's thoughts shifted. They'd moved the rod's vector away from the middle of the Founder's City, but Aza still didn't know the status of the Ashamine databases. Their specific location was classified, so Aza and Em had done the best they could to protect the entire area. *Was it enough?* The debris cloud made it impossible to see far. She knew there would be a massive crater where the rod had impacted. *And millions upon millions of dead, all vaporized.* Realizing that was part of what composed the cloud made Aza feel sick.

"Almost there," Em said, putting her arm around Aza's shoulders. Aza winced, a habit that quickly developed with her injuries. Em didn't notice, her attention completely focused on the forward view screen.

"During the meeting," Ash said, "I need you both to remain in a safe location." Aza tried to break in and protest, but Ash kept going. "Who knows the kind of tempers I'll be facing, and I will be pushing for drastic change. If anything gets out of hand, I need you both to get back up to the Brotherhood fleet. There is a treaty in place between the Ashamine and us, but once the war is officially over, who knows how long it will stand. Many conservatively-minded officers still have lots of influence, and they'd rather see themselves in power instead of creating a democratic consensus. The Ashamine is extremely weak, but it still has teeth. If my negotiations fail, we need to get back to Azak-1. We'll be safe there, and can try to broker a more lasting peace from there."

As Ash spoke, Aza had to agree. *I have no experience with government or negotiations, and besides, no one will listen to a 13-year-old girl.* Ash looked like he was preparing for an argument, and was caught off guard when she said, "Of course. I'll wait wherever you tell me to."

"Don't expect me to agree so easily," Em said, giving Ash a sly smile. "You need me in the negotiations."

"I know," Ash said, shaking his head, "but there is no one I trust to protect Aza more than you. I'll have other Brotherhood officers to support me."

Em took a deep breath. "I *suppose* I can continue baby-sitting, but only this one time. Then I have to get back to real work." Em looked at Aza, winking. The squeeze around her shoulders made Aza wince again, but she appreciated confirmation the older woman was joking.

"Thank you," Ash said, returning his full attention to piloting.

Minutes passed in silence. The shuttle bumped down on one of the palace landing pads. When they exited the ship, a gaunt looking aide was there to meet them.

"This way," he said, without greeting or further explanation.

Ash, Aza, and Em followed. As they entered the building, Aza couldn't help but marvel at the opulence and grandeur of the space.

Huge, living trees lined either side of the massive room. She wanted to walk over and touch one, having only seen them on the Network before, but Aza remained with the group. Fountains trickled and murmured, their liquid movement a contrast to the solidity of the polished stone floor. She felt overwhelmed by the wealth spent to outfit this empty, purposeless room. Memories of the need and poverty of the under city flooded through Aza, making her grimace.

Finally, they stopped in front of a huge set of doors. "Several delegates are already inside," the aide announced, "and others will arrive shortly." He sniffed, turned on his heel, and left.

"What a kind man," Em sneered.

"Stay here," Ash said, "and if you hear or see any signs of danger, get back to the shuttle. Don't wait for me." He pulled on the enormous handle and the door swung open easily. Stepping inside, Ash shut it behind him.

Aza wanted to ask Em about taking care of her long-term, but now that she had the opportunity, she felt embarrassed. *Why would she want to give up a life of adventure to watch over me?* Aza tried to overcome her hesitation, but she couldn't make herself speak. *Em could teach you so much. She could turn you into an agent, just like her.* This thought tapped into Aza's motivation, but before she could speak, she heard the sound of approaching footfalls.

Turning, Aza saw the strange group that had taken out the Breaker leader, walking towards them. The same aide escorted four adults and one child. *And that's the biggest dog I've ever seen,* she thought. *It looks like a wolf.*

Em ran over to Maxar, slamming into him. They hugged, tears once again falling down their faces. The aide seemed angry at the interruption, but remained silent. The rest of the group moved forward, giving the siblings time to be alone.

"Hello," the boy said, smiling. Although Aza guessed he was a few years younger than her, his orange eyes and tired face made him seem much older.

"Hi," she replied, feeling shy. *Orange eyes,* Aza thought, remembering that only Founders and their offspring had that trait. "I'm Aza."

"My name is Lothis," he replied.

"You're the Successor," Aza blurted. "You're supposed to be dead."

"And in a way I am, which means I'm the Successor no longer."

Aza didn't understand exactly what that meant, but part of it made sense. "You're not here to reinstate the Founder's position?" Despite her lack of political training, Aza knew that if the Founder's only heir walked into a room full of Ashamine officers, Ash's proposal wouldn't stand a chance.

"No, in fact I'm here to do the opposite."

Aza exhaled, not realizing she was holding her breath.

Em and Maxar rejoined the group. Em looked overjoyed. "What are the odds we'd find each other again?"

"Blightheartedly bad," the tall, scarred man replied, smiling.

"Good to see you again, Em," the robed, hooded figure of the group boomed. At first, Aza thought it was a trick of the light, but then she realized his irises really were black. He moved and spoke with a fluidity that felt almost too human.

"And you as well, Karthis," Em replied. "We lost track of you after Eishon-2."

"I discovered a few matters I had to attend to."

The tough looking woman in the other group let out a bark of a laugh. "Don't let Dras fool you," she said. "If not for him, we would all be dead, and See'dek would be in this palace, dominating the galaxy."

"Felar, you know we did it as a team. I only did what I could," he said, bowing.

Aza noticed the aide had turned an angry shade of red. "If you have all your reunions and meetings finished, it is well past time for you to join the meeting. You're keeping several important dignitaries waiting."

"Blightheart you and your dignitaries," Felar said, getting in the aide's face. "We saved you and everyone you know. You should be thanking us, instead of being a pompous bugger." The aide took a step back, looking equal parts frightened and indignant. Saying nothing, he turned on his heel once again and walked quickly away.

Aza smiled, liking how the commanding woman handled the situation. "He's probably right though," Felar said, after the aide was out of hearing range. "No use in stirring up even more animosity. We should go inside. We'll have time for reunions later, in a less buggered situation."

Felar opened one of the massive doors and everyone but Aza and Em walked inside. The large wolf-dog stopped at the last second, turning to look at her. Aza couldn't tell if he was friendly or not, so she stood still, waiting to see what he would do. Finally, he trotted over and plopped down next to her. For a moment, she hesitated, then Aza began running her fingers through the course fur.

"Hello, friend," she said under her breath, feeling more relaxed. "Em," she continued, raising her voice. "I have something I'd like to talk with you about."

241

65 – ASH

Ash sat back in his chair and rubbed his face with one hand. "There is no way in the fires of the dark star that I'm going to allow Dareth Adjular to be any part of this government. That man should be tried for crimes against humanity. You know the projects he was a part of. You've read the witness accounts."

"I know," Em said shrugging. "I'm not the one who nominated him to oversee reconstruction."

Ash let out a sigh. "Of course you didn't. I'm sorry, Em. Why do you come here and let me berate you about problems you have no control over?"

"Because you need someone to vent to, otherwise you'll explode. And who else is going to do it? I'm just about your only ally here."

Everything she'd said was true. In the month that had passed since his first meeting on Ashamine-2, Ash had felt constantly overwhelmed. The Ashamine government, despite losing almost all its top personnel, was still a powerful, imposing force. If he hadn't come in at their lowest point, they probably still would have executed Ash as a traitor. *I'm barely hanging on now,* he thought. *But I won't give up. I won't surrender the progress we've made to buggers like Adjular.*

His public status as a war hero and savior of the human race was mostly true. Felar, and the rest of the Harbingers, understanding the situation, had agreed to give him primary credit for taking out See'dek, despite the fact all he had done was keep the friendly fleets from firing on them. *All the people think you're a hero and want to make you the next Founder.* That would have been easier in the short term, but Ash found the idea horrendous. *I will not let humanity be controlled by a dictator, even if that dictator is me.*

Still, he was having a hard time fending off the Ashamine wolves and nurturing thoughts of democracy amongst the public. *You knew this wouldn't be easy,* he told himself, trying to shore up his morale. *This is the best opportunity you could have ever hoped for. You dreamed of this kind of thing when you were back on Azak-1, hunted by the Ashamine.*

"What are you thinking about?" Em asked, her brow furrowed.

He chuckled. "Just feeling sorry for myself."

"You took on a big, dangerous project," she replied, looking sympathetic. "It's understandable."

"I don't deserve someone like you."

"Of course you don't," she said, giving him her characteristic sly smile. "But here I am, all the same."

"I owe you an unpayable debt for rescuing Aza, and for all your assistance towards forming the democracy."

"And for agreeing to be her guardian, and for eliminating the enemies who threaten your safety."

"Yes, obviously," Ash replied, trying to mimic her sly smile. "Is she doing OK?" he asked. "Aza, I mean."

"She's remaining as positive as you could expect. Lots of nightmares. Her focusing on training and education seems to help."

"I wish I could be there for her more," Ash sighed, "but what I'm doing now is for her future."

"I know," Em said, walking over to give him a hug. "And you are doing a fantastic job. I was just giving you a blighthearted time, which probably isn't the best idea right now. We're all making sacrifices, you most of all."

Ash let himself melt into her embrace. "How are all these generationally conditioned people ever going to learn to think for themselves?"

"They're not, at least not all of them. You and I had to work hard get out of the Ashamine system, and we did it with little to no support. There are more people like us out there, and they will come around soon. The rest will just have to die off. Do as much as you like, give them choices, show them the truth about the Founder and the Ashamine, but they'll still hold fast to their old ways. That's where Aza's generation comes in. They aren't set in the ways of the past, not yet. They'll learn to choose for themselves and be part of a freethinking society." Em's words buoyed Ash's spirits, and he felt his determination return.

"They'll learn to love the Entho-la-ah-mines," she continued, "and they'll find a way to unite with them. None of this will be easy, mind you, and it will require years of hard work, but it is what we have to do."

Ash squeezed her harder. "Thank you, Em."

"Don't get too emotional on me," she replied, "you'll tarnish your reputation."

Ash let her go and stepped back, feeling ready to return to the looming challenges. *Stay strong, stay safe,* he thought, taking a deep breath, *and may the wisdom of Azak-so guide me.*

66 – LOTHIS

Lothis stared out the expansive window, seeing the dirty clouds below. Underneath them, he knew the entire population of the under city was struggling to survive. *We're doing the best we can,* Lothis thought, wondering how many would starve to death before the new government could send more aid.

As much as I want to help that situation, he thought, turning back to his terminal, *there is nothing I can do.* Ash, the Brotherhood leader they'd once known as Parick Olvold, had assigned him the task of decrypting and disseminating vast amounts of Ashamine state secrets. It was a mindless job, but one he was uniquely qualified for. *How long until I can be back in public again?* he wondered, tired of seclusion, but knowing it was for the best.

Ash is barely holding on to control as it is. The more people who know of my location and existence, the more danger someone might try to put me into power. Lothis dreaded the thought, so he stayed in his room, relying on Felar and Aza for company.

You could have gone with Maxar and Jaydon back to Eishon-2. The thought still tempted him sometimes, but it would necessitate leaving Felar, something he was unwilling to do. *Ash needs Felar to be his military adviser, so she has to stay here as well.* As of late, she'd been flitting back and forth between Ashamine-2 and 4, the Forces training world. *If anyone can unite the troops under this new government, it's her.*

Lothis directed his full attention back to his own work, going through file after file. Some were mundane, others were full of vital information showing humanity the truth about the Founder and the Ashamine government. A select few files would cause far too much damage to the public psyche, and these, Lothis re-encrypted and transferred to his own, secure file storage, to be reviewed by Ash and his advisors.

Lothis frowned, the file he was currently working on resisting his ability to mentally decrypt it. He studied the document for several moments, drawing on more of his Elrahi connection to permit him to work faster. *Legacy Genetics Project,* Lothis read finally, the title stirring up a sense of foreboding. He deciphered the key, entered it, and selected the open option.

Reading the file's latest entry, Lothis realized why: *Subject is nearly ready for social reintegration. Lothis shows remarkable abilities in all fields, especially with technology. He has exceeded all of my expectations and far surpasses what could be expected of genetic engineering. More study is—* Lothis jabbed the close option, anger and frustration welling up within him.

I don't want to remember that, he fumed. *None of it!* Memories of his time as an experiment, trapped under Haak-ah-tar, flooded through his mind. He tried to stop them, but he couldn't. An overwhelming sense of loneliness crashed down on him, and he closed his eyes, fighting hard not to cry. Visions of stalking monstrosities greeted him. His whole world felt like it was shrinking back to the size of his cage.

"Lothis?" Felar said, her voice breaking him out of his misery. He opened his eyes, shaking his head in an attempt to clear the remaining images. "What's wrong?" Walking around his small work table, she sat on its edge, facing him.

"Flashbacks," he said.

Felar nodded, taking a deep breath. He'd been experiencing them a lot lately, more than he was willing to admit. Felar had told him she was too, that they were an unavoidable side effect of everything they'd experienced.

"What brought it on this time?" she asked. Lothis pointed at the file title, unable to get any closer to the information it contained. "Ah, yes," she sighed. "Understandable. I saw some of that when we were in the Haak-ah-tar facility." Felar put her hands on his shoulders and looked him in the eye. "What's in that file doesn't define you, doesn't make you who you are. It may be a record of your origins, but you decided your own course."

"But I'm a clone of *him,*" Lothis said. "I'm a replica of one of the most evil humans ever to exist." He'd read the secret history of what his genes had done, first as the original Founder, then as each of his direct duplicates.

"So what?" Felar said. Her flippant tone caught him off guard. "You've made your own decisions. You rebelled against every Founder who came before you. Even when given the chance to take your rightful place, you rejected it, choosing instead to tear down the system they created and maintained. You don't even look like them, Lothis. And I'm not talking about subtle differences the LGP introduced to make their lies plausible. Yes, you have the orange eyes, but everything about you is different. You look more and more like Veth each day. At least how Veth would look as a human." She gave him a warm smile, but he could see the concern in her eyes.

"I'm not going down that old path," he said. "I'm maintaining positive self-talk, despite the heaviness of the work."

"Good," Felar nodded. "Good."

"This work just brings up lots of bad memories."

"We both knew it would," she replied, her tone soft. "You still have the opportunity to go to the Entho-la-ah-mines, to be humanity's emissary. Dras is doing the best he can, but he doesn't understand humans like you do, and he is sure to get caught up in studying them."

"Soon," he replied. Lothis wanted to be with the alien species, knew he was the best person for the job. *That also requires leaving Felar.* The thought of losing her support was still too much. "I'm nearly done with the databases," he continued, turning back to the screen. Seeing the LGP file again made him grimace.

"You don't have to keep them all," Felar said, "and you certainly don't have to distribute anything directly related to you."

Lothis' finger hovered over the expunge option. *It is part of human history,* he thought, wavering. *Even if it is about me, about the terrible things done to me, it belongs to our collective existence.* A huge part of him wanted to remove the painful information forever, to never have to see it again, but still he hesitated.

"I can't," he said finally, hitting the distribute option, which would send the file to the developing free media outlets. "I don't want the deeds of my forebears to be safe in darkness, forgotten by future generations. The Ashamine suppressed or twisted everything. We cannot let humanity's new government start in that direction. Someone out there may find my story inspiring, and perhaps, knowing that may help me heal."

"Wise words for someone so young," Felar replied.

"I'm not as young as I look," he shot back, giving her a small smile.

"Let's take a break," Felar said, rising from the desk. "There is a splendid forest park nearby. Not like the palos groves on Lith-elo, but it is something."

Lothis looked back and forth between her and his terminal screen.

"You need to take care of yourself, Lothis. If you work yourself ragged, you won't be helping anyone. I have an overwhelming workload as well, but I'm blowing it off. The new democracy will survive us being absent for an hour."

"OK," Lothis nodded, hitting the logout option on his terminal. He followed Felar out of his apartment, and they turned onto an accelerated walkway. Felar kept moving, her pace brisk, and the surrounding buildings whisked by as Lothis tried to keep up with her.

"All these meetings and shuttle rides have me feeling so stiff," she said. "I miss active duty and open spaces."

Lothis had to agree. Going from on-the-run, life and death situations, to being a secluded hasher and analyst, felt very abrupt. A deep part of him longed for the adventure of the past. *But that cost you.* The memories of his friends' deaths made him feel lonely once again. Despite the month that had passed, his grief was still a raw, open wound.

Felar turned onto another accelerated sidewalk, and they continued in silence. *The Harbingers are all dead or dispersed,* he thought darkly. *Fitting, since the rest of the Elrahi are gone as well.* Maxar had told him about Tremmilly's theories, how the Elrahi had been wrong about the Dawn's true meaning. *Only an energy imbalance,* he thought, *one that we made even larger.*

Lothis felt a deep sadness, knowing that the billions of Elrahi that had fled to the Dawn were now completely obliterated. *Felar, Maxar, and I are the last of our race. Beowulf too, somehow.* A part of him missed his family and friends, but another, more logical part knew it was the way of the universe. *We had our time, our opportunity, just as humanity is currently experiencing. Maybe they will figure it out, maybe not. Either way, I hope the Entho-la-ah-mines can recover. Perhaps they will lead the Akked into a new, peaceful era.*

"Here we are," Felar said, stepping off onto a stationary sidewalk. Lothis followed her, staring up at the large, open gates before them. Huge trees stretched out on the other side, a beautiful vista encompassing the top of an entire building.

They walked past the gates, the alloy sidewalk transitioning to dark, moss covered dirt. Lothis took a deep breath, the smell reminding him of Tremmilly.

"This way," Felar said, leading him off the main trail and onto a smaller path.

Lothis thought about asking where they were going, but he remained silent, knowing Felar was just trying to keep him out of the public eye. *Hardly anybody here anyway,* he thought, as they wound their way deeper and deeper into the forest.

After several minutes, the dense undergrowth opened up, revealing a grove. Felar stepped to the side, leaving him with an unobstructed view. Before him, stood his sister, a broad smile on her face.

"Tremmilly?" he said, heart racing with excitement. He stepped forward, eager to embrace her. But the figure remained motionless, and in the next instant, Lothis realized why. *Only a statue.*

"I commissioned an artist," Felar said.

Lothis tried not to show his disappointment, feeling ashamed for his ridiculous hope. *She's gone, and you know she's gone.*

"Hard to find one, given the current state of the world," Felar continued. "But I wanted us to have a place we could remember Tremmilly."

It had been hard to consign her body to space, in the Elrahi tradition, but it was fitting. *The empress of a million worlds can't rest on just one,* Lothis remembered Maxar saying at her service. *The last time we were all together.*

"I doubt Maxar will come back to see this," Felar said, beginning to look troubled, "but I thought it would be nice. For us."

Lothis took a tentative step towards the holographic form, so vivid and lifelike he thought it might just step down off its podium. *So many things I wanted to say to you, but couldn't in life, or even at your ceremony,* he thought, staring into her caring eyes. *You were so wise, a magnificent ruler and empress. The Accord was lucky to have you. You made mistakes like the rest of us, but you did what you could to make them right. You sacrificed yourself to save humanity, to protect them from the mistakes the Elrahi made as a species. And no one but the last three of us will ever understand the true extent of what you did.*

"Lothis?" Felar said, obviously worried. "I didn't mean to upset you. I know it is a bittersweet thing, but I thought it would be OK to surprise you."

"Yes, it's perfect," he said, tears running down his face. He embraced Felar, allowing the full extent of his emotions to run through him. He kept his face pressed against her chest, taking solace in her presence.

Finally, Felar broke the silence. "There's more," she said, motioning towards the far end of the clearing. Lothis turned to look.

For a moment, he thought he was hallucinating. "Queen Na-ah-co!" he said, seeing her shimmering blue exoskeleton. "What—how?" Lothis stammered, feeling caught off guard. "I didn't sense you!" The monarch approached, followed by a retinue of Entho-la-ah-mines and human guards.

"Lothis," the Queen answered, bowing her front set of legs. Her voice sounded warm and comforting in his mind, banishing his earlier sorrow. "I'm sorry I could not aid your sister in her time of need, could not even be there for her last ceremony."

"No," Lothis replied, shaking his head. "No, you needed to be there for your people. Tremmilly knew what she was doing. And as to the ceremony, it was much too dangerous. How were you able to come to Ashamine-2 now?"

"Felar arranged this," the Queen said. "I must say, I had misgivings, but I've never felt unsafe. The humans keep a close watch on our physical wellbeing, and my attendants make sure a mental shield is always close."

"Things are calmer now than before Tremmilly's ceremony," Felar said, "at least in the public's fervor to exterminate the Entho-la-ah-mines. If nothing else, the Breakers taught humanity some much-needed empathy. I still don't trust the hardline humanitarians. They would happily see the Entho-la-ah-mines eradicated."

Lothis still felt off-balance, his joy threatening to overwhelm him. "I'm just so happy to see you. Will you be here long?"

"Depending on the length of the meetings I'm here to attend, perhaps. I would love to spend my free moments with you, if you have time. There is still much we can learn from each other as well as healing we can share."

"I would love nothing more." Lothis looked to Felar, his huge smile making his face hurt. "Thank you," he said, feeling more complete now than he had since Cazz-ak's death, "for everything."

67 – MAXAR

Maxar inhaled deeply, trying to find a hint of Tremmilly in the forest's scent. He'd been on Eishon-2 for a full week now, looking for something he knew was impossible to find. *Those words were just your own mind, talking in Tremmilly's voice. She's gone, you bugger, and she'll never be back.*

Still, Maxar had returned to Eishon-2, hoping to find some part of his forever love. Jaydon had come with him, but whether that was to wrestle with the darkness of his own past, or to keep Maxar from killing himself, he had no idea. *Maybe it's both.*

In the month that had passed since Tremmilly's death, Maxar had felt like he'd been set adrift in interstellar space. Ash had offered him a slew of jobs and positions, and he'd tried a few, but none kept his attention. Rather than do bad work, he'd resigned, and followed his lonely heart to the only place that still felt connected to Tremmilly.

Eishon-2 was now free of the Breakers. Without See'dek's guidance, the entire race had gone mad, then quickly starved to death. Maxar was unsure what sustained them, but something in their anatomy had failed. *Besides, they didn't leave many troops here anyway.*

When Ash had heard that Jaydon and Maxar were heading for the backwater planet, he'd offered them positions as colony chiefs. Maxar turned the offer down, which he was sure the leader expected, but surprisingly, Jaydon had agreed. "Might as well bring the planet into the democracy," he'd said with a snort. "Not like there is going to be anyone there but us for quite some time anyway."

Ash had asked him to take a cargo ship full of tools and starving people with them. "They are ready and willing to work. They've all been vetted. You won't have any terrorists or under city crime lords with you. The planet needs a fresh start, and Ashamine-2 needs fewer people to support."

Jaydon had reluctantly accepted the task, mumbling about how he'd never get any peace or tranquility now. "My buggering work is never done." Despite his grumbling, Maxar knew he was eager to help humanity's fresh start, otherwise he would have no qualms about declining.

"And here we are," Maxar said, reaching down to pet Beowulf. He still didn't fully understand his connection to the wolf-dog, but he felt anxious whenever they were apart. *And Tremmilly would have wanted us to be together, even without our bond.*

Maxar found an expansive shade tree and settled beneath it. *If I could just find a way to feel more settled.* His mind was always on edge, and he wondered if he'd ever move on.

He closed his eyes, and memories of Tremmilly drifted through his mind. *Her laugh, her smile, her love.* Maxar didn't want to cry anymore, didn't understand how he was still capable of it, but still the tears came. For a moment, he considered pushing thoughts of Tremmilly out, but it felt like a traitorous act. *Besides, memories are better than emptiness, and pain is better than a void.*

Lying back, Maxar tried to find a comfortable position, nestled beneath the huge tree. It reminded him of his times with Tremmilly in the palos groves on Lith-elo, expressing their love to each other. He remembered the tender moments they'd shared, the things they'd laughed at, and the bond they'd created. Memory after memory resurfaced, and he felt the bittersweet agony of it all. *I love you, forever,* he thought, seeing her repeat the words back to him.

Maxar's mind spiraled out, cascading through pain, joy, loss, love, and hope. He could feel his intersecting connections to Tremmilly, Eishon-2, the Akked, and space-time. His entire history, spanning two existences as different beings, played out before him. The consciousness of Empress Aris, of Tremmilly, was intertwined in them both, a binding, positive force, always with him, always inspiring him. Joy soared within Maxar, a feeling he'd thought lost forever. Time seemed to lose all meaning as he floated in the nexus of existence.

Around Maxar, he sensed Tremmilly's energy, flowing and coursing across the universe. It was in the stars, the interstellar spaces, in the rocks and trees surrounding his physical body. Drawing back, he realized she was also in his own mind and body.

I love you, forever, Maxar repeated, knowing that now, he could go on.

251

Want a free, exclusive Dawn Saga short story?

Subscribe to my newsletter, and I'll send you *Jaydon*. I'll also keep you updated on new Dawn Saga releases and short stories:

http://zachariahwahrer.com/jaydon

Dear Reader,

Thank you for investing your time in my fiction! If you enjoyed this book, I'd really appreciate it if you would share the experience with your friends and leave a review online at your favorite retailer.

If you'd like to get in contact with me, you can email: **zachariah@wahreroftheworlds.com**.
My website, **www.zachariahwahrer.com** is a great way to find more of my writing. If you are more of a social media person, I'm on:
Facebook: www.facebook.com/ZachariahWahrer
Twitter: www.twitter.com/ZachariahWahrer
and *Instagram:* www.instagram.com/ZachariahWahrer

May the fires of the black star be quenched in your life,
Zachariah Wahrer

***

ABOUT THE AUTHOR

Zachariah Wahrer spent the first twelve years of his adult life doing various jobs around the United States, such as eBay salesman, punk rock musician, horse halter craftsman, and rock climbing gym route-setter.

Near the end of 2014, Zachariah moved into a Honda Odyssey with his wife, Sarah, and began traveling the United States and Canada, seeking inspiration and adventure while writing and rock climbing full-time. His first novel, Breakers of the Dawn: Book 1 of the Dawn Saga, was electronically published in December of 2014.

When not deeply immersed in imaginary worlds, Zachariah loves to experience the outdoors as well as read about science, futurology, and trans-humanism. He also enjoys home-brewing and creating digital art to accompany his writing.

While writing this novel, Zachariah lived in Bozeman, MT.

www.ingramcontent.com/pod-product-compliance
Lightning Source LLC
Chambersburg PA
CBHW030330200626
46816CB00006BA/2006